PRAISE FOR ISABELLA MALDONADO

A Forgotten Kill

"Dani Vega is the kick-ass heroine we've all been waiting for! Former Army Ranger, current hard-core FBI agent, she can outthink, outfight, and just plain outclass any opponent around. Welcome to your next favorite series!"

—Lisa Gardner, #1 *New York Times* bestselling author

A Killer's Game

"Maldonado keeps the plot boiling and the bodies dropping to the end."

—*Kirkus Reviews*

"Intense, gripping, and compulsively readable, *A Killer's Game* goes from zero to ninety on page one and never slows down. FBI agent Dani Vega is a heroine to cheer for—tough, inventive, and highly capable. A winner."

—Meg Gardiner, #1 *New York Times* bestselling author

The Falcon

"Another great read from [Isabella Maldonado]! I'm a Nina Guerrera fan, and this book is the best of the series so far. Don't miss it!"

—Steve Netter, Best Thriller Books

A Different Dawn

"A horrifying crime, cat-and-mouse detection, aha moments, and extended suspense."

—*Kirkus Reviews*

"Maldonado expertly ratchets up the tension as the pieces of the puzzle neatly fall into place. Suspense fans will be enthralled from the very first page."

—*Publishers Weekly*

"A thrill ride from the very start. It starts off fast and never lets up. It's one of the best thrillers of the summer."

—*Red Carpet Crash*

"*A Different Dawn* is a heart-stopping journey on parallel tracks: police detection and personal . . . Isabella Maldonado has created an unforgettable hero in Nina Guerrera."

—Criminal Element

"A killer of a novel. Fresh, fast, and utterly ingenious."

—Brad Thor, #1 *New York Times* bestselling author

The Cipher

"The survivor of a vicious crime confronts her fears in a hunt for a serial killer . . . forensic analysis, violent action, and a tough heroine who stands up to the last man on earth she wants to see again."

—*Kirkus Reviews*

"[In] this riveting series launch from Maldonado . . . the frequent plot twists will keep readers guessing to the end, and Maldonado draws on her twenty-two years in law enforcement to add realism. Determined to overcome her painful past, the admirable Nina has enough depth to sustain a long-running series."

—*Publishers Weekly*

"*The Cipher* by Isabella Maldonado is a nail-biting race against time."

—POPSUGAR

"Maldonado does a superb job of depicting a woman who's made a strength out of trauma and an even better job at showing how a monster could use the internet to prey on the vulnerable. Maldonado spent twenty-two years in law enforcement, and her experience shines through in *The Cipher*."

—Amazon Book Review

"A heart-pounding novel from page one, *The Cipher* checks all the boxes for a top-notch thriller: sharp plotting, big stakes, and characters— good and bad and everywhere in between—that are so richly drawn you'll swear you've met them. I read this in one sitting, and I guarantee you will too. Oh, another promise: you'll absolutely love the Warrior Girl!"

—Jeffery Deaver, *New York Times* bestselling author

"Wow! A riveting tale in the hands of a superb storyteller."

—J. A. Jance, *New York Times* bestselling author

"Intense, harrowing, and instantly addictive, *The Cipher* took my breath away. Isabella Maldonado has created an unforgettable heroine in Nina Guerrera, a dedicated FBI agent and trauma survivor with unique insight into the mind of a predator. This riveting story is everything a thriller should be."

—Hilary Davidson, *Washington Post* bestselling author

ISABELLA MALDONADO
A FORGOTTEN
KILL

OTHER TITLES BY ISABELLA MALDONADO

FBI Agent Dani Vega series

A Killer's Game

FBI Agent Nina Guerrera series

The Cipher

A Different Dawn

The Falcon

Sanchez and Heron series
(coauthored with Jeffery Deaver)

Fatal Intrusion

Detective Veranda Cruz series

Blood's Echo

Phoenix Burning

Death Blow

ISABELLA MALDONADO

A FORGOTTEN KILL

THOMAS & MERCER

Published by Thomas & Mercer, Seattle

www.apub.com

Amazon, the Amazon logo, and Thomas & Mercer are trademarks of Amazon.com, Inc., or its affiliates.

ISBN-13: 9781662515828 (paperback)
ISBN-13: 9781662515811 (digital)

Cover design by Shasti O'Leary Soudant
Cover image: © Marie Carr, © Beatrice Preve / ArcAngel

Printed in the United States of America

*For Liza Fleissig and Ginger Harris-Dontzin,
whose sage advice, timely intervention, and unswerving
support have guided me through the slings and arrows of
outrageous fortune.*

CHAPTER 1

August 15, 2024, 2:30 a.m.
East Harlem, Manhattan

"Something's wrong," Conner muttered to himself. "She's late."

As he'd done many times before, Conner waited at the Harlem–125th Street station for Angela Dominguez. Only her train hadn't come.

Was there a crash? A shooting? A bomb?

He pulled out his cell phone and had started entering the Transit Authority's website into the search bar when the platform vibrated beneath his feet. He glanced down to see the lights embedded in the floor begin to glow and felt the tension drain from his body. The number 6 train heading uptown had been delayed. Nothing was wrong.

A minute later, his eager eyes scanned the small cluster of passengers making their way onto the platform.

She glanced up at him after he fell into step beside her. When she finally spoke, her words were tinged with a sexy Colombian accent that never failed to heat his blood. "You really don't have to—"

"It's the middle of the night," he cut in. "So yes. I have to walk you home."

Her shy smile told him she was secretly pleased. It was enough encouragement for him to edge closer to her. Should he take her hand?

Conner had first approached Angela two weeks earlier when he'd seen her get off the train. She'd been leery at first, understandably guarded around a powerfully built man who was easily twice her size. She'd asked why he was out so late, and he'd explained that he worked the swing shift as a bouncer at a nightclub on the Upper West Side of Manhattan.

She'd confided that she worked on the opposite side of Manhattan, as part of an office-cleaning crew for a high-rise building on Third Avenue. Like him, her shift ended at two in the morning, and she took public transportation to her apartment in Harlem.

Her beauty had drawn him instantly. Getting to know her had cemented the attraction. His sweet Latina Cinderella scrubbed floors until the wee hours, then rose early to work as a short-order cook in a local diner until the late afternoon. He estimated her age at twenty-five, but her hands already showed the calluses and shiny burn scars from her labor. He longed to take those hands in his own but refrained, unwilling to risk frightening her off.

Instead, they chatted as they strolled along Fifth Avenue from the subway stop in Harlem, which seemed empty compared to the bustling activity of the thoroughfare during business hours.

Without warning, Angela reached out to grasp his arm. He followed her startled gaze to a nearby cluster of honey locust trees lining the sidewalk. A beefy, unkempt man was barreling straight at them, something clutched in his hand.

Conner swept Angela behind him and faced the threat.

A gap-toothed grin spreading across his unshaven face, the man raised a clenched fist and moved his thumb. A silver blade sprang out with a distinctive click Conner recognized.

"Your money," the man said. "And your jewelry." He maneuvered the switchblade into fighting position. "Now."

"Stay where you are," Conner whispered to Angela over his shoulder. "If you try to run, he'll go after you. If you're behind me, I can protect you."

Assuming she appreciated both the danger of their situation and his experience as a bouncer, he moved forward to confront the mugger.

The element of surprise carried many advantages, and Conner made use of them all. He'd learned to confront bullies with an overwhelming show of force as a small boy and, one way or another, had dealt with violence ever since.

He slammed a meaty fist into the mugger's forearm, sending the knife flying. He barely registered it clattering to the ground several yards away as he followed up with a series of punishing blows to the man's head and body.

The mugger stumbled, fell, then scrambled to his feet and took off, hollering obscenities as he fled.

Before he could give chase, a slender set of arms wrapped around Conner's arm, holding him back.

"Thank you," Angela whispered.

He turned toward her, and she buried her face in his chest. He gently pulled her into his arms, saying nothing but stroking her silky black hair as she released a shuddering sob.

After a full minute, he pulled his cell phone from his pocket and started to call 9-1-1. Again, her surprisingly firm grip stayed him.

"Don't call the cops."

He raised an inquiring brow.

She lowered her head. "I'm . . . uh . . . I—don't exactly have my paperwork in order."

He lifted her chin with his index finger, bringing her soft brown eyes up to meet his. "Your work visa expired?" he said gently. When she merely nodded, he tucked her trembling hand into the crook of his arm and turned toward her apartment building. "Let's just get you home."

He stopped after a few feet and bent to pick up the switchblade. "Shouldn't leave this lying around," he said to her. "Kids might find it and get hurt."

Her look of admiration was worth doing battle with a street thug. He pocketed the knife and guided her the rest of the way to her door in silence.

"I want to make sure you get inside okay," he said after she typed her code into the keypad by the main entrance.

"Want some coffee?" She hesitated. "A beer?"

In his dreams, he'd done a lot more than have a drink with her, but that was just his imagination working overtime. Not reality.

"I'll just walk you up to your unit." He kept his voice neutral.

He followed her up to the third floor, where she pushed the door open and turned toward him. Conner could tell she was rattled and didn't want to enter her apartment alone.

Sure enough, she stepped aside to allow him in first. He brushed past her, careful not to make overt contact as he went inside the modest studio apartment.

"Sit," she said, indicating two pieces of mismatched furniture made of faded fabric. "I'll get the coffee on."

He eased himself onto the sofa, watching her graceful movements in the kitchen, which was separated from the tiny family room only by a tile-covered island. She filled the coffee maker's reservoir with tap water, then flicked on the power and reached up to open the cabinet door.

An instant later, her hands flew to her mouth, muffling a scream.

He surged to his feet and was behind her within seconds. "What's wrong?"

She turned wide brown eyes to him and stuttered through shaking fingers still pressed against her lips, "He came b-back."

He drew his brows together. "Who?"

"S-stalker," she choked out, barely holding back tears.

"Someone's stalking you?"

"He broke in once already," she said. "My friends don't believe me." She took her hands from her mouth to point at the open cabinet. "But I swear, I didn't do that."

4

On the upper shelf sat a row of teas, their labeled tins neatly arranged in alphabetical order. The lower shelf had an array of ground-coffee bags, also in alphabetical order, and grouped by variety. Each tin or bag was aligned precisely against the front edge of the shelf, with other bags behind it in symmetrical rows.

"How did it look before?"

"I just shove the coffee and tea in there. Whatever I use most is in front. I don't organize it."

He took her slender hands in his, engulfing them. "How long has it been since you noticed anything else?"

"The last time was four days ago."

"What happened that time?"

"My pantry." She glanced at a narrow cupboard at the far end of the counter. "All the boxes and cans. Lined up in a row. In alphabetical order." She let out a whimper. "Everyone thinks I'm nuts."

He didn't bother to suggest she call the police. She'd already made it clear that wasn't an option. With deliberate gentleness, he pulled her against him. She instantly molded her body to his with a quiet sob.

He stroked her cheek with his knuckles and tried to reassure her. "I believe you."

She tilted her head back to gaze up at him. "I'm scared, Conner." She swallowed audibly. "Why don't you stay?"

He longed to crush his lips against hers, to taste her sweetness, to feel her sweat-damp skin beneath his fingertips.

Summoning all his will, he disengaged from her grasp. "It wouldn't be right," he said softly. "I can't take advantage of you." He paused. "We'll know when the time is right."

She raised up on her tiptoes to plant a tender kiss along his jaw. "You're amazing, Conner."

He stayed a few minutes longer to make sure she was calm. She'd forgotten the coffee, but he didn't want to bring it up again and frighten her. When he started for the door, she made a second veiled invitation.

After another silent battle with his desire, he insisted she lock the door behind him and left.

Fresh night air would clear his head from the pheromone-induced fog that enveloped him. He had walked out onto the sidewalk and made his way to the corner of the building when a shadowy figure stepped into his path.

"Where's my money, asshole?"

Conner instinctively tensed, prepared for another attack. Once the man moved under the streetlight, Conner recognized the mugger from a few blocks back.

They had unfinished business.

"Broke my nose," the mugger went on in a stuffy voice. "Wasn't part of the deal."

Conner reached into his pocket, pulled out a roll of bills wrapped in a rubber band, and extended the money.

The mugger shook his head. "Gonna cost you double. I got doctor's fees now."

"Did I ruin your chance at a modeling career?" Conner said, not troubling to hide his contempt. "Please. A broken nose is an improvement." He dug a hand into his other pocket and pulled out a few loose Benjamins. "There," he said, tossing them in the air between them. "That's all you get. Take it or leave it."

Conner watched the other man stoop to gather up the fallen bills before disappearing into the darkness. His mind was on Angela Dominguez. His sweet Cinderella believed she'd found her prince, but there would be no fairy-tale ending for her.

He'd planned every detail down to the minute. Until then, he would bide his time as the days passed.

The final days Angela Dominguez had left on this earth.

CHAPTER 2

August 15, 2024
Bellevue Hospital, Manhattan

FBI Special Agent Daniela Vega strode through the corridor in the secure psych ward at Bellevue Hospital. The chief psychiatrist, Dr. Ashley Maffuccio, had called Dani with what amounted to a summons yesterday, and offered to personally escort her inside the facility.

An eerie howl from behind one of the locked doors pierced the silence that had been broken only by the steady rhythm of their footfalls. Barely recognizable as human, the unearthly wail crescendoed to a shriek before dying in a whimper.

"We're adjusting his meds," Dr. Maffuccio said, gesturing toward the room from which the sound had emanated. "That sometimes causes residual effects until the transition is complete."

Dani made no response. She was here to speak to a murderer who had requested her by name. She would not have come, but the patient had claimed to have important information for Dani's ears only. The patient had been catatonic upon arrival at the institution a decade earlier, but gradually began blurting random words. Two years ago, the words started to form fragments of Bible verses. Then recently, according to the staff, the patient had a breakthrough, exhibiting lucid moments for the first time.

Dr. Maffuccio came to a halt in front of a door on the left at the end of the hall. "I'll come in with you."

It wasn't a question.

After tapping a series of numbers on the keypad beside the door-frame, Dr. Maffuccio pushed the handle down and walked inside.

Dani followed, noting white sheets of paper with cramped writing in pencil taped to all four walls. There were thousands of words, as if the patient had vomited out mental fragments in a stream-of-consciousness regurgitation of disjointed thoughts.

Her eyes finally rested on the bed, where a woman in a pale-green T-shirt and gray stretch pants sat upright.

"How are you doing, Camila?" Dr. Maffuccio asked in quiet tones. "I've brought the visitor you asked for." Getting no response, she gestured to Dani. "Remember?"

Dani forced herself to look into the woman's dark eyes, searching for a glimmer of recognition. After what seemed like an eternity, she turned to Dr. Maffuccio. "I don't think she has anything to say to me after all."

Camila reached out, empty hands groping the air, and croaked out a single word. "No." Her jaw continued to work soundlessly, like a diver at the bottom of a pool, shouting. The water trapped the sound, allowing only bubbles to find their way to the surface.

"Perhaps direct contact would help," Dr. Maffuccio suggested.

Dani approached the bed slowly, not wanting to startle the patient. She reached out and gently took the woman's birdlike fingers in hand. "What is it, Camila?"

Camila's eyes lit at the contact, which seemed to spark a reaction. "And when these things begin to come to pass, then look up, and lift up your heads," she said in a reedy voice. "For your redemption draweth nigh."

Dani shot a quizzical glance over her shoulder at the psychiatrist.

"When she first begins to speak, it's always Bible quotes," Dr. Maffuccio said. "King James Version."

Dani suppressed a sigh and focused on the patient. If she couldn't get anything intelligible out of her, this would be a wasted trip. "It's me, Dani," she said. "You asked for me. You said you had something important to tell me."

Camila leaned forward. "Judge not, lest ye be judged." Her grip on Dani's hand tightened as she continued. "Every good tree bringeth forth good fruit, but a corrupt tree bringeth forth evil fruit."

Dani tensed. Had Camila just called her a bad seed from a rotten tree? The accusation was all too familiar. One she had heard many times from the aunt who had taken her in after her mother had stabbed her father to death. Whenever Dani had displeased her, which was all too often, tía Manuela would mutter *Como tu madre* under her breath.

In Manuela's eyes, Dani was just like her mother.

Her mother, the evil woman who had killed in cold blood.

Her mother, the woman who sat on the hospital bed clutching Dani's hand.

"Try a more personal connection," Dr. Maffuccio said, taking Dani from her reverie. "See if you can break through."

Swallowing the lump that had formed in her throat, Dani edged closer. She forced out the word she had vowed never to use again.

"Mamá," she said to her mother. "Speak to me. Tell me why you asked me here."

Deemed unfit to stand trial, Camila Vega was committed to Bellevue in lieu of prosecution for the murder of Dani's father ten years ago. At seventeen, Dani had come home from school to find her mother kneeling beside her father's inert form, holding a bloody butcher's knife from their kitchen. Her mother, who had been emotionally fragile as long as Dani could remember, had experienced what the psychiatrists had termed a "mental break."

Once she'd been committed, Camila stayed in her room at Bellevue, entirely mute. After eight years of treatment, she had finally begun to speak. Dani had been in the military on deployment at the time, and her younger sister, Erica, had called to share the news. According to Erica, their mother's therapist asked why her first words were in archaic English, and she had explained that Camila often read an old Reina-Valera Spanish Bible that included a King James English translation, which had been in the family for generations.

Unfortunately, the words Camila uttered consisted of disjointed phrases from scripture. Try as they might, the hospital staff could not connect what she was saying to anything going on around her, and ultimately concluded her speech had no meaning.

After that, Camila made no further progress until a month ago, when she began to make a few coherent statements, but only for a minute or so each time. Things changed yesterday when she asked for Dani. She'd never made a request to see anyone since her arrival.

And after all these years, her first words to her eldest child were an insult?

"Mamá," Dani repeated.

Suddenly, as if flipping a switch, the fog in her mother's eyes cleared. "Dani," she whispered.

"Yes, it's me."

Camila reached out with her free hand to caress Dani's face, a look of wonderment on her features. "All grown."

She had a million questions for her mother, but Dani kept quiet, unsure how long the lucid moment would last.

"There's something . . ." Camila seemed to drift away before coming back to reality. "Must . . . say," she finished.

"What is it?"

Camila lowered her voice again. "Not me. Never me. No matter what."

Dani froze. She wouldn't put words in her mother's mouth. Wouldn't even make a suggestion to someone so mentally susceptible, but it seemed like she was trying to say she was innocent. "Tell me exactly what you mean."

"Your father," Camila said, eyes pleading. "I didn't . . . the knife . . . it was . . ."

"The knife was from our kitchen," Dani said. "And you were holding it." She felt terrible when she saw her mother's pained expression but continued to lay out the damning evidence. "I used my key to unlock the door when I came home. No one else was in the apartment."

Dani's official statements had played a large part in the police charging her mother with the crime.

Camila shook her head, adamant. "Found him like that . . . wasn't me."

"Then who?" Dani asked, trying to keep the frustration from her voice.

Camila's body relaxed. Her eyes assumed a faraway look. "Ask, and it shall be given unto you," she murmured. "Seek, and ye shall find. Knock and it shall be opened unto you."

Back to Bible verses. Somehow, when Camila quoted scripture, her speech flowed freely. When she tried to communicate her own thoughts, the sentences came out in disjointed fragments.

Still holding her mother's hand, Dani turned back to Dr. Maffuccio. "Is this it?"

Dr. Maffuccio gave her a sympathetic nod. "This is the most she's said in a lucid state. It may be days before she's clear again."

Dani straightened and released her mother's hand, which fell limply to her lap. She addressed Dr. Maffuccio. "What do you make of her statement?"

Dr. Maffuccio sighed. "Sometimes patients will rearrange or alter events in their minds to lessen their pain."

"You're saying she's delusional?"

"I'm saying there's no way to know," Dr. Maffuccio corrected. "I can't render a professional opinion."

It would be up to Dani to decide whether she wanted to delve into the past and open old wounds at the request of someone who couldn't separate reality from fantasy.

"Beware of false prophets," Camila said, cutting into her ruminations. "They come to you in sheep's clothing, but inwardly they are ravening wolves."

CHAPTER 3

Ten years earlier, April 10, 2014
Benedict Avenue
Castle Hill, Bronx

When Dani came home from school, her first inkling of trouble was the low keening moan coming from inside her family's Bronx apartment. The second was the scent of blood.

At seventeen, she hadn't smelled it often, but the odor was unique enough to have left a lasting impression.

"Dad?" Her voice sounded as tentative as she felt, and it was met with nothing more than the same sound. Something was very wrong.

Cautiously, she edged from the small foyer into the family room.

Her mother was on her knees, clutching a blood-soaked butcher's knife. On the floor beside her was Dani's father's still form.

Time skidded to a shuddering halt. Her entire universe shrank until it encompassed only the space in front of her. She struggled to make sense of a scene that defied reason. Her mother's face was an eerie mask, reflecting utter madness tinged with unspeakable pain.

Dani looked on, her feet welded to the floor, as her mind refused to process what her eyes clearly saw. There was only one inescapable conclusion, but she couldn't fathom the reason behind the violence.

What had driven her mother to stab her father? The knife quivered in her mother's shaking hand, galvanizing Dani into action.

She dropped her backpack beside the laundry bag sitting on the floor and barreled straight at her mother, determined to stop her before she plunged the blade into her father again.

She slammed into her mother, knocking the woman off her knees and sending the knife flying.

"What did you do?" she screamed at her mother.

Her mother made no response, but lay there where she fell, tucking her legs up into a fetal position.

Dani sank down beside her father. It was far worse than she'd thought. There were four deep stab wounds in his upper body. Her eyes filled with tears, but she blinked them away. Tears wouldn't help. Panic wouldn't help. She gathered her will and forced herself to perform an assessment. She had trained for this.

Worried over her father's precarious health since he'd been medically discharged from the Army, she'd taken a local course in first aid and CPR given by the Red Cross the summer before.

A sense of calm came over her once she had a course of action. She gently felt along the side of his neck.

No pulse.

She bent down low to check for breathing.

Negative.

She rose up higher on her knees, prepared to give chest compressions, then hesitated. Forcing blood to circulate through the heart would only make him bleed out faster. She had to stanch the flow first. She darted a glance over her shoulder. "Get some duct tape, Mom!"

Her mother was still lying in a tucked position on her side, eyes fixed and staring straight ahead. The moaning had stopped, but that was the only change.

Dani cursed and sprang to her feet. She raced to her backpack and fumbled with the zipper twice before she managed to pull out her cell phone. She tapped the screen to unlock it, but the sensor wouldn't read her bloody fingerprint. More curses followed as she typed in the numeric code.

"Nine-one-one, what is your emergency?"

"My mother stabbed my father." She could hear the hysteria in her own voice and struggled to speak clearly. "He's dying. You've got to send an ambulance—please hurry!"

She had run to the kitchen and started yanking open drawers in search of the roll of duct tape her father always kept handy for minor household repairs.

"Is your mother still there?"

"Yes." Her fingers, wet with blood, slipped on the small handle as she pulled open another drawer.

"You need to get to safety right away. I'll confirm your location and send rescue and police, but before that you have to get out of harm's way."

Dani held the phone in one hand while she rummaged in the deep drawer with the other. "No way." She flicked a glance out toward the living room but couldn't see any movement. "If my mother comes after me . . . I'll deal with her."

And she meant it.

"Listen, you need to be safe. I want you to—"

Dani rattled off her address, interrupting the call-taker. "I'm done talking," she said, finally grasping the roll of tape. "I need both hands to save my father. The best thing you can do for me is get some paramedics here fast."

"Don't hang up." The call-taker's voice became urgent. "I'm sending help your way now. Just lay the phone down and put it on speaker. I'll talk you through the procedures until they arrive."

Dani was smart enough to know the call-taker would also be listening in to see if her mother attacked her. She followed all the instructions to the letter, grateful to have someone guide her movements so she wouldn't forget anything.

After kneeling beside her father again, she took his face in her hands and pressed her lips onto his, angling her mouth to get an airtight seal before blowing in two breaths.

The lips that had spoken her name so lovingly, the lips that had kissed her good night for seventeen years, the lips that always held a warm smile, were stone cold.

CHAPTER 4

August 15, 2024
Castle Hill, Bronx

Dani had spent the past hour stuck in traffic, the vehicular chaos around her reflecting the turmoil within. The drive from Manhattan to the Bronx had taken the better part of an hour, and she had spent that time debating her next move.

Whatever Camila's faults, she had always been honest. She must have truly believed she didn't kill her husband.

But belief wasn't fact.

And the facts indicated something completely different from what her mother had just told her. Could the facts have been interpreted incorrectly? Would the addition of more facts shed more light on the situation? Undoubtedly, which was why she was headed to the Bronx.

If she began poking around, her younger siblings would hear of it eventually, and she'd rather they hear it from her. Erica and Axel, each currently attending different universities, were home for summer break.

Home meant their aunt and uncle's apartment in the same Castle Hill neighborhood where they had lived with their parents until the day their lives had been torn apart.

The very unit where Dani now stood, irresolute, on the welcome mat in front of the door. She loved her younger siblings but kept her visits to a minimum. Despite the bold lettering on the doormat, Dani had never felt welcome.

With their father dead and their mother under arrest for his murder, tía Manuela and tío Pablo had obtained custody of all three of her brother's children. Manuela had taken them into her home but had never allowed Dani into her heart the way she had done with the younger children, Erica and Axel.

From the very first night, Dani had been made to feel like an intruder. Try as she might, she would never forget Erica's heart-wrenching sobs and Axel's silent tears on the worst night of their young lives. They had refused to be separated, so tía Manuela had spread out blankets and pillows on the family room floor for them to huddle together. They had lain side by side, with Dani in the middle, whispering in the dark.

"Did Mom really do it, Dani?" Axel asked.

Dani pulled his slender body closer to hers. He was only eleven years old. She couldn't give him all the gory details. "Yes, mi'jo."

"I d-don't understand," thirteen-year-old Erica choked out. "I know Mom's got problems and all, but how could she do something like that?"

"What's wrong with her?" Axel said quietly.

Dani had tried to answer the same question in various forms from the police who came rushing into the apartment with their guns drawn, from the paramedics who tried in vain to resuscitate her father, and from the homicide detective who interviewed her for over an hour.

Her mother, apparently incapable of speech, never uttered a word. So Dani was left to explain the inexplicable.

Yes, Mom had suffered from emotional upset for as long as Dani could remember. Yes, her parents would sometimes argue, but she had never seen it turn violent. Yes, Dad had a traumatic brain injury from an IED when he had been deployed overseas. No, he had never been physically aggressive and never hit Mom.

Grief-stricken herself, Dani held her feelings inside. She had to be strong for her siblings. Today, ready or not, she was an adult. She would be stoic, like her dad. She would not go to pieces in front of Erica and Axel. And no matter what her personal feelings were, she would not tell them their mother was a monster. They would make up their own minds about her over time. It was not for Dani to plant the seeds of hate within their hearts.

"Mom was . . . struggling," she began, feeling her way through a delicate conversation. "I'm sure she didn't want to hurt Dad. I'm thinking she didn't know what she was doing. She's not responsible for—"

"How dare you!" Tía Manuela snapped the lights on. She had been listening from the hallway that led to the main bedroom. "You don't think Camila knew she was stabbing my brother to death?"

Dani felt Erica's and Axel's bodies tense and hugged them closer as they all blinked in the sudden brightness.

Manuela stormed into the room, jabbing an accusing finger directly at Dani. "I haven't seen you shed a single tear all day."

Her aunt had no idea Dani had locked herself in a bathroom stall at the precinct and allowed the grief to surface, her body racked with spasms of anguish before she slumped to the cold tile floor. Throughout the rest of the day, she'd held her emotions in check to honor her father, who, despite intense pain from his combat wounds, never let his children see him cry.

Manuela's eyes narrowed to angry slits. "It's because you're just like *her*." The last word came out in a contemptuous snarl. "Como tu madre," she repeated for emphasis.

It was a phrase Dani would hear often. Her aunt's open hostility was one of two reasons she joined the Army a year later, when she turned eighteen. The other was to follow in her father's footsteps. He'd served in the elite 75th Ranger Regiment out of Fort Benning, Georgia, and she made it her mission to do the same.

She was her father's daughter, not her mother's. She would prove it to the world. She would prove it to her family. Most of all, she would prove it to herself.

Now that her past had intruded on the present, how would it impact her future? She would never find out by standing in the hallway. Best get this over with.

The apartment door swung open at her knock, revealing Manuela, who met her unannounced visit with stony silence. Dani stood her ground, refusing to slink away under her aunt's hostile glare.

"What do you want?" Manuela finally said, speaking with the same Nuyorican accent Dani's father had had.

"I'm here to see Erica and Axel." She offered no further explanation. Manuela was the last person she would confide in.

Manuela had clasped the edge of the door, apparently prepared to shut it in Dani's face, when a voice called out from behind her.

"Hi, Dani," Erica said, smiling at her over Manuela's shoulder. "I'll tell Axel you're here."

Scowling, her aunt stepped aside for Dani to pass. Minutes later, the three siblings were in the tidy family room catching up on the week since they had seen each other.

"I'm headed out for groceries," Manuela said, grabbing her purse from a narrow wooden table by the door. "Be back in an hour." Which was code for *Make sure Dani's gone by then.*

Erica rolled her eyes, and Axel shook his head. They both knew of their aunt's prejudice against their big sister, but past confrontations had led nowhere. They had all resigned themselves to the situation.

Once they were alone, Dani got down to the purpose of her visit. "I went to see Mom today."

The remark was met with raised brows. Dani had not set foot in Bellevue for years. She had maintained that there was no sense trying to communicate with someone who could not engage. Even when she'd heard Camila had begun speaking, the additional news that her words consisted solely of random scriptural quotes kept her away.

Or so she tried to convince herself. And others.

If she were honest, Dani would admit that being in her mother's presence reminded her of the brutal act that took her father's life. The broken shell that was her mother brought nothing but pain—and no small amount of resentment.

"Why did you see Mom?" Axel asked.

She pushed feelings of guilt aside and focused on the conversation. "She asked for me. According to the treating psychiatrist, she started to have lucid moments."

Erica and Axel exchanged glances.

"No one told us," Erica said. "Is she getting better?"

"When I saw her, she was in and out." Dani refused to sugarcoat the situation. "But she was clear for a couple of minutes."

"And?" Axel prompted, impatient to hear details.

"She claimed she didn't kill Dad," Dani said, then held up a hand to forestall the flurry of questions certain to follow. "She had no clue who did it, but insisted it wasn't her." She hesitated before adding, "Granted, this was between quoting Bible verses, one of which was 'seek and ye shall find.'"

After a moment of stunned silence, Erica spoke up. "Sounds like she wants you to figure out what really happened."

Erica looked at her with total faith, as if her big sister could set everything right. Dani kept her doubts to herself. Their mother was not mentally stable. How could her words be trusted? On the other hand, if Camila had been wrongly committed for ten years, Dani would have to face the fact that her own statements had contributed to a massive miscarriage of justice. Did she dare pick at the scabs that had formed over old wounds based on a few blurted comments?

"It's not that easy," she began. "I have no jurisdiction in a homicide committed in the city."

"But you're a federal agent," Erica persisted. "Doesn't that mean you have oversight?"

A common misconception Dani had heard many times before. "The FBI does not investigate murders unless they're committed on federal property or involve interstate abductions. Otherwise, the local police have to request our assistance."

"Then what can you do?" Axel asked.

"The case was closed by the NYPD a decade ago. I'll have to convince them to reopen it—which won't be easy. They'll want evidence. The word of a psychiatric patient won't be enough."

"Can we help?" Axel asked.

"I don't want you two to get involved."

"There must be something we can do," Erica said.

Perhaps there was. The problem that nagged her—the one she'd rather not contemplate—was motive. Had their dad made a deadly enemy? His Ranger contingent had seen heavy action during certain overseas deployments. She'd always thought about how he'd been injured, but he had injured others. Killed them too. That was the nature of combat.

She didn't know of anyone who hated her father at all, much less enough to kill him in cold blood. But how much did anyone know about the private lives of their parents? She ruled out a complicated love triangle for a motive. Dad was too physically unwell to carry on an affair, and the only thing Mom placed above her devotion to her husband was her faith.

She had to be sure, though. Sometimes kids saw things and didn't understand what they were looking at.

"I know it's painful, but think back to the day Dad died," Dani said, shifting her gaze from her sister to her brother and back again. "Is there anything either of you can recall that makes you think someone else killed him?" She paused long enough for them to consider the question. "Did Mom or Dad mention a new friend or acquaintance?"

Since the killer—if it wasn't Camila—had clearly entered without breaking in, Dani concluded the most likely suspect would be someone who had befriended one of their parents.

When they shook their heads, she proceeded with the next logical supposition. "Did you see a stranger in our building, or maybe hanging around outside?"

Negative responses again.

"Did the police tell you anything to indicate they thought there might have been an intruder?"

When the detective had interviewed her, he had asked whether she used a code to access the building and a key to enter her apartment. The questions had seemed like a perfunctory checking of investigative boxes to prove he'd done his due diligence. Not that she blamed him. She had been certain her mother had committed the crime as well—and said so.

Erica answered for both of them. "Nothing."

"The guy who talked to us seemed thorough," Axel said. "Asked if anything was stolen."

The comment jogged Dani's memory. The detective had asked her about electronics, cash, and jewelry to make sure nothing was stolen. He had used the lack of theft to help rule out robbery as a motive and further establish her mother's guilt.

Then she recalled the same detective visiting the family in Manuela's apartment a few weeks later. He had come by to explain that Camila would be committed to Bellevue in lieu of prosecution.

He had also given Dani a box containing her father's personal effects. The detective had attended the autopsy, where he took custody of valuables that had been on the body at the time of transport. Since the items weren't needed as evidence, he had turned them over to the oldest child.

Dani and her siblings hadn't wanted to break the seal and go through what was inside at the time. Touching his personal belongings would make them relive the trauma of his death all over again. They agreed to open the box together on their father's next birthday.

But Dani had left for the Army before that day came. In the intervening years, she had been deployed overseas or stationed in Fort Benning, Georgia. After her discharge from the military, she'd gone straight to Quantico for new agent training. By the time she returned to New York a few months ago, the box had been relegated to the back of her mind.

"Where's Dad's stuff?" she asked.

Erica waved her hand at a nearby bookcase. "Tía Manuela was scared somebody might take it, so she hid it in here." She rose and crossed the room to pull a thick leather-bound tome from the top shelf.

Dani reverently took the treasured volume, inhaling the scent of antique paper. "I don't understand," she said to Erica. "How could anything fit inside Mom's family Bible?"

"Tía Manuela made some . . . modifications," Axel said. "She pulled out the pages and used the cover to make hidden storage."

"She did it when we were at school," Erica added, seeing the expression on Dani's face. "By the time we got home, the damage was done."

"We saved all the pages," Axel said. "They're in a shoebox in tía Manuela's bedroom closet."

Dani looked at each of them in turn, fighting to control the rage that boiled up inside her. Every time she thought their aunt could sink no lower, the woman found another level down. Manuela had practically raised her kid brother and loved him with the fierceness of any mother. Camila had never been good enough for Sergio. Probably no one would have measured up, but their mom had been emotionally fragile even back then. Manuela had made no secret of her feelings and had told anyone who would listen that she'd warned her brother he would regret the day he married Camila.

Now that Dani and Camila were both out of reach of her wrath, it seemed Manuela had found another way to take revenge.

Dani swallowed the lump in her throat before speaking. "You two never told me about this." When they both shifted uncomfortably, she continued. "I'm taking the cover and the pages, and I *will* get this fixed."

She would scour the city until she found an expert in antique book restoration and pay whatever it cost to repair the heirloom that had been passed down for over a hundred years. The 1862 edition of the Reina-Valera Bible documented all the births, marriages, and deaths in their family going back generations.

A bitter silence stretched between them. No one needed to state the obvious. Manuela had deliberately chosen to destroy something that represented the bloodline of her beloved brother's killer. She could have used a fake book but used a convenient excuse to make her point instead.

Dani opened the cover and found, nestled inside, a beige cardboard box big enough to hold twenty-five cigars. When she lifted it out, a torn piece of cellophane tape curled up.

"Who broke the seal?"

Axel gave his head a small shake. "Tía Manuela knew we were waiting for you, but she wanted to see what was inside."

Of course she did.

Dani loosened the drawstring. When she shook it, a rugged tactical analog watch with an olive drab nylon strap tumbled out, landing on her open palm.

She handed it to Axel. "You should have this. He wore it in the field."

He put it on his wrist without a word and waited while Dani shook another item from the pouch.

"Dad's wedding ring," Erica said softly. "I remember the engraving."

Dani tilted the band to see Estás Conmigo Siempre etched on the inside. Camila had engraved the phrase "You are always with me" because her husband was frequently not physically present due to his military obligations.

She handed the ring to her sister, considering how appropriate the sentiment was for the child of a father who could never be present anymore.

After Erica slid the ring onto her thumb, Dani upended the pouch, and a silver chain slid out. Something was missing, though.

"Where's the pendant?" she asked, peering into the empty pouch.

Her father wore a 75th Ranger Regiment pendant attached to the necklace. The design was in the shape of a shield divided into four quadrants, with a sun and a star separated by a lightning bolt. After graduating from Ranger training, she had gotten an identical one, but wore it only on special occasions.

"Tía Manuela wears it," Axel said. "She wanted something of Dad's."

Dani's fist closed around the chain. "Did she at least ask you? It's your inheritance, not hers."

Two sets of downcast eyes told her the answer.

"I'm going to get it back from her and—"

"No," Erica said. "Let her keep it." She raised the hand with the wedding band turned thumb ring. "We all have something now . . . and besides, we'll get it eventually. She's not going to be buried with it."

Dani wasn't so sure. She supposed her siblings had warmer feelings for Manuela, who still provided a home for them during school breaks. Dropping the issue, she opened the catch and put the chain around her neck.

"You're right," she said. "We all have something that was special to Dad now." She reached out, and they each clasped one of her hands. "I'll get to the bottom of whatever happened that day. Even if the truth hurts."

She did not want to raise false hope that their mother might be innocent. Dani was the one who had discovered Camila holding the bloody knife. They had not.

CHAPTER 5

August 16, 2024
26 Federal Plaza, FBI Joint Terrorism Task Force
Lower Manhattan

The next day Dani sat in the interview room fidgeting under the bands strapped across her chest. The man sitting across from her had called them pneumographs, but she knew they were monitoring her respiration for changes in response to the questions he posed. The blood pressure cuff on her upper arm tracked her heart rate, and the sensors wrapped around two of her fingers measured her perspiration. The polygraph examiner, FBI Analyst George Rudd, had been hammering at her for an hour and a half.

"We're nearly finished, Agent Vega," Rudd said, staring at the open laptop on the desk in front of him. He could read more from the machine than he could from her expression.

"But you have just one or two more things to ask me, right?" she said.

She had taken several polygraphs in her life and knew the drill. The examiner would start off with an explanation of how the equipment worked and what topics would be covered. Then the process would begin with innocuous questions to get a baseline.

Is your name Daniela Vega? Are you twenty-seven years old? Were you born in New York City?

The queries—all with yes or no answers—would get more complicated after that, working their way into the heart of the issue. Rudd had delved into her actions during her last assignment, which was under review by the Office of Professional Responsibility, known as OPR, the federal version of Internal Affairs. Now that the interview was ending, the examiner would ask another round of simple questions to record how much her initial baseline had changed during the course of the session.

"Did you join the United States Army when you were eighteen?" Rudd asked.

"Yes."

"Did you receive training in cryptanalysis?"

"Yes."

Her training as a codebreaker in the military had finely honed her already acute ability for pattern recognition.

"Did you later join the 75th Ranger Regiment and attain the rank of corporal?"

"Yes."

Her father, also a Ranger, had been her inspiration. She was among the few women who managed to make it through the grueling process to join one of the most elite special forces units in the nation.

Her thoughts drifted to her mother's claim of innocence. How could an intruder have gotten into the apartment, let alone managed to kill a highly trained combat veteran like her father?

And then she considered how badly he'd been injured during his last deployment. He'd been given a medical discharge after suffering the aftereffects of an IED. The doctors had called it a traumatic brain injury, but teenage Dani understood only that her father had dizzy spells, debilitating migraines, and constant ringing in his ears. Some of the medication had made him groggy. In his compromised state, someone could have gotten the drop on him.

"That's all for now," Rudd said. He pushed away from the laptop and powered off the equipment.

Dani snapped back to the present, curious about how he had ended the examination. "Why did you finish with questions about my past?"

Rudd peered at her over wire-rimmed reading glasses. "I prefer to begin and end each session with questions I know the answers to. That way I can see if there are any deviations in your responses from the initial baseline."

As she'd suspected, he was looking for any disruption to her established pattern. Something she understood perfectly. The secret to deciphering most codes had more to do with pattern recognition than anything else.

"Someone will be in touch if there are any issues or if we need to meet again."

Rudd was allowing the possibility of future sessions. This had happened to her before. Sometimes she had gone over the same material multiple times until the examiner was satisfied with her answers.

She had finished unhooking herself from the equipment when the interview room door opened and the special agent in charge of the Joint Terrorism Task Force walked in.

She got to her feet. "Sir?"

She made it both an acknowledgment and a question. The New York JTTF was the largest of over two hundred such standing units nationwide, a massive organization headed by Special Agent in Charge Steve Wu, who was well above her pay grade. The fact that he was here meant he'd likely been listening in on at least part of the interview.

"Agent Vega," Wu said by way of greeting, then uttered the four words no one ever wanted to hear. "We need to talk."

He took the seat vacated by Rudd, and she followed suit, sinking back down onto her chair.

"The good news is that OPR has nearly completed its investigation into your . . . actions," Wu began, pausing a beat to find the best term to describe what had occurred during her previous assignment. The FBI was still dealing with the fallout.

If there was good news, that meant bad news would surely follow. She held her tongue and waited.

"I'm not sure what their determination will be," Wu continued. "But you need to keep your head down for the next few days. I'm going to keep you on administrative leave."

So this was the bad news. If she had been on the verge of exoneration, he might have reinstated her, but he didn't. Would she be dinged for something? Transferred? Terminated?

"Sir, if there's anything I can do to—"

"That's what I'm telling you, Agent Vega," Wu cut in. "There's nothing for you to do except continue to take time off. Make yourself available for any further interviews, but I don't think there will be any."

The investigators from OPR had made up their minds then. This polygraph must have been the final component to be sure she'd told them the truth during the endless hours of interviews they had conducted.

When she made no response, Wu filled the awkward silence. "Spend time with your family. Relax. Just don't leave the city."

He wanted her to spend time with her family? Fine. She would look into her mother's claim. The only way to do that effectively would be to involve the local police. The detective who had investigated her father's death ten years ago was with NYPD Homicide. She remembered him clearly, but had no idea where he worked now, or if he had retired.

Coming to a decision, she affected an air of nonchalance. "Is Flint still assigned here on a temp?"

NYPD Homicide Detective Mark Flint had been on loan to the JTTF for the duration of their recent investigation. They had worked closely together, making him the logical choice to ask for an introduction—or reintroduction—to the detective who had handled her father's death.

"He's due back at 1PP tomorrow," Wu said, eyeing her speculatively. "Why?"

Flint was a detective first grade assigned to NYPD headquarters at One Police Plaza in Manhattan. She had not been surprised to learn his supervisors would want him back as soon as he had finished making statements and completing paperwork from what everyone was now euphemistically referring to as "the incident."

She lifted a shoulder. "Wanted to say goodbye. Not sure when we'll cross paths again."

Wu's dark eyes hardened a fraction. "You can see him on your way out."

She understood herself to be dismissed and had the uncomfortable sensation that she had said something wrong. Perhaps her boss assumed her interest in Flint was romantic. If that were the case, there was no violation of protocol. The FBI prohibited fraternization among fellow agents working on the same unit, but there was no rule against dating someone outside the Bureau, especially if that person worked in an entirely different location.

She hesitated in the doorway, considering whether she should confide her real intentions to Wu. He was familiar with her background and might even help her uncover the truth.

No. This was too personal. She had no desire to dredge up her past, especially when she was the subject of an internal investigation. Bringing up the fact that both insanity and murder ran in her family was not a good idea right now. Or ever.

She walked through the door without looking back, determined to find Detective Flint and talk to him alone. She would tell him the whole story, and he would help, or he would not.

CHAPTER 6

Dani tilted her head back a fraction to glance up at Detective Mark Flint. He had walked with her out of 26 Fed, and they now stood facing each other in the square adjacent to Thomas Paine Park.

He lifted an inquiring brow. "What's going on, Vega?"

She had planned what she wanted to say on the elevator ride down from the fourteenth floor. She decided to approach the situation from an oblique angle, feeling her way before fully opening up about her situation.

"What would it take for the NYPD to reopen a closed murder investigation?"

His eyes widened in surprise. "Depends on how it was cleared. You talking about a case that was closed by arrest, by exceptional means, or unfounded?"

She understood the distinction. Cases were cleared by arrest when someone was formally charged. A case would be closed as unfounded if further investigation revealed that no crime was committed. When a death was involved, that could happen if someone who appeared to have been murdered died by suicide, accident, or natural causes.

"I'm talking about exceptional means."

"Then the suspect is deceased?"

She was not surprised Flint had drawn that conclusion. Cases were closed exceptionally only when a perpetrator had been identified but could not be prosecuted for the crime. Often this was because the suspect had died. If someone was charged and fled to a country with no extradition or simply could not be located, the case would be classified as *inactive, warrant on file* until the individual was in custody. Then the disposition would become *closed by arrest*.

She shook her head. "In this case, the District Attorney's Office declined to prosecute."

Flint crossed his arms. "Because?"

"A suspect was arrested but deemed unfit to stand trial due to mental incapacity."

"And now the perp has recovered?"

Another logical assumption, but the wrong one.

"Possibly, but that's not the point," she said. "What if the person who was charged never committed the murder?"

"You're talking in riddles, Vega," Flint said. "Stop dancing around and give it to me straight." He frowned. "That's why you asked for this little chat, isn't it?"

Aware she would have to trust him to get anywhere, she started through the park, and he joined her. They spent the next twenty minutes going through her father's murder and her recent visit to see her mother at Bellevue.

"I'm sorry this happened to you, Dani," he said when she finished.

His use of her first name and sympathetic expression made her think of all the times he must have uttered similar words of comfort to the grieving family of a murder victim. This also indicated he was shifting into investigative mode.

"I can't say I've made peace with it," she told him. "You never make peace with something like this, but I'm prepared to discuss the case."

He seemed to take stock of her, then relented. "On the day of the murder, was the apartment door locked when you arrived home from school?"

She had captured his interest. It was a start.

"I had to use my key to get in," she said. "Sometimes my dad would open the door for me, but not if he was having dizzy spells."

She explained how he had been discharged from the Army after a traumatic brain injury.

"You said the apartment was empty except for your parents." He made it a statement, then followed up with a question. "Where did the murder weapon come from?"

"The knife came from our kitchen," she said. "No one brought it to the scene."

He hesitated a moment, then lowered his voice. "How confident are you that your mother's recent . . . statement is grounded in reality?"

He had gotten to the heart of the matter. She had to be completely honest with him.

"She seemed clear when she spoke to me, but I can't be certain," she said. "Her treating psychiatrist wasn't sure either. My mother is no longer the woman I knew growing up—and even then, she wasn't the most stable person." When Flint made no response, she continued. "After my father died, it took years for my mother to speak at all. Then she eventually quoted scripture. She only started making sense a couple of days ago, so I figure what she's saying must be important—and she asked for me."

"Does she know you're a federal agent?"

"I doubt it. She probably wanted to tell me because I'm the only one who was there that day." She glanced down. "I'm the one who found her. The one who made a statement against her."

"Is that what this is about?" he asked gently. "You feel guilty because your words helped get her arrested?"

"My younger brother and sister are counting on me to find out the truth."

"And if that truth means you were wrong?"

"Then I'll set things right."

"And if that truth means you were right?"

"Then my mother is either lying or delusional," she said. "No one is any worse off."

He regarded her for a long moment. "Who was the detective who interviewed you?"

"Stan Chapman."

"Old-timer," Flint said. "I've met him a few times. Kind of a legend in the Bronx."

She had hoped Flint might know him well enough to ask a favor but considered herself lucky Chapman hadn't retired to Florida like many of his colleagues. "He's still on the force then?"

"Probably not much longer," Flint said. "He's got to have over thirty-five years on the job."

She dropped a not-so-subtle hint. "It was a long time ago, but maybe he'll remember me."

Without coming out and saying it, she'd asked for an introduction. She waited to see what Flint would do.

After a long moment, he slid out his phone and tapped the screen. "This is Flint. I need a cell number for Detective Stan Chapman." He paused to listen, then added, "Bronx Homicide."

CHAPTER 7

Bronx Homicide Squad
Simpson Street, Bronx

After showing her credentials to the desk sergeant, Dani followed Flint through a wood-paneled hallway that harkened back to an earlier era. Formerly the NYPD's 41st Precinct—better known as Fort Apache—the century-old neo-Renaissance building had been repurposed to house the Bronx Detective Bureau.

Flint halted in front of the heavy wooden door that led to the Homicide Squad. "Let me make the introduction," he said to her over his shoulder before grasping the handle and pushing the door inward. "He may not recognize you, and I didn't explain why you're here."

Fine with her. Chapman had invited them to come, but, according to Flint, the detective had sounded harried over the phone and had agreed to carve out time to meet with them only as a professional courtesy after Flint explained that they wanted to look into one of his old cases.

She trailed Flint into a bullpen with four desks covered in police-related flotsam. The walls were similarly festooned with signs, posters, and papers.

The area was empty except for a barrel-chested balding man Flint introduced to her as Detective First Grade Stan Chapman. She had recognized him immediately but did not let on, allowing Flint to choose when to reveal her relationship to the case they intended to discuss.

While the two men caught up, Dani studied the space. She was surprised to see stacks of papers piled beside each computer, considering that everything was digitized. A plastic novelty skull sat on top of a battered credenza beside a coffeepot that had seen better days.

Adding to the retro vibe were massive corkboards covered in papers held in place with pushpins. A poster was tacked to one of the boards.

"There is no hunting like the hunting of man, and those who have hunted armed men long enough and liked it, never care for anything else thereafter." —Ernest Hemingway

These detectives were indeed hunters. Judging by Chapman's apparent age, he was the type who would have trouble giving up the chase for retirement.

Pleasantries over, Chapman gestured to a pair of metal-framed faux-leather swivel chairs. "What's this about a case from ten years ago?" he asked. "You got some new information?"

"A murder in Castle Hill," Flint said. "Victim was Sergio Vega."

Chapman leaned back in his chair and closed his eyes in thought. "Oh, yeah," he said, after a moment. "I remember that one." He gave his head a rueful shake. "Tragic. The wife did him. She got committed and never went to trial."

Dani, who had braced herself for a blunt discussion of the case, knew Chapman would have been more tactful if he knew who she was. Before she could clarify, he turned a startled gaze on her, then narrowed his eyes on Flint. "Hold up a sec. Did you say her name was Special Agent Vega?"

She responded before Flint had the chance. "I'm Daniela Vega."

"You're the oldest daughter," Chapman said. "I didn't recognize you."

Hard training in the military had wrought many changes, especially to her appearance. She bore little resemblance to the teenager he had interviewed a decade earlier.

"I'm—uh, sorry for your loss," he said to her, then flicked an accusing glance at Flint. "You should've told me you were bringing a victim's family member when you called."

"Mea culpa." Flint gave him a disarming smile. "Figured we could explain when we got here."

"You said something about looking into one of my cases," Chapman said. "You got a problem with the investigation?"

"Not at all," Flint said quickly. "It's just that Agent Vega might have new information that could put things in a different light."

Chapman turned back to her. "If memory serves, the last time we spoke was at your aunt's apartment. I went to let you know about the disposition of the case and return your father's personal effects."

Her hand drifted involuntarily to the chain around her neck. "You were very kind. Thank you for that."

"Your father's case is closed," Chapman said quietly. "There are no grounds to reopen it."

"My mother's talking now," she said, unsure how much to reveal. "Says she didn't do it."

Chapman looked sympathetic. "I've worked hundreds of murders in my time. More often than not, the suspect claims innocence. When they do, their family believes them. It's not a reason to spend time I don't have investigating a settled matter."

Disappointed but not surprised, she plowed on. "I'm only asking to look at the files."

He raised a skeptical brow. "And when you look at them, you'll have questions. You'll want to go through the whole investigation with me." He swept a hand out, encompassing the computer, inbox, and piles of notes covering his desk. "I've got twenty-three unsolved murder cases going back over twelve years. Those victims have loved ones who are counting on me to make an arrest. Three of them might have been committed by the same perp. I can't take time away to dig through a closed case without compelling evidence."

Dani thought of the grieving families waiting for Chapman to call. She couldn't distract him from his duties.

But maybe she could help him go faster.

"Three of them might be related?" she said, thinking out loud. "A serial killer?"

He held up both hands, palms out. "Don't go spreading that around. That's all I need."

"I'm trained to identify patterns," she said simply. "It's what I do."

Flint grinned. "She was a military codebreaker. I've seen her in action, and she's good."

"This isn't a code," Chapman said.

"You suspect three of your open cases may be connected," she said. "That means they have elements in common. I can spot a pattern that computer algorithms or experienced detectives might not detect." She lifted a shoulder. "There's no harm in letting me have a look."

He paused to study her before he responded. "You're wrong about that."

Sensing the detective was sifting through the pros and cons of allowing her access, she waited for him to continue.

"You would have heard of one of the three cases," he said, dragging a hand through his thinning hair. "Because it happened in your old apartment building."

She sucked in a breath as the memory came flooding back to her. "Luna Delgado."

Luna had lived in the unit one floor above theirs. Despite holding two jobs, she was always asking around the building if anyone needed things done. Dani's mother had occasionally paid her to sew torn clothes or hem pants.

"Who's Luna Delgado?" Flint asked, looking from Dani to his colleague.

"She was murdered the day after Sergio Vega," Chapman said. "Another detective on my squad, Pete Morrow, caught it. When Pete died of a heart attack two months ago, I inherited most of his open cases."

It was sad to think that some investigations lasted longer than the detectives who worked them. Dani knew it was common practice for unsolved crimes to be passed on to others, eventually ending up in Cold Case if they weren't closed.

"That's what started me down this damned rabbit hole," Chapman went on. "Something about Delgado's murder seemed vaguely familiar. I went through my unsolved files and pulled two others from that same time frame, but I haven't had time to dig deeper."

Flint seemed more intrigued by the close proximity of her father's death to Luna Delgado's. "Did you and Pete think it was strange to have two murders in the same building a day apart?"

Chapman shook his head. "One was a domestic where a wife stabs her husband." He flashed Dani an apologetic look for the blunt characterization of a crime that had devastated her family before summarizing his fellow detective's case in the same frank manner. "The other was a rape where the victim was suffocated. The cases had nothing to do with each other."

She remained pointedly unfazed. If she wanted in, she had to prove her ability to remain objective and focused.

"Obviously," Flint said. "But still, what's up with that building?" He flushed and turned to Dani. "I didn't mean . . . that is to say, I—"

Now they were both feeling awkward. She had to put them at ease.

"There weren't any Park Avenue penthouse suites available back then." She lifted a sardonic brow. "So my parents figured Castle Hill was the next best thing."

As intended, her remark broke the tension.

She addressed Chapman. "I didn't know Luna well, and as you can imagine, I had other things on my mind when she died."

Like moving out of her apartment, being interviewed by mental health experts about her mother's condition, and helping care for her younger siblings.

She gave them a moment to absorb her meaning before continuing. "I wasn't aware her case was never solved, and I'd like to help."

It was the least she could do.

Chapman's gaze locked with hers. "You're offering me a deal."

She nodded. "I'll tell you if you have a serial killer, and you let me see the Sergio Vega murder book."

He jabbed a finger at her. "Not until you give me your analysis."

She didn't hesitate. "Deal."

CHAPTER 8

Dani sat beside Flint at a conference room table in the Homicide Squad briefing room. Three huge binders rested on the table's scarred top, but Chapman had directed their attention to a printout containing a summary of the cases they held.

"You see what I mean?" Chapman asked them. "The murders were all in the Bronx and took place in the same year. The vics were young, single, Puerto Rican females who lived alone in modest apartments and had two or three jobs."

A polite way to say they were members of the working poor.

"Not sure what to make of the demographics," Flint said. "The Bronx has a large Puerto Rican community." He shrugged. "May not mean he's targeting a particular ethnicity—could just be his environment."

"Agreed," Chapman said. "But there's more." He reached across the table to tap the printout with his pen. "Look at the rest of the victimology."

Shifting into analytical mode, Dani scanned the list of dispatched police responses. "Luna Delgado was the first victim. She and the second victim both called in stalking complaints in the weeks before they were murdered."

"Exactly," Chapman said. "Unfortunately, neither of them could describe their stalker very well, mostly just gave a description of an athletically built male."

Frightened, the women had probably tried to put distance between themselves and the sinister figure trailing them. Dani could picture them ducking their heads to avoid eye contact and scurrying in the opposite direction. No wonder they couldn't provide a good description.

"I was lead detective on the second two cases," Chapman continued. "Sofia Montez was killed over three months later on the opposite side of the Bronx. She was the other one who reported a stalker, but her case had an added twist."

That was one way to put it.

"Someone broke into her apartment two weeks before her death," Flint said, reading over Dani's shoulder. "But nothing was stolen."

"At the time, I didn't connect the burglary with the stalking," Chapman said, a note of self-recrimination in his voice. "I couldn't be sure the same perp was responsible. Frankly, I still can't prove it."

"What about Jennifer Trejo?" Dani had moved down to the third victim. Her case was months later. The day before Halloween.

Chapman's face darkened. "That's one of the strangest homicides I've worked. And it's the case that convinced me I was looking at three crimes with one perp."

"Trejo didn't have a stalker, though," Dani said, looking for similarities.

"But she had a burglar," Chapman said. "Check out the summary of the police report."

She read a synopsis of the complaint form. Jennifer Trejo's apartment was burglarized about a month prior to her death. Instead of stealing valuables, however, the intruder entered while she was at work to rearrange items.

The suspect reorganized the bedroom closet, categorizing clothes by season, then subdividing them by color and size. Shoes were similarly sorted.

"I'm familiar with breaking and entering," Dani said. "Never seen breaking and organizing."

"Neither had the dispatcher or the patrol officers who handled the burglary complaint," Chapman said. "They took a report, dusted for prints, and knocked on the neighbors' doors, but there was nothing to follow up with after that. None of the doors or windows showed any sign of forced entry, and the only thing missing was a pair of panties. One of the officers indicated in his report that the alleged victim might have lost her underwear in the laundry and imagined the break-in."

Flint grimaced. "That doesn't put us in a good light, but you can understand what they were thinking at the time."

"Not me," Chapman said. "I called their sergeant and gave him a ration of shit, which I'm certain he passed on with an extra helping." He dragged a hand through his hair. "I couldn't let it go. Spent hours going through all the notes and crime scene photographs. That's when I saw it."

Dani consulted the paper. "The pinholes?"

"Two small holes in the wall of the main bedroom in the Trejo case," Chapman said. "I went back and enlarged the photos taken at the Montez crime scene and found the same thing." He held his thumb and index finger about an inch apart. "There was about this much space between them. At first I thought they might have been from hanging a picture, but they were the same size and in roughly the same place in both bedrooms. So I had a team of evidence techs go back to all three apartments to double-check."

"New tenants would've moved in by then," Flint said.

Chapman gave him a tell-me-something-I-don't-know look. "I'm not saying it was evidence that would hold up in court, but it was all the confirmation I needed."

Dani was beginning to appreciate the toll investigating murders had taken on the veteran detective. He must have had situations where he could not solve the crime or, worse, the guilty had escaped justice based on a technicality. How many families had wept as he tried to explain the vagaries of a criminal justice system that allowed their loved one's murderer to go free?

"What did the techs find?" Dani asked.

"They found the holes in both of my cases. Told me someone could have installed pinhole cameras inside the walls, but there wasn't any sign of surveillance equipment."

"And Luna Delgado's apartment?"

"That wasn't my case at the time, but I convinced my squad mate to check it out. There were no holes anywhere in her apartment."

"Could the drywall have been patched or painted over before he got in there to have a look?"

"That's exactly what I think happened," Chapman said. "But I can't prove it."

"Delgado only had a stalker, none of the other bizarre stuff," Flint said. "Why do you think her case is related to the other two?"

"I'm still betting holes were there and got patched," Chapman said. "But even if they weren't, her case was the first one." He shrugged. "Maybe the perp evolved."

He was right. Criminals learned from experience and adjusted their techniques. If the unsub—FBI speak for unknown subject—felt compelled to murder young women in their apartments, his MO could adapt over time to avoid capture. That was how the smart ones got away with it. Sometimes for years.

Dani steered the discussion back to pattern recognition. "Aside from gender, ethnicity, and living alone in the same general location, what do all three cases have in common?"

"They were all sexually assaulted before their deaths," Chapman said.

"How were they killed?"

"I went through the autopsy reports, and that's one of the things that isn't consistent," Chapman said. "Delgado was suffocated with a pillow, Montez was manually strangled, and Trejo was bludgeoned with a blunt instrument. They were all restrained, but with different types of bindings." He leaned forward. "Get this. In the Trejo case, the ME determined the perp had swung the murder weapon with his left hand. And before you ask, neither of the medical examiners in the other two cases could be certain whether the doer was right- or left-handed."

"So in the first two cases he stalks the women ahead of time," Dani summarized. "In Delgado's case, that's the only police report before the murder. But in the Montez case, he also breaks in and installs hidden cameras."

"We think," Chapman cut in. "There's no way to prove the same person who stalked her broke in to install surveillance equipment—or that he was her killer. Technically, they could be three separate crimes."

"Noted," Dani said, acknowledging the comment with a dismissive air that showed she didn't believe it any more than he did. "In the Trejo case, there's no stalking complaint, but he burglarizes her apartment to install cameras and organize the closet before taking a pair of her underwear on his way out." She paused. "And the suspect might be left-handed."

"Assuming he hid cameras in the second two apartments," Flint said, picking up the narrative, "he could watch them from the comfort of his own apartment, and they'd have no clue."

"Finally, when he kills them, he removes the video equipment," Dani finished, "leaving no trace he was ever there."

"That's what's so frustrating," Chapman said. "The guy's a ghost. We've got no fingerprints, no semen, no forensic evidence at all." He appeared to reconsider his comment. "At least nothing viable."

Flint frowned. "What do you mean?"

"I'm sure he wore gloves and used a condom," Chapman said. "But we collected some microscopic fibers and a few hairs. Sent them to the crime lab in Queens, but we had no luck. We got some DNA in the most recent case, but the lab report said the sample was insufficient for analysis."

"This guy knows what he's doing," Dani said. "And he's intelligent."

"I'm going to have trouble proving it's a series," Chapman said. "Plenty of women attract stalkers, and only two of the three filed a stalking complaint. Besides, we can only be certain there were pinholes in two of the cases. There's no consistent thread through all three cases."

Dani put down the paper. "I think it's a series." She leveled him with a hard stare. "And so do you." When he made no response, she continued. "There's a pattern in there somewhere, and I'll find it."

Chapman didn't deny her assertion. "Do that, Agent Vega, and I'll pull all the evidence in your father's case out of storage and share it with you—along with my notes and whatever I can remember." He returned her gaze. "But first, three innocent victims were murdered on my watch. It's been ten years, but I can't let it go. And you're right. I do think the cases are related. He's never been caught, and he's still on the loose." He leaned back in his chair and eyed her speculatively. "I've investigated serial killers before, and they don't just wake up one morning and decide they're done murdering people. Once they become active in a certain area, there are only three ways it ends."

She waited for him to elaborate.

"They go to jail, they die, or they move to a different hunting ground."

"And you're worried this unsub isn't dead?"

Chapman nodded. "If he went to prison for some other crime, he could get out anytime and pick up where he left off. On the other hand, if he moved away, he's probably been killing people all these years. Hell, he could be stalking his next victim right now. Just because he's not operating on my turf right now doesn't give me a free pass. If I can ID him, I can lock him up and stop him before anyone else dies."

Dani couldn't argue. An unsolved serial killer case took priority over a single murder that had been closed a decade earlier. "I'll do whatever I can to help you catch him."

She did not add that she would investigate her father's case at the same time.

CHAPTER 9

Benedict Avenue
Castle Hill, Bronx

Dani pivoted without warning and crossed Benedict Avenue, offering Flint no opportunity to mount an argument before she reached her objective.

"Yo," Flint called out from behind her. "What gives?"

After leaving Detective Chapman's office, they'd driven out to the scene of the third murder on the list, Jennifer Trejo. The crime had occurred the day before Halloween ten years earlier, and Dani hadn't expected much from canvassing the apartment building's residents, but they decided to get eyeballs on the location anyway. She also hoped its proximity to a spooky holiday might make a murder stand out in people's memories.

After finding most apartments empty, with their occupants at work, Dani and Flint had agreed to grab lunch before the next set of interviews when she made an abrupt change of course.

"We're in the neighborhood," she said, striding purposefully along the sidewalk.

He hustled to catch her as she reached the five-floor walk-up at the end of the block.

"What about our lunch plans?" He shook his head. "You just can't wait to get started on the Luna Delgado case, can you?"

"Chapman wasn't the lead detective on that investigation," she said. "So he only knows what's in the report. Just like us."

"And she was killed the day after your father, so we're going to ask the tenants about both cases." He made it a statement rather than a question.

She made no apologies. "Why not?"

He gave her a side-eye. "Chapman's not going to be happy when he finds out you were poaching without his knowledge or consent. Your father's case is still his. He didn't give you the green light to poke into that one."

"Then it's good you won't tell him."

She wasn't optimistic a canvass in her old building would be any more productive than the one they had just conducted down the street, but she wanted to know how many of the old tenants were still there. One person in particular could be a gold mine of gossip.

Nearly a century old, the beige brick building's front held the metal scaffolding that comprised a fire escape down the middle. Air-conditioning units jutted from many of the casement windows, and others were open to tempt in a fresh breeze.

Dani climbed the two short steps, coming to a halt at the reinforced glass entrance. She reached for the keypad set into the brick facade on the left and hesitated. If the same lazy superintendent still maintained the building, he might not have bothered to delete old codes from the system. Taking a gamble, she punched in a series of numbers.

A blue light accompanied by an electronic click confirmed her suspicions. She pulled the door open and crossed the threshold, then spoke to Flint over her shoulder.

"You don't have to join me if you're worried about stepping on Chapman's toes," she said to him, still holding the door open behind her. "I can catch the subway back to my place when I'm finished here."

Flint, who lived in Brooklyn as well, had offered to drive her home since she had no access to her Bureau car while she was on admin leave.

"I'm helping you with the Delgado case," he said, following her inside. "If you start asking questions about another investigation, that's on you." The corner of his mouth quirked up. "But the last building was a bust. I don't know what you expect to find here."

"Not what," she said, making her way down the dimly lit hallway. "But who."

She made her way to the second floor, explaining her objective to Flint as they went.

"The neighborhood snoop lived in our building," she said. "Hopefully she's still here. Her name's Rosa Sanchez, but everyone calls her Rosa la bochinchosa."

"Come again?"

"A bochinchoso is a gossip—but in this case, a female since there's an 'a' at the end of the word rather than an 'o.'"

"So Rosa Sanchez is a busybody?" Flint asked.

She nodded. "And who better to ask for the scuttlebutt about two nights everyone in the building would have talked about for months?"

Arriving at apartment 2B, she rapped her knuckles against the metal door, dislodging flecks of peeling red paint. Shuffling sounded from inside, and Dani pictured Rosa peering through the security lens.

A heavily accented voice finally responded. "Who is it?"

"Daniela Vega and . . . a friend."

Flint shot her a quizzical look but said nothing. At the previous building, Flint had taken the lead and introduced them with their job titles. This, however, was her turf, and she had her own strategy—which involved finding out how much Rosa knew before sharing anything.

The door swung open to reveal a rail-thin woman holding a half-smoked cigarette between fingers with chipped red nail polish that resembled the door's paint. "Dani Vega, is that you?"

"Have you got a minute?" Dani said by way of greeting.

She needn't have bothered asking. Rosa la bochinchosa would never miss a chance to find out why the long-lost daughter of the building's most infamous tenant and the man she murdered was on her doorstep. Such a source of juicy rumors would not be turned away.

"Come in," Rosa said, stepping back. "And you must introduce me to your novio." She gave Flint a wink.

"He's not my boyfriend," Dani corrected. "We're colleagues."

Rosa's gaze turned shrewd as she continued to study Flint. "Ah, then you are un federico."

He shook his head. "I'm Mark Flint."

"'Un federico' is Puerto Rican slang for a federal agent," Dani explained before turning back to Rosa. "He's NYPD."

The exchange told Dani that Rosa had already heard about her career with the Bureau after leaving the Army.

"We're here to ask about what happened here back in April of 2014," she said.

Rosa's head bobbed vigorously. "That was when they started calling this building el matadero."

Flint's brows furrowed in confusion. "The bullfighter?"

"That's el matador," Dani said. "El matadero means 'the slaughterhouse.'"

"Two killings in two nights," Rosa went on. "It took months to get new tenants. Nobody wanted to live here for a long time."

Dani and Flint spent the next half hour trying to get useful information out of Rosa. Unfortunately, la bochinchosa lived up to her nickname and peppered them with questions of her own. She seemed to sense there was a serious reason for their sudden visit and tried to wheedle it out of them.

By the time they left, Dani was mentally drained from the verbal sparring and had little to show for their efforts regarding either case.

"That woman was like a dog with a bone," Flint said, lifting the NYPD placard from his car's dashboard and stowing it in the console. "We should have her teach Interrogation 101 to the rookies."

"Which is why I wanted to talk to her," Dani said. "It's one-stop shopping for info. If anyone knew anything they hadn't told the police, Rosa would have heard about it."

"Did you learn anything new?"

She considered the question. "Not today, but Rosa will start ferreting around. She knows we're interested, so she'll be interested again. Unfortunately, soon everyone will hear about our visit."

"So the price of admission is we lose the element of surprise," Flint said.

She glanced away, thinking about what she would say to Wu and to Detective Chapman if either of them found out that she had wrapped her father's case into the other investigation. No matter what they had told her, Rosa would make all kinds of inferences—and share them with anyone who would listen.

"The price of admission may have been too high," she said quietly.

CHAPTER 10

Twenty-one years earlier
Zaladon Military Academy for Boys
Upstate New York

Conner was nine years old. The man towering over him seemed like a giant. An angry giant. He'd been trained to address him as "instructor," or "sir," but neither seemed adequate when speaking to someone who wielded absolute power over all the students at the academy.

The instructor threw the contents of the last locker onto the enormous jumble of clothing heaped in the center of the barracks.

"Do you know what this is?" The instructor's face gleamed with sweat. He pointed an accusing finger at the mountain of shoes, uniforms, and textbooks he'd yanked out of each of the thirty-six lockers that lined the wall.

His own prepubescent voice came out in a squeak. "Sir, yes sir."

"What is it?"

"It's a pile of shit, sir."

"And what likes to live in a pile of shit?"

"A maggot, sir."

"Then you must be a maggot."

"Yes, sir. I am a maggot, sir."

"I won't tolerate any stinky, smelly, shit-eating maggots in my barracks. You will clean this entire place, do you understand?"

"Sir, yes sir."

"I can't hear you, maggot."

"Sir, yes sir!"

"You will clean and scrub every inch of this room. Then you will organize everything as it should be. Not just your belongings." He pointed at the others standing at attention. "Everyone else's too. I will come in here with a ruler to check your work. You will not eat, you will not sleep, you will not stop to take a piss until every object in this room is perfectly spaced and aligned. Do you understand me, maggot?"

"Sir, yes sir."

After witnessing his public humiliation, the other boys filed out to fill their bellies in the mess hall. They returned after emptying their bladders in the group latrine at the end of the hall. Their final entertainment for the evening came shortly before lights-out. They had gathered around to watch him crawl on his hands and knees with a ruler, checking the space between each boot and shoe lined up inside the bottom of everyone's locker. He had already counted each garment hanging on the rods above, performing a quick calculation to ensure every piece of clothing was evenly separated.

"Oops," a boy named Frank called out from behind him. "Bumped the door. Clumsy me."

The others guffawed as he turned to see Frank standing in front of his locker, its contents now crumpled on the floor. Laughing, the rest of the boys followed Frank's lead, pulling their clothes out of their respective lockers to toss them down.

Filled with impotent rage, he could do nothing but watch as hours of painstaking labor was destroyed in less than sixty seconds.

Frank curled his lip in an exaggerated show of disgust. "Guess you're not going to bed anytime soon, are you?" Then he waited until he was sure everyone was watching before he added, "Pervert."

As he spent the remainder of the night cleaning the barracks by flashlight while the others slept, he realized the instructor had told the others what the nature of his infraction was. Normally discipline was kept private, but this time every boy in the academy had been recruited to ensure punishment would be meted out. And that he would serve as an example to the others.

His crime had been getting caught with a magazine. One that featured glossy pictures of beautiful women. Full-figured, curvy women. Naked women who made his fevered nine-year-old mind run wild with impulses he barely understood.

That had been his stated crime, anyway, but his actual offense had been something quite different.

He had discovered the magazine a month earlier, tucked inside the front cover of an outdated encyclopedia on the bottom shelf of the academy library. He figured one of the students had hidden it there, confident no one would find it.

But he had found it. Students were not allowed internet access, so he'd used the antiquated volume to look up the original New York state flag for an essay. After taking a good long look, he'd carefully returned the magazine to its hiding place, then come back nearly every day to sneak another peek.

Until today.

He'd gone to his usual spot to find the instructor already there with the encyclopedia open in his hand. The instructor's head had snapped up, and their eyes met. In that moment, he'd known the magazine had belonged to the instructor, who clearly didn't want it found among his possessions when the students cleaned his quarters.

Rather than admit his guilt, the instructor found a ready scapegoat to pin it on. Unable to prove any of this, he had been forced to endure the torment of his peers, who would have looked at the magazine if they'd found it, and his instructors, who hoped he had "learned his lesson."

But the only lesson he'd learned from the instructor that day was to find a way to frame others for his crimes.

CHAPTER 11

August 16, 2024
Queens, New York

As always, Conner began the inspection of his apartment with the closet.

Precisely two inches separated each hanger on the rod. Footwear was grouped by color, material, and function, with an inch between the heel of each inward-facing shoe. He was about to close the door and move on to the medicine cabinet when something caught his eye.

Something out of place.

A black leather boot at the far end of the row looked to be off by a fraction. Sweat prickled his hairline as he bent down to study the row of shoes. Heart racing, he reached into his pocket for the retractable measuring tape.

He dropped to his knees and pulled the tape out, stretching it flat on the closet's parquet floor directly behind the offending bootheel.

It was skewed four millimeters to the left. Without any roommates or pets, there was no one to blame but himself. The toe of his shoe must have brushed against the boot as he was adding a new outfit to his collection.

He'd taken care to align the new hanger, spacing it properly with the others. Apparently his attention had been fully engaged at eye level, and he'd neglected to double-check what was on the floor.

And now he would pay for his oversight.

Still on his knees, he grabbed the boots and hurled them from the closet. With gathering speed, he grasped each pair of shoes and flung them after the boots to land on the bedroom floor.

When the closet floor was empty, he stood and surveyed the pile he'd created. The visual chaos reflected the disorder that had intruded into his life thirty minutes earlier.

He pulled out his cell phone, cursing as he opened his monitoring app again. He had set up an alert through a third-party app that would scour all social media platforms for certain hashtags appearing together. Half an hour ago, he'd gotten an alert that someone named Rosa had posted one of the monitored combination hashtags on her Facebook page.

#CASTLEHILL COMADRES, GUESS WHO DROPPED BY? DANI VEGA FROM 4C. SHE'S ALL GROWN UP & ASKING ABOUT #MURDERS IN OUR BLDG. DM ME IF U REMEMBER ANYTHING & I'LL PASS IT ON.

The pairing of #Murders and #CastleHill had triggered the alert. A quick Google search of three keywords from the post—Dani Vega, Castle Hill, and murder—took him to news stories about Sergio Vega, whose wife had been charged with his murder but never stood trial due to mental illness. He was familiar with the case, like many fellow New Yorkers who had avidly followed the lurid headlines back in the day. Gradually, however, public interest had shifted to the next tragedy, and the media moved on.

The Facebook post indicated that Dani was "all grown up," which led him to conclude she was one of Sergio's kids. More searches focusing on Dani confirmed his suspicions.

He learned she had followed in her father's footsteps, joining the Army at eighteen. That would have been the year after Sergio's death. A neighborhood paper wrote an in-depth story about the hometown hero who joined the Army after graduating from Bronx Compass High School. She was trained in cryptanalysis and earned a bachelor's degree before becoming one of the first females to join the 75th Ranger Regiment at Fort Benning as a fully qualified Ranger.

This had surprised him. He had never heard of a woman in any of the military's elite special forces units, but he had confirmed it through other news articles. There were even pictures of Vega, covered in mud and sweat, on an obstacle course. At the time the photo was taken, her head was shaved, making her brown eyes appear large and luminous. His pulse kicked up as he studied the image. She was fierce, feral, and— there was no other word for it—hot.

He read that Vega had left the Army and joined the FBI about ten months ago. And now she was sniffing around her old apartment building, asking questions about her father's death. Why? And how long would it take her to look into another murder in the same building on the following day?

He'd been so careful. Planned everything to the smallest detail. And now disorder had crept in, threatening to destroy the perfect symmetry of his world. He shoved the phone in his pocket and shifted his gaze back to the closet. Once disarray violated a space, a purge was necessary to restore order.

Thoughts of a purge took him down dark corridors. Places he didn't want to go. Places best left in the past. The echo of an angry voice reverberated in his mind.

The voice of the instructor.

Conner shook his head to clear the disturbing memories. Forcing himself back to the present, he strode inside the closet again, this time grabbing handfuls of hangers, yanking them off the rod with the clothes still on them. He threw them on top of the pile of shoes, then went back in for more. He would not stop until he had emptied the space, and then he would spend the rest of the day placing every item back in its proper location before he left. He would use the time to consider the new variable that had altered the equation.

Dani Vega.

From his deep dive on the internet, he concluded that Special Agent Vega was smart, determined, and trained to be lethal. He could not deal with her as he had other women in the past. Instead, he would use his unique skill set to analyze her, find any weaknesses, and exploit them.

She would never see him coming. No one ever did—until it was too late.

CHAPTER 12

Brooklyn Heights, Brooklyn

Dani watched Flint tip his head back to swig the last of the amber liquid from the bottle. "I'd offer you another beer," she said to him. "But you've got to drive home."

She had invited Flint up to her Brooklyn Heights condo after learning he lived a short distance away in Red Hook. They had discussed Detective Chapman's murder cases while sitting in traffic on the Brooklyn Bridge, and both felt the need to review the digital files on the flash drive he'd given them.

Her brother, Axel, had designed a computer program to capture digitized data from various systems. A subroutine converted the material into a standardized format, scanned for nexus points, and organized it into a searchable spreadsheet. When she described the customized program to Flint, he wanted in.

Aware he'd been reassigned to his regular duties and would be back at his desk at 1PP the following morning, she took advantage of the opportunity to have Flint help her upload the files and discuss the cases. As a seasoned homicide detective, he had a lot more experience investigating murders. She might recognize a pattern, but he could determine whether what she detected was significant or mere coincidence. They had spent the past half hour inputting the case information and were ready to dig into the data.

"I'll be here at least another hour," Flint said, setting the empty bottle on the desk that took up a good portion of her apartment's second bedroom.

Taking the hint, she retrieved two beers from the fridge and handed one to Flint before resuming her seat.

With no roommate sharing her space, she had converted the extra room into a home office for those frequent times when she continued working after hours. Twin oversize monitors perched on matching pedestals were connected to her laptop, providing the ability to multitask.

"We sure as hell didn't learn much from knocking on doors today," she said. "So now that we can manipulate the data, I'm hoping we'll at least be able to confirm whether the three cases Chapman gave us are related."

Flint looked at the screen to the left. "We already went through the victimology with Chapman. How about filtering for timing?"

She entered the commands Axel had taught her to change the parameters. "I'll start with the year, then the month, date, day of the week, and time window."

Flint looked on while a spreadsheet formed, populated with subsets of data. "These were all in 2014," he said. "In April, July, and October, at different times of day."

"The one in October happened during daylight hours," Dani said. "The ME estimated the time of death between noon and three in the afternoon." She glanced at Flint. "He commits some of the crimes in broad daylight."

"And on different days of the week," Flint said. "Was the Delgado case at night?"

Dani nodded. "Between nine in the evening and midnight. There's no pattern there." She recalled a detail from the case file. "If the killer had waited a few more hours, she might still be alive today."

When they were inputting data from the original report, they'd included the building superintendent's statement indicating the victim was due to move out in the morning. It was her last night in the apartment, and someone had murdered her.

"Coincidence." He waved a dismissive hand. "Neither of the other two women planned to move out."

She didn't like coincidences and random events, which always skewed her attempts at pattern detection, but she accepted that they sometimes happened. "Probably."

They continued to study the chart in silence for several minutes.

Flint spoke first. "The killings are spread over six and a half months, roughly three months apart." He cut his eyes to her. "Does that count as a recurring sequence?"

"Hard to tell with only three data points," Dani said. "Unless . . ."

Flint was saying something, but she had tuned him out to concentrate on the screen. Something floated at the edge of her conscious mind, then bubbled to the surface.

"The murders were not actually three months apart," she said. "Look at the dates. They were separated by exactly 101 days."

Flint caught on immediately. "What date is 101 days after the last murder?"

She keyed a search into the computer. "February 8, 2015," she said. "Can you access the NYPD case management system?"

"I can," he said, pulling out his cell phone. "But don't you think Chapman would have noticed a similar case?"

"Maybe the body wasn't found," Dani said. "Or maybe it happened in another part of the city. Chapman only covers the Bronx."

"It's likely that a murder occurred somewhere in New York on any given day based on population alone," Flint said. "Over eight million people live within the city limits, and millions more come here to work."

She wasn't deterred. "Can you check to see if any involved a similar victim and MO?"

Flint gave her a skeptical look before tapping the screen on his phone. She listened to his half of the conversation while he explained what he wanted to whoever was on the other end of the call. After several rounds of clarification, he listened and disconnected.

"There were 352 homicides in 2015," he told her. "None of those occurred on February 8."

She'd been wrong. The key was not 101 days between murders. Codebreaking involved trial and error, and this had all the earmarks of a code. She wasn't prepared to give up. "This has to mean something," she said, mentally recalibrating. "There must be a different pattern."

She navigated away from the program and pulled up the digital case files they had collected the data from. She divided the screen into three sections, putting the first page of each report side by side.

"What are you doing?" Flint asked.

"Looking for commonalities," she said, scrolling through each case.

She got to the lab sheets, scanning the items that had been submitted for forensic analysis.

"It's like Chapman told us," Flint said, indicating each lab sheet in turn. "The bindings used are all different. One zip tie, one rope, and one nylon cord."

Dani's attention had been drawn by something else. "What's that number at the top of the lab sheet? It's not the case number."

Flint followed her gaze. "That's an accession number used by the lab."

"The Army uses a similar format." Dani's skin prickled with recognition. "Those are Julian dates."

In the Julian calendar, the days of the year are numbered from 001 to 365, or in leap years, 001 to 366. The entire date would be expressed with the digits of the year first, followed by three digits representing the specific day within that year.

"Why does the Army use Julian dates?" Flint asked.

"They stamp the packing date on their MREs," she said. "That way troops won't get food poisoning from eating expired rations."

"So what are those dates telling you?" Flint asked.

Rather than answer, she pulled up a Julian calendar on the computer and consulted it. "Can you call back and ask them if there were any murders with a similar MO on April 14, 2015?"

He repeated the process, making the same request. After a brief wait, his eyes widened.

It took every ounce of discipline not to yank the phone out of his hand to hear what had surprised him. "What did they find?"

Flint laid the phone on the desk and tapped the speaker icon. "Could you repeat that?"

"There was a murder matching your parameters in Queens on April 14, 2015," an efficient voice announced. "Victim was a white female, twenty-seven, raped and strangled in her apartment. No suspects."

"Could you cross-check to see if the victim ever filed a stalking report or something similar?" Flint asked.

The sound of a clacking keyboard lasted an eternity before the response came. "Two complaints," the voice said. "One was for a prowler in her neighborhood a week earlier, and the week before that she called in a suspicious event."

"What was the nature of the suspicious event?" Flint asked.

"The complainant alleged someone entered her apartment and organized her purses, shoes, and scarves while she was away at work. No sign of forced entry. Nothing stolen. No prints found."

"Can you send me the case number for the murder?" Flint asked. "And the name of the homicide detective who caught it?"

By the time Flint disconnected, Dani had already added the new information to the chart. "This has to be our guy," she said.

"Spill," Flint said. "How did you know?"

She glanced at the cell phone. "I want to check one more to be sure before I explain. Ask if there was a matching murder in Queens on July 24, 2015."

He gave her a quizzical look but made no objection and did as she requested. Minutes later, they had another case.

"This time you knew the exact date *and* the borough," Flint said after he disconnected.

Now confident in her analysis, Dani filled in several more rows of the chart.

"You're identifying a buttload of cases over the past ten years," Flint said when she was finished. "We don't even know if they exist."

"I'm laying out new parameters for our search," she said. "Look at the Julian dates."

He followed her gaze. "He hits three times a year in one borough before rotating to a different one, where he hits another three times. I don't get what else you're seeing."

She moved the cursor as she narrated. "The cases Chapman gave us had Julian dates of 101, 202, and 303," she said. "That sequence got my attention. There can't be a Julian date beginning with a four, so the next one had to begin with one."

"I get it," Flint said. "April 14 was 104, and July 24 was 205." He glanced at her. "You think the one after that will be 306, which would be November 2."

"The killer keeps a schedule," she said. "Now all we have to do is find the cases that fit."

His jaw slackened as he gazed at the screen. "So you filled in the rest of the dates on the spreadsheet by counting up from 101." He shifted to face her. "If he's still out there, that means he's killed thirty-one people so far."

They both looked at the chart she had made, which showed the most recent Julian date as 131, or May 10, 2024, only three months ago.

"Who would commit murders on a strict timetable like this?" Flint murmured.

She was ready with her answer. "Someone who stalks his victims for weeks, planning every aspect of the crime ahead of time. Someone who breaks into his victims' apartments to touch, rearrange, and organize their belongings according to his own specifications. Someone who installs hidden cameras to watch their every move."

"You're saying he's compulsive." Flint's expression darkened. "Something drives him."

She gave voice to the unspoken implication hanging in the air between them. "Which means he'll never stop."

CHAPTER 13

August 17, 2024
Bronx Homicide Squad
Simpson Street, Bronx

"We need to reconstruct the timeline to see how many cases we have," Dani said to Chapman the following morning.

She and Flint had arrived at his office at the Bronx Homicide Squad to show him a printout of the spreadsheet with the information they had entered the night before.

Chapman had immediately comprehended her description of the series but had his doubts about the specific dates. In his experience, serial murder was usually a crime of opportunity or passion rather than a planned event. Like Flint, he had investigated hundreds of deaths, and she couldn't blame him for being skeptical. For her, the proof was in the pattern, which was why she left most of it blank so he could see it come together for himself.

"Can you log in to the citywide homicide record system?" Flint asked him. "We'll know if Agent Vega's theory is correct in a matter of minutes."

"Agreed," Chapman said, turning to face his computer. He used the mouse to navigate to a blank data-entry form. "What's the next date and location we're looking for?"

She read from the sheet. "November 2, 2015."

Chapman filled out the fields on the digital form, narrowing the parameters as much as possible to weed out extraneous cases. He had to resubmit the query twice before he finally sat back in his chair and swore.

Dani wheeled her swivel chair closer to peer around him. "Should be in Queens."

"We'll go through the details later," Chapman said, saving the file and opening a new blank form. "Give me the date after that one."

"April 16, 2016," she said. "That one shifted because it was a leap year. It will also be in a different borough. He's already hit the Bronx and Queens. I'd try Manhattan or Brooklyn because Staten Island is a lot harder to commute to for frequent stalking."

With the search narrowed to two boroughs, the results popped up faster.

"Got a match in Manhattan," Chapman said, then saved the file and cleared the form. "Next."

"July 26, 2016," she said. "Also in Manhattan."

Moments later, he was adding another case to their growing collection.

"I bet he goes to Brooklyn in 2017," Chapman said, now clearly on board.

She gave Chapman an appreciative nod while he went to work. Nothing was more convincing than being able to use the system to predict the next sequence.

"We got a problem here," Chapman said halfway through 2020. "Can't find a case matching Julian date 220."

Dani peered at the screen. "That should be on August 7 in Manhattan. I see you found a match on April 28 on the Upper West Side, which was the one before."

Flint crowded in beside her. "Maybe he broke his pattern."

"One way to find out," Dani said. "Check the next date. Should be November 16 in Manhattan."

In less than two minutes, Chapman located a match. "Got one in Chelsea."

Dani watched the detective log in the data while she pondered the missing case. "He always killed his victims inside their apartments, so it's not like there's a body we didn't find."

"I checked a few days before and after August 7 and came up empty," Chapman said as he finished entering the case number for the November murder. "I say we finish this table and circle back to that one later."

It took less than twenty minutes to fill out the rest of the spreadsheet.

"He started in the Bronx, then switched to a different borough each year," Chapman said, swiveling to face her. "Next was Queens, then Manhattan, then Brooklyn. After that, he rotated back to the Bronx. Why didn't I see this?"

Dani cut his self-reproach short. "No one would have seen it."

He wasn't mollified. "You did."

"Vega's a special case." Flint tipped his head toward her. "Her brain doesn't work like most people's."

Was that a compliment, an insult, or merely an observation?

She decided to take it as the latter. "Uncle Sam spent a lot of time and money training me to think this way. It doesn't matter how we got here. We're onto him now and we're putting a stop to his agenda." She didn't add that she would have to convince her supervisors to let her work off the clock, an unorthodox practice—probably against policy and procedure—but she'd find a way to convince them. First, of course, she'd have to make sure she still had a job after the actions of her last assignment.

She pulled her buzzing cell phone from her pocket. Had her mother said something new? She glanced at the screen and saw Special Agent in Charge Steve Wu's name. Throat suddenly dry, she tapped the screen to read the text.

OPR INVESTIGATION IS COMPLETE. REPORT TO MY OFFICE IMMEDIATELY.

CHAPTER 14

Conner adjusted his binoculars, bringing the woman into sharper focus. A sudden breeze sent a dark-chocolate tendril of hair tumbling down from the loose knot at the back of her head. She swept it away from the smooth caramel skin of her face. She was a feast for his eyes, and the urge to taste her made his mouth water. He licked his lips.

Watching had always been his guilty pleasure. His secret addiction. He'd learned that exposure to certain stimuli during a child's formative years had a lasting impact. For him, it had been the photographs his friend Tommy had shown him on the school bus ride home.

They were in third grade. Only eight years old. Tommy had gotten a Polaroid camera for his birthday and used it to take pictures of high school girls at his older sister's pajama party.

Photos of scantily clad girls, taken without their knowledge, had mesmerized him. From that day on, he had begun to spy while at school. Once he had "accidentally" gone into the girls' bathroom. Another time he'd tried to sneak into their locker room, but he'd been busted by the gym teacher. A letter home to his parents had landed him in hot water.

The final straw occurred three months later over the summer. His parents had sent him to Bible camp in the hope of cleansing his sinful nature. Instead, he'd taken the opportunity to cut a hole in the wall and peek into the girls' dormitory. Unfortunately, the girl who caught him was the preacher's daughter.

He'd been sent home from camp early to find his parents looking at brochures for military boarding schools. To his surprise, they took students as young as seven years old. The next month, he was dropped off at the Zaladon Military Academy in Upstate New York.

The strict daily regimen of the academy had made it nearly impossible for him to indulge his cravings. With the exception of the magazine hidden in the library, he hadn't been able to see any girls except in his dreams—and the instructors hadn't figured out a way to monitor those.

By the time he graduated at eighteen, he believed he'd been cured. In the years that followed, he had gone about his life, getting a job, settling into an apartment, even dating a few women, though nothing lasted after they moved in with him.

None of his girlfriends had been willing to use his systems. They kept their closets in disarray, left makeup and other female paraphernalia all over the bathroom counter, and stuck food in the fridge, freezer, and pantry without the proper labels. Growing up in the academy, he'd often been assigned kitchen duty. For everyone's safety, the instructors used a military date system to rotate the food so no one ate spoiled rations. Conner had taken the time to teach his girlfriends the Julian date format, showed them how to use the label maker, and expected compliance. Still, they screwed up, forgot to do it, or outright refused. When that happened, he would tell them to pack their stuff and get out.

He'd resigned himself to bachelorhood, accepting that he might be a bit demanding, but seeing no need to change. Numbering systems were necessary. Why couldn't everyone see that? Rotation according to a fixed schedule ensured success in all aspects of life. Over time, he'd settled into a routine, and everything was on track.

Until that night he saw the video.

When it was over, his pulse raced, his body was drenched in sweat, and he knew there was no cure for him. All those years, he'd merely been in remission, and the contraband footage brought all the old obsessions back in a heated rush. From that moment on, however, simply watching would not satisfy the new desire that had formed in his fevered brain.

Conner's arms grew tired from holding the binoculars steady, pulling him back to the present. He had decided to avoid direct contact today. Instead, he would observe her from a distance. Aware of where she worked, he had stationed himself in the perfect position to watch her leave at the end of the day.

He picked her out effortlessly. No one else moved with such lithe, supple grace. He was a connoisseur of the female anatomy, and hers was perfection.

She reached up to tuck the escaped wisp of hair behind her ear. The movement momentarily widened the opening of her pale silk blouse to reveal her lovely vulnerable throat and a tempting glimpse of cleavage. He dialed the lenses, zooming in closer.

Unbidden, an image of his hands around that slender neck rushed into his mind, quickening his pulse and heating his blood. He expanded the view of her throat until it took up his whole field of vision. A trickle of perspiration coursed down her throat. He followed its progress past her collarbone until it disappeared behind the silk top.

The sight filled him with frustrated rage. He'd have to pay special attention to Dani Vega, who had just become equal parts dream and nightmare.

After learning from the news article about her appointment to the FBI's New York Joint Terrorism Task Force, a quick online search informed him it was housed on the twenty-third floor of the government building at 26 Federal Plaza in Lower Manhattan. Further research revealed the area around the building was under constant video surveillance.

When choosing his vantage point, he had selected a place well hidden by the foliage of the trees in Thomas Paine Park across the street. His objective had been to size her up and learn how she traveled back and forth to work. Could he follow her? Better not. Agents were presumably trained in countersurveillance. He had come here in the hope that he might discover valuable information about Dani Vega that could come in handy later.

And he most definitely had.

He lowered the binoculars, dug into his pocket, and fished out the burner phone he saved for emergencies. He tapped the first speed dial, and the gravelly voice of Donovan Dewitt carried through the small speaker.

"What do you need this time, Conner?"

"A favor."

"Favors don't come cheap," Donovan said. "And the last one ended up costing me. You fractured my guy's nose with that little hero stunt you pulled." He let out a disgusted snort. "According to him, you didn't even stay in the chica's apartment long enough to get laid—so what the hell was that about anyway?"

Conner ignored the question. "I can pay." He paused a beat. "The job I have in mind would need three people. You got a couple of associates you can trust?"

"Three's going to be steep."

"You know I'm good for it."

"Tell me what you want, and I'll give you a price. You pay me cash up front, and I'll make it happen."

Conner spent the next several minutes outlining his strategy. He elected not to share all the details. No sense in spooking them—or, more likely, giving them an excuse to jack up their fee. By the time he disconnected, he'd decided to keep Vega in sight. She may have taken a course or two, but he'd spent more than a decade perfecting the art of invisible observation.

If he caught her looking at her reflection in storefront windows as she walked by, if she crossed the street for no apparent reason, or if she stopped more than once to check out her surroundings, he would consider himself under suspicion and break off the surveillance. If need be, he could always make another phone call and set up a rotating tail, which was extremely hard to notice even for a trained observer.

He could not allow Dani Vega to interfere with his plans. Not when he had a schedule to keep.

CHAPTER 15

SAC Wu had secrets. He was bound by his position as the second-highest-ranking FBI official in the nation's largest city and also by his own ethics not to reveal certain information to Agent Vega.

She sat in one of the two leather chairs that faced his desk, looking at him expectantly. He chafed at the constraints that bound him, preventing him from leveling with her.

"Your text said the investigation was concluded, sir?" she said.

She tried to hide the signs of stress, but he noticed the fidgeting hands that smoothed a nonexistent wrinkle from her black slacks and the slight crease furrowing her forehead.

"The Office of Professional Responsibility found you in compliance with all laws, regulations, and policies."

She blew out a noisy breath, and he felt a smile tug at the corners of his mouth as he observed her relief at the news. He did not, however, share that it had been a close call. Her last assignment had been unprecedented in the history of the Bureau. Wu had been able to convince everyone that her actions were justified, with the notable exception of his immediate supervisor, Assistant Director in Charge Scott Hargrave, who insisted that she'd reverted to her special forces training a bit too readily.

Personnel regulations prevented Wu from telling Vega that his supervision of her operation had also been under review by Hargrave, and that the assistant director had not been pleased with him either. Their fates were inextricably intertwined, but she couldn't know that.

"I wouldn't hold my breath waiting for any commendations," he told her. "But I'm officially reinstating you to full duty."

She gave him a knowing look. "I suppose you aren't up for any awards either?"

Perhaps she had figured out more than he'd realized. "All that matters is that it's over. We can get back to terrorists, cyberattacks, and bomb threats. You know, business as usual."

He'd intended to lighten the mood, but she shifted in her seat, clearly uncomfortable. He tried to make eye contact, but her gaze kept sliding away. Normally forthright, Vega appeared to be hiding something.

He opted for a direct approach. "What aren't you telling me?"

Still not meeting his eyes, she focused on the front of his desk when she spoke. "I was with Mark Flint meeting with a Bronx homicide detective when you texted me."

He squelched the questions on the tip of his tongue to let her talk.

"He requested my assistance to see if I recognized a pattern in a series of cold case murders." She finally looked up. "I found evidence that a serial killer has been operating throughout the city for over a decade."

Nothing was ever simple or straightforward when it came to Daniela Vega. "What makes you think you detected a series that has escaped everyone else's notice?"

He listened in growing disbelief as she outlined a murder schedule he could describe only as bizarre.

"No one else believed me at first, either, sir," she said, apparently reading his expression. "Until I had them use the progression of Julian dates to predict the next case. You can do it, too, if you—"

He waved a dismissive hand. "I trust you."

And he did. He had seen her at work, cracking codes and detecting patterns that included numerical progressions. If anyone could connect these cases, it would be her.

"How many?" he asked her.

"Thirty."

He did a quick calculation. "Based on what you told me, shouldn't there be thirty-one cases?"

"He apparently skipped August 7, 2020. We can't find any matches in the database."

Thirty murders were more than enough to cause a citywide panic. "This is going to grow hair," he said. "Word will inevitably get out."

"Flint is meeting with his chain of command right now," she said. "He thinks they'll want a task force."

Of course they did. The NYPD was about to get lambasted for failing to detect a prolific serial killer flying under the radar for years. They needed to get in front of it as soon as possible, and a multijurisdictional task force was an ideal way to show the public they were making up for lost time. He did not envy his counterpart at One Police Plaza, who must be reaching for some antacids about now.

"I'll get on the phone with the chief of detectives and offer the Joint Operations Center as a base for the group."

This would take finessing. Since Vega had broken the case, the PD would want her involved going forward. Rather than loan her out, he intended to keep her with his team. To do that, he'd have to stretch the definition of "domestic terrorism" to include a serial killer, but he was confident the high body count combined with the inevitable public outcry would get everyone on board.

Vega got to her feet.

"Where do you think you're going, Agent Vega?"

She sank slowly back down into the chair, eyeing him warily.

Like most inherently honest people, she wasn't good at deception.

"You might be able to kick nearly anyone's ass, but you should never play poker."

"Thought I unhooked myself from the polygraph machine yesterday," she said, attempting humor. Failing miserably.

"I don't need fancy equipment to detect stress responses." He let the statement hang in the air between them. He wanted her to know he could read her. Wanted her to know she'd better come clean. "I'm only going to ask you once. Why were you working with a Bronx homicide detective while you were on administrative leave?"

A pinkish glow suffused her tan skin. "You know about my father's death." She made it a statement rather than a question.

He did, of course. It had been part of her background check when she joined the FBI. He'd read her entire file recently, and the circumstances surrounding her tragic past were fresh in his mind. He nodded.

"I went to see Detective Chapman." Her words were halting, as if she spoke around a lump in her throat. "I still have . . . questions about the circumstances, and he was the lead detective on the case."

She was one of the strongest people he'd ever met, but at that moment she looked as grief-stricken as any surviving family member he'd dealt with in his career. Her situation was not like the others, though, and digging into the past would only bring more pain to her and the rest of her family.

"I don't see how dredging all this up could help." He gentled his tone. "It's not an unsolved case, Dani." He deliberately used her first name, personalizing their conversation. "Why open old wounds?"

She looked at him for a long moment. An inner battle seemed to be raging inside her, but this time, he couldn't tell what was causing the turmoil.

"I was only seventeen when it happened," she said. "The detectives kept a lot from me at the time, and now I'm ready to know the truth."

She wasn't telling him everything. He was highly skilled at interrogation and contemplated using the tactics to force her to come clean.

Then he recalled the grilling he'd recently received from Hargrave and OPR. He'd vouched for Vega, assuring those investigating her actions that she was honorable.

She would have good reasons for keeping certain details to herself. He always insisted on full disclosure from his agents but, for the first time in his career, he saw the value of plausible deniability. Vega was protecting him as much as herself from scrutiny. If her investigation landed her in trouble, she did not want him in the hot seat with her.

It all came down to trust, and she had earned his many times over. "Let's focus on the serial killer case," he said. "When it's over, if you still want to revisit your father's murder, come see me and we'll talk. Until then, keep away from it."

"Yes, sir."

Fortunately, a major case would occupy her time while he decided whether her curiosity about the past was warranted, and what he should do about it. "This is still an NYPD case, but I want you to start the briefing for the task force first thing tomorrow morning."

They took each other's measure in silence. Finally, Vega stood once again. This time, Wu did not stop her as she left his office.

He had entered into an unspoken alliance and, once again, would end up answering for her actions. Whatever happened, they would rise or fall together.

Steeling himself for another unpleasant confrontation, he picked up the phone and pressed the extension for Hargrave.

CHAPTER 16

The following morning Dani stood at the head of a crowded conference table in the FBI's Joint Operations Center, known as the JOC.

Wu had ordered key personnel to come in for an initial briefing, and now Dani found herself in the awkward position of addressing a room full of law enforcement personnel who had more experience than she did. She recognized Flint, Chapman, and her FBI colleagues, but she didn't know the lead detectives for the remaining unsolved murders.

In preparation for the meeting, she'd come in an hour early to meet with Sanjeev Patel, the JTTF's top cybercrime specialist. Brilliant in his own right, his tech skills were formidable. She'd given him the flash drive containing the spreadsheet, and Patel had asked her who programmed the operating code that incorporated nexus detection analytics into the standard subroutine.

"You've got to convince your brother to become an FBI analyst," Patel had told her. "We seriously need people like him."

She'd always known Axel was talented, but praise from someone with Patel's expertise confirmed that her opinion wasn't biased by love. She'd spent the rest of the hour before the meeting going through each case, making sure every entry on the chart was correct. She and Patel had entered additional data from autopsies, interviews, and police reports, discovering another possible link. Now she was ready to share her conclusions.

At her signal, Patel uploaded her spreadsheet to the massive wall screen for everyone to see. She spent the next twenty minutes reconstructing the timeline for her audience before the questions started.

"How do we know the guy started in April of 2014?" a Brooklyn detective asked. "Maybe there's another set of cases with a different numbering system that goes back further in the past."

Dani had prepared before the meeting began. She glanced at Patel, who took the nonverbal cue, opening a second tab on the digital spreadsheet.

"Specialist Patel has compiled cases throughout the entire metropolitan region involving similar victims and MOs going back twenty years," Dani said. "There are no obvious correlations, but they need to be checked out individually to be certain."

The secondary chart was filled with scores of entries.

"We'll divide up into investigative teams to save time," Wu said, addressing the group for the first time since the meeting began. "But we'll focus our energy on the thirty cases we're confident are related to see if we can develop any leads now that they're linked."

A detective who worked out of the Manhattan Homicide Squad spoke up. "Speaking of linking cases, why didn't NCIC pick up on the pattern?"

The National Crime Information Center, a nationwide computerized database maintained by the FBI, contained data about all kinds of crimes. All federal, state, and local law enforcement agencies were mandated to enter details from police reports to form a massive clearinghouse designed to help apprehend fugitives, locate missing persons, return stolen property, and detect similarities among cases separated by distance and time. Many serial offenders who traveled around the country had been identified using the system.

Patel responded quickly. "Unfortunately, the database is only as good as what's entered into it," he said. "Also, this unsub changes key elements of his crimes. Not all the victims were stalked—or, at least, many of them never called the police to report anyone following them."

"Same thing with the break-ins," Dani added. "Less than half the victims filed burglary reports. My guess is that he either didn't always rearrange their belongings, or the women were afraid no one would believe them if they came forward about those incidents."

"He varies the way he commits the murders too," Patel said, explaining what he and Dani had concluded earlier. "Sometimes he uses an edged weapon, like a knife, but then he's also strangled, suffocated, and bludgeoned his victims."

She interrupted to reveal the new commonality they had discovered an hour earlier. "The method he used to kill his victims may have varied, but the autopsy reports show blunt force trauma from a left-handed attacker using an object, his fist, or the heel of his palm in seventeen of the cases. The remaining ones were strangled or suffocated."

"If our perp is a southpaw, that'll be useful to eliminate potential suspects," Chapman said.

"When we have some," Wu said dryly. "Sounds like the only weapon he didn't use was a firearm, which makes me wonder if he knows a thing or two about ballistics and wouldn't risk leaving that kind of evidence at the scene."

A woman Dani recognized as the Queens detective chimed in from the opposite end of the conference table. "Or maybe he likes the intimacy of watching his victims die by his own hands."

The room fell silent as all heads turned toward Dr. Portia Cattrall, who headed the Behavioral Analysis Unit for the FBI's New York Field Office. SAC Wu had introduced her at the outset of the briefing, but Dr. Cattrall had withheld her opinions so far.

Dani sat down, intrigued to hear what the forensic psychologist had to contribute.

"I read through the cases last night," Dr. Cattrall began. "Unlike most psychologists, I don't have the luxury of direct analysis—or any interpersonal contact at all. Therefore, my theories are just that. Theories. Not facts. What I am about to tell you is based on two decades of experience, but, where the human psyche is concerned, nothing is certain."

With so many unfamiliar people in the room, Dr. Cattrall apparently felt the need to provide a disclaimer. She looked around the room as if waiting for comments. Receiving none, she continued with her analysis.

"One key element of the killer's methodology stands out." She paused as if deciding how best to explain her theory. "This unsub is—first and foremost—a voyeur. I arrived at that diagnosis due to the hidden video equipment he installed in the victims' apartments."

Everyone in the room was doubtless familiar with the general concept of voyeurism, but Dani had the sense the psychologist had a different perspective.

Dr. Cattrall slid her glasses off and placed them on the table. "Clinically speaking, a voyeur is aroused by watching people who don't know they're under surveillance, especially when they're doing things that are normally private, such as showering, dressing, or having sex."

"So it's critical that the person he's watching has no clue?" Chapman asked.

"It's the spying that excites him," Dr. Cattrall said. "He feels compelled to do it."

"Speaking of compulsions," Flint said. "What about the B and Es?"

Dr. Cattrall nodded. "Breaking and entering to organize the victims' personal belongings demonstrates both an extreme form of control-seeking behavior and the likelihood that we're dealing with someone suffering from obsessive-compulsive disorder."

Dani wanted to confirm her own assumption. "Could OCD explain his need to stick to a regular routine?"

"Yes," Dr. Cattrall said. "Especially considering the fact that he commits his crimes on sequential dates rather than when an opportunity presents itself or when a particular target triggers him."

"So did he create a system to count his victims and keep an exact schedule?" Dani asked. "Or was it because he was afraid to lose track of his crimes?"

There had been cases where prolific serial killers had murdered scores of people, forgetting their names and where the bodies were buried. Tragically, grieving family members could never be certain their loved one's killer had been caught and had no way to literally or figuratively put the victim to rest.

Dr. Cattrall lifted a shoulder. "Could be either or both."

The notion of prearranging violence on a fixed timetable continued to bother Dani. Other crimes, such as bank robberies or art heists, required advance planning, but murder felt different. Individuals, unlike banks or museums, were unpredictable.

"What happens if his preselected target goes on an unexpected trip, or has an accident, or changes jobs and moves away?"

Dr. Cattrall looked thoughtful. "I wondered the same thing. The only explanation I could come up with was that he selected more than one victim."

"He actively stalked several different women at the same time?" Flint gave his head a disbelieving shake. "When would he have time to go to work?"

"He could have a few candidates, then focus on one close to the deadline," Dr. Cattrall said. "For all we know, some of the women he ended up killing weren't his first choices." She shrugged. "It's impossible to be sure until he tells us . . . and frankly, we may never know."

"Let's get to the profile," Flint said. "Who are we looking for?"

The newly formed task force was about to embark on an investigation that could yield hundreds of leads. While nothing was certain, an analysis from the BAU could help narrow the search from a pool of potential suspects.

"The unsub is of above-average intelligence, as demonstrated by his ability to conceal the fact that his crimes were related until now," Dr. Cattrall said. "We already know he's compulsive, but the ability to stalk his victims and wait until the appointed time to attack shows self-discipline and restraint. The lack of forced entry in the apartments indicates he either has experience picking locks—which wouldn't work with electronic keypads—or that he's cunning enough to obtain a key or the combination in advance of his crime. If that's the case, then he's far more dangerous."

"How so?" SAC Wu asked.

"It means he's figured out how to manipulate his victims to gain their trust," Dr. Cattrall said.

Dani thought of Ted Bundy, who had used ruses to maneuver his victims close enough for him to overpower and abduct them. His feigned helplessness and charm penetrated their natural defenses, and they let their guard down for just an instant—which was all it took. Was this the type of killer they were dealing with now?

"When you're interviewing persons of interest, look for someone physically strong," Dr. Cattrall added. "There were no drugs in his victims' systems, so he had to use brute force to restrain them and, in some cases, manually strangle them."

"Most of the victims are Hispanic," Chapman said. "Are we looking in that community for our perp?"

"That's less certain," Cattrall said, consulting her notebook. "Out of thirty known cases, ten of the women self-identified as Latina, nine were White, six were Black, and five were Asian. Notably, they were all physically fit and had long, dark hair, so that could be a preference, but it's impossible to tell his ethnicity based on victimology."

"There's something we haven't talked about," Dani said, gesturing toward the wall screen. "Take a look at the killer's schedule." All eyes turned toward the chart. "Regressing the dates and locations shows us the past, but *pro*gressing the numbers tells us the future."

A murmur went around the table as everyone absorbed her meaning.

"The next murder will take place in Manhattan on August 19," she said. "Tomorrow."

"Shit," Chapman said. "He's probably stalking his next victim as we speak."

Wu glanced at Patel. "Can you access the NYPD database and search for any recent stalking complaints involving single women living alone in Manhattan?"

"Already on it."

"Broaden the parameters," Chapman added. "Look for breaking and entering, burglaries, prowlers, trespassers, and suspicious persons or events."

Dani agreed. This close to the appointed time, the killer had doubtless already selected his target and installed cameras. She could only hope the woman in his sights had called the police to report suspicious activity.

A sense of frustration permeated the room. They knew when, they knew how, and they knew where—but they still might not know enough to stop the killer before he took another innocent life.

CHAPTER 17

Brooklyn Heights, Brooklyn

The sun was setting by the time Dani walked along the sidewalk toward her Brooklyn Heights apartment. Now partnered with Flint, she had opted to park her Bureau car in the FBI's automotive garage on 26th Street near the headquarters building and ride with him. Overenthusiastic city parking enforcement officers were less likely to ticket and tow a vehicle with an NYPD placard on the dash.

Since she was without wheels, Flint had offered to give her a lift home. She declined, not wanting to wait around while he met with the brass at 1PP at the end of the day. Unlike some of her colleagues, she enjoyed riding the subway and walking through the city. As a native New Yorker, the traffic sounds, the exotic smells wafting from restaurants serving every imaginable ethnic food, and the warm summer breeze on her skin brought her senses alive.

She reached the end of the block and was preparing to cross the street when a plaintive cry drew her attention. Coming to an abrupt halt, she pivoted to her left and zeroed in on a construction site halfway down a small side street, where a man in a business suit stood near the site. He appeared to be looking for help, but no workers were present.

"You okay?" she called out, starting toward him.

He spun to face her, clutched his chest, and fell to his knees.

She rushed forward, pulling out her cell phone. She glanced down at the screen and started to tap in 9-1-1, but got only as far as the first digit when a hard object crashed down on the back of her head, sending her sprawling to the ground as the phone flew from her grasp.

Darkness clouded the edges of her vision. She fought to remain conscious as rough hands tugged at the right side of her belt. She reached for her Glock, only to find an empty holster.

Whoever had clobbered her was now in possession of her service weapon.

Gloved fingers scrabbled at her neck, and she caught a glimpse of a barrel-chested mountain of a man leaning over her. The part of her mind that still functioned understood that he planned to strangle her rather than shoot her in the back.

As her systems came back online, she made her first move, which was to put distance between herself and her attacker to perform a threat assessment. She drew her knees up and tucked into a ball, rolling out of his reach.

Going with the momentum, she rolled over again, this time coming up on her feet. She had enough experience ground fighting to know it was not to her advantage to remain at a lower place than her opponent.

Correction . . . opponents.

Three men faced her. One was the oaf who had been trying to choke her, the second held the crowbar he'd used on the back of her head, and the third was none other than the man in the business suit— who now held her Glock. All wore black leather gloves.

"Your money and your jewelry," the man in the suit said, training the pistol on her.

She'd been in life-threatening situations before and had experienced the same peculiar sensation of time slowing down. She sized up the opposition in the same instant she processed new information. Oaf, Crowbar, and Suit were a team of muggers who had figured a woman walking alone at dusk for a soft target.

They were about to learn otherwise.

"Now," Suit said, motioning with the pistol.

Moving the gun off target for an instant gave her the opening she needed. She sprang forward, using the element of surprise to plow directly into him, grabbing the muzzle and aiming it toward the darkening sky.

Suit's index finger, trapped in the trigger guard, bent at an unnatural angle. He howled in pain, using his free hand to throw a punch at the side of her head. Anticipating the move, she spun away from his fist and twisted the gun harder, eliciting another shriek.

From the corner of her eye she saw the hook of the crowbar swinging in a vicious arc toward her head and managed to duck an instant before the heavy metal bar whistled past her ear and collided with a sickening *thunk* into the side of Suit's head.

Suit crumpled to the ground, and she had bent over him to wrench the gun from his slackened hand when Oaf bear-hugged her from behind. Meanwhile, Crowbar, apparently realizing she was about to gain control of the Glock, swung his weapon of choice again, this time aiming to knock the pistol away.

She had a split second to decide whether to continue prying the gun from Suit's unnaturally bent fingers or release her grip to deliver an elbow strike to Oaf, who was moving one of his beefy hands up to wrap around her throat again.

If she timed it wrong, the crowbar would pulverize her hands, rendering them useless in a fight. She released her grip just before the crowbar smashed into the gun, sending it hurtling through the air.

She immediately drove her elbow backward into Oaf's chest. He let out a grunt, and the hand around her throat loosened enough for her to take a half step forward, creating enough space to snap her head backward into his chin.

He let go of her completely, and she darted away, performing a quick reassessment. Oaf was clutching his jaw, Crowbar was lining up for another swing, and Suit was unconscious on the ground. Her Glock was nowhere in sight, but she'd had plenty of training in hand-to-hand combat.

Crowbar swung again, and she spun out of the way, using the movement to launch a counterattack in the form of a roundhouse kick that landed solidly in the center of Oaf's midsection just below the sternum. He dropped to his knees, coughing and sputtering, unable to suck in air. He would be out of the fight for the next couple of minutes.

And then there was one.

She and Crowbar squared off, circling each other. She made sure to keep out of swinging distance. She realized he wasn't attacking, and if the standoff continued long enough, Oaf or Suit would recover. Clearly Crowbar was buying time so they could gang up on her again.

The thought of time passing made her consider her surroundings. No one had entered the narrow side street in the ninety seconds they'd been fighting.

But Crowbar didn't know that.

She made a show of directing her gaze behind him. "Hey," she called out, waving her arm as if trying to get the attention of a passerby. "Call the police!"

The instant Crowbar glanced over his shoulder, she launched herself at him. One of the key strategies in mortal combat was not to allow an adversary reaction time. Delivering an unrelenting onslaught of blows made it difficult for the opponent to mount a counterstrike—or effectively defend himself.

She moved in close, making it impossible for him to take a swing at her with the crowbar. He grasped the hooked part with both hands and aimed the sharp end at her belly, telegraphing his intention to skewer her with it. He failed to appreciate the fact that both his hands were occupied while hers were free, and his range of motion was limited, while hers was not. Lastly, he was focused on offense rather than defense.

Taking full advantage, she swiveled her body sideways, parrying the metal bar with her forearm. The beefy man's momentum carried him past her, and she gave him a mule kick to the hamstring. Before he could turn around, she brought her leg back and swung her foot up directly into his crotch from behind him.

The crowbar clattered to the ground as the man who had wielded it doubled over and swore. She was about to pick it up when Oaf barreled into her from behind.

He had recovered faster than she'd thought possible. She allowed the blow to propel her away, spun, and shifted into a fighting stance.

Expecting a renewed attack, she was surprised to see Oaf and Crowbar half dragging Suit across the street toward an idling black van with its side door open. They heaved Suit inside and scrambled in after him.

As the van peeled out, she craned her neck to see the license plate, but it was covered in mud and unreadable. She turned in a circle, scanning the ground until she spotted her Glock and her cell phone several yards away.

She secured her service weapon first, then snatched up her phone and tapped out three numbers on the cracked screen.

"Nine-one-one, what's your emergency?"

Dani quickly outlined her situation, carefully describing the getaway van and its occupants before disconnecting at the sound of approaching sirens. Now that the immediate danger was over, her main concern was cutting off the van's escape. The muggers were dangerous and had to be stopped.

She could only hope she'd made enough of an impression to make them consider another line of work.

CHAPTER 18

SAC Wu understood leadership principles. He always responded in person when one of his agents was injured and never left until he'd dealt with the situation.

After getting to the scene, his first order of business had been to check on Vega, who'd suffered a blow to the back of her head. He'd taken her to a nearby streetlight to get a better look at her in the gathering darkness. She'd downplayed the injury, joking that she was hardheaded and explaining that paramedics had checked her out before he arrived.

He wasn't buying what she was selling. "I'll be satisfied when I get a report from the emergency room doc," he told her.

"I'm not going anywhere without my gun." She motioned to a pair of crime scene detectives talking to the patrol supervisor coordinating the response. "They collected it to send to the lab for forensic analysis."

The police personnel clustered around a group of sector cars included Flint, who had cut short his meeting at 1PP to assist in the investigation.

Wu turned back to Vega. "No one fired the weapon, and you said the muggers all wore gloves. I don't understand why they need it."

She'd given him a quick account of the attack when she called to notify him about it.

She nodded. "CSU wants to test it anyway. We fought over it. There could be trace evidence."

The NYPD's Crime Scene Unit wouldn't normally be called out for a relatively minor street crime, but Flint's sergeant had put in the request upon learning the victim was a federal agent.

Wu knew the FBI was occasionally accused of bigfooting local police and went out of his way to avoid any appearance of highhandedness. He would not, however, allow them to confiscate his agent's service weapon when it wasn't necessary.

He strode over to the group and introduced himself, then spent several minutes convincing the crime scene detectives to swab Vega's service weapon for DNA and check it for latent prints using a field test kit rather than taking it to the lab. They bought in when he mentioned the inordinate amount of paperwork for everyone involved, agreeing their time would be better spent scouring the immediate vicinity for blood spatter or any signs of trace evidence.

That settled, the patrol sergeant gave him an update. "They located an abandoned van a few blocks away matching the description Agent Vega gave," he told them. "It was reported stolen about four hours ago."

Wu figured it wouldn't be easy. "Any trace evidence inside?"

"Another CSU team's going through it now," Flint said, after reading a text on his phone. "We're isolating images of the perps ditching the van from traffic cameras." One corner of his mouth curved into a wry smile. "They were limping, hobbling, and leaning on each other when they got into a blue SUV. The video unit is attempting to track that vehicle now, but there was mud on the tags that prevented the license plate reader system from capturing the numbers."

Wu shifted his gaze to Vega. "You didn't mention that you kicked their asses."

He caught Flint's eye, sharing a knowing look with the detective. They'd both seen her in action on a previous assignment, and the men who'd attacked her should consider themselves lucky she'd held back.

Like others he'd met who had served in special forces, Vega was humble. She never bragged about the years of advanced combat training that made her so formidable. She let her actions speak for her, quickly and efficiently taking care of business.

He'd get a detailed report from her about her use of force later. Now his main focus was on why she'd been targeted. Flint had started his career in uniform walking a beat before working his way into the detective ranks, and Wu appreciated his insight into the types of criminal activity that didn't normally concern federal agents. Instinct told him the encounter was out of the ordinary, but he wanted a street cop's perspective.

"How many muggers have you heard of that worked as a team, set up an ambush ahead of time, had a getaway vehicle standing by, and a second car in the area in case the first one got burned?"

Flint tilted his head to one side, considering the question. "None," he finally said. "Muggings are usually crimes of opportunity."

Vega looked at him. "You think I was targeted," she said flatly. "And I agree. The guy in the suit had already started faking a heart attack before I was in his line of sight."

"So one of the other two men—or maybe a fourth person you never saw—would have to act as a spotter, giving the crew a heads-up when you were close," Flint said.

"They could predict that anyone in law enforcement would render assistance," Wu added, then paused. "It was the perfect trap, assuming they knew you were an agent."

"That's a major assumption," Flint said. "Her creds aren't visible, and her gun is concealed under her suit jacket."

"But why would someone go after a federal agent?" Wu asked. "It's asking for trouble."

Vega was ready with an answer. "To stop the agent from discovering something."

"I don't mean to be insensitive, but I've got to put it out there," Flint said. "If they wanted to stop you, why not just put a bullet in your brain?"

His bluntness did not appear to upset Vega in the least. "They didn't bring a gun," she said. "They came with a crowbar, so they planned to put me in the hospital rather than the morgue."

"Which wouldn't bring as much heat as killing you, but sideline you for a while," Flint said.

"Right now, the only case I'm investigating is the serial killer," she said to him. "And I'm partnered with you."

Wu wasn't sure what she was getting at. "You think Flint will be next?"

She raised a brow. "He should be sure to watch his six."

He was on board with the notion that this was more than a common street crime but wasn't ready to connect the incident to the serial killer case. Did Vega know more than she was sharing, or was she simply warning Flint to stay on guard?

She was something of an enigma to him. He understood her on many levels, but she kept a lot of things to herself. A trait they both shared, whether she knew it or not.

CHAPTER 19

Conner's back slammed against the brick wall, forcing the air from his lungs. The move should have made him breathless, but it served only to anger him further. He had agreed to meet Donovan behind the gym to pay him the second half of his fee. Apparently Donovan wanted to exact a pound of flesh in addition to his payment.

"Three of my crew are laid up," Donovan said. "One of them has a broken hand." He shoved Conner harder. "And it's your fault, asshole."

Conner made the conscious decision to let Donovan blow off a bit more steam, but there was a limit to his patience, and Donovan was reaching the end of it.

"They couldn't go to the hospital either," Donovan went on. "It's the first place the cops would look. So you're going to pay the ten grand for the private doc I sent them to."

"I'll give you an extra five," Conner said. "And if you don't take your hands off me, you'll be the doctor's next patient."

Donovan released his grasp of Conner's shirt collar and pulled out a switchblade. "Nobody talks to me like that and lives," he said.

Conner ignored the knife. "You know what I've done for you," he said quietly. "And you know what I could do to you—even if you kill me."

Both men glared at each other. Conner watched Donovan's expressive face as the threat sank in. Donovan was smart, which was why he'd risen through the ranks of his criminal organization to a second-tier leadership position. He had to assume Conner would take precautions to ensure someone else could access—and release—evidence of Donovan's long list of crimes.

"Five thousand, then," Donovan said, pressing the release to snap the spring-loaded blade back inside the handle. "But we're even now."

Conner shook his head. "We're finished when I decide we are."

"Then we're only doing surveillance for you from now on," Donovan said. "At least when it comes to her." His dark eyes narrowed. "You lied to me about Vega."

"I didn't lie," Conner corrected. "I just didn't share all the details."

"Details?" Donovan shot back. "I wouldn't call special forces training a detail. That bitch nearly took my guys out for good."

Conner had told Donovan that the target was a rookie FBI agent, which was accurate. They needed to know she would be armed so they could plan an ambush. If they had been aware she had advanced combat skills, they would have demanded even more money up front.

It had been hard enough to get Donovan on board with attacking a Fed. He'd leveraged every bit of dirt at his disposal to convince Donovan to go through with it. The idea that the target was young, female, and new to the job had gone a long way toward selling the plan.

"I told you to put your best men on it," Conner said. "Maybe your best isn't good enough."

Donovan's fists clenched hard enough to whiten his knuckles. "You told us to take her gun instead of using our own. That was bullshit."

"I told you how to get the drop on her," Conner said. "It's not my fault your guys couldn't pull it off."

His cell phone vibrated with an alert. "Are we done here?" Conner reached into his pocket with deliberate nonchalance. "Places to go, people to see."

He waited for Donovan to stalk off before checking his phone. Another one of his monitored social media hashtags had popped up. This time it was #JESSICAFONTAINE.

He tapped the screen and quickly navigated to the post.

GOT A CALL FROM NYPD DETECTIVES ABOUT JESS. LOOKS LIKE THEY HAVE NEW LEADS. #NEVERFORGET #JESSICAFONTAINE

A response appeared as he was reading.

WE SHOULD HOLD A VIGIL AND CALL THE MEDIA. DM ME TO MAKE PLANS. LET'S GET AS MANY PEOPLE OUT THERE AS POSSIBLE. #NEVERFORGET #JESSICAFONTAINE

Jessica had died in 2020. The fact that cops had reached out to a friend or family member with a new lead could mean only one thing. They were onto him.

Soon enough there would be headlines about a serial killer stalking the city, and everyone would be on high alert. Cursing, he began to recalibrate. He would start with Agent Vega, who was the key to everything. Next he would set a plan in motion to make sure no one ever came knocking at his door.

CHAPTER 20

August 19, 2024
FBI Joint Operations Center
Lower Manhattan

Dani was among the first to arrive at the Joint Operations Center the following morning. Wu had insisted on taking her to the emergency room last night. By the time the ER doc had cleared her, it had been close to midnight. A night of broken sleep punctuated by unsettling nightmares had left her fatigued, and her body was still sore from the fight. Nothing a steaming cup of black coffee with a shot of espresso couldn't fix.

"We're out of time," SAC Wu said to the room at large. "No one goes home until we have a break in the case."

Today was August 19. If the killer kept his schedule, another innocent life would end before the day was over.

"I want to wrap up last night's incident before we move on to team reports," Wu said, turning to Patel. "You have the final update from DAS?"

The NYPD's Domain Awareness System included police CCTV and private security cameras that combined to form a network giving them access to thousands of cameras in the city. Wu had requested shared access, which had been granted via a secure communications link.

Patel, who controlled the wall screen, clicked an icon to open a digital file. "This is the last image they obtained of the SUV."

A grainy feed of a highway filled the screen. Cars and trucks raced in and out of view before the boxy profile of an SUV digitally tagged with a glowing X passed through.

"The vehicle was identified as a Chevy Suburban," Patel continued. "Last known direction of travel was southbound on I-95."

Interstate 95 stretched from Maine to Florida, with hundreds of exits along the way. Once he left the city, the driver would have thousands of avenues of escape.

"We put out a BOLO for the vehicle," Flint said. "The state police won't have a legal reason to arrest whoever's inside if they manage to locate it. Best the troopers can do is ID the occupants for us so we can get arrest warrants."

"Any word on the getaway van they used before they got in the SUV?" Wu asked Flint.

"CSU had the van towed to the crime lab in Queens. It's in one of the examination bays. They'll finish processing it later, but they took preliminary swabs and collected some fibers."

"When will we hear back?" Wu pursued.

"It's not at the top of their to-do list," Flint said, a slight flush coloring his cheeks. "They prioritize murders and felony sex crimes." He flicked a glance at Dani. "I could put in a request to expedite if we knew Vega was targeted based on the serial killer case we're working now."

A murmur went around the room. Dani hadn't shared her suspicions with anyone other than Wu and Flint. Clearly, the detective wanted the others to know there may be more to the situation.

Wu raised a hand, bringing the sidebar discussions to a halt. "We cannot confirm that," he said.

"Which in FBI speak," a baritone voice straight out of Brooklyn piped up from the back of the room, "translates to 'that's for sure what happened.'"

The comment was met with a few chuckles.

"The muggers demanded cash and jewelry," Wu said. "Exactly what you'd expect."

Flint offered his take. "But the crime was way too coordinated for your average skel. A strung-out street hood wouldn't have the ability to plan this far in advance. And he wouldn't have multiple partners and two vehicles on standby."

Dani wanted a behavioral profiler's opinion about her assumption. She found Dr. Cattrall among the others in the room.

"Do you think the series of murders could have been committed by more than one person?"

If her attack involved a coordinated team, perhaps the killings did too.

"I do not," Dr. Cattrall said without hesitation. "The signature is highly idiosyncratic." When her remark was met with silence, she elaborated. "The unsub's behavior is very specific to his personal tastes, quirks, and desires. Others would not have a need to reorganize and straighten their victim's personal space. Additionally, the way the items are arranged is consistent. Look at it this way," she continued, warming to her subject. "If you live with someone else, have you ever found yourself reloading the dishwasher after they put things in?" Her comment was met with knowing smiles all around. "Others would likely have had different ways of straightening. In these cases, though the items varied, the way they were arranged was consistent."

"You don't believe my mugging was related then?" Dani asked bluntly.

Dr. Cattrall shook her head. "I can't say that conclusively, but there are no obvious indicators of a connection."

Wu seemed anxious to move on. "Let's wait to see if we get anything back from the crime lab," he said. "In the meantime, I'd like to know how many of you found evidence of pinhole cameras at the murder scenes?"

The question had the desired effect, refocusing everyone's attention on the priority investigation.

Several of the detectives whose cases previously had no indication of audiovisual surveillance spoke up. They had reviewed the crime scene photos, enlarging them until they could identify what would have appeared to the naked eye like holes from a thumbtack in the walls of the primary bedroom and also the living room.

"I called the crime scene detective who photographed the scene," a Manhattan homicide detective named Robinson said. "When I sent him enlarged images, he told me they looked like holes for hanging small pictures or posters. He couldn't see any electrical wires, so he never made a connection with spy gear. Once we told him what to look for, he noticed the outlet covers in the living room and bedroom looked like they'd been removed and replaced. That must be how he got behind the walls to plant the cameras without anyone noticing."

Other detectives shared similar stories, but Dani wanted further confirmation. "Did all of you find two holes about an inch apart?"

"That was the first thing I asked too," Chapman said. "To see if they matched the ones in my cases." He glanced around at his colleagues and spoke for the group. "The answer is yes. We checked with our video unit, and they think one hole was for the camera's lens, and the other was for a microphone."

Another link to add to the growing list of connections, but not for every case. Several crime scenes showed no signs of any hidden cameras in the apartments of their victims. No one could tell if the unsub simply didn't install surveillance cams in those cases, or if it had gone unnoticed and wasn't in the crime scene photos. Dr. Cattrall, however, had her own theory.

"Just because we didn't find them doesn't mean cameras weren't there," she said. "For this personality type, watching is more than half the fun." She paused. "To put it bluntly, he gets off on it—literally and figuratively."

Apparently concluding that aspect of the discussion had ended, Wu pressed for another angle. "Any other commonalities in the cases?"

"The vics all lived alone and had no pets," Chapman said. "And they were all sexually assaulted. The bodies were left on the bed naked."

"He was careful not to be interrupted," Flint said. "Another reason to watch them ahead of time."

"I'm sure that was part of his target-selection criteria," Dr. Cattrall put in.

Wu turned to Patel. "Let's add that to the spreadsheet. We want to check out every nexus between the victims and the crimes." He turned back to the others. "What else?"

A detective from Queens spoke up. "This doesn't apply to all the cases, but in the ones that involved a stalking complaint prior to the murder, we found similar suspect descriptions."

"I'm sure it's too much to hope for that the guy wore a patch over one eye or had a unique facial tattoo."

"I wish," the Queens detective said. "You know how eyewitness descriptions go—we're lucky they all agreed on him being male, tall, and pretty buff."

"No agreement on race?"

The detective shook his head. "A few vics said he was white, but the rest said they couldn't be sure. I'd hate to rule anyone out based on something as flimsy as that."

"Agreed," Wu said. "Let's stick with unknown ethnicity." He glanced around again. "What else do the cases have in common?"

At first no one answered. Then Chapman spoke up in a tired voice. "Luck."

"You think this unsub got away with all these murders by chance?" Wu said. "Because I don't. He's damned clever."

Chapman shook his head. "I'm talking about stuff he couldn't control. Stuff that happened to the evidence."

Wu's brows furrowed. "What happened to the evidence?"

"We've been comparing our files," Chapman said, indicating his fellow detectives. He consulted a legal pad covered in handwritten notes. "Turns out the DNA samples were damaged during analysis in eight cases, hair and fiber samples collected were deemed insufficient for analysis in nine cases, and the results of rape kits performed on the victims were lost altogether in six cases." He looked up from his notes. "If you add all those up, it leaves only seven cases where the perp was successful in removing all traces of his presence."

Dani could tell Wu was choosing his words before he responded. The NYPD crime lab had been caught up in a scandal several years back when a routine audit revealed that a few technicians had repeatedly mishandled evidence. The NYPD brought in new management to overhaul the system from top to bottom, but the public and the media had long memories when it came to the embarrassing situation.

Wu appeared to be thinking along the same lines. "Did some of these cases occur before the lab was restructured?" he asked, keeping any hint of censure or judgment out of his voice.

Chapman nodded. "The lab's squared away now, but it's too late for some of these cases."

"So he was smart," Dani said. "But also lucky." She privately wondered how many investigations had been compromised but didn't pile on when the detectives were clearly as frustrated as she was.

"UFB," Flint muttered. "This asshole should play the lottery."

"Plenty of other cases went down the crapper too," Chapman said. "He wasn't alone. In fact—"

"Excuse me," Patel interrupted her before turning to Wu. "I've got an alert based on the parameters you set, sir. A woman was just found dead in Manhattan. Female, Hispanic, living alone. Her coworker came to her apartment to check on her when she didn't show up for work this morning. Responding officers said it looks like she was strangled."

His words echoed like a death knell through the room. They had believed they had hours before the killer struck. With sickening clarity, Dani realized that August 19 had technically begun last night after the stroke of midnight.

They were nine hours too late.

CHAPTER 21

Dani hated interviewing friends and family of murder victims. The grief and anguish stamped on their faces and evident in their body language mirrored the expressions her brother and sister had worn years ago.

When Death claimed a victim, no prayer or supplication ever brought anyone back. Dani had seen many casualties during her military career, but felt no more comfortable with it than the shocked and angry young woman who stood before her in the hallway outside the victim's apartment.

Cynthia Blakely had come to the apartment when her best friend, Angela Dominguez, failed to show up for her shift. Both women worked at a nearby restaurant, where Angela was a short-order cook and Cynthia waited tables. According to Cynthia, Angela was never late.

"I know this is difficult," Dani said to Cynthia. "But we need to know more about why you came over to her apartment this morning."

She had sensed Cynthia's hesitation when she described her reasoning. Something was missing from the account.

Cynthia looked at her shoes. "I was, you know, worried about her. Like I told you. She's never late."

"You didn't wait to see if she would get there in another hour or two," Dani pressed. "You took the morning off—something you never do—to check on Angela." She leaned in close, subtly invading Cynthia's space. "You suspected something had happened to her, didn't you?"

Cynthia lifted her head to meet Dani's gaze. "Yes."

"You've got to level with us," Dani said. "Help us find out who did this."

Cynthia took a shuddering breath, apparently steeling herself. "I feel like shit," she began. "Angela had been acting kind of weird lately. I finally got her to tell me what was going on. What she said made no sense, though."

Dread prickled the back of Dani's neck. She had an idea where this was going but allowed Cynthia to tell the story without interruption.

"She said someone was doing stuff inside her apartment when she wasn't there. She'd come home after work and find her kitchen counters cleaned and the food in her pantry lined up all straight. I mean, real weird, like with the boxes set up according to food type and size. Same with the cans." Cynthia gave her head a rueful shake. "Asked her how many edibles she'd had that night and if they were the legal kind. Then I told her someone should bust in and clean my place for free." She dabbed at her brimming eyes. "Angela didn't think it was funny."

Dani glanced at Flint, who was on his phone, murmuring instructions to the crime scene detectives going through the apartment. He gave her a slight nod. She took it as her cue to continue. Now that she'd finally established a rapport, he would want her to wring out every detail she could. Her first order of business was to get more actionable information for CSU.

"How long did Angela say this was going on?"

Cynthia shrugged. "About a month or so."

"Did Angela consider calling the police?"

Cynthia looked away, tears streaming down her face. Dani handed her a tissue and waited through a series of sobs.

"I talked her out of it," Cynthia finally said. "Told her everyone would think she was nuts."

Cynthia dissolved into tears, and Dani stepped back to give her some space. She was about to approach her again when Flint's gentle tap on her shoulder drew her attention. She turned to see him crook his finger and walk toward the other end of the hallway.

"What's up?" she whispered when they were out of earshot.

Flint jerked a thumb at the closed apartment door. "Just got off the phone with the crime scene detective," he said. "We need to gown up and go inside."

CSU was careful to document everything at the scene with pictures even before they fully entered the immediate area where a murder had occurred. Strict protocols were in place to ensure the preservation of evidence. Cross contamination was also a concern, and no one wanted to risk damaging the integrity of any stains, fibers, or even microscopic elements that could help identify the killer. If CSU wanted them inside, there had to be a damn good reason.

Moments later, they were each handed a clear plastic bag containing a full Tyvek suit. Dani kept her questions to herself as she covered herself from puffy cap to bootied foot in loose white material. The clear face shield went on last before they stepped carefully inside the apartment.

A slender man similarly clad in forensic garb approached. "You're the FBI agent who's also a codebreaker?" he said to Dani.

Perplexed, she merely nodded.

He held up a sheet of lined notebook paper with untidy writing in ballpoint ink. "We photographed this and will attach it to the case file as a JPEG," he said. "But I wanted to give you the chance to get eyeballs on the original document before we seal it up for processing at the lab."

Dani extended a hand, but the CSU detective pulled the paper back. "Eyes only," he said.

She leaned forward to examine the page. Two lines of verse were scrawled in shaky handwriting.

FATHER TO ALL, YET FATHER TO NONE.

TO US, HE IS ALWAYS NUMBER ONE.

"It's a riddle," Dani said. "In the form of a rhyming couplet with nine syllables in each line." Her eyes traveled halfway down the page to a series of apparently random letters.

DODSMLHXBPDNGYBU

"The letters are an encrypted message. I'm assuming the answer to the riddle will crack the code."

"We think so too," the CSU detective said. "And it looks like he forced her to write it before he killed her."

Dani glanced up at him. "This is the victim's handwriting?"

"It matches what we found in her journal," he said. "There are two crumpled sheets near the body with the same stuff on it and then some scribbled-out letters at the end," the CSU detective said. "She must've made some mistakes, and he forced her to start over again on a new sheet. The pages look like they were torn out of her diary, and the pen appears to be from a loop attached to the side. We can confirm this at the lab with handwriting experts."

"He didn't want to bring anything that belonged to him into the scene," Flint said.

"At least, nothing he intended to leave behind," Dani said. "If this case is like the others, he would have brought restraints and possibly a weapon, but took them with him."

"Along with any pinhole cameras he'd already hidden in the walls," Flint added.

"Got your text about the cams," the CSU detective said to Flint. "We found evidence of punctures in the drywall in the main bedroom, bathroom, and the living room. We're processing those too."

As far as Dani was concerned, any doubt that this was related to the other cases had just been eliminated.

"There's another reason I wanted to show you the original note," the CSU detective said. "The first two attempts on the crumpled sheets had no blood on them." He pointed a gloved fingertip at the center of the paper. "Look at the blood spatter on the last one."

She immediately saw what he meant. "The droplets are on top of the ink."

He nodded. "My guess is he promised not to hurt her if she wrote out what he told her. When she finally got it right, he killed her."

The layering of the droplets indicated writing first, then bleeding second.

"Cause of death?" Flint asked.

It wasn't CSU's job to determine the official cause of death, but the teams had investigated hundreds of fatalities, and their assessment would likely match the medical examiner's findings after the autopsy.

"Blood loss," the CSU detective said without hesitation. "He sliced into her femoral artery, and she bled out fast."

The woman had complied with his demands in the hope that he would spare her, but in the end, he had shown himself to be cruel, manipulative, and a liar.

"There's a major problem we're not talking about," Flint said. "Why did the perp change his MO to leave a coded message?"

Both men turned to Dani, saying nothing. They didn't have to. The implication hung in the air between them.

Dani addressed Flint. "You think this is about me. The fake mugging too."

"I'm not saying this murder is connected to the mugging," Flint clarified. "But I am saying both crimes involved you in some way. And I don't believe in coincidences."

Dani jerked her chin in the direction of the bedroom where Angela Dominguez's body had been discovered. "How do you figure her death involves me?"

"Not necessarily her death," Flint said. "That happened on the killer's schedule and had been planned months in advance." He gestured to the note. "It's the message that's directed at you. Somehow the perp knows we have a cryptanalyst on our team. He's jumping up and down waving his arms in the air to get your attention. He's pulling you into the investigation. What I want to know is why." His eyes bored into hers. "I'd lay odds it's someone you know, or someone you've had dealings with before."

The ominous words struck a nerve. Flint was one of the premier homicide detectives on the force. His opinions carried weight, and he had concluded that she and the killer had crossed paths. If she could figure out how, where, or when, then she could figure out who.

"Then it's up to me to solve this riddle," she said to Flint. "Sooner rather than later."

"I'll be tied up here awhile," he said. "I'll catch up to you after I clear the scene."

CHAPTER 22

An hour later, Dani strode through the main door of the Joint Operations Center. Flint had asked one of the uniforms to expedite her trip from the crime scene. Determined not to waste time, she had taken a screenshot of the page and come up with a solution for the rhyming riddle while riding in the patrol car.

"Did you get the image I sent?" she asked Patel by way of greeting.

"Nice to see you too," he responded, scrolling his mouse to open a file on the wall screen. "Uploaded the image and converted the text."

The right side of the screen displayed the handwritten note, and the left showed the content as printed letters and numbers in a Microsoft Word document. Patel had anticipated her request before she made it. Now she could manipulate and rearrange components of the phrases any way she wanted. She focused on the first pair of lines, reading them again.

FATHER TO ALL, YET FATHER TO NONE.

TO US, HE IS ALWAYS NUMBER ONE.

She was startled out of her reverie by Wu, who had come in behind her. "Do you have an analysis?"

"I wondered why the word 'us' was underlined," she said. "That broke the pattern, and it was intentional, so I started there."

"Interesting," Wu said. "I would have started at the beginning."

"I assumed the rhyming couplet should be considered as a whole unit," Dani said. "And the word 'father' is used twice."

Wu narrowed his eyes. "You've figured out the first part, haven't you?"

She nodded. "The word 'us' is underlined to emphasize it. That implies more than the straightforward meaning." She strode to the screen and pointed. "Take each letter separately, and you come up with 'U' and 'S.'" She moved her hand to indicate the first word in the clue. "When you think of 'father' combined with 'U' and 'S,' what comes to mind?"

"The father of the US," Wu said, dawning comprehension evident in his tone. "George Washington."

She looked at her boss. "To the US, he's always number one. He is considered the first founding father. He was the first president." She lifted a shoulder. "He's on the one-dollar bill."

"Number one," Patel said from the computer controls where he stood. "I get it, but how is he father to none?"

"That threw me off at first too," she said. "Look up George Washington's children."

Everyone waited while Patel split the screen again to perform a Google search. "I never knew he had no biological offspring," he said a moment later. "His descendants all trace back to his wife, Martha Custis—but not to him."

"I didn't realize it either," Dani said. "But Martha was a widow when he married her. She had two children and a grandson that he adopted and raised as his own. He and Martha could not have kids, and he never had any with another woman."

"That certainly fits the description," Wu said. "If you take the narrow-minded view of restricting your definition of 'father' to biological lineage." He turned to her. "Let's say you're right. What about the rest of the clue?"

Everyone focused on the screen again.

DODSMLHXBPDNGYBU

"I assume the riddle provides a key to the next part of the code," Dani said. "I'm going to simplify the answer to 'Washington,' and use that. The hard part is to figure out what kind of cipher was used to encrypt the message."

"What do you mean?" Wu asked.

"I don't believe the killer has a background in cryptanalysis," she said. "If he did, he would have used such an unusual skill to leave codes at each crime scene."

"He started doing it at this scene because of you," Wu said. "Somehow he knows about you and is getting your attention."

"If that's true, he would probably do some research and choose one of the more famous encryption methods. I doubt he would use a computer to do it. He wants to challenge me personally in a battle of wits."

Patel's fingers were poised over the keyboard. "What encryption methods are you talking about?"

"There are all kinds of ciphers. Some are simple—you just swap letters. On the other end of the spectrum are ones that require supercomputers to perform multiple calculations per second," she said. "And there's a lot of variation in between."

"Put yourself in his place," Patel said. "What would you choose?"

She gave it some thought, pacing back and forth as she discarded one idea after another. She'd cracked hundreds of codes while in the military, mostly during training but sometimes out in the field where failure was not an option—like now. Not wanting to confuse her colleagues with details of how various encryption methods worked, she waited until she'd reached a conclusion before sharing her plan of action.

Since the unsub knew who she was, he'd know she'd been trained in cryptanalysis. He was playing with her by creating a code for her to break, so how would he do it? If he wasn't a pro, he'd either use an online program or look something up. He must be using this as a delaying tactic, so he'd most likely avoid an online program that would need a digital key.

No, he'd go old school, forcing her to match wits. For that, he'd do some research, and there were a handful of codes that had become famous. If he selected one of those, which would be the most likely?

"Let's start with the Caesar cipher. It's the simplest. You substitute letters by shifting the alphabet."

After several minutes spent working through various possibilities, she knew her first guess had been wrong. "Looks like he's making it more difficult. The Caesar cipher uses one alphabet. There are tougher ones that use multiple alphabets."

Everyone waited while she paced, thinking out loud. "The Alberti cipher," she muttered, then shook her head, realizing her second guess was also wrong. "That one requires a disk to decode the message, and we didn't find anything like that."

"A computer disk?" Patel asked.

"Alberti created it in the fifteenth century, so no." She explained the concept as simply as possible. "It's two concentric circles. You have to rotate the inner circle to the right place to get the letter on the outer circle. There's a lot more to it, though."

Wu frowned. "Is there a multi-alphabet cipher that doesn't need a separate piece to solve it?"

"There's the Vigenère cipher." She considered the famously tricky code that had been popular for centuries. "It's nicknamed *Le Chiffre Indéchiffrable*—the unbreakable cipher."

"If it's unbreakable, how do we crack it?" Patel said.

Her response was straightforward. "Pattern analysis. And thousands of hours of practice."

She instructed Patel to create a table with twenty-six columns across and twenty-six rows down. Next, she had him put one letter of the

English alphabet in each square on the x-axis and on the y-axis. This left a rectangular grid with a total of 676 spaces. She then had him fill in the remaining 624 empty spaces by lettering them in order from x-axis down beginning with the letter in the top row.

A grid appeared on the screen with the entire English alphabet on both the x-axis and the y-axis, creating 676 individual squares, each containing a letter.

"This is called a Vigenère square tool," she said to Patel. "To use WASHINGTON as the key, we find the intersection of those letters."

"But the message has more than ten letters," Wu said.

"You just keep repeating the keyword from the beginning until you've accounted for all the letters in the encrypted text," she said.

She called out each letter to Patel, who copied and dragged them individually to a space below the table. Everyone studied the new text.

HOLLEYBENCHNORTH

"A different keyword would yield different results," Wu said. "We can't be sure this is the correct interpretation."

"You can assign the Crypto team to work on various permutations using other keywords," Dani said. "Since this decryption doesn't lead to gibberish, I'm going with it." She addressed Patel. "Separate the letters into the words HOLLEY, BENCH, and NORTH. Search the web for any intersection of those words with WASHINGTON."

In less than a minute, Patel had replaced the decryption tool with a picture of an iconic landmark.

"The Arch of Triumph," Wu murmured. "In Washington Square Park."

Modeled after L'Arc de Triomphe in Paris, which was based on L'Arco di Tito in Rome, the stunning marble arch had been designed to celebrate the centennial anniversary of George Washington's inauguration as the first president.

"That park is practically right around the corner from here," Dani said. "My sister goes to NYU. I've been there plenty of times, but I don't recall anything about Holley."

Erica was now in her final year at New York University. The main campus bordered on the famous park, which had become a hangout for students.

Patel replaced the arch with the image of a bronze bust perched atop a white limestone plinth. "This is Alexander Lyman Holley," he said. "His monument is tucked away toward the back of the park."

Dani concentrated on the next part of the clue. "Is there a bench beside the Holley bust?"

Patel switched to a satellite view of the park. "There are two benches along the curb behind the monument." He glanced up, grinning. "One of them is on the north side of the base."

"It's a dead drop," Wu said.

Dani agreed. Spies and others who wished to transfer information to others without being detected were known for leaving an envelope or a package hidden in a public location after providing directions to the receiver.

"See if there are any cameras in that part of the park," Wu said to Patel. "If it's not monitored, pull any satellite feed you can find going back twenty-four hours. I want to know who sat on that bench."

"I'm guessing we'll find something taped underneath the bench to the north of the statue." Dani was eager to make progress. Flint would probably be finishing up at the murder scene. He should be there to help investigate the new lead. She pulled out her cell phone and tapped one of the speed-dial presets. "Meet me at Washington Square Park," she told him. "We've cracked the code and—"

"Hold up a second," Wu said. "This could be a trap. A package taped under the bench could contain anything from an IED to anthrax. Or the unsub could be getting you into position for a headshot from a building across the street."

She couldn't deny his logic. "Correction," she said into the phone. "Meet me *and the cavalry* at Washington Square Park."

CHAPTER 23

Washington Square Park
Greenwich Village, Manhattan

Dani stood beside Flint fifty feet back from the wooden park bench on the north side of Alexander Holley's monument. Out of an abundance of caution, Wu had insisted on calling out all manner of law enforcement toys to Washington Square Park.

"I don't see the bomb dog sitting," Flint said.

Explosive detection K-9s were universally trained to sit when they caught a target scent. A dog who pawed at explosives was a liability in that line of work. In this case, the black Labrador's nose was the only thing lowered to the ground as it circled the monument and bench, thick tail wagging.

"Looks like they're done," she said, watching the handler lead his dog away. "CSU's next at bat."

Two Crime Scene Unit detectives covered in white suits and wearing masks approached. One bent down to peer at the underside of the bench. He gave a quick thumbs-up to his partner, who readied a digital camera.

Clearly he'd spotted something, but he wouldn't touch it before documenting its exact position with photographs. After that, Dani assumed they'd check for latent prints and other trace evidence.

She groaned. "This is taking forever."

As she'd expected, they waited a quarter of an hour before the first CSU detective reached under the bench and tugged at something. After a full minute, he straightened, holding a white business envelope with silver duct tape on either end. The second detective began taking rapid-fire pictures of the envelope.

"These two are like crime scene paparazzi," Flint muttered, apparently sharing her impatience. "We don't need forty-seven angles of the same piece of evidence."

Before entering the park, CSU had agreed to send pictures of any materials they found to the JOC so the task force could add it to the growing mountain of information they were gathering. Finally, the second tech lowered the camera and grabbed his cell phone.

A minute later, Dani tugged the buzzing cell phone from her pocket. "Vega."

Wu's voice greeted her. "Patel is sending a photo to you now."

Dani tapped the screen, navigating to a newly arrived text. She opened the image.

"Shit."

"My thoughts exactly," Wu said.

Flint peered over her shoulder as Dani reread the words printed on the back of the plain white business envelope.

Agent Vega

"What's up with this guy?" Flint said.

"He's got my attention," Dani said. "Can the CSU team open it here instead of waiting to take it to the lab?"

"They brought a portable chamber," Wu said. "They'll open it now."

She glanced up to see the second detective reach into a duffel and lift out a clear plexiglass box the size of a small aquarium. A pair of blue gloves were attached to two holes cut into the sides. The first detective opened the top and placed the envelope inside before sealing the tank shut. They rested the container on the bench and squatted beside it. The second detective inserted his hands into the blue gloves and picked up the envelope.

They were taking no chances. If any airborne contaminant was inside the envelope, it would not be carried on the wind.

After an eternity, the second detective eased the last part of the glued flap open and was unfolding a sheet of white copy paper. His partner repeated the previous procedure, first taking pictures of the page with his camera, then his phone.

"Patel's forwarding the image to you now," Wu said, still on the phone with her.

Flint's breath brushed against her temple as he resumed his previous position to read over her shoulder.

CATCH ME

OR ANOTHER ONE DIES.

NOT MUCH TIME LEFT.

NEXT DEADLINE IS

ENCODED IF YOU SOLVE FOR X.

RUN, DON'T WALK.

Below the text was a mathematical equation.

$$\left(\left(-3e^{\pi i} \times (\cos^2 x + \sin^2 x)\right)\right)^5 - \left(\left(\sum_{k=0}^{\infty} \left(\tfrac{7}{8}\right)^k\right) - \lim_{x \to 6} \frac{x^2 - 36}{x + 6}\right) = x$$

"He's changing his timetable," Dani said.

"And it sounds like the new deadline is coming up sooner rather than later," Wu responded. There was a brief pause and the sound of a squeaking swivel chair in the background. Then his voice sounded muffled, as if he'd pulled the phone away from his mouth. "Find me a mathematician," he called out to someone in the JOC, then added, "ASAP."

"Someone from Cryptanalysis can break that down pretty fast," Dani said to him. "Or I can start working on it right now."

"Someone here can crunch the numbers," Wu said. "I want your entire attention on the scene."

"He could have simply told us the new date, but instead he comes up with a complex equation to slow us down," Flint said. "Then he warns us to hurry up." He gave his head a frustrated shake. "Makes no sense."

"It's a distraction," Dani said. "He creates a sense of urgency to make us scramble. While we're rushing around, he's setting up his next kill."

"Agreed," Wu said. "We'll have to multitask to avoid losing time. Patel is coordinating with the PD to check the feed from cameras in the park, but unfortunately that monument doesn't have any nearby. It's out of the way."

"I'm sure the unsub knew that," Dani muttered.

"The lab will process the envelope, paper, and duct tape for prints, DNA, and trace evidence," Wu continued. "And you two can report back here. We'll have the equation solved by the time you arrive."

"You can also start running some names." She deliberately made the comment cryptic, testing her hypothesis.

After a brief pause, Wu's voice carried over the phone's speaker. "What names?"

She glanced at Flint, who shrugged.

The first part of the message hadn't led either of her colleagues to the same place she'd reached moments ago. Then again, neither of them had worked as many puzzles and codes as she had.

She posed the question to both of them. "Did you notice the strange phrasing of the text before the equation?"

"The wording's weird," Flint said. "But it didn't mean anything to me."

She directed them to look at the message again, this time paying special attention to the first letter of each phrase.

CATCH ME

OR ANOTHER ONE DIES.

NOT MUCH TIME LEFT.

NEXT DEADLINE IS

ENCODED IF YOU SOLVE FOR X.

RUN, DON'T WALK.

"Conner." Flint glanced at her. "You think that's his name?"

"We'd never get that lucky," she said. "But it's a clue. Maybe a street name, or a hometown, or a code name, or an anagram. It means something to him."

"I'll get Patel on it," Wu said. "And Cryptanalysis. We'll run every permutation of that name and those letters. If there's a needle in that haystack, we'll find it."

"We'll head your way after we do a final sweep." Dani disconnected and began a slow 360 perusal of the immediate vicinity.

"You feel him watching you?" Flint asked her.

She nodded. "He's a voyeur, remember?" she said. "And he needs to know we picked up his message. He's good at hiding cameras, so he could have planted one somewhere. I'm guessing he'd prefer to see us in person, though." She stopped turning to face Flint. "Above all else, our guy likes to watch."

CHAPTER 24

Conner dialed the binocular lenses, keeping Agent Vega in focus. The K-9 and forensic team were obviously NYPD, as was the detective standing beside her with the gold shield around her neck. That meant they must have set up some sort of task force.

The observation confirmed what he'd suspected. After operating in the dark for years, he'd bleeped onto the radar of two of the largest law enforcement agencies in the world. Between them, they could throw a shitload of resources at this investigation. Enough to penetrate some of his defenses if he didn't act quickly.

His first strategy had been to slow them down so he could get everything in place. He'd learned to use the tools at hand, and in this case, it was New York University. He'd headed for the NYU math department and quickly found a grad student hard up for cash. After introducing himself to a tall, skinny twentysomething man with Coke-bottle glasses and a close-cut Afro, Conner had asked him to design a multifactor polynomial equation leading to a specific integer. The grad student had been satisfied with Conner's explanation that it was for a friend who had bet he could solve any math problem in his head and without a calculator. As Conner had expected, the grad student had taken it as a personal challenge to make it difficult.

Twenty minutes later, Conner had his equation. The next part of the preparation was far trickier and took him the rest of the day to complete. Once everything was ready, he had come out to the park, careful to arrive before it closed at midnight, and blended in with the crowd around the arch, listening to music. He had managed to slip away from the group unnoticed, placing the envelope under the bench and leaving without encountering any curious passersby or any cops.

Now that Agent Vega and her cohorts had gotten his delivery, it was time to set the rest of the plan in motion. They would crack the code soon enough, and then they would have some decisions to make. He wondered how they would react.

He followed Vega's progress as she strode confidently through the park. Despite his need to hurry, he took a moment to admire her toned physique, evident even in business attire. She would be even more difficult to deal with than he had first supposed, but he had been devoting extra time to his training in preparation for the final phase of his operation.

As before, her long dark hair was twisted up into a slightly mussed knot high on the back of her head. It left her neck bare, and when she turned, his eyes were drawn to her lovely throat. An oath escaped his lips as his grip tightened on the binoculars.

Whether Vega knew it or not, their fates were linked.

CHAPTER 25

FBI Joint Operations Center
Lower Manhattan

Wu had divided the task force personnel by area of expertise, assigning each subgroup a different task. They'd spent the past hour combing through their existing files as well as other databases to follow up on the new lead. He'd just reconvened everyone around the conference table when Vega and Flint arrived from the park to join them.

He brought the newcomers up to speed as they took their seats. "We've solved the math equation."

Vega looked at him. "And?"

"The answer is 235," he said as Patel switched the screen to show the equation with the solution.

$$\left(\left(-3e^{\pi i} \times (\cos^2 x + \sin^2 x)\right)\right)^5 - \left(\left(\sum_{k=0}^{\infty} \left(\tfrac{7}{8}\right)^k\right) - \lim_{x \to 6} \frac{x^2-36}{x+6}\right) = 235$$

"That's supposed to be our new deadline," Patel said. "Crypto believes it's—"

"A Julian date," Vega cut in. "But without the year."

Wu figured she'd get there right away. "The year wasn't necessary since he said the deadline was soon." He gestured to the screen, where

Patel had posted a Julian date calendar. "The 235th day of 2024 is August 22."

"That's three days from now," Flint said. "He wasn't bullshitting about us not having much time to catch him."

It was the reason Wu had divided the work, saving time. Now he wanted progress reports. He addressed the analysts who had hunkered together at one of the terminals lining the room. "Any hits on the name Conner?"

A sharply dressed woman with razor-cut blonde hair spoke for their subgroup. "We've run the name through the investigative files for all thirty-two cases we've now attributed to this guy. No witnesses, friends, or persons of interest by that name in any of them. Then we tried street names, cities, and other locations. No connection to any of the cases there either."

Wu wasn't ready to let it go. "I'm convinced Conner refers to his identity somehow . . . like an alias." He turned to Dr. Cattrall, who was seated opposite him. "Or maybe an alternate personality?"

Dr. Cattrall considered the idea before responding. "You're referring to dissociative identity disorder, or DID," she said. "Separate personalities operating within the same person."

He nodded. It was a long shot, but he wanted a professional to weigh in.

"Genuine DID is extremely rare," Cattrall told the group. "Most people with the disorder have spent over seven years in the mental health system before they get a diagnosis, because the symptoms can mimic other things. The alternate personalities are referred to as 'alters,' and help the person cope with trauma and stress." She slid off her glasses and laid them on the table. "In reviewing the crime scene information from all the cases, I cannot rule out DID, but it wouldn't be my first hypothesis. The person committing these crimes is not only a killer, but a serial rapist, a voyeur, and a burglar," she continued. "The obsessive-compulsive tendencies displayed by the rearrangement of his victims' items indicates a different personality type than someone who suffers from DID."

He pressed for clarification. "What if one of his 'alters' was a rapist, one was a killer, another had OCD, and so on?"

"The kind of switching between alters that would account for the entire constellation of behaviors is not substantiated by the crime scenes," Dr. Cattrall said. "He would have to flip back and forth between alternate identities while in the act of committing his crimes. Each alter would have no idea what was going on."

One of the Brooklyn detectives raised his pen to get her attention. "Why would that be a problem?"

"Imagine waking up to discover you're in a stranger's apartment with no idea why you're there. Looking around, you see things out of place and feel compelled to organize. Suddenly you wake up again, with no memory of what happened before, and this time, you're beside a dead woman you've never seen before. Then you wake up watching a video of yourself sexually assaulting someone." She spread her arms, palms up. "You'd be terrified, alarmed, and overwhelmed. You wouldn't have the presence of mind to clean up the crime scenes so effectively that no viable forensic evidence has been discovered so far. You wouldn't understand enough about the entirety of the crimes to successfully evade detection from the most advanced forensic experts and the most experienced homicide detectives in the country. In my opinion, we're dealing with one individual who has one identity." She shifted her gaze to Dani. "The question uppermost in my mind is, Why did he address the note to Agent Vega?"

A question Wu had wondered about as well. Vega reddened under the weight of everyone's attention, clearly not liking the spotlight. He was about to press the issue when his phone chimed with an urgent email alert.

Everyone knew he wouldn't interrupt the meeting unless something important was happening. All conversation stopped as he tapped the screen and scanned the message. This was the last thing they needed right now. He scrolled to the bottom, then addressed the group.

"The NYPD's deputy commissioner for public information is giving us a heads-up. Reporters are swamping the police with requests for information about a serial killer we failed to notify the public about."

The announcement was greeted with a colorful array of obscenities from around the room. Wu gave them a moment to vent before continuing.

"It seems Angela Dominguez's friend, Cynthia, called every media outlet who would listen and told them Angela was the victim of a serial killer who's been running loose in the city for years. She accused the PD of withholding information that could have saved lives. Specifically, that he stalked his victims and broke into their apartments ahead of time."

"How would she know that?" Dani asked. "We never told her about the stalking."

A frustrated groan escaped one of the homicide detectives. "I did an in-depth interview with Cynthia after you and Flint left," he said. "She found the body, so I had to document everything for the case file."

Wu knew one of the detectives would conduct a follow-up interview, but he hadn't read the report yet.

The detective's tone was apologetic. "Since Angela had told her about the break-ins, I asked her if she ever mentioned anyone following her or stalking her. She wouldn't answer the question until I told her why I was asking, so I let her know there *might* be related cases that involved stalking . . . emphasis on 'might.'" He grew adamant. "But no way in hell did I tell her we had a serial killer running around."

"Did she mention anyone stalking Angela?" Flint asked.

"Turns out she told Cynthia that a man had followed her a couple times. When I asked her why no one reported it, Cynthia admitted she talked her friend out of calling the police."

"Same thing Cynthia told me when I asked her about the burglaries," Vega said.

"She got pretty mad after that," the detective said. "Blamed the cops for not warning women about a stalker that had killed two women. I tried to calm her down, but she ended the interview by telling me to do something anatomically impossible and slamming the door on her way out."

"It's projection," Dr. Cattrall said. "Cynthia feels responsible for convincing her friend not to make a report. Instead of blaming herself, she's shifting the responsibility elsewhere. Now she can vent her anger about Angela's death on law enforcement. If anyone ever asks her about it, she can claim it was our fault for not telling the public about the threat."

The fact that Cynthia's version of events wasn't accurate made no difference. The story was already out there, and they had no choice but to get in front of it.

"The director was giving me a courtesy call," Wu told them. "The NYPD is hosting a news conference at 1PP in an hour. This investigation is about to go public."

CHAPTER 26

NYPD Headquarters
One Police Plaza, Lower Manhattan

Dani stood on the steps behind Ivan Dobransky, the three-star chief of detectives who headed the NYPD's Detective Bureau. Dobransky had concluded his prepared statement and was fielding questions in front of a bank of microphones attached to a lectern in front of the headquarters building. She was one of many in law enforcement who formed a backdrop behind him.

Their plan was twofold. First, they wanted to show a united front to the public, who should see that the authorities were putting their full attention on the identification and arrest of the killer who had been stalking their city undetected for years. Second, they planned to scan the crowd, which was precisely what Dani was doing while the chief spoke.

Before leaving the JOC, the task force had discussed the possibility that the killer might attend the news conference to personally witness what he had caused. Dr. Cattrall had agreed that—as someone who enjoyed watching—he might want to see and feel the undercurrent of fear swirling around the plaza. They had arranged for multiple cameras to feed a live stream of the crowd into the JOC, where they could analyze it in real time and save the footage for later.

Unsure exactly what she was looking for, Dani was perfectly placed to see all the reporters, camera people, and passersby who had paused in their daily routines to see what was going on.

"Is it true that the serial killer is responsible for over ninety murders?" a television reporter from a local television station called out to Dobransky.

Dani knew the tactic. Throw out an impossibly high body count to bait the police into revealing exactly how many murders there had been. That information would come out later in court, but they didn't want it released yet. No one in the public seemed to have caught on to the killer's schedule and numbering system, which was a detail they didn't plan to release yet.

"I don't know where you heard that number," Dobransky said, clearly irked. "But we have nothing to substantiate that information."

Someone who had attained the rank of chief of detectives was too much of a pro to take the bait.

"Are the victims all single women who live alone?" another reporter asked.

They had hotly debated how much to release to the public. There was the classic dilemma in speaking about a crime before an arrest or a trial. A good defense attorney could make use of any official statements if they were later proved to be incorrect assumptions on the part of the police. Worse yet, the killer could be spurred to change his behavior or escalate his crimes in reaction to something he heard. The chief was not only speaking to the public, he was creating a record of the investigation, and he was communicating with the killer at the same time.

"They were," Dobransky said. "But we want everyone to remain vigilant whether that description applies to them or not."

"Is it true the killer breaks into his victims' apartments and organizes their rooms?" another reporter asked. "And what does that say about him?"

This detail had no doubt come from Cynthia, making it likely that pundits and armchair profilers would take to the air to offer their opinions about the suspect. The behavioral profile was something they wanted to keep to law enforcement circles, but certain inescapable facts were out in the public now. Dobransky had no choice but to lean into it.

"Some of the victims' apartments were burglarized, but that was not the case every time," he said. "The same is true for stalking."

"So you're confirming that the victims were stalked weeks before they were killed?" the reporter followed up. "Why wouldn't you alert the public about the danger so that potential victims could be on the lookout for stalkers?"

The classic no-win question. If the chief said they had chosen to withhold that information, the police would be held responsible for preventable deaths. If he said they were unaware of the pattern, the department appeared incompetent.

"We only linked the cases together and discovered the pattern recently," Dobransky said, going with the truth. "And as soon as we had enough evidence to believe the cases could be attributed to the same perpetrator, we set up a task force and dedicated resources to arresting the person responsible."

"Are you setting up a special tip line?"

Dobransky nodded. "It will be staffed 24/7, and we welcome anyone who has any information that could be helpful to this investigation to call. Right now, we have no description other than a male who is above-average height with a muscular build."

Dani had been scanning the crowd for anyone fitting that description, but it was too vague to be definitive. She resorted to relying on her training to watch for anyone who did not fit in. Someone who stood out from the media members and onlookers.

A tap on her shoulder drew her attention. She turned her head slightly to see Flint beckoning her. Instead of being part of the window dressing for the news conference, he had been prowling the perimeter, observing the crowd.

She edged backward and sidled away from behind the chief, who was still taking questions. Flint would not have pulled her aside in full view of the cameras unless something important had happened.

"We got a notification from the crime lab," he said to her in a low voice once they were away from the others. "They managed to lift a partial print off something from the park."

"Good enough to run through AFIS?" she asked, catching his excitement.

The Automated Fingerprint Identification System required a minimum number of distinguishing features in a latent print to compare in the database. If the prints were only partial, or if they were smudged, there might not be a solid match.

"The first test was inconclusive," Flint said, then grinned. "But they tried a new technique, submitted it a second time, and managed to get a hit."

Dani allowed herself a moment of satisfaction. For the first time since the nightmare had started, a tiny bud of hope began to grow.

CHAPTER 27

Conner watched Agent Vega step away from the wall of blue uniforms lined up behind the NYPD's head mouthpiece. Assuming the entire plaza around police headquarters would have extra security in the form of barriers and surveillance cameras, he had taken precautions to attend the news conference.

He'd purchased special reflective glasses years ago, wearing them only when he was concerned about facial recognition. The lenses looked ordinary but blocked infrared sensors, shielding his eyes and the area around them. As a bonus, they had a reflective coating that scattered light waves from flashguns, defeating most of the current tech used to map facial features. A ball cap and baggy clothes completed the disguise while still allowing him to blend in with the crowd.

He moved slightly to keep Vega in sight after she turned to lean in close to a man in a suit. The two put their heads together in what looked like an urgent conversation. Who was she talking to?

He edged closer, straining to overhear them, but he couldn't risk drawing attention to himself by getting too close. The man talking to Vega shifted, and Conner recognized him as the detective who'd been with her in Washington Square Park. Dozens of news articles online had featured the storied career of Detective First Grade Mark Flint, who was awarded the medal of valor last year at a huge ceremony.

Flint seemed animated, like he had news to share. Maybe a breakthrough in the case. Had they solved the equation he'd left for them at the park?

Of course they had.

Had they figured out their new deadline?

Ditto.

They should have figured those things out fairly quickly, so what was all the excitement about now?

Vega started to head out of the plaza at a jog, with Flint trotting beside her. Something big was happening.

He would have to make it his business to find out what. He'd been so careful, but the smallest mistake could spell disaster, and the next death might be his own.

CHAPTER 28

Dani and Flint had hurried from the news conference to join the rest of the task force at the JOC. She took a seat and looked up at the massive screen that spanned most of the wall on the far side of the conference room.

One-third of the space was occupied by an arrest photo of a man in his midthirties. His dark eyes peered out from under thick black brows that matched his hair. His face bore a five-o'clock shadow that gave his smooth tan skin a slightly rough appearance.

"We're sure this is our guy?" Flint said to no one in particular.

They had come in after the others and missed the beginning of the briefing.

Wu picked up a printed lab report. "I'll give you a quick rundown." He scanned the page, summarizing key facts. "The text was printed on standard office paper using a laser printer, but the math equation was handwritten. Then he made a copy of the entire note with the equation and put it in a standard white business envelope, which was self-adhesive, so he didn't leave DNA from saliva by licking the seal. The duct tape he used to stick the envelope to the bench was cut, so he didn't tear it with his teeth, and he wore latex gloves throughout the entire process." Wu looked up. "Bottom line, he was careful as hell."

How had such a meticulous criminal missed something?

"Except?" Dani prompted.

"Except the gloves turned out to be the problem," Wu said. "A tiny fragment of latex stuck to the duct tape. Our working theory is that he didn't want to draw attention to himself by crawling under a park bench, so he sat on it and put the precut pieces of duct tape on the envelope. When the coast was clear, he bent forward and reached down to press it onto the underside of the seat directly beneath him. He'd have to do it by feel, and a bit of the glove's fingertip got snagged by the sticky tape."

She could picture it clearly. "The maneuver would take him seconds, and he'd get up and leave. But he had to feel the glove get stuck. He'd know it was torn."

"Maybe not. He was under stress and in a hurry to leave. Even if he did, though, once he saw how tiny the piece of latex was, he'd figure there was a good chance he'd leave more trace evidence trying to pry it from the adhesive. Most importantly, he wouldn't know about the NYPD crime lab's newest tech."

The homicide detective from Queens spoke up. "The lab's in my borough. I took a tour a few months ago, and I've seen what they can do. Pretty freaking amazing. And I'm guessing they couldn't have pulled that print before this new equipment came."

"How does it work?" Dani asked.

"There's a technical description on the report," Wu said. "Basically, it involves putting the fragment of latex inside a vacuum chamber, then vaporizing particles of silver nitrate to coat it in an atomic layer that reveals the partial print. After that, the system uses predictive analysis to expand the ridges and whorls far enough out to establish enough data points to run it through AFIS."

If the hit had come from the Automated Fingerprint Identification System, that meant the matching person probably had a criminal record.

Dani turned back to the image of the suspect on display. "What do we know so far?"

Patel highlighted the name under the photo. "His name is Wilfredo Garcia-Ochoa, but the arrest documentation says he goes by Fred Ochoa."

"Interesting rap sheet," Flint said.

Dani latched on to a detail noted on the intake form. "He's left-handed."

"Thought you'd spot that," Patel said. "Fits with the injuries to the victims. And look at this."

Another section of the screen was devoted to Ochoa's arrest record, which included a stalking conviction.

"He was dating a woman named Giana Mancini in Brooklyn back in January of 2019," she said, reading from the compiled case notes at the bottom of the screen. "Met her at a New Year's Eve party. That means he would have killed his most recent victim just a few weeks earlier on November 11, 2018." She turned to Dr. Cattrall. "Would he switch targets so quickly, considering he must have been obsessed with Giana?"

"Totally plausible," Cattrall said. "In fact, he might have selected Giana as his next target, but when she pressed stalking charges, he chose someone else."

"Not just that," Flint said. "She also bugged out. He couldn't very well stalk her in Italy."

The detective's report indicated that Ochoa had begun dating Giana in January. By mid-February, she had filed a stalking complaint. NYPD patrol caught Ochoa in the process of leaving flowers and a note on her doorstep. A search conducted later revealed his cell phone had a file with pictures and video of Giana that appeared to have been taken without her knowledge. Right after the trial concluded, Giana went to live with relatives in Sicily. She never returned to the States.

"I'm sure that's how his attorney convinced the judge to give him a suspended sentence," Wu said. "The target of his obsession was unavailable, and he had no prior convictions."

"Maybe no convictions, but there was a serious charge in his background," Flint said. "I know the court is not supposed to consider dismissed cases, but this situation screams for an exception to that rule."

Ochoa had been arrested and charged for raping Andrea Yarbrough in 2011 long before the current series of homicides started. Andrea became uncooperative with the prosecution during the trial. The judge ended up dismissing the case with prejudice. At that time, Ochoa's record was clean.

"Looks like he assaulted two women and never served time in prison for his crimes," Dani said. "And now there are many more victims—only they're all dead."

"We should reach out to Andrea Yarbrough," Flint said. "Maybe she can shed light on his personality."

"I'd like to interview her if she's willing to talk," Dr. Cattrall said. "I could glean a lot of information about Ochoa from her recollections of his behavior."

"We can try," Wu said. "But the case file indicates she developed a sour taste in her mouth regarding law enforcement and may not cooperate." He frowned. "I wonder what happened."

"What else do we know about his background?" Flint said. "His personal history."

Patel opened another panel on the screen and narrated the information that appeared. "Ochoa was born and raised in Yonkers."

Yonkers, a suburb of New York City, was just north of the Bronx. Since it appeared he started his crime spree in the Bronx, it would make sense that he selected an area in close proximity to a familiar environment.

"He graduated from Pace University with a BA in communications and a minor in computer science," Patel continued. "After that, he bounced from one small start-up tech company to the next. Right now he's employed at Fool's Dream Technologies, which is based in Brooklyn. They develop apps but haven't had any that hit the jackpot so far."

How did this background fit into what they knew about the unsub? He was clearly comfortable with mathematics, and computer science involved computations for various types of programming.

"Currently, he has an apartment in Flushing, Queens," Patel went on. "There's no record of him ever being married, and we're doing a deep dive on his social media and other information to determine what his relationship status has been over the past fifteen years. That way we can see what he was posting about before the murders began and while they were going on."

It would be interesting to learn if he had a bad breakup that instigated the first attack. Was he the type who couldn't take rejection? Would he be involved in a serious relationship and commit murders on the side to fulfill fantasies that real life couldn't satisfy? She had trouble picturing what would be going through someone's mind while they lived a double life, going to work every day in a standard office environment, yet committing heinous acts in their off hours. Plenty of serial killers had managed to do just that—most famously Ted Bundy, who fooled everyone he worked with.

Her musings were interrupted when Wu posed the most important question of all. "Do we have enough for a warrant?"

It was a comment every agent asked sometime during an investigation. The answer often depended on a variety of circumstances and factors. There was no checklist that guaranteed a judge would sign off on an affidavit for a warrant.

Wu had been looking in the direction of Flint and the contingent of NYPD detectives at the far end of the table when he spoke. Since all the known homicides had occurred in their jurisdiction, the police would make the arrest and the New York District Attorney's Office would prosecute. This was their show. And their call.

"I'll talk to the DA's Office," Flint said after glancing at his colleagues. "We're running short on time, so we don't have the luxury of tying this up with a pretty bow the way the lawyers always like it."

"If nothing else, we for sure have enough for a knock-and-talk," Detective Chapman said. "I vote we pay Ochoa a visit at his apartment when he gets home from work today."

Dani was all about action. "We interview with or without a warrant," she said. "It will either be consensual or not, but either way we move forward. And I'd like to go with."

"We need to strategize about your involvement in the initial interview, Agent Vega," Wu said. "He's fixated on you for some reason, and we don't know why."

She had anticipated the objection and prepared for it. "That's the best reason for me to see him in person. We want to provoke a reaction from him. If he's been thinking about me, how shocked will he be to find me on his doorstep?"

Wu appeared to give the matter consideration. She knew not to interrupt as he weighed the decision.

"I agree with Vega," Flint said to Wu. "I like to keep interviewees off balance, and this should do the trick." He shrugged. "If we don't get a warrant, Ochoa will be a lot less likely to slam the door in our faces if Vega is there."

That argument apparently sold Wu. "Go with Flint," he said to her. "But we'll be taking extra precautions."

Fine with her, as long as she got to be in the mix.

CHAPTER 29

Early the following morning, Dani stood at the reception desk of a newly constructed apartment building holding out her creds for the doorman's inspection. He had already eyed Flint's shield and cast a wary glance at the small contingent of tactical officers accompanying them.

The task force had spent the remainder of the previous day writing affidavits for search warrants and arrest warrants, only to have the judge refuse to sign them. It had been a frustrating exercise that lasted well into the night. They had all agreed it was imperative to make contact with Wilfredo Ochoa, even if only for a consensual interview. Hoping to catch him before he left for work, they had gone straight to his residence rather than reporting to the JOC.

Dani had been impressed by the towering structure, which was part of a new complex. The developers had razed an entire block of buildings and replaced them with a cluster of high-rise condos surrounding a green space. Flushing, like many places in the city, was experiencing a revival of sorts.

The doorman must have been nervous when they arrived en masse soon after daybreak. He had tried to contact his supervisor, who did not respond. Now it was up to him, and he looked like a man who desperately wanted to pass the buck to someone else.

"Um . . . why did you need to see Mr. Ochoa?" the doorman asked.

"Police business," Flint said in a tone designed to discourage further questions.

"I'll need to contact him and ask if he's available to see you," the doorman said, reaching for a button on the front desk panel. "I can show you up if he agrees to—"

"No need to call." Dani stepped forward, crowding him. As she predicted, he instinctively backed away from the panel. "And we can show ourselves up."

"That's against policy," the doorman said. "I've at least got to notify the building superintendent, or it'll be my job."

She didn't like the idea of someone outside of law enforcement tagging along.

Flint opened his mouth, an objection forming on his lips, but this time the doorman surprised them by tapping the white earbud wedged in his ear and explaining their situation to whoever was receiving his transmission.

A moment later, his eyes widened. "Really?" He looked from Dani to Flint and back again. "The super says he just got a noise complaint about that unit."

"What kind of noise?" Dani asked.

"The unit next door called to report that Mr. Ochoa's TV was turned all the way up. He wouldn't answer his door when the neighbor rang the bell. We've never had any noise complaints about him before."

Dani exchanged a glance with Flint before turning to the doorman. "Can you access the apartment?"

The doorman nodded. "All residents sign an agreement that staff can access their unit for emergencies, to check on their safety, or for noise complaints. It's spelled out in the contract."

"Have the super meet us up there," Flint said. "And tell him not to knock on the door or make entry until we get there."

The doorman looked relieved to have specific instructions to follow that weren't against procedure. He activated the elevator, and they crammed themselves inside. A brief ride took them to the tenth floor. As soon as the doors opened, the sound of an action movie playing at maximum volume reverberated through the hallway. No wonder the neighbor had complained.

A short, stout man in a gray work uniform got off the second elevator and hurried toward them, pounding to a stop before introducing himself as Gary Tucker.

"I'm the super," Tucker said, as if he needed to explain.

"Do you know Mr. Ochoa?" Dani asked, gesturing toward the source of the racket a few doors down from the elevator.

Tucker shook his head. "I've never had to deal with him. He doesn't cause any trouble."

Except killing people.

"Here's how this is going to go," Flint said. "You wait here, and we'll see if he answers the door." He shifted his gaze to the small tactical team. "We don't have paper on this guy, so it's strictly a knock-and-talk as of now." He waited for the team leader to nod his understanding. "If he answers, Vega and I will go in and talk to him, and everyone will stand by out here in case this turns into a shit show."

Dani planned to leave the door open a crack when they went inside so everyone could hear them and so they didn't waste time unlocking it if they needed backup. The judge had not found enough probable cause to issue an arrest or a search warrant. Under normal circumstances, they wouldn't bring the cavalry, but this suspect had murdered at least thirty-two people and had shown himself to be strategic. He might have orchestrated surprises for any law enforcement who came to his door. At issue was the show of force. They could not go in heavy on a consensual interview. The team had to keep out of sight completely unless they were needed. And it had damned well better be an emergency.

Flint turned back to the super. "If Mr. Ochoa doesn't answer, that's where you come in."

Tucker nodded eagerly and held up an electronic key. "This will open any door, and the residents aren't supposed to add their own locks or chains," he said. "That's why we have a secure building."

"Good," Flint said. "And you have the right to unlock and enter the apartment because of the noise complaint, right?"

Another nod from Tucker. He looked like a bobblehead. "I can go in and turn off whatever's making the sound."

Flint gave him a knowing look. "And we can assist you, because there's a noise ordinance violation."

Tucker hesitated, then seemed to catch on. "Right."

Dani and Flint walked to Ochoa's unit. Her training, both military and law enforcement, would have her stop and listen before knocking. But the blaring television drowned out any other sounds she might have detected inside.

She pushed the buzzer.

Nothing.

Flint pounded on the door.

Still nothing.

They repeated the exercise twice more before beckoning Tucker.

"You're up," Dani told him.

They waited as he waved the fob in front of the electronic lock. A green light popped on, and Tucker pushed down the door handle.

Dani laid her hand on top of his. "We'll take it from here," she said.

"But—"

Dani shot him a quelling look, and the protest died on his lips. He stepped back, and Dani wrapped her right hand around the grip of her pistol and slid it out of the slim leather holster attached to her belt.

She pushed the door open and moved inside, Flint close on her heels. After entering the small foyer, she followed the sound of the television through the galley kitchen. Once she passed the refrigerator, the studio apartment opened into the main living space. She saw the television and started toward it, then stopped short. Flint bumped into her from behind.

They both stared at the body of a man lying motionless on a queen-size bed that took up most of the room. His head was encased in a clear plastic bag taped tightly around his neck. Despite his bluish hue and the blurring of his features from the bag, Dani could identify the corpse.

Wilfredo Ochoa, their prime suspect, would not be answering any questions.

CHAPTER 30

Two hours later, Dani was wedged beside Flint in the space where Ochoa's narrow galley kitchen opened into the main living area. The NYPD crime scene detectives had allowed them that far after they had photographed and processed the front part of the studio apartment.

The super, acting under management policy, had called paramedics. Dani and Flint intercepted them in the hallway when they wheeled a gurney stacked with a small mountain of medical equipment out of the elevator. No way were they going to let anyone destroy the integrity of the crime scene and haul the body away when the victim was obviously deceased.

A fire department lieutenant turned up and insisted on examining the body. A quick inspection of the lividity caused by pooling of the blood satisfied him that Ochoa's heart hadn't been beating for several hours. Rescue personnel packed up their equipment and left.

From her vantage point at the edge of the kitchen, Dani now watched the crime scene ballet of the Tyvek-suited detectives moving around each other in a methodical examination of the main room. The apartment was incredibly neat and tidy. Everything was perfectly organized.

Of course.

One of the crime scene detectives opened the closet and raised his camera. Dani craned her neck to peer around him. Sure enough,

Ochoa's clothes were precisely arranged, categorized by season, color, and style. Even a boot camp drill sergeant would have been impressed.

"Same as the cupboards and pantries," Flint said. "Certainly fits the profile."

Her gaze followed the crime scene detective, who had moved from the closet to photograph a floor-to-ceiling entertainment center that occupied most of one wall in the main room. "Look at how deep the shelving unit is on either side of the television," she said to Flint. "That has to be a Murphy bed."

"And a high-end one too," he agreed, looking around. "In fact, this whole place is loaded with designer appliances." He glanced down. "This tile floor is expensive, and so are the marble countertops."

She had to use two remotes to turn off the television. One for the large flat screen itself, and the other to cut off the throbbing bass of the stereo system connected to it. No wonder the noise had permeated the entire floor of the building.

The thought brought another question to mind. "Do you think the TV was turned up to be sure someone found the body before too long?" she asked Flint. "Ochoa lived alone. If he sometimes worked remotely, it could have been days before anyone missed him."

Flint nodded. "We were supposed to find him sooner rather than later. He probably didn't want his body to lie here and decompose." He grimaced. "Can't blame him."

One of the CSU detectives crossed the room, holding a piece of plain white copy paper sealed in an evidence bag. "He left a note. Found it in the printer on that desk in the corner."

Dani was forcibly reminded of the writing recovered with the last victim. She braced herself, dreading seeing her name on the page. This time there was only one short sentence.

DEATH IS BETTER THAN LIFE BEHIND BARS.

She exchanged glances with Flint. "No riddle, no equation, no code," she said. "Lacks his usual flair."

"The note implies he knew we were onto him," Flint said. "According to the neighbor who called in the noise complaint, the TV started up a few hours ago. That's not long after we got a forensic hit on Ochoa. How would he know we were coming?"

It was a damned good question, and she had no answer. She craned her neck to see around the page. Two of the other techs were pulling the sheets up from the corners of the bed. Next, they hoisted Ochoa's body up and walked him to an open black body bag. They gently placed him inside before tucking the sheets around him and zipping the bag closed. This method preserved any trace evidence that may be in or on the body. Even tiny fibers, flakes of skin, or hair would be transported with the body so it could be separated and analyzed in a sterile environment. Cross contamination was a huge problem, and anything that could be done to minimize the introduction of foreign materials was critical.

Aware they were nearing the end of the process, Dani directed her question toward the lead crime scene detective, who was still holding the paper. "I'd like to fold the Murphy bed up if you're finished processing it."

He shook his head. "We'll do it."

She didn't argue, because her request had the desired effect. The techs moved to the bottom of the stripped bed and pulled the latch at the bottom. The entire bed frame swung noiselessly upward until it snapped into place. She was now looking at parallel rows of wooden slats that formed the underside of the bed framed by a pair of bookshelves.

"Slide the bookshelves together," Flint called out to them.

Two of the techs moved to opposite sides of the shelves. They pushed from the outside in, and the shelves slid inward until they met in the middle. Now it looked like four equally sized bookcases lined up together, with no indication of a bed.

"Slick," Flint said.

"Can you open the bottom cabinets?" Dani asked them.

Each of the techs went to a pair of cabinets that had been concealed when the bed was down.

"Holy shit," one of them said after opening the door.

His colleague squatted down to peer inside the cabinet on the opposite side of the shelving unit and let out a low whistle.

"What did you find?" Dani said, starting toward them.

Flint laid a hand on her arm, holding her back. "You'd better show us."

They each stood, pivoting away from the open storage compartments. Rows of clear plastic bins sat neatly arranged on shelves inside. Even from across the room, she could see a sticky label with printed numbers on each container.

The sinking feeling in her gut told her the answer, but she asked the question anyway. "Are those Julian dates?"

One of the techs began taking photos while the other one responded. "They're a match for the list you gave us when we arrived. There are sixteen containers in this cabinet." He shifted his gaze to his colleague. "How many in yours?"

"I got fifteen over here," the tech said as he continued taking pictures.

"And we just happen to have thirty-one known victims," Flint muttered.

Dani caught his eye. "There would be thirty-two except for the missing case from the spreadsheet. We'll have to wait for forensics to match all the victims through DNA to confirm what we have."

He leaned forward, squinting. "And are those ladies' panties I see inside those tubs?"

Dani didn't need to hear the response to know Flint was right. She recalled that most of the women who filed burglary complaints had not reported anything missing. They had probably assumed a pair of underwear had been lost in the wash and not linked the disappearance with the stalker—if they even noticed they were being followed—or the break-ins. Instead, it turned out that Ochoa had not been satisfied with watching his victims, organizing their possessions, and recording their private moments. Even their deaths had not been enough. He had stolen a trophy from each of them to relive whatever sick fantasies his dark mind harbored. She glanced at the body bag on the floor.

Ochoa's murder schedule had come to an end.

CHAPTER 31

"I'd rather be here than attending the autopsy," Dani said to Flint as they walked through the front doors of the NYPD's crime lab in Queens the following morning. "I've seen enough dead bodies to last me a lifetime. It's forensic science that interests me."

"Then you've come to the right place," a tall man in a white lab coat said as he approached and extended a hand. "Brad Howell, senior criminalist supervisor."

She was vaguely aware of the pecking order for civilians who worked at the lab. They ranged from an entry level I to a supervisory level IV, which must be what Howell was. Flint had called ahead to arrange for a meeting with someone in a position to provide the latest information about the evidence collected in the park and in Ochoa's apartment.

After the introductions, Howell escorted them through a series of hallways with windows into examination areas. She passed forensic examiners in lab coats and protective eye coverings squirting fluids into test tubes with nitrile-gloved hands.

"We were able to perform a rapid DNA test from the samples collected in the apartment," Howell said after stopping at a window looking into one of the examination rooms. "By protocol, the DNA profiles of all murder victims must be entered into the database, so it only took a short time to verify that the underwear recovered in the apartment was a match."

She saw one of the criminalists examining a slide under a microscope. A cotton swab and a pair of black lace panties were on a sterilized section of the table beside him.

"You were able to confirm all thirty-one known victims?" Flint asked. "Some of those cases are a decade old."

"Forensic science has come a long way in recent years," Howell said. "If the material's been reasonably preserved, we can extract usable DNA many years later, even after clothing has been washed." He glanced through the window at the criminalist hunched over the viewing lens. "Our preliminary analysis revealed no extraneous samples."

"You mean there was no DNA from a victim we didn't know about?" Dani asked.

"Correct," Howell said. "And there was no DNA from any potential suspect other than Ochoa."

She wanted to be certain. "Was Ochoa's DNA on all the victims' panties?"

"It was," Howell said. "In each case, only his and the victim's. No one else."

Relief flooded through her. The lab had confirmed what the crime scene indicated. Another dot connected.

After a few more minutes of discussion, Howell escorted them from the building. She and Flint reviewed the case as they walked to his car. The task force would continue to wrap up all the loose ends, digging into Ochoa's background, verifying his whereabouts at the time of each murder, and attempting to get video evidence of him in the vicinity of the most recent cases.

"A few things still bother me," Flint said as they reached the parking lot. "Ochoa committed the murders on a set rotation, now we can't ask him why he skipped over one of the Julian dates."

She agreed. "According to Dr. Cattrall, he was obsessive about the timing." She thought back to the numbers, which, as they always did, came easily to her. "The missing case was 220 the twentieth victim. Not the first or the last, but somewhere in the middle. Ochoa picked right back up on the next date in the sequence."

"What if Dr. Cattrall was wrong, and there were no backup victims?" Flint said. "Something happened to the one he'd picked out, and he didn't have a replacement lined up. Or, hell, maybe he was in jail, or sick, or out of town."

Her thoughts went to a darker place. "Or maybe there's a body out there we haven't found."

"Now that we can put a name to the perp, we can check to see what he was doing at the time. If he was traveling, we can check for a matching MO in that location."

"There's more." Dani changed the subject, bringing up something else that had nagged at her. "I kept expecting to find the videos Ochoa made of his victims. As a voyeur, you know he'd watch those repeatedly. He wouldn't destroy them."

Flint's brows drew together. "And the audiovisual equipment," he said. "That stuff is pricey. Maybe he has a locker somewhere that we'll find out about, and that's where we'll recover the rest of his stash."

"We have a lot more to investigate before this case is put to bed," Flint said. "Like, how did he come up with the name 'Conner'? We still haven't found any association with that yet."

Dr. Cattrall and the FBI would conduct an extensive postmortem on his behavior and background to add to their ever-expanding serial killer database. Before they were finished, every aspect of Ochoa's life would be examined with microscopic scrutiny. The answers lay somewhere in Ochoa's background, waiting to be unearthed.

Dani pulled her buzzing cell phone from her pocket. "Agent Vega."

Wu's response was quick and agitated. "Are you and Flint finished at the lab?"

"We just left. What's up, sir?"

"Someone just reported another stalker," Wu said. "And his MO is identical to the series we're investigating."

"Could it be a copycat?" Dani asked, thinking of all the details Cynthia had leaked to the media.

"He's doing things that were never released to the public," Wu said. "And there's more. I'll fill you both in while you drive to Hoodwinx Café."

Dani had eaten there before. "You want us to go to Hell's Kitchen? It's a bitch to get through Queens at this time of day."

"Tell Flint to step on it," Wu said. "If you get stuck in traffic, hit the lights and siren. Do whatever you have to, just get there fast."

CHAPTER 32

Dani held out her phone with Wu on speaker so Flint could listen as he maneuvered through traffic.

"Panties?" she said into the microphone. "We're on red alert for stolen undies?"

While she and Flint sped along, Wu had explained that a woman named Gloria Gomez had called the tip line to report a stalker and a burglary. An unidentified man has been following her for weeks, and this morning she arrived at her apartment to discover someone had broken in and taken a pair of underwear from her dresser drawer.

"Ms. Gomez gets off work at two in the morning," Wu said. "The ME's analysis at the scene indicated Ochoa was dead by midnight. The stolen lingerie was a detail never made public. Fortunately for us, Angela Dominguez never missed any underwear, so she didn't tell Cynthia it was taken."

"Okay, so maybe Ochoa broke in earlier and stole Ms. Gomez's lingerie, but she didn't realize it until now," Dani said.

"She has a kind of low-tech security system," Wu said. "She's had a problem with stalkers and other men following her home and coming to her apartment unannounced, so she's set up certain things to let her know if someone's been inside."

"Cameras?" Flint asked.

"No such luck," Wu said. "She can explain it to you when you interview her. That's who you're going to meet."

"There's got to be more," Dani said. "Does the ME think Ochoa's death wasn't a suicide?"

"The ME won't get Ochoa on the table until later," Wu said. "We don't have a definitive answer yet, but in the meantime, Detective Robinson was checking on the cases from Manhattan since that's his area." He paused for emphasis. "Jessica Fontaine was murdered on April 28, 2020. Her DNA was found on the underwear collected from Ochoa's apartment. She's definitely one of the series."

"What's the problem?" Flint asked.

"Wilfredo Ochoa was in Florida from April 27 through the 30th. There are other people with that name, but we confirmed it through flight manifests with the appropriate documentation required to fly commercial planes. It was Ochoa."

The Joint Terrorism Task Force had representatives from many government agencies, one of which was Customs and Border Patrol. Air carriers had been mandated to submit passenger manifests to Customs on an ongoing basis since 2005. After a call from Wu, Robinson would have access to all the information he needed within a matter of minutes.

"Could he have taken another flight back using an alias?" Dani asked. "If he planned things out so well, he might have included the trip to Florida as misdirection."

"He attended his sister's wedding," Wu said. "We checked her social media history. She posted dozens of pictures throughout the reception. Her brother was in several of them, including one where he's standing in a crowd waving goodbye while she and her new husband leave for their honeymoon." He shook his head. "Face rec matched him. Ochoa was in Tampa, not Manhattan. He could not have killed Ms. Fontaine."

"Then someone framed Ochoa," Dani said. "And now the real killer is at large."

"It gets worse," Wu said. "The deadline he gave us in the note at the park is coming up after midnight tonight."

They had been caught short last time by thinking he would strike later in the day. They would not make the same assumption again.

"Gloria Gomez is his target then," Dani said. "And we have to come up with a plan to stop him."

"She's waiting for you at the café now," Wu said. "I've given her your descriptions. She'll approach you if she knows she's not being followed."

"How could she know?" Dani asked. "She's not in law enforcement, is she?"

Wu let out a humorless laugh. "Let's just say she's gotten pretty good at countersurveillance."

"And that part about a lot of men following her home," Flint asked. "What the hell is that about?"

"Best you get the details from her," Wu said cryptically. "I can't do it justice."

CHAPTER 33

Hoodwinx Café
Hell's Kitchen, Manhattan

Dani and Flint had no sooner walked inside the café than a woman sitting alone with her back to the corner raised a hand, fluttering her fingers.

Dani scanned the environment as they crossed the room and noticed no one paying any attention to them. She didn't pick up on any threats or danger cues as they navigated their way around the scattered tables.

"Gloria Gomez?" Dani asked when they were beside the woman.

Dani and Flint had worked out their strategy during the drive over. According to Wu, Ms. Gomez had been subjected to male strangers following her and attempts to burglarize her apartment. They decided she might be more trusting with another woman and Dani should take the lead in the interview.

"Call me Glo," she said, gesturing for them to sit down.

Knowing that Flint would prefer a seat where he could watch the door, Dani sat directly opposite Glo so she could study her facial expressions and body language while the detective watched their backs. She and Flint were developing the unspoken rapport that comes with partnership.

"You reported a break-in at your apartment and a stalker you believe is related to the murders we're investigating?" Dani asked.

"There's been, like, a lot of guys who follow me when I leave work," Glo said. "But this latest one totally creeps me out."

Perhaps she should back up a bit and find out more about the complainant. "Where do you work?"

"I'm a dancer at the Pink Velvet Strip Club," Glo said. "Some of the customers get a little . . . riled up during the performances, you know? They see me make eyes at them, and they don't quite make the connection that it's a show. Faking like I'm interested gets me better tips." She gave her head a small shake. "So they get it in their heads that I'm into them or something, and they wait for me behind the club when I leave."

Glo was an exotic dancer. That explained the stalkers. "And some of them break into your apartment?"

Glo nodded. "Once or twice I didn't lose them on the way to my place, and they figured out what building I was in. I guess it wasn't that hard to get someone to point out my unit. Most everyone in my building knows where I work. Hell, some of them come to see me perform."

"Your building doesn't have a doorman?" Dani asked.

"Stripping is good money. I live in a nice place, but it's not swanky enough for a doorman. There's a keypad to unlock the front door." Glo rolled her kohl-lined eyes. "But if anyone wanted to get in, they'd just have to wait for someone to leave the building and walk inside before the door closed. No one pays much attention." The corners of her mouth lifted in a self-satisfied smile. "I can't afford one of those camera systems in my apartment, either, which is why I came up with a way to tell if someone got in while I was out."

Based on the profiles of the other victims, Dani knew the answer but had to ask anyway. "You live alone, then?"

"I don't have time for a pet, and roommates bring too much drama into my life," she said. "Which is why my little system works. Every time I leave, I put a tiny piece of clear tape high up on the outside of my door. If it's broken, the door's been opened."

"Clever," Dani said. "You found it broken when you came home this morning?"

Glo nodded. "I got out my pepper spray and went inside. No one was there, but when I went into the bathroom, all my makeup was lined up in a row. The foundations were all on the left, mascara and eyeliner in the middle, and lipstick on the right."

A chill went down Dani's spine. Out of the corner of her eye, she saw Flint tense. They both understood Wu's urgency now.

"Did you touch anything?" They had never had any luck getting latent fingerprints, but it was worth it to find out.

"I know better than that," Glo said. "I watch *CSI*."

Whoever entered the apartment probably did, too, but Dani didn't say that. Instead, she stuck to the interview.

"How did you discover your underwear was missing?"

"I keep a knife and an extra can of pepper spray in my underwear drawer in the bedroom," Glo said. "It's there in case anyone gets in while I'm home alone—especially when I'm asleep at night. Anyway, I saw right away that my purple G-string was missing. It was on top of the pile because I was going to wear it and changed my mind at the last minute."

She couldn't help but admire the thought and preparation Glo had put into hardening her home as a target, as well as her observational skills. She would have done well in counterintelligence.

"Were you inside your apartment when you called the tip line?"

"Hell no. I got out of there as fast as I could. Walked straight to this café and called from a safe place. Been here ever since."

Dani wanted to be sure they weren't dealing with a copycat. Given how smart and resourceful Glo was, perhaps she could answer a key question.

"Did you notice any small holes in the walls?" Dani asked. "I'm talking dot size."

Glo frowned. "It's weird you mention that. When I was going through my underwear drawer, I did see a little hole in the wall. I don't remember it being there before either."

"Was it across the room from the bed?"

"Yeah, why?" She narrowed her eyes. "I saw that look you two just gave each other. What does the hole mean?"

Flint spoke for the first time. "It means your instincts were right. And we've got a problem on our hands."

CHAPTER 34

Ten years earlier
February 3, 2014
Queens

Trembling with anticipation, Conner loaded the flash drive into his tablet. The video started with a beautiful Latina woman who was clearly what Conner had heard some people refer to as a "stroller." He might occasionally pay for sex, but not with anyone who plied her trade on street corners.

The woman slowly took off her clothes, giggling and flirting as she tossed them into the air. When she finished the show, a naked, muscular man walked into the frame, scooped her up, and carried her to the bed.

She seemed to be into it, letting out excited squeals when he joined her on the mattress. Conner watched in fascination as the man proceeded to go at her with the rough brutality of a stallion mounting a mare. In the midst of what could only be described as rutting, the man wrapped his hands around her throat and began to squeeze.

She opened her mouth to scream, but no sound escaped her compressed throat. She thrashed, eyes popping, but he had her completely pinned down. Completely at his mercy. And this man had none. He did not stop until he was satisfied, and she was dead, which happened at roughly the same time.

Conner's heart pounded as he watched the man calmly get up, cross the room, and turn off the camera.

He was sick, giddy, and aroused all at the same time. He had never killed anyone. Had never even witnessed someone else being murdered in real life. Was this real?

Hard to be sure. Maybe he should view it again. And again.

He watched his bootlegged copy of the show in the privacy of his apartment every night for two months.

And then he saw her walking down the street one day. He did a double take, not trusting his eyes. It was the woman in the video. The woman whose death he had witnessed.

He forgot everything—where he was going, what he was doing, how to breathe.

He followed her as if in a trance. He could no more have stopped trailing her than he could have stopped his heart beating by sheer force of will.

Had he seen an actress playing a role in an underground porn movie? No, the woman in the movie was dead. There was no mistaking the man's fierce grip on her throat. Zooming in, he'd been able to see the man's knuckles whiten as he dug his large fingers into her slender throat. Her violent thrashing gave way to convulsions, and the man had held her in his grasp a long time after she lay motionless on the bed. Conner had witnessed her death, and he knew it.

The woman he was following now must be a lookalike. There was no other explanation. But the mere fact that he had watched someone who looked so much like her die on film made him certain she had come into his life for a reason.

He continued to trail her as she took the 6 train to the Bronx. He kept her in view when she made her way to Castle Hill. He watched her go inside an apartment building on Benedict Avenue, and decided she must live there.

He left to go home but, try as he might, he couldn't get her out of his mind. He continued to look at the show on his tablet, imagining his sweet senorita in the place of the one who had been murdered. After that, it hadn't taken long for him to contemplate what it would be like to be the man in the video. To feel his lover's life force ebb from her body as he climaxed.

He wasn't sure exactly when his fantasies morphed into plans, but it hadn't taken long. He'd gotten a pair of spy cameras from an electronics store a few blocks down, planning to set them up and record the show just like the man in the video had done. Only he wanted to see more than just what happened in the bedroom. He wanted to see everything unfold from start to finish. And he would be able to view the private performance anytime he wanted. Forever.

He followed her enough to learn her patterns. Today he'd waited around in a coffee shop where she stopped for a latte on most days. She had come to the counter for her drink when the barista called out the name Luna. Now he knew her first name, and her schedule.

He was getting off shift for a three-day break. It was time to act on his plans. He learned her routine well enough to break in while she was at work and install the cameras in her living room and bedroom ahead of time.

He would need to devote all his energy to subduing her and wouldn't have time to set up the equipment and check to be sure all the action would be in view. No, he wanted everything in place in advance. Unlike in the bootlegged video, this woman wasn't a prostitute, and getting close to her required deception. The show would be so much better if he could capture her reaction when she realized he'd tricked her.

His pulse quickened in anticipation. He was one of the few people in the world who had the opportunity to live out their wildest fantasy. And the will to make it happen.

The bond of death was far more intimate than any other. He was about to create this special relationship with her, recording it for his viewing pleasure.

Luna would be his first. His last. His forever love.

CHAPTER 35

August 21, 2024
Queens

Conner sat in his apartment, fuming. He'd been forced to cash in his insurance policy—Wilfredo Ochoa. He believed in planning, organization, and order. He rotated to a different borough annually, selecting all three targets for that year in advance, assigning each of them their place on the schedule.

This year's Julian dates were 131, 232, and 333, and the targets were in Manhattan. Gloria Gomez was slated for November 28, but he had to move up her date, giving him just enough time to include her in Ochoa's pool of victims.

And then that plan had gone to shit too.

Two days ago, he was supposed to break into Glo's apartment after midnight when she was dancing at the club. He'd install the cameras, organize some of her belongings to see her reaction, and steal some underwear to leave in Ochoa's apartment with all the other evidence.

But she hadn't gone to work that night. He couldn't pin her death on Ochoa, but he wasn't about to let her miss her new date. Instead, he broke in the next night and set everything up. When he returned for a personal visit tonight, he'd arrange the scene to aim the cops at someone else and use the G-string to frame him.

Satisfied with his new plan, Conner turned his attention to the video feed playing on the screen. Gloria Gomez was stunning. The kind of woman fantasies were made of. She had snared his attention in the way she surely did with most men who looked at her.

Only this show was for him alone. No one else was watching. And no one would interrupt their time together. He would occupy himself with the sumptuous dancer while the FBI spent every waking moment on Fred Ochoa.

He'd taken care to set the stage down to the last detail, including organizing Ochoa's apartment. The man had been fairly neat, but nowhere near his own exacting standards. He'd been pressed for time but had still emptied every drawer, cupboard, and closet to place the contents back the way they belonged. The way the FBI would have expected them to be.

The way the instructor would have expected them to be.

Even if the Feds and cops eventually caught on, he figured the deception had bought him a night with Glo and time to wrap up any unfinished business before he moved on and set up shop in another city.

He continued to study the video. She had entered her apartment with wide eyes and a small canister of pepper spray in hand. Curious. What had spooked her? He'd have to adjust his strategy based on this new information. It was all about doing the research before taking action. Something he'd learned the hard way ten years earlier.

Next she'd methodically cleared the apartment, using techniques he recognized from cop shows on TV.

Cute. Sexy too.

He switched camera feeds to follow her progress into the bathroom. Moments later, she stumbled out, knees weakened by shock. Her supple body trembled in fear.

He felt intoxicated. Drunk with anticipation.

She went straight to the underwear drawer in her bedroom and checked to be sure the second canister of pepper spray and a knife were there. He hadn't bothered to take them. When he came for his visit in a few hours, they would do her no good.

He saw the instant she noticed her G-string was missing. Her gorgeous brown eyes widened, and his pulse raced at the thought of their shared connection. At that moment she was thinking of him. Soon he would be all she would think about. He would become her world.

The thought of her looking at him with fear and awe reminded him of the woman who had changed everything. He'd believed Luna would be the only one. But there had been a problem with the audio in the bedroom. When he replayed the video, he hadn't been able to hear her strangled cries. Or the sound of her heels thudding against the mattress while she thrashed.

It hadn't been perfect. And he needed perfection. Especially after all he went through to get to Luna. So he planned the next one with exquisite care, and the execution had been flawless. In the process, however, he'd discovered his newly created beast needed regular feeding.

For a decade he had enjoyed total success, only occasionally having to tweak things a bit due to unforeseen circumstances. His plans for the dancer would fall into place as well. Soon she would be his.

He watched her back away from the dresser, then turn and rush out of view. He switched to the camera in the main living area to follow her. He had expected her to bolt, but she pulled open a drawer in the kitchen. He shuddered with revulsion at the disarray inside the junk drawer but forced himself to keep watching. She picked up a plastic cellophane tape dispenser and tore off a one-inch strip, then put the dispenser back, closed the drawer, and left the apartment quickly, locking the door behind her.

Baffled by her actions, he paused the video. Why would she need a small scrap of tape? He slid the mouse to click open another video file from earlier that day and watched her do the same thing.

"What the hell?" he muttered, going back sixty seconds to review the footage a second time. Then a third.

He had to figure out the reason behind the odd behavior, because he was certain it was significant.

Apparently, she intended to use the tape right away, because she had to juggle her purse, the pepper spray, and her keys, with the sticky scrap of cellophane pinched between two fingers. It was awkward, so she wouldn't have bothered when she was clearly afraid for her safety.

Her safety. The words echoed in his mind. He considered the possibilities a full minute longer before the solution came to him.

She must put the tape from the edge of the door to the doorjamb. If it was broken or unstuck, she would know the door had been opened while she was gone.

The pretty kitty was clever. Had she gotten the idea from another cop show on TV or come up with it on her own?

Of course, her extra precautions wouldn't make any difference for tonight's plans, but at least he now knew she was capable of surprises. Then again, so was he.

Tonight, Gloria would put on a show just for him. It would be her curtain call. And it would be one to remember.

CHAPTER 36

Dani caught the sense of urgency that permeated the conference room at the JOC. She and Flint had taken Gloria to a nearby apartment the NYPD occasionally used as a safe house, advising her to keep her cell phone charged and ready. They would call her with instructions as soon as they had finalized a plan.

"You're convinced the unsub will keep the deadline he gave us at Washington Square Park?" Wu asked Dani.

She nodded. "Any time after midnight is fair game, and Gloria gets off work at two in the morning. If he sticks to his pattern, he'll be waiting inside her place when she gets home."

"Gloria didn't call the tip line from her apartment, where he could listen in," Flint added. "He probably has no idea she called, and even if he did, there's no reason he'd suspect we found other reasons to think Ochoa was framed."

"There's one thing that's been bothering me since Ms. Gomez called," Wu said. "Why would he risk another attack so soon after setting up Ochoa? Even if he didn't get caught, he might leave a clue behind and undo his entire plan."

Dr. Cattrall was the first to respond. "Because he's compulsive," she said. "And because the killer's MO was made very public, thanks to the friend of the victim who called all the media. Someone with his personality would watch all the reports. Between his knowledge of the real crimes and the info released to the public, he could get enough details wrong to make his next murder look like a copycat."

"We'd still be looking for him, though," Wu said.

"But not with all the assets of a task force," Dr. Cattrall countered. "The serial killer case would be closed, and the new one would be just another death in the nation's biggest city." She tapped her chin with a long finger. "Or he might change his MO and abduct Ms. Gomez, taking her somewhere else to record her death before disposing of her body."

Dani couldn't argue with Dr. Cattrall's logic. She reevaluated her previous observations from their interview at the café. "According to Gloria, he's been stalking her while she walks home from the club recently. He's established a pattern. Based on that, combined with what Dr. Cattrall just told us, he might decide to attack her on the way home from the club instead of waiting inside her apartment."

"We can't rule out either possibility," Cattrall said. "But one thing he can't change is his voyeuristic tendencies. He'll set up a camera somewhere along the way in advance or have video equipment on his person to record whatever he does to her."

"That reminds me," Wu said to Dani. "Good job asking Ms. Gomez about the pinholes in her wall."

"She's observant," Dani said. "Figured she'd notice."

"With luck, we'll get an image of this guy's face when we recover the surveillance equipment from her apartment," Flint said.

Patel crossed the room to join them. "I wouldn't count on that," he told them. "Cameras that small probably stream the video. We'd have to access his cloud storage to see it."

"After we arrest this guy, I'll send ERT to recover the cameras, and you can head up a team of video forensic specialists to track down the server," Wu said to Patel. "CSU can process the rest of the scene."

The FBI's Evidence Response Team was the federal counterpart of the NYPD's Crime Scene Unit. Wu's comment could be taken as an insult since both agencies had state-of-the-art facilities and highly trained personnel.

Apparently sensing the sudden tension in the room, Wu glanced at the contingent of homicide detectives. "We just got some new equipment. This would be our first chance to try it out."

That seemed to satisfy everyone. No matter what kind of law enforcement you were, cutting-edge tech was always appreciated.

"As long as you share." The edge in Flint's tone said he was only half-joking. "Bad enough you guys get all the newest toys and a bigger sandbox to play in. We won't let you keep secrets too."

The long-standing complaint had merit, and Wu was gracious enough to acknowledge the issue. "We'll have some of your detectives work directly with us." With that crisis averted, Wu addressed the room. "For the first time, we know precisely who, where, and when the killer will strike." He glanced around the table. "I want ideas about how to take him down, whether it's in her apartment or walking home." He narrowed his eyes. "And those ideas cannot include allowing her to be the bait. It's far too risky."

"We could deploy one of our rapid-response tactical units to her apartment right now," one of the NYPD detectives said. "They could get inside and set up hours ahead of time, then make an arrest as soon as the perp enters the apartment."

Dani recalled a detail from the interview and pointed out the flaw in the plan. "Gloria saw a pinhole in the bedroom wall. We have to assume he planted other video equipment in the apartment and that he would see the team set up."

"We could jam his signal," the detective said.

Flint responded first. "That'd spook him. He'd abort, and we'd lose our best chance at catching him."

"Let's see if we can find a vacant apartment in the building to set up shop," Wu said. "And I'll get one of our undercover surveillance teams to attach listening equipment to her apartment's windows."

She had to admire Wu's resourcefulness. The FBI had specialists who could deploy devices without drawing attention. They had an array of disguises that included municipal workers, telephone repair persons, mail carriers, maids, and many others.

"Her building has a brick facade," Wu continued. "By code, the mortar needs regular maintenance. We'd have to arrange for the scaffolding, but we could get right outside her window. Otherwise, maybe exterminators spraying for roaches, but that would have to be inside only."

"I'll put a call in," Patel said, standing and heading for his terminal. "Whatever play we make has got to be expedited."

"With luck, we'll catch him breaking into the apartment," Dani said. "Then we can hold him on burglary charges while we see what else he's been up to."

"But that still doesn't address the issue of an attack on Ms. Gomez before she makes it back to her place," Wu said. "If he's watching from outside this time and doesn't see her walking home from the club as usual, he might change his plans." He gave Dani a meaningful look. "Unless, of course, he *does* see her."

A moment later, she grasped his meaning and stiffened.

She'd be far more comfortable running headlong into a raging gun battle than posing as a stripper.

CHAPTER 37

Wu had seen the instant understanding dawn in Vega's eyes. She had her soldier face firmly in place, and he couldn't read her reaction to his idea.

"You want me to take Gloria's place," she said flatly.

All eyes in the room were focused on the exchange between the special agent in charge and his most junior agent. He'd rather have this discussion in private, but there was no time.

"We have other agents with more experience undercover, but we don't need that kind of skill for this assignment." He didn't add that locating an agent who was female, Hispanic, available within the hour, and could pass as an exotic dancer would be a tall order on short notice.

Vega remained stoic. Her military background clearly made her hesitant to refuse what she would perceive as an order from a superior.

Flint, however, weighed in with his own concerns. "Whoever the unsub is, he has a lot of experience looking at women." He motioned toward the psychologist. "Like Dr. Cattrall told us, he's a voyeur. He's watched videos of Gloria, and he's been stalking her on the street. He's also seen Vega. How could she possibly fool him?"

Wu had been wrestling with the same problem when the idea had first occurred to him. He addressed Flint directly, aware everyone was listening. "He'll never see Agent Vega up close or in the light.

We'll sneak her into the club through the back door ahead of time. Then she'll put on Ms. Gomez's outfit and leave when she's finished performing, taking the same route she usually does and leaving at the same time."

Apparently unconvinced, Flint began to pick apart his argument.

"He'll see her face."

"It'll be dark."

"What if she walks under a streetlight?"

"She'll avoid them."

"Won't he find that a bit strange?"

Wu was surprised when the Manhattan homicide detective chimed in. "She could pretend to get distracted and walk away from the direct light to check something out," Robinson said. "And keep her head moving so he never gets a solid look at her." When Flint cut his eyes to him, Robinson shrugged. "Worked undercover a couple years. Learned a few tricks."

"I don't walk like a dancer," Dani said, finally speaking. "I'm not exactly graceful."

She couldn't have been more wrong. He would never say it out loud, but her physical attributes were among the reasons he'd thought of her for the assignment. Years spent conditioning her body had left her lithe and sculpted without unnecessary bulk to weigh her down. Combat training that incorporated martial arts had given her an economy of motion that appeared smooth and effortless.

"Actually, you are," Wu said. "Although you might be more comfortable with the word 'stealthy.'"

She had no retort, apparently considering his appraisal of her prowess. Now that he'd dealt with the objections, it was time to close the deal.

"You only have to fool him long enough for us to catch him watching you," he told her. "Once we pick him out, it doesn't matter if he doesn't go through with it. We'll tail him until we figure out who he is and take the investigation from there. There's no downside."

She paused, and he assumed she was assessing the mission, calculating the odds of success versus the potential for failure.

"I'll do it," she said.

CHAPTER 38

"Seriously?" Dani said to Gloria. "Your stage name is Glo-go?"

Gloria put a hand on her glitter-dusted hip. "If Jennifer Lopez is JLo, then Gloria Gomez would be Glo-go, right?"

No way to argue with impeccable logic like that. "How long will your last set take?"

Wu had arranged for an agent dressed as a cab driver in a taxi to transport Glo from the safe house apartment to the club in time for her to dress for her performances as usual. Meanwhile, Dani had disguised herself in a white chef's jacket to pass herself off as one of the cooks who arrived at the club's back entrance to work the night shift. She had pinned up her long dark ponytail, tucking it under a short auburn wig topped with a white cap to complete the transformation, rendering her nearly invisible among the other workers who came and went to the establishments clustered in the bustling Hell's Kitchen area with its active nightlife.

Glo, who had been waiting for Dani inside the rear entrance, quickly ushered her to a small dressing room off the greenroom backstage. Glo had undergone a transformation of her own. The straight long black hairpiece she had worn during the day had been replaced by a hot-pink spike-haired wig sprinkled with the same silver glitter that covered her body, which was barely contained in a pink mesh G-string and two matching pasties. Dani watched Glo strategically drape seven filmy scarves over herself to remove during her dance.

Dani regarded Glo with apprehension. Could she pass herself off as the uber-sexy exotic dancer? Then she remembered how Glo looked when she met them at the café. Her long sheet of glossy black hair, faux-leather leggings, and filmy leopard-print top had drawn a few apprecia-tive glances, but no overt gawking. If that was how she dressed walking home, maybe Dani could pull it off.

Glo noticed her looking and gave her a slow smile. "Like what you see?" She winked. "Because the feeling is mutual."

"Thanks for the compliment," Dani replied, face flaming. "But I was just trying to figure out how I was going to walk to your apartment in six-inch spike stiletto heels."

"Are you kidding?" Glo chuckled. "I don't wear my show clothes walking home." She lifted a shapely leg to show off her black patent leather pumps. "I change into sneakers. The FMPs are for the stage."

That was a relief. Combat boots were more her style, but running shoes would do fine.

"And to answer your question," Glo continued, "I'll be finished with this set in twenty minutes. Then I get a fifteen-minute break before my last set."

Dani took off her chef's jacket, cap, and wig, stashing them in a plastic bag she'd brought in her pocket while she waited in the green-room through both sets. Each time Glo sashayed off the stage, another woman strutted on to take her place. The nightclub ran like clockwork. No one in the audience was ever without an overpriced beverage to drink, a beautiful dancer to ogle, or a tasty bite of food to eat.

Glo hurried into the greenroom after her final set. "Glad that's over," she said, shaking off a flurry of glitter. "Damn pole was sweaty as hell. Almost lost my grip twice."

Dani supposed every job had its downside. She followed Glo into the cramped dressing room.

"Here," Glo said, thrusting a knockoff Gucci beach bag into her hands. "It's what I wore coming in tonight."

Peering inside, Dani saw that it was the same outfit Glo had on at the café, including the waist-length silky black wig. She would have liked more of a disguise, but a hoodie would have been a dead giveaway on a hot summer night. Plus he would have seen her on the video and known what she was wearing.

"Here's my outfit," Dani said, handing over the plastic bag containing the chef's garb.

Glo reached in and fished out the bulky white jacket. "Is this a disguise or birth control?" she asked.

"It's meant to make you blend in," Dani said. "You could be anybody in that getup."

Glo arched a brow. "You got that right."

Dani lifted the formfitting black leggings up for inspection. "These, on the other hand, don't leave much to the imagination." She met Glo's gaze. "I couldn't carry so much as a credit card in the pocket."

"Nice thing about spandex is that it's stretchy," Glo said. "Hugs the curves."

They each put on the other's clothes and studied their reflections in the full-size mirror. Glo was unrecognizable in the shapeless white jacket. She wore Dani's gray tank top and yoga pants underneath. The cap and auburn wig completed the deception. She would leave from the back door, where agents in various disguises would take turns shadowing her until she was far enough away to slip into the same fake taxi that had taken her to the club hours earlier. Countersurveillance measures would ensure she went unnoticed.

Dani's journey would be quite different. She, too, would exit from the rear of the club at the same time Glo always did after work. She would walk back to the apartment, taking Glo's usual route. A wireless transmitter hidden in Dani's ear would ensure the surveillance team following her would be aware of her movements at all times.

If she made it back to the apartment without incident, she would enter using Glo's spare key. The tactical team staged in a vacant apartment down the hall would also be monitoring all communications. One word from her—or any alarming sound—would bring them crashing through the door.

They had gone over all possible scenarios. Whether the unsub approached her on the street, in the building, or in the apartment, they would have him.

Dani turned away from the mirror to face Glo. "Your show's over. Mine's just getting started."

CHAPTER 39

Dani waited twenty minutes after Glo left in the chef's outfit, monitoring the comm system to be sure the team picked her up safely. Phase one of the operation had gone seamlessly. Time for phase two. She tousled the long black wig, pulling strands of hair forward to cover part of her face, counting on the darkness to obscure the rest of her features.

"It's Vega." She kept her voice barely above a whisper, but loud enough for the wireless microphone to pick up the transmission. "I'm leaving out the rear entrance."

"Affirmative." Flint's response carried clearly into her earbud. "Alpha team will pick you up."

It took less than a minute for her to sense it. She could not see anyone watching her but felt the weight of someone's gaze on her. She forced herself to continue mimicking Glo's gait, which the two had practiced in the greenroom. She kept her head forward and angled slightly down, but darted her eyes left and right, taking in as much in her periphery as she could.

"Feels like someone's watching me," she said, then added, "besides you all, that is."

She deliberately avoided looking at the homeless man who shuffled in her vicinity for a block before turning to start down another street. By that time, a woman walking a Labrador had strolled along, keeping close until she was replaced by a young man in a baggy T-shirt, carrying a skateboard. None of them stayed in her vicinity long, but any one of them could have rushed in to help if the need arose.

Not that she was likely to need it. She was confident Wu had selected her for the assignment because of her special forces training, nothing more. They had all seen her take down three attackers a few days ago, and they had watched video of her doing much worse in her last assignment.

"I've got someone," one of her fellow agents said over the comm system. "White male, dark hair, in his thirties, six feet tall, two hundred pounds, wearing a black T-shirt and blue jeans." A short pause. "He's about twenty feet behind Vega. Not too close, though—he's being careful."

Dani hadn't detected the man's proximity, which told her he was no amateur.

"Disregard my last," the agent said. "Subject turned onto another street."

This was why she had to keep up her role until the stalker made a move. Not only would a pile of cops swarming all over an innocent bystander put them all on the wrong side of the table at a review board, but it would also ruin their best—and possibly only—chance of catching the unsub before he hurt someone else. She continued along Gloria's normal route another ten minutes before the next transmission.

"He's back."

Dani made a conscious effort to keep her pace unhurried at the ominous words.

"Must've walked along a parallel block and cut back here," the voice continued. "Pretty damned smart."

She agreed. The maneuver served two purposes, making it more difficult for the woman he was targeting to notice him stalking her, and also making it easier for him to pick out anyone trailing him.

An NYPD detective's voice followed. "I'll see if the vic can ID him as soon as we get eyes on him."

This had been part of the plan. Along Dani's route, a detective would be parked with Glo in the back seat. He would hand her binoculars equipped with the latest night vision, which was full color and made it look like broad daylight. She would look at whoever was trailing Dani and tell them if it was her stalker.

Dani walked past the place where she knew Glo was waiting in the detective's unmarked car. She deliberately slowed her pace, checking her shoe as if she had inadvertently stepped on some chewing gum, allowing Glo to get a good long look at whoever trailed her.

"It's him," the detective's voice sounded in her earbud. "Positive ID from the vic."

She could hear his heavy footfalls between the noise of passing cars. Darting a glance over her shoulder, she judged the distance between them in preparation for the takedown. A gust of wind blew between the tall buildings, catching her hair. Long strands rippled back, exposing her face to the wide beam of a passing truck's headlights. She heard an expletive behind her and spun to see the suspect break into a run.

She reached for her creds. "Stop, FBI!"

He sped up and she charged after him. He was in fairly good shape and motivated by fear. He veered to the left, darting across traffic. He was heading straight toward a bus and showed no signs of stopping.

"Look out!" Dani shouted, a few yards behind him.

The bus driver leaned on his horn and braked hard, causing the massive vehicle to slew sideways, colliding with empty parked cars lining the far side of the street.

The chaos spurred the man to an all-out sprint, and he cleared the bus by inches, blocking Dani's view of his retreat. Tires squealing, the bus skidded to a shuddering stop. Purely focused on her quarry, Dani raced around the rear of the vehicle in time to see the suspect disappear around the block.

A cacophony of voices erupted in her ear as agents and police called out their locations and joined in the hunt. No one had expected him to make a suicidal run through traffic, but they were recovering their positions quickly, with Dani in the lead.

She rounded the corner and spotted him trying to open the door of a building, but it was locked at this late hour. He moved on to the next, with the same result. He flashed a wide-eyed look over his shoulder and started to run again. He'd lost precious seconds attempting to get inside a building, giving her a last chance to catch him.

He was fast, but she had endurance as well as speed. Within seconds, she launched herself onto his back, tackling him to the pavement.

Footsteps thundered toward her as she wrestled with the burly man, who was driven by panic, rage, or a combination of both. They tumbled in a heap, clawing and scrabbling. He brought a meaty fist down toward her face, but she dodged the blow, twisting away. The fist struck out at her again, and she caught the glint of metal for an instant before it connected with her upper left arm.

She grabbed his forearm and pulled him closer, a counterintuitive maneuver that caught him off guard, allowing her to deliver an elbow strike to his jaw. His head snapped back, and he slumped on top of her, unconscious.

"Damn, Vega," Flint said. "You could have let us help."

"You can help by getting this son of a bitch off me," she said, gasping from under his inert bulk. "And we need to check his vitals."

The stalker was already coming around. He took a swing at Flint, who, along with the undercover agents, forced his hands behind his back and handcuffed him.

She was surprised to see Wu walking toward her, then realized she shouldn't have been. Unlike most special agents in charge, he found every opportunity to go out in the field, and this operation was important enough to give him a good excuse.

He extended a hand and pulled her to her feet. "Good work, Vega."

"The takedown was the easy part," she said. "Stuffing myself into Glo's skintight leggings was the real challenge."

He started to laugh, then narrowed his eyes. "You're bleeding."

She followed his gaze and glanced down at her upper left arm. Sure enough, a trickle of blood oozed through the sliced fabric of Glo's leopard-print shirt. She whirled, calling out to the others. "He's got a knife."

Flint held up a six-inch folding knife in his latex-gloved hand. "Already took it off him."

A streak of crimson smeared the sharp edge of the blade. In the throes of the fight, she had registered the weapon but hadn't felt it cut into her.

"That needs stitches," Wu said. "And you'd better get a tetanus shot and some tests." His eyes met hers. "I'll have an agent take you to the emergency room."

She had no interest in sitting in a hospital for hours while the rest of the team interviewed Glo's stalker—a man who might be the serial killer who had slipped through their net once before. "Slap a Band-Aid on it," she said. "I'll be fine."

His eyes narrowed. "Or would you prefer to ride in an ambulance? Because that's your other option."

"It's a scratch," she said. "I've had worse and still carried out my mission."

"That's when you were in the military," Wu replied. "You're in the FBI now, and we have policies about injuries sustained in the line of duty." His tone sharpened. "Let me put it in a way you'll understand. I am giving you a direct order. Do not report back to duty until you have had that laceration treated by a doctor. Am I clear?"

"Crystal, sir."

Wu lifted a hand to signal one of the agents, who loped over to them. "Take her to the ER," he said, then turned back to Vega. "Let me know what the doctor says." His voice softened. "I want to be sure you're okay."

She followed the agent to his car, which had been parked a block down. Clapping a hand over the gash on her arm, which now bled freely, she cursed under her breath and climbed in the unmarked sedan.

As they pulled away from the curb, she glanced back to see the rest of her team march the handcuffed prisoner to the transport vehicle that had pulled up from the staging area down the street.

Frustration bit at her. Glo was both smart and observant. Her positive identification of the stalker, along with his behavior tonight, made a solid case. They could hold the suspect for hours, asking questions and catching him in lies, slowly closing the net around him until he saw no way out and finally confessed.

But she wouldn't be there when it happened.

CHAPTER 40

Mount Sinai West Emergency Room
10th Avenue
Manhattan

Two hours later, Dani watched the surgeon's gloved fingertips pull the skin of her wound taut. A shot of local anesthetic delivered ten minutes earlier had ensured she felt nothing more than pressure while the nurse irrigated and cleaned the wound in preparation for closing it. Now the surgeon angled the tip of the medical glue gun at the top of the laceration.

"Hold still," he told her. "The tissue adhesive needs to be placed perfectly to close the wound and prevent infection."

She had undergone field dressings without the benefit of anesthesia. She wasn't a flincher.

He pulled the trigger and clear, gelatinous goop oozed out. "The glue takes only a few minutes to set," he said, deftly directing a line of adhesive along the reddened seam of the cut. "It will fall off on its own in a couple of weeks, but you need to be careful not to pick at it or do anything to make the skin separate again."

He was gone a minute later, and she was waiting for the nurse to discharge her. Glancing at the livid cut again brought her thoughts back to the incident that had caused it.

She replayed the fight in her mind, recalling the instantaneous flash of light from the overhead streetlight glinting off the blade tucked into his hand.

She sat up ramrod straight.

The stalker had swung the knife with his right hand. During the fight, she had observed that the man was not skilled with edged weapon combat. Had he been more proficient, he might have done more damage, despite her training.

Only a highly experienced knife fighter with extensive training would attack with his nondominant hand, something even skilled fighters wouldn't ordinarily do. That meant the stalker was either right-handed, like 90 percent of the population, or he was one of less than 1 percent of the population that was completely ambidextrous.

According to the autopsy reports compiled by the task force, more than half of the serial killer's victims had shown evidence of trauma inflicted by a left-handed attacker. The remaining cases had not indicated a right-handed attacker—the ME hadn't drawn a conclusion one way or the other. To Dani, that meant the killer was left-handed.

Not ambidextrous.

Not right-handed.

But Glo had identified the man following Dani from the club as her stalker. Then again, Glo had also told them she'd dealt with several stalkers over the two years she'd spent as a dancer. Not hard to imagine given that the audience was plied with alcohol while they watched her strip. Not a good combination for rational behavior.

They had concluded the killer stalked his victims weeks in advance, and that because he kept to a timetable, he might have more than one woman under observation in case his primary target was unexpectedly not available at the appointed time. This allowed for the overlap when he would have been stalking Angela Dominguez and Glo at the same time.

But what if Glo's stalker wasn't the killer? An idea occurred to her. Since the killer had never left obvious signs of a break-in, that meant he must have either burglarized his victim's apartment and waited for her to come home, or he had used a ruse to get her to allow him inside before overpowering her. He always committed his crimes in a controlled environment, where his hidden cameras allowed him to be certain his victim was alone and at his mercy. Tonight, however, he had attacked out in public.

Another change in pattern.

They had planned for the possibility that he might do things differently after framing Ochoa, which was why they had her under surveillance, but now she was seeing the situation in a new light.

Had they arrested the wrong man?

Flint had reserved an interview room at the Midtown North Police Precinct. They would have taken the suspect there on assault and stalking charges. Then they would begin questioning him about the murders. She glanced at her watch. Five thirty in the morning. The takedown had occurred three hours ago.

Given the time it took to transport the prisoner to the precinct, formally charge him, take his prints and DNA, then get him into the interrogation room and Mirandize him, they would be right in the middle of the interview now, and Flint would not be taking phone calls or checking texts. Breaking the flow of such a critical discussion was unthinkable. At least she could call Wu and brief him.

She pulled out her cell phone. Cracked screen. Sending up a silent prayer for divine intervention from whichever patron saint watched over technology, she pressed the power button.

Nothing.

She swore in two languages and jabbed the button three more times with the same result. Another thought occurred to her, pushing the interview from her mind.

If they had not arrested the real killer, Glo was still in danger. Before Dani had handed her comm equipment over to the agent who dropped her off at the hospital, she'd heard Flint dismissing the tactical team standing by in the apartment down the hall from Glo's. Wu had also called off the undercover agents deployed around the building. They had the suspect in custody, and the arrest operation was over.

Now she had a new theory. She could be totally wrong but would rather look like a fool than gamble with Glo's life.

She had to tell Glo to get the hell out of her apartment and go to the nearest police precinct. She knew Flint's and Wu's numbers by heart, but Glo's had been programmed into a device that had essentially become an expensive paperweight. There was no way for her to reach out, but Flint or Wu could.

She jumped off the table, ran from the treatment room, and scanned the area for her nurse. Unable to locate her, she snagged the first hospital employee she could find. "I'm with the FBI," she said to another nurse, this one a pale young man with red hair.

When he merely raised a brow, she remembered she was wearing Glo's faux-leather leggings and leopard-print top. She reached down, pulled up her left pant leg, and slid her creds from her high-top sneakers. The nurse examined them closely, clearly unsure whether he was being scammed.

"I was on an undercover assignment," she said by way of explanation, not sure whether that made her even less credible. "This is an emergency. I need to use the hospital phone."

"I'm sorry, but I can't let you do that."

She considered her options. Should she tell him to call 9-1-1 and request the nearest patrol officers to go to Glo's apartment? The dispatcher would see the call originated from the hospital, not the FBI. She couldn't show the call-taker her credentials and had no way to verify her identity without going through a lot of steps a busy dispatcher may not be willing to navigate.

Her mind raced, struggling to come up with alternatives.

She couldn't simply call in a bomb threat so they would evacuate Glo's building. First, that was a crime, and second, the nurse would snatch the phone from her hand and tell the dispatcher she was lying. A stunt like that would also end any more cooperation from him and might land her in a four-point restraint tied down to a gurney.

The fastest way would be to apprise her boss, who could deploy all kinds of resources in a matter of minutes.

"Then you do it," she said to the nurse, desperate. "Call the Midtown North Police Precinct on West 54th. Tell whoever's at the desk that Special Agent Vega with the FBI needs to speak to Special Agent in Charge Steve Wu. He and some NYPD detectives will be in the viewing area, watching one of the interview rooms."

Looking as if he were acting against his better judgment, the nurse picked up a nearby phone and hit a button connecting him to the hospital switchboard. "Can you put me through to the Midtown North Precinct?" He paused. "Someone claiming to be an FBI agent needs me to call them." He cut his eyes to her. "I know. She says it's an emergency."

She waited an eternity, thinking about Glo. Was the killer already in her apartment? Was he with her now? She glanced at her watch again.

The nurse finally got an answer and outlined the situation. Even without hearing the other side of the conversation, Dani could tell he was getting nowhere. She fought the urge to yank the receiver out of his hands and shout into it.

"Ask for a supervisor," she urged.

He rolled his eyes. "I'm talking to the desk sergeant. He *is* a supervisor."

She hit her breaking point. "Tell the sergeant to take down this information," she said. "Special Agent Vega is on her way to Gloria Gomez's apartment." She waited for the nurse to repeat her words, then rattled off Glo's address. "Detective Mark Flint, SAC Steve Wu, and other homicide detectives have a prisoner in the interview room now. Let them know that I believe Ms. Gomez is still in danger. I'm headed to her place to check on her."

The nurse conveyed the information, then turned to her. "The sergeant wants an explanation about what's going on. Who is Gloria Gomez and what prisoner is in custody?"

She was not about to stand there for the next half hour relaying the particulars of a lengthy investigation to the sergeant. Not when he could simply repeat her message to someone who would understand it instantly. Not when Glo might be fighting for her life right now. The apartment was a little over half a mile away on foot. This early in the morning, the sidewalks and streets would be relatively empty. She could run there in less than three minutes without worrying about getting flattened by a car.

"I'm out of here," she said to the nurse.

Wu would either get her message or he wouldn't. Backup would either come or it wouldn't. Either way, she was going to protect Glo until they figured it out. She turned on her heel and strode out, leaving the nurse and the desk sergeant to sort through the red tape.

She was done talking.

CHAPTER 41

West 52nd Street
Hell's Kitchen, Manhattan

Dani listened at the door to Glo's apartment, checking for sounds of distress inside before she announced her presence by knocking. She heard the deep rumble of a man's voice but could not make out the words. An instant later, she recognized Glo's trilling laugh.

Surprised Glo would have a visitor so early in the morning after being up late, but relieved she did not appear to be in danger, Dani rapped the door with her knuckles.

"I'm so glad you're okay," Glo said after opening the door. "Detective Flint said they took you to the hospital to get stitched up."

"I'm fine," Dani said, gesturing toward her arm. "But your shirt isn't. Sorry about the cut and the bloodstains."

"I couldn't care less about the shirt," Glo said. "But I would miss the leggings, so I'm glad they didn't get sliced to ribbons."

Dani appreciated the sarcastic deflection hiding the concern. Glo had been worried about her, and it showed in the lines furrowing her brow.

"You have company?" she asked.

Glo stepped back. "Why don't you join the party?"

Dani strode past her to find Brad Howell, senior criminalist at the NYPD crime lab, standing in the living room area, wearing a white lab coat and blue nitrile gloves. His wide-eyed stare told her he was equally surprised to see her. Either that or Glo's low-cut leopard-print top exposed enough cleavage to snag his attention for a moment before his eyes traveled north to meet hers.

"Are you here with the crime scene detectives?" she asked him, recalling that Flint had told them to process the apartment after he had taken the stalker into custody.

"They already left," Howell said. "I'm here to do a secondary sweep. As a supervisor, I personally conduct a follow-up analysis of all high-profile cases."

What he said was logical, but something still troubled her. "Why wouldn't you respond with the detectives and oversee the evidence collection in progress?"

"I didn't hear about the arrest until first thing in the morning when I got to work," he said. "The crime scene team had just left here and were headed to the lab. We must have passed each other going in opposite directions." He shrugged. "I can examine their analysis compared to mine as soon as I get back."

"I was just going to offer him some water or a soda," Glo said, walking past them toward the kitchen. "Can I get you anything, Agent Vega?"

"Nothing for me, thanks," Dani said, then turned back to Howell in time to catch him staring again. His gaze drifted down below her chin, lingering a moment before he glanced away. She had the urge to stoop to meet his eyes and remind him that her face was several inches above where he was looking.

It was unsettling. In fact, this whole scenario was unsettling.

"I'll take some water," he said, starting toward the kitchen. "The sun's barely up, but it's already getting hot and humid. Today's going to be a scorcher."

She had just come over from the hospital, and it hadn't been that hot yet. She watched him take the clear plastic bottle of water from Glo, wrapping his gloved hand around hers as he did so. Most people would only touch the bottle. When he did not release his grip immediately, Dani reached for her gun.

Howell spun, jerking Glo against him, her back to his chest.

Dani was bringing her Glock up to level the sights on Howell.

Her body had reacted on pure instinct, without conscious thought. Her mind caught up an instant later. Brad Howell was the killer who had deceived everyone for a decade. Suddenly it all made a terrible and twisted kind of sense. Who better to tamper with evidence, access police files, and monitor investigations than someone on the inside?

Everyone had missed it, but she felt personally responsible. She was the one who detected patterns, spotted clues, and noticed deviations that others missed. Her well-honed skills had not served her this time. And Gloria Gomez was about to pay the price.

A gleam of metal caught her eye for the second time in a matter of hours.

"Drop it," Howell said, ducking behind Glo as he pressed a knife into the side of her neck.

In the instant it took Dani to draw her weapon, he had snatched a chef's knife from the wooden block on the kitchen counter.

Howell, a seasoned forensic expert, was clearly aware that a gunshot to his forehead would drop him to the floor before his brain could transmit the electrical impulse across the synaptic gap between his neurons, rendering him unable to cut Glo's throat.

She would have time to analyze her failings later. Focused on the immediate threat, she looked for the slightest opening to get a clean shot, but he was taking no chances. She was trained to aim for center mass, but the only exposed parts of his body were nonlethal targets, which were useless when a quick flick of his wrist would open Glo's carotid artery. Apparently aware of her proficiency with firearms, he had also taken care to angle the knife in such a way that even a sharpshooter couldn't shoot his hand without the round hitting Glo's throat.

"Drop it," he repeated, digging the edge of the blade deep enough to draw bright-red droplets of blood.

Had the nurse and the desk sergeant figured out a way to verify her identity and get her message to Wu and Flint? Would the sergeant send officers to the address she provided to check on the situation? Eventually someone would come, but when?

Rule one: Never give up your weapon.

But what were her options?

"I'm not playing," Howell said, moving his arm a fraction to draw the sharp blade across her smooth skin. The droplets became a steady trickle coursing down her throat.

Glo screamed.

This was not part of the plan.

Slowly, Dani bent her knees and placed the Glock on the floor.

Her Ranger squad staff sergeant had a quote for every occasion. One he'd used often from world heavyweight champion Mike Tyson came to her now.

"Everyone has a plan until they get punched in the mouth."

CHAPTER 42

Dani straightened after placing the Glock on the floor beside her feet.

Howell stood from his crouched position behind Glo but kept the knife's edge pressed against her throat. "Kick the gun over to me," he ordered.

Dani mentally played out various actions she could take and the possible outcomes. If she turned her Glock Gen5 semiautomatic pistol over to him, he would have fifteen rounds in the magazine and one in the chamber, plenty of firepower to kill both of them and shoot his way past any police who might be on their way.

A knife, however, reduced the number of people in imminent danger down to one. Glo was still in peril, but Dani's training had included disarming enemies with edged weapons. If she could get Glo out of the way, Howell would be hers.

Unless she gave him her pistol.

She swung her foot to the side, kicking the gun with the edge of her sneaker. Rather than sliding over to Howell in the kitchen, it clattered across the floor into the bedroom.

Howell bellowed a string of obscenities and wrapped his free hand around Glo's slender throat. When he squeezed, droplets of blood oozed out between his fingers.

"Let her go," Dani said.

"Like hell," Howell said. "She's going to walk to the bedroom with me."

He intended to keep Dani at bay by holding the knife to Glo's throat until he could substitute the blade for her service weapon. And once he got the gun, she and Glo would serve no purpose whatsoever. They would become liabilities. Loose ends in need of trimming.

Dani watched Howell march Glo toward the bedroom door, their feet in lockstep. He had to keep his knife in position, hold Glo tight against him, keep an eye on Dani, and look for the gun all at the same time. An opening would come, even if it was only a fraction of a second, and she would be ready when it did.

The pair edged to the doorway. Howell darted a glance inside the bedroom in search of his objective.

Without a sound, she launched her body through the air, slamming into both of them. Glo went sprawling, the force of the impact sending her to the floor out of Howell's reach.

Keeping her eyes riveted on Howell, Dani shouted at Glo. "Run!"

When she saw no corresponding movement in her peripheral vision, Dani spared a second to glance at Glo, who lay motionless by the closet. Had Howell slit her throat? No blood spurted from her neck. Perhaps her head had struck the floor, knocking her unconscious.

Concern for Glo had distracted Dani a moment too long. Howell dived for the gun, and she barely had time to fling herself onto him as he landed heavily on top of it.

The pistol was trapped beneath him, and her sole objective became to prevent him from getting his hand around the grip and aiming the muzzle toward her.

Extensive experience ground fighting with large men had taught her to leverage her strengths. Most males had powerful upper bodies, and Howell had clearly spent time in the gym. Women, however, had considerable strength in the core, hip flexors, and legs.

She planted her feet and wrapped her arms around Howell's torso, trying to get a grip on his left wrist. He could use his right hand to shoot, of course, but he would be more accurate with his left.

He writhed and cursed, desperately clutching for the weapon. With a different goal in mind, she focused on gaining control of him. She finally managed to wedge her fingers between his left hand and his body and grasp his thumb. She pulled back with every ounce of force she could muster.

Howling in pain, Howell grabbed her throat with his free hand and squeezed. Dani had mere seconds to act before she lost consciousness. She released her grip on his thumb to claw at the hand throttling her. He redoubled his efforts, wrapping his other hand around her neck. Apparently, he'd decided to choke her out before retrieving the gun, which was still trapped between his body and the floor.

With both of his hands occupied, Dani was free to deliver a palm strike to his temple. The move was meant to stun an opponent, but his beefy arms were in the way, preventing the blow from connecting with full force. Undeterred, she balled her hand into a fist and brought it down on the bridge of his nose, eliciting a grunt of pain and loosening his grip enough for her to plant her hands on his chest and push.

They rolled away from each other before springing to their feet and squaring off. The Glock remained on the floor between them. Dani lowered her center of gravity and raised her arms in a fighting stance.

"You're going to die," Howell said, breathing hard. "And then I'm going to take my time with the dancer before she joins you."

She allowed no trace of fear in her voice. "You don't know who you're messing with."

"If you're talking about your little stint in the Army, I know about it," he said.

He had done his homework, but how much did he really know?

"I was in the 75th Ranger Regiment, asshole."

"Who gives a shit?" he said. "I'm a hell of a lot bigger, stronger, and smarter than you."

"You want to know what a Ranger can do?" She narrowed her eyes. "Fuck around and find out."

He lunged for the gun again, and this time she was ready. She lashed out with her foot, catching him in the jaw. He staggered backward, barely managing to stay on his feet. One of the techniques she had learned in hand-to-hand combat involved timing. Once an initial strike landed, a fighter would continue a relentless attack without giving the enemy a chance to recover, much less mount a counterattack.

Rather than maintain distance, Dani advanced on Howell, kicking his leg along the large nerve that ran along the outer side of the thigh. He lurched backward again, his eyes wide with shock and pain. Instantly she closed the distance between them to deliver an elbow strike to his solar plexus, knocking the wind out of him. His mouth guppied open and closed, but no sound came out.

She slammed the heel of her palm into his throat. When he doubled over, she clutched the back of his head, pulling him toward her as she drove her knee into his groin. His legs buckled, and he crumpled to the floor, where he tucked himself into a fetal position.

She stepped to the side and retrieved her service weapon, sliding it back into its holster. She had no handcuffs with her but remembered Glo telling her about the tape in the kitchen drawer that she used as a low-tech security device. Scotch tape wouldn't hold a prisoner, but maybe Glo had something else that would do the trick.

Thoughts of Glo pulled her attention to the slender form lying prone on the floor, but she knew better than to give aid to a fallen comrade before the environment had been rendered safe. She raced to the kitchen, tugging open drawers until she found one filled with random household items. She rummaged through the contents, grabbed a roll of silver duct tape, and trotted back to Howell, who was still curled up and moaning.

Her toughest job was prying his hands from between his legs. He did not respond to any commands, and she had to resort to digging her index finger into a pressure point at the notch in the center of his collarbone that housed a cluster of nerves. When he reached one of the hands, cupping his crotch to grab at her, she quickly bent his wrist in a control hold, forcing it behind his back. She increased the pressure until he gave her his other hand. She tugged his wrists together and wrapped the tape around them, taking care to cover the skin above the blue nitrile gloves so he couldn't slip free. Satisfied, she bent to tear the strip off with her teeth and secure the end in place.

Once Howell had been restrained, she crawled to Glo and gently rolled her over. A quick check of her vitals revealed that, while unresponsive, Glo was breathing and had a pulse.

Dani placed her knuckles on the center of Glo's chest and dragged them firmly up and down. Known as the sternal rub technique, the method would revive an unconscious person when smelling salts weren't handy. After more than ten seconds of the pain stimulus, Glo's face contorted in a grimace.

"Ow," she groaned, slapping at Dani's hand. "What the hell are you doing?"

A noisy breath escaped Dani's lips. If Glo had not regained consciousness, her prognosis would have been far worse. Even so, she needed an evaluation at the hospital.

"Where's your phone?" Dani asked her.

"Purse," was all Glo could manage.

Dani got to her feet and scanned the apartment in search of a pocketbook. Her efforts were interrupted by pounding on the apartment door.

"Police!" a male voice bellowed from the other side.

Dani crossed the room to open it. "About damn time."

CHAPTER 43

NYPD Midtown North Precinct
West 54th Street
Hell's Kitchen, Manhattan

Dani watched Howell's body language closely as he protested his innocence. She and Flint had been verbally sparring with the senior criminologist for the past ten minutes without making any headway.

Unfortunately, a trip to the ER for a medical checkup had given Howell hours to come up with an alternate interpretation of what had occurred in Glo's apartment. By the time he had been pronounced free of broken bones or internal injuries and taken to the Midtown North Precinct interview room, he was not only ready to talk . . . he had insisted on providing his side of the story.

"She should be sitting on this side of the table," Howell said, jabbing a finger at her. "Not me."

"I didn't hold a knife to anyone's throat," Dani said.

"You aimed a gun at me," Howell said. "You tried to kill me. I did the first thing I could think of." He paused a beat. "And it worked. You didn't pull the trigger, did you?"

"Let me be sure I have this straight," Flint said. "You're saying you took Gloria Gomez hostage in self-defense?"

Howell nodded vigorously. "I was at the apartment conducting a follow-up analysis of the crime scene. Suddenly Agent Loony here shows up and starts waving her gun around for no reason." He dropped his voice and leaned toward Flint in a conspiratorial whisper. "I think she's disturbed. Maybe too many combat tours overseas. You know . . . PTSD."

His strategy was brilliant. If Dani responded to his clear provocation by so much as raising her voice, she would confirm his diagnosis of instability. If she failed to deny his accusations, that could be interpreted as tacit agreement. The only avenue left to her was to pick apart his story in calm, measured, rational terms.

She took a breath before embarking on that path. "The FBI's Evidence Response Team is the equivalent of the NYPD's Crime Scene Unit."

He gave her a disdainful look. "And?"

"The ERT collected the pinhole cameras you concealed in Gloria's apartment." She made a show of looking at her watch. "They should have video clips to share with us any minute now. Then we'll know who's telling the truth."

Patel had already gotten word to her that his assumption had been correct. The cameras weren't big enough to hold data within the unit. She was deliberately baiting Howell, who clearly prided himself on his cleverness, in the hope that he would say something to give the video forensics team a place to start in their hunt for the digitized files.

Howell did not appear ruffled in the slightest. "I've read the files, and this killer—whoever he is—has avoided leaving any physical signs of his presence at every scene," he said. "I can't be certain, but I would imagine someone like that would be clever enough to have the equipment designed to stream videos directly to an untraceable server in the cloud. For extra protection, he would probably encrypt the whole process." His mouth twisted in a wry grin. "Hell, he might even infect it with malware designed to wipe the entire database if the wrong code was entered."

Howell was bragging. He was so sure he couldn't be caught that he was coming right out and telling them how he did it. He was daring them to prove his guilt.

She looked at Flint, saw the red scald creeping up his neck, and knew he was thinking along the same lines she was.

"That's why there was no video in Wilfredo Ochoa's apartment," Flint said. "You planted the panties, but you couldn't very well download a hard copy of the videos and put them there as well."

"Of course he couldn't," Dani said, then turned to face Howell. "Or we would have seen you raping and killing those women instead of Ochoa, the man you framed."

Howell shrugged, palms up. "I was merely speculating based on my experience."

"You were rubbing our noses in it," Flint said. "But there's bound to be trace evidence on those cameras. And I'll bet we'll track the purchases of sophisticated surveillance equipment back to you."

Howell's smug expression stayed in place. He either had a great poker face or he'd already covered his tracks. As a forensic expert, he could have checked for latent prints, fibers, hairs, or other trace evidence right after installing the cameras. And, having read enough police reports over the years to be aware of investigative techniques, he could have taken measures to obtain the equipment through back channels.

She came at him from a different angle. "You are a civilian criminologist and a supervisor at the lab. The only ones who normally go to crime scenes are sworn police detectives certified in evidence collection. When I arrived at Gloria's apartment and kept questioning why you were performing a task outside of your duties, you realized I was too suspicious. You panicked and took a hostage to get my gun away from me."

"If you check the records, you'll find that I have responded in person many times over the years," Howell said. "The crime lab has been the subject of lawsuits and internal investigations due to missed evidence at scenes and the mishandling of materials that have been collected. You're criticizing me for doing my job?"

It was true. The lab had undergone a complete overhaul of its policies and practices after several of these instances came to light. Howell could easily defend his behavior.

Flint followed up on her new line of questioning. "While you were getting your medical checkup, we had the opportunity to look into your history," he said to Howell. "You did respond to several scenes. Homicides, in fact. Specifically, homicides involving the deaths of every woman attributed to the serial killer."

"And to several other murders as well," Howell added.

"You're too smart to draw attention to yourself by only going out on certain cases," Dani said. "You didn't want those to be linked to each other at all, and if they ever were, you didn't want your name to be associated with only those crimes. No, you made sure to be present at lots of high-profile cases, didn't you?"

"I'm very conscientious about my job," he said.

She tried to break through his veneer of calm. "That's why the murders were committed without a shred of physical evidence," she said. "In fact, I recall the day we met. You told me there was no 'viable' forensic material left at any of the scenes. At first, we all thought it had to do with that lab scandal a few years back, but now we know what really happened." She leaned across the table, invading his space. "You screwed up and left traces behind at some of the scenes, didn't you? But hey, no one's perfect. Sometimes you've got to find a way to clean up your own mess." She let the implication hang for a moment before posing the key question. "When we inspect the logs, how many times will we find that you checked out the evidence?"

He steepled his fingers. "I keep trying to tell you two. I'm a supervisor. Making spot checks is in my job description. I'm sure my name is listed logging out hundreds of pieces of evidence in the course of my duties. Maybe even thousands over the years."

He had an answer for everything.

"You told me I was under arrest for abduction and attempted murder," Howell went on. "By the time my attorney gets finished, you'll be lucky if you have a misdemeanor assault left."

"You sliced into her neck," Flint said. "One millimeter deeper and she—"

"That was an accident," Howell cut in. "I think a judge or jury would understand that anyone's hand would be shaking when they were looking down the barrel of a gun." He gave Dani a considering look. "And I think a civil jury would be inclined to find in my favor when I file a lawsuit against the FBI for violating my rights. First, there's excessive force, and next, you try to make me a scapegoat for crimes I didn't commit."

"Like you did to Ochoa?" she said.

He didn't take the bait. "I haven't called my attorney yet because I have nothing to hide. I'm talking to you because I choose to. I am quite certain, however, that when I do call her, she'll expedite the arraignment and see to it that a reasonable bail is set."

He was far too canny to come out and say it, but he'd spelled out his escape plan. His attorney would appear before the judge to explain away the only charges they had on him at the moment as a giant misunderstanding combined with an overreaction on Dani's part.

The judge would take Howell's position of trust, his ties to the community, and his spotless record into account and set a bail that he could easily post. Even if the judge included travel restrictions, Howell could escape to a country with no extradition before they managed to scrape together enough evidence to charge him with any of the murders.

Dani got to her feet. Rather than grabbing Howell by the lapels of his white lab coat and shaking the truth out of him, she stalked out of the interview room, determined to clear her mind and think.

The sound of Howell's laughter reached her as she closed the door behind her.

He had won, and he knew it.

CHAPTER 44

Dani leaned her forehead against the smooth wall of the hallway outside the interview room, trying to get her blood pressure down. If she didn't think of a way to outmaneuver him, Howell would be a free man within hours.

"I was watching in the observation room," a voice said from behind her. "I'm shocked you didn't knock out that arrogant prick's teeth."

She turned to see Detective Chapman's sympathetic smile. "That would only raise the dollar amount of his lawsuit," she said. "And he'd still get away with murder. Literally."

Chapman grew serious. "You hide it well, but I'm a trained observer. I can see how much this investigation is affecting you. Don't make my mistake." His voice sounded strained. "There are ghosts that follow me around. Ghosts of every victim who hasn't gotten justice. That includes the unsolved cases, and the ones where there wasn't enough evidence to prosecute but I know damn well who did it." He rested a fatherly hand on her shoulder. "Let it go, Dani. If you don't, it'll eat you up inside."

He spoke with the conviction of bitter experience.

Faced with his total honesty, she opened up. "This man is a monster. He's compulsive. He'll never stop. More people will die." She forced out the toughest words. Words that had lodged in her throat. "And it's on me. If I could have—"

"No." Chapman frowned at her. "Don't you dare take this on yourself." He lifted his hand from her shoulder to tap his chest. "I'm the one who should have seen the pattern years ago. You made the connection, not me. How many people would still be alive if I'd picked up on it as fast as you did?"

He wasn't being fair to himself. He hadn't been trained in pattern recognition the way she had. She understood that he was talking about inappropriate guilt. And she appreciated him for baring his soul to do it.

"I've decided it's time to retire," he said, then added, "My hunting days are over."

At first she wasn't sure what he meant. Then she recalled the Hemingway quote on a poster in the Bronx Homicide Squad.

"There is no hunting like the hunting of man, and those who have hunted armed men long enough and liked it, never care for anything else thereafter."

She couldn't picture him relaxing on a beach. Retirement would not come easily for Chapman, who, whether he admitted it to himself or not, was the job. He'd devoted his entire adult life to seeking justice, a goal she shared. Would decades working in the constraints of a system that often seemed arbitrary take the same toll on her years from now?

He dug into his pocket and pulled something out. "We had a deal." He opened his hand to reveal a flash drive resting on his palm. "You held up your end of the bargain and then some. Not only did you tell me whether the first three cases were linked, but you also solved them. And a whole lot more."

Her heart began to pound. "The case files for my father's death are on this drive, aren't they?"

He'd chosen the only thing that might distract her from spiraling into a toxic combination of guilt and remorse, and she knew it had been intentional on his part. In military terms, she had received a new mission, one that would demand her attention.

"I've been carrying this around since you first came to Bronx Homicide," he said quietly. "Knew I'd give it to you sometime, but couldn't find the right moment." He took her hand and placed the drive into it. "Nothing can bring back your father, but you and your family deserve answers." He paused. "I don't expect anything will change, but at least you'll know all the facts."

She thought back to the visit with her mother at Bellevue. The treating psychiatrist, Dr. Maffuccio, couldn't be certain whether anything Camila Vega said was reliable, but something about her earnest claim of innocence had moved Dani. Now she finally had a way to settle the matter once and for all.

"Thank you," she said simply. "This means more than I can say."

"The least I could do." He jerked his chin toward the closed interview room door. "Unfortunately, we still have to deal with this assclown before you can get started on anything else."

"What else would Agent Vega be starting on?" Wu said, joining them.

How much had her boss overheard? Wu had made it clear she needed to come to him for permission to look into her father's murder. And that he might not agree to let her do it.

She answered before Chapman could respond. "We were talking in general," she said to Wu, directing his thoughts toward the most pressing problem. "Howell's going to keep us busy. He all but told us he's going to bolt, and we can't stop him. I'm racking my brains trying to come up with something to link him to the murders. Hell, even just one murder." She sighed. "Tell me Patel and the video forensics team located Howell's cloud storage."

Wu gave his head a rueful shake. "They're still trying to trace the feed, but they have to go slowly. Howell knows how to destroy evidence to cover his tracks. They're operating on the assumption that he'll have virtual safeguards set up to protect the files or—worst case scenario—delete them." He looked every bit as disappointed as she felt. "Justice and the law do not always go hand in hand," he said. "We have to follow the law and hope that justice prevails."

"Is this where you tell us this is why Lady Justice is blindfolded?" Chapman said. "Because that feels pretty weak just now. Especially when I can hear the victims calling out to me . . . like I do every night." He looked down. "If I could put cuffs on the man who killed those women, I could retire feeling like I'd done my part."

Years of confronting the worst humanity had to offer had taken their toll on the detective, who had been the voice of so many victims who couldn't speak for themselves. He looked weary, burdened by the weight of every unsolved case in his extensive career.

"We'll figure something out," she said to him, then cut her eyes to Wu. "And it will be a righteous conviction."

"If we can connect him to one crime, all the others are linked," Wu said. "Those links will form a chain."

She had never heard the boss wax philosophical about an investigation and was about to tell him so when Chapman snapped his fingers.

"That reminds me," he said to her, fishing something out of his pocket with his other hand. "This chain is yours."

She looked at the clear plastic baggie in his outstretched hand and saw her father's silver necklace inside. It must have broken during the scuffle with Howell.

"Where did you find this?" she asked, absently touching her bare throat. She had a dim recollection of Howell trying to choke her, which must have been when it came off.

"Gloria Gomez found it on the floor of her apartment. She gave it to one of the uniforms while the paramedics were checking her injuries. Told him you must have dropped it and asked him to make sure it got back to you." Chapman frowned. "The uniform was fresh out of the academy. He wasn't sure what to do, so he brought it to me."

She looked from Chapman to Wu and back again. "How did Glo know it was mine?"

"She told the officer you wore it when you met her at the café," Chapman said.

Wu peered at the necklace. "It's a plain silver chain. How could she tell it was the same one?"

"It's not exactly plain," Chapman said. "I'm sure she recognized it the same way I did." He indicated the black torpedo-shaped connector that held the silver chain together. "I've never seen a clasp like that one. Looked it up. It's called a bayonet closure. This is the second time I've had to repair it."

"Second time?" she asked, taking the baggie from him.

"I never told you because I didn't want to remind you of your father's last moments," the detective began. "But one of the rings connecting the closure to the chain was bent open, and the chain fell off your dad's neck." His hand went back into his pocket, this time retrieving a bright-red Swiss Army knife. "I always carry this. Used the pliers to close the ring and bend it back into shape. Good as new."

"Kind of you," she said, examining the unusual closure. She'd noticed the clasp when she took the chain out of the box at her aunt's apartment, but Erica and Axel hadn't seemed surprised by it. Of course, none of them had seen the necklace for over a decade, and their father always wore it tucked under his shirt, so she didn't give it another thought.

"Maybe it's bad luck," Chapman said. "Maybe you should wear the other one."

"I don't follow," she said. "What other one?"

"Your father's other necklace," Chapman said. "You know, the one with the Army Ranger pendant on it."

She opened the top and tipped the baggie, letting the chain slide into her open hand. "My aunt Manuela has the pendant," she said. "I got the chain that went with it."

Chapman shook his head. "There were two silver chains. One had the pendant on it and the other one had this clasp."

This made no sense. "My father only wore one necklace."

Chapman pointed at the closure. "There are the marks from the pliers I used to fix it the last time."

A cascade of thoughts and memories crashed in on her. She considered everything she had known—or thought she had known—in a new light.

"I need wheels," she said to Wu. "Are there any agents from the surveillance team here?"

Wu pulled a set of keys from his pocket but held them in his closed fist. "What's going on?"

She hadn't expected him to offer up his assigned car. All the other agents must have headed back to the JOC. "There's no time to explain, but if I'm right, I'll have all the answers we need." She stretched out her hand. "I'm asking you to trust me."

He opened his fist and dropped the keys into her waiting palm.

CHAPTER 45

Benedict Avenue
Castle Hill, Bronx

Forty-five minutes later, Dani gazed into fathomless dark eyes that held no warmth. At least, not for her. Manuela looked upon Dani's younger siblings with genuine affection. The fact that her aunt was capable of love made Manuela's rejection even more pointed. It was one of many things that had hastened Dani's departure for the Army at eighteen.

"It's mine," Manuela said, pressing a protective hand over her chest, where the pendant was concealed under her blouse.

Dani stifled a groan of frustration. "I just want to see the necklace. I promise not to take it."

"Sergio would have wanted me to have it," Manuela said, still defensive. "He never took it off, and neither will I."

Dani had learned that the reason she never knew Manuela had taken her father's chain from the box of his personal effects was because she always wore it under her clothing. Invisible to the world, but close to her heart.

Her father's parents had died young, and Manuela, ten years older than Sergio, had practically raised him. She looked upon him more like a son than a kid brother. The only thing Sergio had ever done wrong, according to Manuela, was to marry Camila. Manuela treated her sister-in-law with the same unrelenting contempt she did Dani. Looking back on the situation, Dani understood that Manuela took out her anger at her brother's killer on the only reasonable facsimile that presented itself. Not only did Dani physically resemble her mother, but she also shared Camila's penchant for puzzles and patterns.

Right now the only puzzle that concerned Dani was the mystery of the two necklaces. She turned to her siblings, Erica and Axel, in a silent appeal for help.

Erica took the tacit cue. "You don't have to take the necklace off," she said to Manuela. "Just pull it out and let us have a look at it."

Manuela's response was directed at Dani. "Why do you need to look at mine? You have one just like it."

Giving up on the necklace for the moment, Dani switched tactics. Instead of easing into the question at the heart of the matter, she plunged into the deep end.

"When you opened the box Detective Chapman gave me, did you—"

"He might have handed it to you, but it was meant for the whole family," Manuela cut in.

Dani realized her mistake too late. The question had sounded like an accusation of theft. This was going from bad to worse.

"Dani didn't mean it that way," Axel said, rushing to her defense. "Why don't you tell us about the box?"

Dani gave her brother a grateful smile. Without a cell phone, she hadn't been able to call her family ahead of time and set the stage for her visit. Axel had clearly picked up on her demeanor and grasped that this line of questioning was important. Aware that Manuela was unlikely to respond to Dani, he and Erica were doing their best to facilitate the interaction.

"It was the day after that detective turned over Sergio's things," Manuela said. "I wanted to wear his Ranger charm, so I opened the box. I knew it would be there because he always wore it."

Dani asked the next question with a deliberately casual air, using the same word her aunt had used to avoid confusion. "Did you take the charm and put it on your own chain?"

Manuela frowned. "What difference does that make?"

For the second time that day, Dani had to fight the impulse to shake a straight answer out of someone. "It could make all the difference in the world."

Manuela continued to glare mulishly without responding.

"Please tell us, tía Manuela," Erica said softly.

Erica's pleading succeeded where Dani's insistence failed.

"I took the chain that had the charm on it," Manuela finally said. "I left the other one in the box."

Dani's antennae went up. Here was another reference to a second chain. "There were two silver necklaces then?" she asked. "One with a Ranger charm on it and the other one just a chain?"

Manuela nodded. "I didn't care about the other one."

With trembling fingers, Dani pulled the chain Chapman had returned to her out of her pocket. "Was this the other necklace in the box?"

Manuela shrugged. "How should I know? They were both ordinary silver chains. You know, the kind men wear. They all look pretty much alike. That's why I wanted the one with the charm. That was special."

"Do you ever remember my dad wearing two necklaces?" Dani asked.

"No," Manuela said. "I figured maybe the second chain was new. Maybe Camila had bought it for his birthday." Her lip curled. "That was another reason I wanted nothing to do with that one. I took the one that mattered."

Dani glanced at her siblings. "Do either of you remember Mom giving Dad a necklace for his birthday?"

"She gave him a new wallet," Axel said. "We still have it."

Dani recalled the gift. It was brown leather and embossed with his initials. She held up the chain so they could examine it. "Did you ever see Mom or Dad wearing a chain with a clasp like this?"

"Mom never wore any jewelry but her wedding band," Erica said. "Not even a watch. No way did that belong to her."

"I don't remember the clasp," Axel said. "But it would have been in the back of his neck under his hair. We wouldn't have seen it."

True, but sometimes a clasp would work its way around to the front during the course of the day, as this one had when she'd worn it. She recalled sliding it around to the back of her neck several times since she had put it on.

Her pulse picked up. Another clue had fallen into place, bringing yet a different part of the picture into focus.

She got to her feet. "Axel, I need to borrow your computer."

CHAPTER 46

"I'm sorry," Dani said to Axel. "But I can't let you see this."

"I'm an adult," he said. "Whatever it is, it can't be worse than some of the virtual reality combat games I play. And besides, it's my computer."

Her brother naturally assumed she wanted to view crime scene–related images and case files. He was correct, but what he didn't know was that the case in question was that of their father's murder. She had already seen the carnage in person ten years ago and had no intention of allowing those harrowing images to haunt Axel's nightmares the way they occasionally did hers.

"I can always go back to my apartment and look at the files on my own computer," she said. "But that's all the way over in Brooklyn, and I don't want to waste time. This is important, and if I can't get what I need in time, a killer might walk."

He raised his hands in a placating manner. "All right, I'll leave you to it."

"Close the door behind you."

Once alone in Axel's bedroom, she pushed the flash drive Chapman had given her into the USB port and clicked open the folder icon that popped up on the screen. Numerous documents, JPEGs, and video files appeared in a date-stamped list.

She scanned down until she found the crime scene photos. Steeling herself for what she was about to see, she began clicking and scrolling. One of the first images showed her backpack just inside the front door, where she'd dropped it beside the laundry bag.

She recalled the clean laundry folded in the bag, and another puzzle piece fell into place. The murder had occurred on a Thursday. The day her mother always took their clothes to the laundromat around the corner before the kids got home from school. Her father would have been home alone for a couple of hours.

It took Dani another five minutes to locate the picture she'd initially been searching for.

One of the crime scene detectives had rolled her father's body over. On the blood-soaked carpet underneath lay the silver chain with the black clasp. The very necklace she had been wearing over the past few days. The closure had not come apart, but a link connecting it had twisted open. Made sense. The metal would give at its weakest point, which was not the reinforced clasp.

She closed the photo file and clicked open the medical examiner's report. She scrolled down to find a notation that mentioned an impression on the decedent's back. The ME had matched it to the chain that had been brought to the morgue along with all the other jewelry on the body.

A separate form regarding the disposition of the victim's personal effects was signed by those who transported the deceased, the ME, and Detective Chapman. This was done to maintain a chain of custody for the items. Chapman secured everything in marked bags and took them to the evidence storage unit. Three days later, he signed the log to remove them, noting their final disposition as "returned to decedent's family."

Dani clicked on Chapman's supplemental investigation for more details. The detective had been unable to interview the prime suspect, Camila Vega, who was catatonic. He had interviewed the seventeen-year-old daughter, Daniela, who said she came home from school to find her mother kneeling beside her father, holding a bloody knife later confirmed to be from the family's own kitchen. The daughter had confirmed she used her key to unlock the door, and that no one else was in the apartment when she arrived home.

The report said there was no bruising or abrasions to Sergio Vega's knuckles indicative of a physical altercation, and only one defensive wound in which he appeared to raise his arm to ward off the knife, resulting in a deep laceration to his right forearm.

Chapman concurred with the ME's finding that Sergio had been surprised and had not had much of a chance to defend himself. In his report, Chapman went into more detail. He researched Sergio's background and learned that he had been an Army Ranger. He also learned about his medical discharge and the debilitating symptoms he dealt with, including migraines, tinnitus, and vertigo following a traumatic brain injury on active duty. Chapman surmised that these injuries had made it difficult for him to resist an attack from anyone, especially his wife, with whom he had no history of domestic violence or any altercations whatsoever.

The wife in question, however, had a history of mental instability. Chapman had learned this by interviewing the victim's closest relative, his older sister, Manuela. She had described her sister-in-law as very disturbed and added that she had always believed her to be capable of harming herself or others. She went on to say she had warned her brother not to marry Camila, whom she considered to be a ticking time bomb.

Of course Manuela would put Camila in the most negative light. Chapman would have relied on her statements, as well as the evidence at the scene, to make deductions about what happened. He made a note of the freshly laundered clothes in the bag and determined that Camila had come home from the laundromat, gotten into an altercation with her husband, and stabbed him to death with a knife from the kitchen.

With the case closed by arrest, he had returned Sergio's personal effects to his next of kin, which was Daniela.

Chapman would have no way of knowing—and no reason to suspect—that the necklace found under Sergio's body did not belong to him, but to his killer. Armed with new information Chapman did not have at the time, Dani played out the scene in her mind.

An intruder had entered the apartment. Her father had probably been lying down with one of his migraines, possibly in the dark, as he often did when it was bad, and his tinnitus had likely masked the sound of a break-in. The burglar had not expected to find anyone home in the middle of the day and grabbed a knife from the kitchen. He had attacked before her father knew what was going on, and his vertigo would have made it impossible for him to jump to his feet and mount the kind of defense he had been capable of before his injury. There must have been a brief struggle, however, causing the killer's necklace to break and fall to the floor an instant before her father did.

The killer either did not know his necklace had come off, or he looked around and couldn't find it. Not wanting to linger too long at the scene of the crime, he took off. Whether at the time of the murder or sometime after, he would have realized the chain was missing. He would have been in a panic until he read the news stories about the wife who had murdered her husband on Benedict Avenue.

Dani opened the final supplement, which was a document Chapman had filed four months after her father's death. He had changed the final disposition of the case from "closed by arrest" to "closed by exceptional means," because the district attorney declined to prosecute due to the defendant's mental state. Camila was transferred to Bellevue, where she would remain until she had recovered enough mental capacity to stand trial for murder.

Dani stopped reading when unshed tears blurred the screen. Her mother was innocent and had spent the past decade locked away for a crime she did not commit. Dani had been angry with Manuela, but her own statements had been every bit as damning as those of her aunt. She had told Chapman about coming home to her mother wielding the murder weapon. She had described her mother's complete inaction while she tried in vain to save her father. She had confessed that her mother had always been emotionally fragile.

She swallowed the lump that had formed in her throat. She was there. Her words had been more instrumental than anyone else's in carrying out the travesty of her mother's arrest. The blame was hers, and hers alone.

What she had done, she must now undo.

Would the necklace be enough? She began clicking on the crime scene photos again, looking for anything else that might support her theory. She thought about everything she had learned, and everything she suspected.

She had examined hundreds of crime scene photos over the past few days. She felt like she had become an expert herself. What could the images tell her that others might have overlooked?

An idea slipped between her roving thoughts. Insubstantial at first, then gaining traction. She began to click through the pictures faster, intent on the one thing that might elevate her theory past all doubt.

Finally, she found pictures of the remaining rooms in her family's old apartment. As she had seen in the other cases, the CSU documented the entire apartment rather than just the immediate area where the murder was committed. The idea was to document the state of the environment in case other information came to light—as it now had.

She reviewed each room until she got to the primary bedroom. Heart pounding, she zoomed in, magnifying the image as much as possible without causing it to pixilate.

And then she saw what she was looking for.

"I've got you, you son of a bitch."

She raced from the room to find Axel sitting on the living room sofa beside Erica.

She stuck out her hand. "I need to borrow your cell phone."

He unlocked it and handed it to her without a word.

Afraid he wouldn't answer a call from a strange number, she texted Wu.

THIS IS VEGA. I FOUND PROOF HOWELL IS THE SERIAL KILLER.
I'LL BE AT UR LOCATION ASAP. DO NOT LET HIM LEAVE.

Her supervisor's terse reply came less than a minute later.

HE'S ALREADY GONE.

CHAPTER 47

Stunned to learn Howell had slipped through the net again, Dani had followed her text to Wu with a phone call.

Her boss explained that Howell had exercised his right to counsel, and Cassie Flock had swung into action, using her vast network of connections to get her client on this afternoon's arraignment docket. Without any additional charges pending, Wu had been forced to hand him over to the US Marshals to await the hearing.

In the meantime, Wu had called everyone back to the Joint Operations Center for an all-hands-on-deck emergency meeting. Dani had used the forty-five-minute drive from Castle Hill in morning rush-hour traffic to plan her strategy. Wu had asked her to open the briefing with an explanation of what she'd learned. After returning the borrowed Bureau car's keys to her boss, and handing Chapman's flash drive to Patel, she took the empty seat left open for her at the head of the conference table.

She directed her most urgent question at Flint before sharing her theory. "What's the status of Howell's hearing?"

"I called my contact at the court clerk's office. Word is Cassie Flock's going for dismissal. If that doesn't work, she'll try for an unsecured bond."

Dani doubted such serious charges would be dropped outright, but an upstanding police department employee with an impeccable record and a plausible explanation for his actions would easily qualify for release without posting bail. Either way, the end result would be the same. Howell would disappear before they could bring the kind of charges that would keep him in custody until trial. Murder charges.

Flint glanced at his watch. "I'll have to head to the courthouse soon so I can be on hand to answer questions."

They were in a race against the clock, and they all knew it.

"I'll get right to it then," she said, signaling Patel, who had uploaded the contents of the flash drive she gave him five minutes earlier. "This is Detective Chapman's investigation into my father's murder ten years ago."

Chapman startled. "You said you'd found evidence against Howell. Why are we talking about this case?"

Everyone else's dubious expressions mirrored Chapman's. After getting the text from Wu, she had followed up with a phone call asking him to convene the task force at the JOC immediately. She left Axel's phone with him and was not able to explain on the drive to Manhattan.

Wu, who had taken her on faith, looked like he was beginning to question his decision. "Perhaps you'd better explain yourself," he said.

She pulled the baggie containing the necklace out of her pocket and held it up. "I got the idea when Detective Chapman returned this chain to me."

She went on to explain that she had gone to see Manuela and learned that two silver chains had been transported with her father's body to the morgue. At her prompting, Patel displayed the various documents on the wall screen.

Within minutes, everyone understood that the necklace found under the body had apparently belonged to the killer.

"Obviously, we need to reopen your father's case," Flint said. "But I still don't see how this gets us to Howell."

"He killed young women who lived alone," Chapman added. "Your dad was the complete opposite of his profile."

"That's why we never connected that case to the rest of the series," Dani said. "Until now." She addressed Patel again. "Zoom in on the chain found under the body."

She stood and walked to the screen.

"This is called a bayonet closure," she explained for the benefit of others in the room who hadn't heard her prior conversation with Chapman. "And this one is not only unusual, but also black, so it stands out from the silver chain."

"I know this is leading somewhere," Flint said. "But you need to speed it up. I'll have to leave soon if I'm going to make it to the courthouse."

"You can run there in less than ten minutes," Dani said to him. "You'll want to hear this before you go." Aware she had bought only a short reprieve, she forged ahead. "I began wearing the necklace just before we connected the cases and attributed them to a serial killer. According to Dr. Cattrall, he's a voyeur and would likely watch our investigation whenever he could. If he had blended in with onlookers at any of the scenes, or if he looked at media coverage of us, he might have seen the necklace on me."

"I get it," Chapman said. "If that clasp had worked its way around to the side or the front, he would have recognized it immediately."

She reached around to gather up her hair, twisting it up against the back of her head. "We've had record heat and humidity these past few days. I've been wearing my hair up a lot. That clasp would have been visible no matter where it was."

"So you think the killer knows you're in possession of evidence that could prove your mother was innocent?" Wu said. "Where does that lead?"

"Do you remember when I was mugged a few days ago?" she asked.

"Of course, but what does that have to do with—"

"We all agreed that it was not a random street crime," she continued. "The men who attacked me demanded my money and my jewelry. But what if their real objective was the necklace?"

Flint looked skeptical. "One of them killed your father and they were trying to recover the evidence?"

She shook her head. "They were sent by Howell to get the necklace. Anything else they got off me was theirs to keep."

"Howell again?" Chapman said. "Why?"

"He would know the real significance of the necklace." She pointed at the screen again. "If the killer wore it when he was committing the crime, he probably had it on all the time under his shirt, like a lot of people do."

"Howell's a senior criminalist at the lab," Wu said. "He'd see hundreds of tight-fitting links. The perfect receptacle to trap and store DNA. Even after ten years, there could still be sufficient residual traces to get a match."

She had reached the same conclusion. "He would do anything to make sure we never had a chance to analyze it."

"Then he probably cleaned it at the lab right after it arrived there for analysis," Chapman said. "I didn't sign it back out for three days."

"I had the same thought," she said. "So I called the lab before I came here. Howell worked a four-to-three schedule back then. Four ten-hour days rotating through the week. He went off shift the day of my father's murder and wasn't back on duty until three days later. He wouldn't have had the chance to tamper with the evidence."

"That makes no sense," Flint said. "He would have made damned sure he came to work to get it—if it was actually his necklace, which I'm still not sure about."

"Howell was only a junior-level criminalist at the time," Dani said. "He couldn't just waltz into the lab on his days off and pull evidence out."

"Like he can now as one of the highest-ranking civilians," Wu said dryly. "He's got free run of the place, but back then he couldn't have gotten access without sneaking in, and he knew all the evidence would be logged in, and the lab is full of cameras. It would have led everyone straight to him."

"We need to get an arrest warrant for murder before he's released," Dani said.

"The crime lab will have entered Howell's DNA profile into CODIS," Wu said. "One of our ERTs could perform a rapid test right now."

The Combined DNA Index System was the FBI's database containing the profiles of those convicted of qualifying criminal offenses. Since criminalists were the ones who analyzed the samples, their DNA profiles were also entered to eliminate them in the event of accidental cross contamination.

Because forensic material obtained from the necklace could be compared to a known sample in the database, rapid DNA testing could confirm a match in less than an hour.

Wu pulled out his phone and tapped the screen. "I need an ERT tech with a portable test kit in here ASAP." He disconnected and turned to Dani. "If the tech gets a match on Howell's profile, that'll go a long way toward establishing probable cause. We'll have to get samples from you, Detective Chapman, and anyone else who might have handled the necklace for elimination purposes later." He paused to consider. "Fortunately, it's been stored in a box until recently."

Chapman paled. "If you're right, there's a problem. You said Howell choked you during the fight. He might've been trying to grab the necklace but only succeeded in breaking it."

"That's exactly what I think happened. What's the problem?"

"That means he touched the chain." Chapman shook his head. "He could say he left his DNA on it today, not ten years ago."

She recalled a significant detail. "Except that he claimed to be there in his official capacity. He was wearing blue examination gloves the whole time. I saw his hands when I taped his wrists together. The gloves were still intact."

"Back up a second," Flint said. "Even if we get a hit on Howell, we've lost the chain of custody—no pun intended."

For the necklace to be entered into evidence, they would have to account for its whereabouts at all times. Once Chapman signed it out and gave it to Dani, there was no official record of what had happened to it, which meant the evidence might be deemed inadmissible. No judge or jury would hear that Howell's DNA was found at the scene of a murder, something he could not possibly explain because he never had an opportunity to touch it in the course of his duties.

"I hit the same snag an hour ago," she said. "So I looked for more evidence." She turned to Patel again. "Pull up the crime scene photos from the apartment and enlarge photo number 197."

As Patel hunted for the image, the conference room door opened to reveal a young woman in khaki pants and a blue polo shirt with the FBI seal on the front. She entered with a bulky black pelican case and turned to close the door, revealing the letters ERT on the back of the shirt.

"What do you need, sir?" she said to Wu.

He signaled Dani, who lifted the baggie out of her pocket. "Can you check for a match from a known sample in the database?"

The tech took the baggie from Dani's outstretched hand. "You need me to extract the sample first?"

"Can you do it here?" Wu asked. "Or do you need to take it to the lab?"

Her brows furrowed. "Do you know the name of the suspect in the database, and did that person wear this necklace?"

"Yes, and yes," Wu said. "We believe the suspect lost it at a murder scene ten years ago." He gestured to Dani. "It was stored in a box shortly after the crime, but Agent Vega has worn it for the past several days."

The tech opened her mouth as if to make a comment, then appeared to rethink what she was going to say. "Is there anything else connecting the suspect to the case?" she asked him.

Wu answered for the team. "It's a long story, and we're short on time. Bottom line, we need to know if you can recover any DNA trapped in the links and search for a match in the database."

More than ever, Dani appreciated her boss. Others found his no-nonsense approach intimidating, but she preferred strong leaders who spoke directly.

The tech considered her answer for a long moment before framing her response. Clearly wanting to accommodate a request from the special agent in charge, she also couldn't afford to mess up what she would assume to be a high-profile investigation.

"Any residual skin cells may be degraded," she hedged. "But the best chance to extract a viable sample would be at the lab in Quantico. We should send it there."

"Can you put a rush on it?" Wu asked.

"Yes, sir." She turned to Chapman. "If you're the lead detective, I'll need you to fill out the paperwork."

The process of shipping the materials to Quantico and waiting for results could take weeks. A word from Wu would push things along, but not fast enough to stop Howell's escape.

"I've got the photo you wanted," Patel said, as the tech sat down beside the homicide detective on the far side of the table.

Dani directed everyone's attention to the screen again. "This is what convinced me beyond any doubt," she said. "The same person who murdered all thirty-one women and Ochoa also killed my father."

CHAPTER 48

Dani waited impatiently while her colleagues studied the enlarged picture on the wall screen.

"Is that the main bedroom in your childhood apartment?" Flint asked, crossing the room to stand by her side.

"It is," she said.

"Zoom in as tight as you can," Flint said to Patel.

Everyone but Chapman and the tech got to their feet to examine the photo close up. With the image magnified, the telltale signs were clearly visible.

"Those are just like the pinholes we found in the serial killer cases," Flint said. "Same location in the room, same size."

"I'm sure Patel can confirm it," she said.

Patel quickly divided the screen into multiple sections, each one containing a close-up of the distinctive pattern of two small holes in the primary bedrooms of the murder victims. They had previously surmised that one hole was for a tiny lens, and the other was for a microphone.

"They're an exact match in diameter, and the distance between the holes is identical in every case." Patel looked up from his terminal at Dani. "Including the ones at your old apartment."

"I'm sold," Chapman said from his seat at the far end of the table. "But that's not going to be enough for a conviction even if we get a DNA hit for Howell on the necklace."

All eyes swiveled to the ERT tech, who was sealing the evidence envelope. "I'll tell them it's top priority."

Dani watched her leave before turning back to Chapman. "Right now I'm not looking for a conviction," she said in reply to his earlier comment. "And we won't even get to trial if Howell leaves town after he makes bail." She glanced around the room. "We just need enough for a search warrant."

"Writing up an affidavit and getting in front of a judge can take hours," Wu said. "If Howell is released before we get to his apartment with paper in hand, he could destroy the evidence before we get there."

"And he would know how to cover his tracks better than anyone else," Flint said.

"If we somehow managed to get to Howell's place before he does, you're gambling that he hasn't already done that," Chapman said. "We could get there to find nothing at all."

"I disagree," Dr. Cattrall said, speaking for the first time since the meeting began. "You never found any of the videos he made for two reasons. First, because they directly incriminate him, and second, because they are his primary trophies. He was willing to part with the victims' lingerie—his fetish objects—to frame someone else. He'd been involved in enough investigations to know of other offenders who stole underwear." She grew adamant. "Never forget that he's a voyeur. The videos are his real obsession, and I'm certain he couldn't bring himself to destroy his last vestige of control over his victims."

"He basically told us they were streamed directly to the cloud," Flint said. "There's no film to destroy."

"I'm saying he would not permanently delete the video," Cattrall clarified. "He's also OCD. If you look in the right place, you'll find his secrets are still there, but hidden or secured somehow. Your challenge is to access them."

"Any suggestions, Doctor?" Dani asked.

"Since he lives alone, he probably views them on his home computer. That way, he could . . . enjoy them by himself."

She did not elaborate, apparently concluding further explanation wasn't necessary by the expressions of revulsion that followed her analysis.

"Take me with you when you serve the warrant," Patel said, flexing his knuckles as if warming up for a piano concerto. "I'll get past any security he's got on his computer."

Wu held up his hand, bringing all discussion to a halt. "Just got a text from one of the marshals. They've moved Howell to the holding area."

This was close to the last stop. Howell had been placed with other federal prisoners awaiting arraignment. Within the next couple of hours, he would be escorted to the courtroom where he and his attorney would appear before the magistrate conducting the bail hearing.

"There's nothing stopping us from putting a tail on him," Flint said. "I'll get some undercover detectives to stick with him wherever he goes if he makes bail. We'll know when he gets to his apartment, and wherever he goes after that."

His comment gave Dani an idea. "Can you request some uniforms to stand by near his apartment building, but out of sight?" she asked Flint. "That way the minute the warrant is signed, we can post them at his door until we get there."

They had no legal grounds for denying someone access to their residence without a warrant. If they posted an officer outside Howell's apartment door now and barred him from going inside before a judge signed the warrant, any evidence obtained afterward—even with a valid warrant—would be thrown out of court as fruit of the poisonous tree. Worse yet, it would never be admissible in the future, practically guaranteeing Howell would get away with all the murders he had committed.

"And if he makes it home before we have the warrant?" Flint asked.

"Then we tell the uniforms when we have it, and they can go in and hold everything in place for us." She grimaced. "I know what you're thinking, and I agree. We'd better get to a judge before he gets to his apartment."

CHAPTER 49

Howell understood why the US Marshals referred to the holding area as a pen. Handcuffed, he waited beside people charged with fraud, securities violations, and other white-collar crimes. He'd assaulted a federal agent, which had landed him in federal court, so at least he wasn't holed up with drug dealers, robbers, and gangbangers. He had standards, after all.

An exceptionally large marshal stood at parade rest, feet slightly apart, hands clasped behind his back, watching them. His close-fitting uniform put his powerful physique on full display, no doubt an intentional reminder to all the bulls in the pen that they shouldn't even consider making trouble.

Something about the marshal rankled Howell. At first he couldn't place it. Then he realized the lawman had roughly the same build as the man who killed the prostitute in the video.

Ten years ago, when he was a junior tech working second shift at the crime lab, a detective had arrested a suspect for murdering a prostitute. Part of the evidence recovered from the suspect's apartment was a flash drive containing video evidence of his crime. Howell had been designated to process the exterior of the drive for latent prints, DNA, or trace evidence to show it had been in the suspect's possession.

He'd finished processing the exterior, lifting a partial print sufficient to get a match for the suspect. Curiosity overcame him, and, fingers trembling, he uploaded a copy of the video to his tablet before submitting the flash drive, along with his report, to the case file.

What he saw that day had rocked his world. It was like the moment in *The Wizard of Oz* when the film went from black and white to Technicolor. Nothing had looked the same after that—and he could never go back to his previous monochromatic existence.

He'd heard of those kinds of videos before, but always assumed the so-called snuff films were fake. Probably they were . . . but not this one. The detective had charged the man with murder, and the woman had really died. That fact, more than anything else, had catapulted his former fascination into a full-blown obsession.

His journey had taken many turns, and could have led in many directions, but that single moment had set him on a course that had taken him to this place.

He was dragged back to the present when a second marshal poked his head into the room. "Bradley Howell," he called out, scanning the room. "Your attorney is here."

This was not what he had planned for today. Or any day. If the truth ever came to light, he would be labeled a monster, studied like an insect, and caged like an animal.

Fortunately, he had a plan to make sure he would not end up as anyone's bitch in prison.

He got to his feet and made his way to the rear door that led to a corridor lined with small interview rooms. He was led into the room on the left. He offered no resistance as the marshal attached his handcuffs to a loop bolted to the center of the table.

He imagined the prisoners charged with money laundering weren't subjected to such extra restraints, but he'd been treated as a violent offender.

"Is this really necessary?" his attorney asked the marshal.

She knew damned well it was, but was already making a show of indignation on his behalf. He liked that. He added to the performance with a wince of discomfort. Unwilling to engage in a debate with a lawyer who made a living by arguing, the marshal left without responding.

"How are you doing, Brad?" she asked when they were alone.

He liked the sound of his given name coming from her lush lips. He also liked the sound of her name.

He lifted his hands as much as the cuffs would allow. "I've had better days, Cassie."

He had selected Cassandra Flock as his attorney nine years earlier. He didn't need a lawyer at the time, but he wanted to pick someone out and have the contact info handy should the need arise. Like everything else, he left nothing to chance. Cassie had been unaware of his existence until this morning, when he called her. He, on the other hand, knew a great deal about her.

He had followed her periodically over the years. After a contentious divorce, she had moved into a swanky apartment on Park Avenue with a doorman and plenty of security. Rising to the challenge, he disguised himself as a census taker in 2020, complete with a government ID badge that included an expiration date, his photograph, and a US Department of Commerce watermark. Once inside the building, he had gotten inside Cassie's apartment and concealed two cameras inside the walls. In the years since, he had occasionally indulged himself while he watched her.

"I've gotten you on the docket for a bail hearing as soon as I could," she said, snapping him out of his lustful ruminations. "But it will probably be another hour or two until we can get before a federal magistrate."

Not good. Vega and Flint had accused him of all the murders during the interrogation. He had cooperated just long enough to learn what evidence they had before cutting off the interview.

Right now, they would be racing to get search warrants for his apartment, his computer, and his cell phone, which the marshals had already taken from him. They could dig through the phone all they wanted and would find nothing incriminating. He had been careful not to link his phone to his encrypted video cloud in any way. Unfortunately, the added precaution left him unable to remotely delete the video files. He needed his computer for that.

The phone did, however, have an app for the security camera he had installed on the door of his apartment. Once he got it back, he would know when Vega, Flint, and a team of evidence techs arrived at his place to search for anything connecting him to the crimes. Ironically, Vega was wearing the evidence around her neck.

He recalled the day he'd zoomed in on her throat with the binoculars when she was leaving her office. With her hair pinned up, the silver chain was on full display, and the black bayonet clasp stood out. The fact that Sergio Vega's daughter was wearing it removed any doubt from his mind about where it came from.

Donovan's crew had failed to retrieve it, and he'd been obsessed about getting it back ever since. He even tried to take the chain back during their fight this morning, but she'd arrested him. It had been lying on the floor, broken. So close, but he'd been unable to free his hands to grab it. The thought disquieted him. What the hell happened to that damned necklace?

"I already spoke to the AUSA, and they're not offering any deals," Cassie continued. "Frankly, I'm surprised."

Only because she didn't know that the assistant US attorney would have received a briefing from Vega and the task force by now. Convinced Howell was a serial killer, the AUSA would do everything in his power to delay the proceedings. When the hearing finally occurred, the prosecutor would argue that the defendant should be held without bail until his court date, which could be weeks or months away. If that strategy failed, the prosecutor would refuse to make deals or plea bargains. That way, when the magistrate set bail, it would be for the most serious felonies possible. Cassie would dutifully argue that the bond should be unsecured, meaning he wouldn't have to pay it up front.

Even if forced to make bail, he had access to plenty of funds and could also put up his condo as collateral. One way or another, he'd be out soon. But would it be soon enough?

"Are you still planning to plead not guilty?" Cassie asked. "I recommend it if they're not willing to break the charges down. Maybe I can work out a deal before the case comes to trial."

He'd be long gone before that day ever came. "Sounds good, but my main concern is getting out of here as fast as possible."

"All my clients feel the same way," she said. "If there's a way to make it happen, I'll get it done."

And she would. Her outstanding track record was the reason he had chosen her. The shapely legs and tight ass were a bonus.

"You should be prepared in case things don't go our way, though," she hedged.

He hadn't flown under the radar for more than a decade without careful planning and plenty of backup strategies.

"I've set up safeguards."

She raised a brow. "Do you need lead time for your safeguards?"

He nearly laughed. She was planning to help him despite the fact that she must have known he was referring to thwarting any further investigation. He gave a slow nod of assent, aware that she needed to maintain the appearance of propriety. After all, attorneys could not knowingly assist their clients in the commission of crimes—in this case, obstructing justice.

"I have a contact in the Federal Magistrate's Office," she said. "I don't know what may be coming, but I'll ask him to contact me immediately if anyone swears out an arrest warrant for you—or a search warrant for your premises."

He held her gaze for a long moment. She was doing everything possible within the law to assist him. The irony was not lost on him, although she had no clue how close to the edge she was.

"I'm very grateful," he said, meaning it. "But they took my phone. How can you call me?"

"They have no legal authority to keep your phone." She straightened. "I'll make sure you get it back when you leave."

"Then I'll wait for your call," he said, reassured.

"Whatever bail amount is set, I'll argue to make it unsecured," she said. "I'm optimistic, but we can't take anything for granted."

Vega and Flint had to swear out a warrant before they could do anything. He had enough experience with police procedure to know the process would take an hour or two. He might be able to get there ahead of them.

As always, however, he had a backup plan. If they managed to beat him to his apartment and find his computer, a surprise awaited them.

Agent Vega would activate his safeguards without realizing what she was doing until it was too late.

CHAPTER 50

Dani and Flint had spent the past twenty minutes going through the affidavit line by line, answering the judge's endless questions.

To prevent herself from shouting, Dani clenched her jaw hard enough to make her molars ache. Unlike the charges they had placed on Howell this morning, which were federal, the serial murders were all NYPD cases. Flint had the lead. She was only assisting in the investigation and shouldn't let her temper get the better of her.

The situation had gone from irksome to infuriating when Flint received a text message five minutes earlier informing him that Howell's bail hearing had begun. Dani and Flint had explained to the judge why they needed him to sign the search warrant quickly.

The judge, unmoved by their pleas for haste, peered down at the paper through half-moon reading glasses perched low on his nose and proceeded through the document at the same plodding pace.

"Invading someone's privacy is a serious thing," the judge said, glancing up from the paper in his age-spotted hand. "And I don't take it lightly."

"Murdering thirty-three people is also a serious thing, Your Honor." She included Ochoa in the body count. "And if the suspect destroys the evidence before we get to it, he'll get away with it."

The judge's face tightened in response to her words, which had come out a bit harsher than she'd intended.

"And if the probable cause in the search warrant can't withstand a legal challenge, then he'll get away with it too," he said.

Flint shot her a repressive look before addressing the judge. "You know me, Your Honor," he said in a placating tone. "I always bring solid cases, and this is no different."

A not-so-subtle reminder that Flint, who had written hundreds of affidavits in his exemplary career, knew what he was doing.

"True," the judge allowed. "But the stakes are as high as they can get. Everything about this case will be picked apart by experts from every field for years. We can't afford any screwups."

Meaning he did not want to be second-guessed or embarrassed. She stifled a groan and spent more precious minutes answering questions concerning details in the document.

Flint elbowed her. "Just got this from the undercover guy," he said, holding out his cell.

She read the text message on the screen.

UNSECURED BOND. MARSHALS ARE PROCESSING HIM OUT.

It was the worst-case scenario. The federal magistrate had not required Howell to post bail, the equivalent of releasing him on his own recognizance, dramatically accelerating his exit from the courthouse.

"I can't believe the magistrate didn't consider Detective Chapman's testimony about possible future charges," Flint said.

"Maybe he didn't allow it," she said. "What matters now is beating Howell to the apartment. Tell your guy to stay on him. We need to know when he's getting close."

"I'm calling the uniforms we posted outside Howell's apartment building," Flint said. "I'll tell them to go inside and wait in the management office, where Howell can't see them. That way they can get to his unit in less than a minute once I send them a scanned copy of the search warrant." He cut his eyes to the judge. "As soon as it's signed, that is."

Flint crossed the room with his phone to his ear and spoke in low tones to the officers while Dani answered more questions. A few minutes later, Flint returned to show her another text.

PERP GOT IN A CAB. AM FOLLOWING IN UNMARKED CAR.

She edged closer to Flint. "I've got an idea," she whispered.

He followed her a few steps away to where the elderly judge couldn't overhear.

"We need to slow Howell down," she said. "Ask a squad car to find a reason to pull the taxi over."

He seemed to give it some thought. "The cabbie is bound to commit some sort of infraction between here and Queens." He lifted the phone back to his ear. "Running checks on the driver and verifying his hack license ought to eat up about fifteen minutes. Any violations the officer finds will tack on more time."

"If it goes on too long, Howell will get out and hail another cab," Dani said. "But we might just buy enough time to get the warrant signed."

She left Flint to make his call and returned to the window where the judge waited with what she sincerely hoped would be his last question. If it wasn't, she might not be responsible for her actions.

CHAPTER 51

Howell jammed himself into the back of the cab. "Two hundred dollars if you can get me to Rego Park in less than fifteen minutes. I'll tell you which building when we're in the area."

He knew it wasn't possible but wanted to be sure the driver would get him there quickly.

The cabbie eyed him in the rearview mirror. "I try," he said in heavily accented English. "Try very hard." He threw the vehicle into drive and peeled away from the curb, only to slow to a crawl within two minutes.

Howell glanced out at the gridlock, determined to get to his apartment before Vega and Flint. They had cars with lights and sirens. All he had was a cabbie desperate for a big tip. Of course, in New York City, that might go a long way toward evening the odds.

"Can't you find a faster route?" he said to the driver.

"Much traffic." The cabbie waved a hand, indicating the area around them. "All streets, same."

When he'd left the courthouse, his top priority had been getting a taxi. Checking his phone could wait until he was on his way. He pulled out his cell and tapped an icon on the home screen to open his surveillance app, revealing a live-streamed video of his living room.

No raid-jacketed Feds or cops poking around. No forensic detectives boxing up his possessions. No movement at all.

He released a long breath. They hadn't gotten inside yet. He toggled to the video feed from his front door, showing the hallway outside his unit.

No one there.

Were there cops lurking nearby, prepared to swoop in and arrest him the moment he arrived? No way to tell. He could only be certain they weren't inside.

His attorney hadn't called to let him know of an outstanding warrant for his arrest. Could he get to his apartment, cover his tracks, and leave before the paperwork was signed? Could the police prevent him from entering in the meantime?

He groaned in frustration and pulled more bills out of his pocket. "I'll double my offer."

He didn't want to rely on his safeguards in the event that Vega and company got to his place first. Devastating but effective, the plan was extreme, like a narcotrafficker burning down his own house to prevent the police from locating a massive shipment. Not a good option, but better than decades in prison.

Maybe it wouldn't come to that. Maybe he could keep what he'd worked so hard to accumulate. He reflected on the lessons he'd learned at nine years old. That day in the academy was not the last time he'd possessed contraband, but it was the last time he'd been caught with it. He'd learned to be sneakier. In woodshop, the other boys had constructed birdhouses, model planes, or jewelry boxes for their parents. He'd built a hidden compartment, passing it off as a cigar box for his father. Instead of sending it home the next day, he'd secured it underneath his bunk. And no one had ever discovered his secret hiding place.

"I try to get you there fast," the cabbie said, executing a sharp right turn onto East Houston Street toward the Manhattan Bridge. Hard to tell which route would be quickest, but the man had been sufficiently motivated to work whatever magic he could.

The next light turned yellow, and the engine roared as the taxi accelerated through the intersection a second after the signal switched to red. Moments later, harsh guttural sounds coming from the driver's seat startled Howell. When a short siren blast squawked behind them, he realized the cabbie had begun swearing in his native tongue when he saw the flashing red and blues in the rearview. When he hadn't pulled over quickly enough, the cop in the sector car behind them had chirped the siren.

When the taxi came to a stop, it took all Howell's self-mastery not to fling open the side door and run, but he didn't want the patrol cop's attention focused on him. Instead, he'd wait to see what happened. If the cop gave the driver only a warning, Howell would make better time staying put than getting out to hail another taxi.

The patrol officer strode to the cabbie's open window. "You know why I stopped you, sir?"

The cabbie shrugged.

"All right, let's see your hack license, registration, and driver's license."

His phone vibrated, distracting him from the discussion between the cop and the driver. His heart stuttered an extra beat when he saw the caller ID.

"What is it, Cassie?"

"My contact at the Magistrate's Office called. There's no arrest warrant yet, but they've obtained a search warrant for your residence. They've got seventy-two hours to execute it, but it's a safe bet they won't wait that long."

Working at the crime lab had given him a comprehensive understanding of the law pertaining to processing evidence, but he was not a detective and had never served a search warrant. His attorney, however, had reviewed hundreds of affidavits, and knew every obscure legal means to get judges to rule recovered items inadmissible in court. He'd be a fool if he didn't take ten seconds to pick her brain.

"Can they stop me from going inside my apartment?"

"Technically you can still enter," she said. "But now that they've got a warrant, they have a right to go in too. They'll stick with you the whole time, preventing you from destroying any evidence before it's collected."

"Shit."

"It gets worse," she said, so quietly he had to strain to hear over the traffic noise. "If they find something incriminating, they can arrest you on the spot if—"

"I won't be there," he finished, coming to a decision. "I'm headed somewhere else."

"They can use any evidence they find pursuant to a lawful search to obtain an arrest warrant," Cassie said in her best legalese. "And if they do, I'll make arrangements for you to turn yourself in. Don't worry. I'll be by your side the whole way."

He disconnected without making any commitments regarding her offer. It wouldn't come to that.

He tossed a wad of cash to the driver, who was still debating with the cop, and opened the door.

"I've got a business meeting." He spoke loudly enough to be sure both of them heard. "This should cover my fare." He didn't want the cop running after him for defrauding a taxi driver—or whatever it was called when you ripped off a cabbie.

He jumped out and started walking down the sidewalk at a fast clip. He wouldn't break into a run until he was out of view. In the meantime, he was already recalibrating, enacting his contingency plan.

CHAPTER 52

Howell's Apartment
Rego Park, Queens

Dani felt underneath the raised bed frame in Howell's bedroom. Her fingers brushed against a small catch. With a slight tug, a hidden drawer slid out to reveal a slender black laptop and power cord.

She turned to the K-9 handler standing just outside the bedroom door. "Jackpot."

The handler reached into a pouch at his waist and pulled out a small treat. "Good job," he said to the black Labrador sitting beside his left foot.

Wu had arranged for an FBI electronics tech to meet her at the condo, and Flint had requested an electronic-sniffing dog from the K-9 unit. A quick sweep of the premises indicated a hidden surveillance camera in the living room wall, cleverly concealed behind stenciled wall art. The dog continued his sweep into the bedroom, where he sat beside the bed.

Familiar with concealed spaces from her covert overseas missions, Dani had offered to conduct the search to find the device that had triggered the animal's sensitive nose. She didn't tell the others that such searches might end with nasty surprises, which was why she'd insisted they wait in the other room—away from a potential blast.

"I've got it," she called to the others after safely lifting out the laptop. She and Flint had met Patel, Wu, Chapman, and two members of the FBI's Evidence Response Team at Howell's Rego Park apartment in Queens.

At first she'd been surprised to see that Wu had responded personally, but she decided the case had far-reaching implications. A high-ranking civilian employee of the NYPD was a serial killer. When they placed charges, Wu would field questions from the media, the police commissioner, and the FBI director.

Given that Howell was a supervisor at the NYPD crime lab, everyone had agreed that any evidence they recovered should be analyzed by unrelated personnel at a separate facility.

As soon as the judge had signed the warrant, Flint scanned and uploaded it to the PD server. The officers posted in the management office had rushed upstairs with a digital copy and stood outside the door to the condo, holding the scene for investigation.

The plainclothes detective following Howell had called Flint to let him know the sector car they had detailed to follow Howell's taxi had pulled it over after the cabbie ran a red light. The officer overheard snatches of Howell's phone conversation. He mentioned the name "Cassie" and appeared agitated. According to the officer, Howell said, *"Can they stop me from going inside my apartment?"* He couldn't catch any more of the discussion before Howell disconnected, tossed fare money to the cabbie, and got out on foot.

The detective assured Flint the surveillance team was hanging close to Howell and would be prepared to move in as soon as they had a green light to make apprehension.

This made sense when Flint relayed it to Dani, who assumed Cassie Flock was on the other end of the phone call. His attorney must have advised him of the warrant, and he'd decided not to be present while they conducted the search.

This told her two things. First, that something inside the apartment was incriminating enough for Howell to be arrested immediately. Second, that Howell was already on the run.

They had yet to find any evidence, however, so they had no arrest warrant or any probable cause to detain Howell. Cassie Flock would look for any excuse to get the case thrown out of court, so they were taking extra precautions with every part of the investigation, especially the searches and the arrest. The plainclothes detective had been ordered to keep tailing him while more detectives were added to the surveillance.

Dani and the task force were in another race, this time to find incriminating evidence on Howell's laptop. Patel was the best they had, but he would need time to get through any firewalls, not to mention any viruses, honeypots, malware, or other virtual booby traps Howell might have set up to defend his digital collection. Every minute that passed carried the possibility that he might figure out a way to elude his followers.

Patel walked into the bedroom. "Where was he hiding his computer?"

"Under the bed frame," she said. "In a secret compartment."

"That's a good sign," Patel said, taking the laptop from her. "Means he didn't want to make it easy to find."

She followed him out to the kitchen. "Increasing the likelihood that there's stuff on there he doesn't want anyone else to see."

"My thoughts exactly," Patel said, placing it on the counter and opening the top. "Let's see what I'm up against."

The home page flickered to life, revealing a white rectangle containing the image of a fingerprint against the backdrop of a starry night sky that filled the rest of the screen.

"Figured he would have it set up to open with his fingerprint," Patel said, turning to Wu. "Were you able to get it?"

Wu opened a small manila folder and tipped the contents onto the counter. "You'll need to put on gloves before you handle this."

Dani watched in fascination as Patel pulled on latex gloves before carefully picking up a clear strip of plastic that resembled cellophane tape.

"We reproduced Howell's fingerprints from the AFIS database," Wu said to Dani. "These were 3D printed."

Ingenious. Just like forensic examiners entered their DNA into the Combined DNA Index System for elimination purposes, they also entered their fingerprints into the Automated Fingerprint Identification System for the same reason.

Patel pressed the fingerprint directly in the center of the white rectangle. An instant later the screen shifted to a desktop with the same starry night sky in the background as the home screen.

"We're in," Patel said, laying the clear tape back on the countertop and pulling off his gloves. "Let the hunt begin."

Dani looked at the screen, which was peppered with digital folders, pdf files, and one icon she didn't recognize. "What's that?"

"See the ring in the center of the square that looks like a swirling letter 'O'?" he asked her. "That's the symbol for a portal."

Wu crowded in beside her to get a look. "What are the odds that's how he accesses his cloud?"

"Pretty damn good," Patel said. He took out a flash drive and inserted it into one of the ports on the side. "Before I start messing around, I'll replicate the hard drive and transfer the data to my laptop." He slid an index finger around the touch pad, moving the cursor from one icon to another, each action followed by an obscenity. "The bastard installed anti-copy software," he announced. "Won't let me copy any data without a password." He typed commands on the keyboard. "I can't even open anything in read-only mode."

"What kind of password does it need?" Dani asked.

Patel typed in more commands. A text box popped onto the screen.

SEVEN DIGIT CODE REQUIRED FOR ACCESS.

"This is tricky," Patel said. "It's not like we can try his pet's name or his kid's name. This is asking for numbers."

"His DOB?" Flint offered.

People often used their date of birth as an easily remembered numerical password.

"Howell was born on April 9, 1994," Wu said after glancing at his computer tablet. "But I don't see how that gets us to seven digits."

He was right. Any combination of 4, 9, and 1994 in any order only resulted in six numbers. Adding a zero in front of the 4 and the 9 would make an eight-digit code. Placing a zero in front of the month and not the day or vice versa would be inconsistent and make no sense.

"What other numbers might be significant to him?" Dani asked no one in particular.

"His EIN?" Chapman suggested.

Anyone who worked for the city would have an employee identification number that remained with them throughout their career.

"Got it," Wu said after consulting his tablet again. "And it's seven digits."

"Might as well give it a try," Patel said. "If it doesn't work, we've eliminated it as a possibility." He tapped the keyboard as Wu rattled off the numbers. "Fingers crossed," Patel said, then pressed ENTER.

The text box flashed red, and a new message appeared.

INCORRECT PASSWORD.

"It was a good guess," Flint said. "Any other ideas or should we just try random—"

"Oh shit," Patel said, eyes riveted to the screen, which displayed a countdown clock and new message.

A VIRUS HAS BEEN UPLOADED TO THE CLOUD. IF THE CORRECT PASSWORD IS NOT ENTERED IN 60 SECONDS, ALL FILES WILL BE DESTROYED.

CHAPTER 53

Dani fought mounting frustration as she stared at the screen. They'd spent half the day racing to beat Howell to the computer, only to find that he'd engineered a way to obliterate their best evidence against him. He had manipulated, contaminated, and purged forensic materials for years. Now he was doing the same with digital evidence.

"If you turn the computer off, would that stop the clock?" Chapman asked Patel.

They had already lost two precious seconds.

0:58

"I wish," Patel said. "The five-second lag time between the incorrect password and the message with the countdown clock was the time it took to upload the virus. It's already there. Shutting the laptop down will cut off our only way to stop the malware from deleting everything in the cloud." He turned to Dani. "We need to come up with that password. Now."

0:52

Everyone else followed his gaze. She was the codebreaker. There was no time to consult with the Crypto team. This was all on her.

She had been in a similar situation years ago when she'd been deployed overseas, and it had not ended well. Her Ranger unit had entered a large compound in the hunt for terrorists who were planning to blow up an Army base. She had been tasked with decrypting their coded plans and documents, but did not do so fast enough to warn her fellow Rangers that bombs were hidden in the building. Several people lost their lives that day, and she had never fully come to terms with it.

Now more lives hung in the balance. Brad Howell needed to be stopped. The victims and their families needed justice. Her mother needed to be set free.

0:46

"A telephone number without the area code is seven digits," Chapman said.

"He would want something special for him," Dani said. "Phone numbers can change and be reassigned to anyone."

"Social security numbers are unique," Flint said. "But they have nine numbers."

Wu held up his hand, palm out. "Quiet, everyone," he said, tipping his head toward Dani. "Let her think."

The condo fell silent.

0:29

To understand what he would use for a password, Dani had to get inside Howell's head. "According to Dr. Cattrall, he's arrogant and selfish," she said, thinking out loud. "And he's highly visual." She looked at the laptop. "The home screen and the desktop both have a starry sky as the background. How many stars are there?"

Patel squinted at the screen. "A lot more than seven," he said.

0:22

"Wait a minute," she said, edging closer again. "That looks like a constellation."

During her Ranger training, she had been dropped in a wooded area alone at night. Part of her mission was to find her way to the base camp before the deadline. Without a GPS or any visual cues visible in daylight, she had been forced to rely on the stars to guide her over the thirty miles across unfamiliar terrain.

"That's Aries," she said. "The ram."

"I'm an Aries," Chapman said. "Born on April Fool's Day." He glanced at Wu. "You told us Howell was born on the ninth. He would have the same zodiac sign."

"That's it," Dani said, gaining confidence in her theory. "Flint's first instincts were right. The password is Howell's birthday."

"How can you be sure?" Patel said.

"Howell has no significant other, no kids, and no pets," she said. "It's all about him. And what would be more important than the day he graced the earth with his presence?"

"I'm with you," Wu said. "But what about the seven digits?"

0:14

The answer came to her with total clarity. It had been right in front of them all along. Now that she saw it, she knew she was right.

She put a hand out to Wu. "I need your tablet."

Wordlessly, he activated the screen and handed it over. She took it from him and performed a keyword search.

0:09

She tapped on a link and a chart filled the small screen. She scanned down the rows and found what she was looking for.

0:03

"Enter the following numbers," she said to Patel. "1-9-9-4-0-9-9."

Completely out of options, no one questioned her. Patel's fingers flashed over the number keys.

0:01

He pressed ENTER.

CHAPTER 54

The screen went dark, and Dani sucked in a breath. An instant later, it glowed to life again, displaying the desktop. Had they managed to enter the correct password in time to deactivate the virus and preserve whatever Howell had streamed to his cloud?

"Click on the portal," Dani said to Patel. "Let's see what's there."

Patel shook his head. "I'm going to mirror everything in this laptop first," he said. "We need to back all this data up in case we trigger another virus."

The fact that he was correct didn't make it any easier to wait. She glanced at Flint. "What's the status of the surveillance team?"

He checked his phone. "Just got another text. After exiting the cab, Howell hoofed it to the Bleecker Street subway station. They're trying to track him without making it obvious, but it's harder down on the platforms with all the trains coming and going."

"By the time we go through video feeds from the Transit Authority, he'll be long gone," Wu added, then shifted his gaze to Patel. "Any progress?"

The laptop held their best chance at finding probable cause for an arrest. If the portal led to videos of Howell committing murders, Flint could direct the surveillance team to take Howell into custody before he boarded a subway car.

"I'm going as fast as I can," Patel said. "Give me another minute."

"Howell is an expert at conducting surveillance," Dani said. "He would know the best way to lose anyone trying to follow him."

In other words, they may not have a minute.

Patel pulled the flash drive out of the port. "Done with the backup," he said. "Now let's see if the link to the stream has been corrupted."

They all watched in silence as he guided the cursor to the portal icon and clicked. A new window opened displaying rows of icons resembling strips of motion picture film.

"Look at how he's labeled them," Dani said, recognizing the pattern that had launched her on this journey days ago. Each icon bore three numbers beneath it.

101, 202, 303, 104, 205, 306, 107, 208, and so on. Three others were at the bottom. X100, X220, and X333

"The first one should be Luna Delgado," she continued. "Murdered on April 11, 2014. Julian date 101."

Patel clicked it open, then maximized the window to take up the entire screen. A lovely young woman Dani immediately recognized as Luna from the crime scene photos walked into view, very much alive. She was in her living room, opening her front door.

The footage had clearly been edited to include only the parts Howell would have found interesting. Luna could be heard asking someone standing outside what they wanted.

"I'm from Los Brokis Movers," a male voice replied. "There's a problem with our crew. A bunch of them are out with the flu. I need to see if we can load your stuff with just two guys."

Luna stepped aside, allowing a man in coveralls with a moving company logo and a matching ball cap to enter. His face was obscured by the bill of the cap as he pulled out a clipboard and began looking around the room.

"That's the moving company she hired," Chapman said. "I checked into all the employees when I inherited the case."

"But how would he know it was Los Brokis?" Dani muttered.

No one had an answer. They looked on as the man finally turned toward the camera. It was Brad Howell.

"He conned his way right in," Chapman said. "He looks like the real thing. He's even got something that looks like a company ID clipped to the front of his outfit." He turned to Flint. "You should tell the surveillance team to scoop him up right now."

"Not yet," Wu said. "We need to see exactly what he does."

Wu was playing it safe. He wanted hard evidence that Howell had done more than talk his way inside her unit.

Patel fast-forwarded the video. The images blurred by before coming to a halt at Wu's sharp command. Howell had delivered a devastating blow to the side of Luna's head, catching her as she slumped. The video cut to the bedroom, where the other camera showed him carrying her to the bed as a low-level hum droned in the background. He laid her down and removed her clothes before binding her hands and feet to the four bedposts. Luna started to come around. She opened her mouth to scream, and he slapped her with brutal force.

"What happened to the sound?" Dani said. "We could hear everything they said in the living room, and that slap should've been audible, but all I can hear is that humming noise."

"Nothing I can do," Patel said. "The microphone must've malfunctioned."

They continued to watch. The unearthly sound made the scene more disturbing.

Once Luna was secured, Howell pulled something out of his pocket before unzipping the coveralls and shucking them off. He was angled slightly away from the camera, and it took her a moment to realize he was putting on a condom.

Lip curled in disgust, she watched with the others as Howell dragged a pillow over Luna's face to muffle her screams and climbed on top of her. She recalled the details of the autopsy and knew what would happen next.

She wanted to look away from the agonizing scene before her. She had seen plenty of death before, but never like this. Howell was a monster who had taken his victims' dignity before taking their lives. He had dehumanized them, but she would give them the respect they deserved. She would not turn away. Instead, she steeled herself to see Luna Delgado's last moments.

Howell continued pressing down the pillow until his climactic shudders convulsed in rhythm with her death throes.

"Tell the team to lock the son of a bitch up," Wu said quietly, his voice uncharacteristically thick with emotion.

When Dani heard no acknowledgment from Flint, she glanced up to see the detective staring down at his cell phone.

"Just got a text," he said, the color draining from his face. "They've lost him."

CHAPTER 55

April 11, 2014
Benedict Avenue
Castle Hill, Bronx

Howell had royally fucked up yesterday. No getting around that ugly fact. And now he had returned to the scene of the crime like a B-movie villain.

He stood outside the door to the superintendent's office at the Benedict Avenue apartment building, hoping like hell his new plan would work. He still chastised himself for not doing more research when he first saw Luna, the beautiful doppelgänger of the woman from the video, walking down the street.

His blunder had nearly cost him everything. Once he realized he'd lost his necklace at the scene of Sergio Vega's death, he'd cooked up a scheme to get it back. It was daring to the point of recklessness, but he had nothing to lose—except the rest of his life.

A news item the following morning about the bereaved family had been the inspiration. Sergio Vega's wife had been arrested for his murder, and their children were effectively orphans. They would need to move in with relatives immediately.

He found some coveralls at a uniform store and used a fabric paint kit to stencil a moving company logo on the chest and matching ball cap. He'd come to see the building superintendent and con his way into Sergio Vega's unit. The plan was desperate, and he wouldn't have attempted it if the police didn't already have a culprit in custody. No one would be looking for a killer on the loose.

He plastered on a fake smile and knocked.

A pale, scrawny man with the slender, boneless appearance of a ferret opened the door. "What now?" He looked tired and cranky, like a man who'd been up all night answering questions from the police.

"The moving company sent me." Howell tapped his chest just beneath the freshly painted stencil, hoping it wouldn't run. "I came to get an estimate so we have enough guys for the move."

"I don't think she has that much," the super said, scratching his head. "Most of her stuff's already gone, from what I saw yesterday during the final inspection."

Something wasn't adding up. "Which tenant are you talking about?"

The super frowned. "Luna Delgado. She moves out tomorrow." He leaned forward to squint at the logo again. "Oh, wait. She's using Los Brokis. Who are you here for?"

He'd heard of Los Brokis Movers, but the super's comment sent his mind careening in a completely unexpected direction. His woman was named Luna. What were the chances the super was talking about someone else with the same unusual name in the exact building where she lived?

Howell took advantage of the opportunity, switching gears on the fly. "Los Brokis had to back out, and we've got the contract for Luna Delgado's move now, but I'm also supposed to check out Sergio Vega's apartment. Our company is handling both units."

He was taking a calculated risk, but Luna didn't get off work until late in the evening, so there was little chance of this man talking to her tonight.

The super put his hands on his hips. "I feel sorry for those kids. Their mom's locked away and their dad's dead. What the hell's supposed to happen to them now?"

He didn't have the time or inclination to dwell on collateral damage. Sergio Vega had brought on what happened. If his kids were in trouble, it was his own damn fault.

"Yeah, well, I need to get a look at their unit to see how many guys it's going to take to haul everything out."

"Can't help you," the super said. "Detectives told me they're still holding it as a crime scene for another day or two. No one's allowed in till they release it."

He gave up on finding the necklace and focused on the new crisis. "Miss Delgado then," he said, thinking fast. "I've got to talk with her about the crew too. Might only be able to get two guys for the move tomorrow."

"Don't you have her cell number?" The super looked skeptical. "And wouldn't you already have a list of what she's taking in the moving contract?"

"Spoke to her an hour ago," he said, taking another gamble. "She's at work. Told me she has more boxes than she thought, and I should go ahead and make a new inventory."

"Sorry, pal. Can't let you in without the tenant present. Too much liability." His brows furrowed. "I'm surprised she has more, though. She's been giving her winter clothes and boots to neighbors. Says she won't need that stuff in Miami."

He struggled to hide his shock at the revelation. He'd have to break into her place to install the cameras today, but he needed one key piece of information he'd been lacking yesterday. Getting it out of the super, who already seemed suspicious, would take finesse.

"We just did the contract over the phone. I haven't had a chance to look around. This building's a walk-up, so how many stairs are we talking?"

The super's expression made it clear he thought Howell was not too bright. "Can you do basic multiplication?"

"Come again?"

"You go up two sets of stairs for each floor, so five times two equals what?"

Howell knew more math and science than this asshole could even imagine. He fought the urge to punch him but did not want to be memorable in any way. If feigning ignorance helped, that was what he would do. He had to think of it as another con. He now knew Luna lived on the fifth floor, and he thought he finally understood how yesterday's mistake had happened.

He adopted a look of bewilderment. "Paperwork says she's in unit 5C. Doesn't mention a floor." He was making an educated guess based on a hypothesis, something he'd been trained to do for years.

"Each story has six apartments." The super took on the tone of a kindergarten teacher explaining basic colors. "A, B, and C in the front, and D, E, and F in the back. She has the front corner unit on the fifth floor."

Hypothesis confirmed. He'd broken into 4C yesterday, exactly one level below his target location. A wave of nausea ran through him. He'd come to recover evidence that could link him to Vega's murder, only to discover Luna was moving out tomorrow. Not across town, either, but over a thousand miles away. He'd lose her forever if he didn't act fast. The super had given him another critical piece of information. It wouldn't take long to cover the stenciled moving company name on his coveralls with the Los Brokis logo. Luna would open the door if someone from the moving company she hired showed up in uniform to discuss a problem with tomorrow's move.

Logic told him he should lie low and try to find an excuse to get into the lab during his off hours, when he wasn't supposed to be there. But he couldn't even get to the parking lot without being recorded, and there were cameras everywhere inside.

But there was Luna. The woman he had obsessed about every waking moment for the past two months until he'd finally worked up the nerve to make his dreams a reality. He was self-aware enough to understand his behavior was often compulsive and used it to his advantage, conducting tests in the lab. No one was more rigorous or exacting.

But there was a dark side to compulsion. He could not simply let Luna go. Whatever the consequences, he would have his night with her.

And it would have to be tonight.

CHAPTER 56

August 22, 2024
Rego Park, Queens

As a Ranger, Dani had been in situations where plan A failed, plan B fell apart, and plan C was no longer an option. She had learned that no amount of training guaranteed a mission's success. When circumstances conspired against her, clear thinking offered the best chance for turning the situation around, which meant she did not have the luxury of giving in to rage.

"Where was the last place the surveillance team saw Howell?" Wu asked Flint, who had lifted the phone to his ear to contact the detective leading the plainclothes squad tailing him.

Flint repeated Wu's question, then listened before sharing the response. "Howell took the 6 to Grand Central Station, where he got off and caught the 4 train uptown toward 59th Street. Next, he boarded the R train toward Queens, but hopped off right before the doors closed. He kept changing trains, jumping on at the last second. Eventually, they couldn't keep up." He gave his head a frustrated shake. "The last place they saw him was on the platform at the 59th Street station. They're not sure where he is now."

"We can't shut down the system," Chapman said. "Not even for this mope."

On any given day, more than five and a half million passengers ride the New York City subway. The idea of shutting down one of the world's longest systems with over 850 miles of track running between 472 stations was a nonstarter.

"We could ping his cell phone," Flint suggested. "We already have a search warrant for all his electronic devices. We could just extend it to include location."

Law enforcement had technology that could narrow down the vicinity of where a specific cell phone was located by triangulation between cell towers or deviating the cell signal to a trapping device, but a judge would have to sign off on the additional invasion of privacy. Even for a serial killer.

Dani had another idea. "Can you plant a Trojan horse in Howell's cloud account?" she asked Patel.

"He's restricted the portal app so it can only be accessed from his laptop," Patel said. "That's why he couldn't use his cell phone to scrub everything from the cloud before we got here."

"He has to have a backup system," Dani persisted. "What if his laptop crashed or was stolen? He wouldn't risk losing his most precious video."

Patel seemed to give it some thought. "I recall Dr. Cattrall's assessment of his personality, and I see what you mean. But he would also make damn sure there was no way to get to his video collection from his cell. He would have to . . ."

He trailed off, apparently lost in thought. Dani knew better than to interrupt him. Discussion stopped as everyone gave the computer forensics expert time to think.

"He's denied permission for his cell phone to access his laptop," Patel said. "That way, he could be sure that—even if we obtained a search warrant for his phone before he was released—there's no way we could use it as a back door to access his device as a work-around for the self-destruct sequence he set up on his laptop."

He closed his eyes and leaned back in his chair. Dani could practically see the gears turning.

Suddenly Patel's eyes opened. "You're right," he said to Dani. "He would have a backup. It would be another laptop, and it would be in a secure location totally unconnected to him."

"A spider hole," Dani said, thinking of the places terrorist leaders had concealed themselves when they were on the run. "Or a compound."

"It would have to be in someone else's name," Wu said. "We've checked every database, and this is his only property."

"Then he's got another identity," Dani said. "Think about how meticulously he plans. Part of his escape would involve a hideout with cash, a change of clothes, and a disguise. Why not another laptop?"

Wu gave her an appreciative nod. "Howell will be desperate to check his cloud account as soon as possible. He'll want to know whether his virus worked, and we wiped all video files when we couldn't come up with the password in time. If it did, he doesn't have to run. His attorney will have a fair shot at poking holes in our case without the video evidence."

She was pleased, but not surprised, at how quickly her boss connected with her thought process.

"And when he logs in to the cloud to check," Wu continued. "Patel will have a surprise waiting for him."

Patel flashed a wicked grin as he began typing on the laptop. "I've got a nice little piece of code that will literally worm its way into his computer," he said. "With a GPS signal that will lead us right to him."

CHAPTER 57

East Harlem, Manhattan

Brad Howell rushed inside the apartment, slammed the door shut behind him, and threw the dead bolt. He leaned his back against the door, forcing his breathing to slow. This was the fastest way to reduce a pounding pulse and regain mental clarity after a frantic race through the subway system.

He knew all the kinds of capabilities the NYPD and the FBI could bring to bear. Soon enough, they would review camera footage and figure out which subway station he'd exited to get to street level. They could follow him for a while as he walked through the crowds, but he needed only a bit of a head start to pull off his final plan. Certain they had lost track of him in the subway, he'd circled back to his Manhattan safe haven.

Every quarter, he paid the landlord in cash to keep the apartment. The landlord, another one who owed him a favor due to "lost" forensic evidence, ensured the apartment remained vacant and pocketed the rent money Howell gave him.

The symbiotic relationship worked for all concerned, because Howell had been able to maintain a base of operations that could not be easily connected to him. He didn't come here often and was not surprised when he had to plug the backup laptop into a power source before booting it up.

It needed a minute to come online, giving him a chance to use his cell phone to check the door camera.

Two uniformed police officers now stood guard outside his unit. Not good.

Heart pounding, he tapped an icon that connected him to the cameras in his living room and cursed. Law enforcement types in Tyvek suits were crawling all over the place.

Including Agent Dani Vega.

A quick review of the footage showed that they'd brought in a dog to sniff out his electronic devices. The last thing he saw was Vega disabling his cameras. Then all he got was static.

He tossed the phone on the table when the laptop opened to the lock screen, which was a duplicate of his main computer. Without the ability to see what the cops and Feds had done, there was only one way to know what his situation was. He entered the password.

The desktop flickered on, but he hesitated. His laptop was also connected to the cameras he'd set up inside and outside his apartment. With the larger screen, he recognized most of the people who had entered his unit, but two of them were unfamiliar. At least one of them had to be a computer forensics expert. Would the expert have been able to defeat the safeguards?

No way.

But Dani Vega was a codebreaker. He had read about her exploits in the Army when she had used her talents on covert missions. Had she been able to figure out his password?

Possible, but highly doubtful considering she had only sixty seconds to do it.

He had to open the portal to the cloud to find out how much they knew. If the video files were wiped, he would know they had failed. He would contact his attorney, and Cassie would work her magic. With no hard evidence, she would have to make only one juror have a reasonable doubt about his guilt. And he had seen how effectively she had sown doubt before. She served many purposes for him, most without her knowledge.

On the other hand, if he opened the portal to find that all the files were still there, he would check the time stamp that indicated when the files were last opened. If they had not been opened since yesterday, his files had not been compromised, and he could delete them before they were found.

Who was he kidding? He could no more destroy his life's work than he could cut off his leg. He would download the files to a flash drive and hide it, then wipe the cloud clean.

But what if the time stamp showed him the files had just been opened? Then he would know that Vega had cracked his encryption—it would have to be her—and the Feds had broken into his cloud account. In that case, he would have to enact his emergency backup plan.

Aware the next few seconds would determine his fate, he clicked on the portal app. His video files appeared, still intact. He felt a rush of relief, but then reminded himself that he had to be sure. A few more clicks switched the view. His mouth went dry. Every video file had been opened within the past hour. Only one person could have done this.

Dani. Fucking. Vega.

All his careful planning. All his work. All his private information. She had ruined every bit of it. She had ruined his life. It would do no good to delete the files now. The FBI had them.

They knew his worst secrets. Shared his most private memories. Witnessed his darkest fantasies. He was exposed, naked, and humiliated. They would judge him without any knowledge of his personal demons. They would condemn him without understanding that he had only been reacting to the compulsions that had driven him and the circumstances that had forced his hand.

The image of a cracked shield flashed on his laptop's screen, pulling him back to the present. He was so sure he'd outwitted them, but now his computer was telling him the FBI was more resourceful than he'd thought. He clicked open the malware alert and saw that he had inadvertently opened his laptop to a Trojan horse virus when he'd accessed the cloud.

They had known he would open the portal and had planted a worm, and he had no doubt that it would contain coding showing them the exact location of his laptop. He slammed the lid shut, fully aware that it would do no good. The GPS signal had already been sent. He could shut the computer down, he could reformat the hard drive, or he could smash the thing with a hammer, and it would make no difference. They would be on their way in seconds.

Heart pounding, he shot to his feet. The urge to bolt nearly overwhelmed him, but he forced himself to calm down and think clearly.

He had planned for this.

He strode to the bedroom and yanked open the closet door. He glanced at the outfits hanging at perfectly spaced intervals in the small space. Pushing aside the moving company coveralls, the exterminator's uniform, the census taker's golf shirt and khakis, and several others he'd used over the years, he groped for the one disguise he'd been saving for a moment like this.

He found the hanger at the far side of the closet and pulled it out. To escape, he would have to live up to his chosen code name now. This would be his greatest con ever. He would need to be on his game to pull it off, but if he managed it, he would be long gone before anyone figured out what he had done.

Before he put New York City behind him, however, he had unfinished business to take care of.

CHAPTER 58

102nd Street
East Harlem, Manhattan

Dani shifted her feet, anxious for action but stifled by protocol and procedure. She stood between Wu and Flint, waiting for the all-clear sign from the NYPD Emergency Service Unit tactical operators. She would have been much more comfortable making entry with the team, but this was the PD's case, and they had plenty of resources.

They had traced the tracking signal to an apartment at 102nd Street and Lexington Avenue in Manhattan. Patel had been in his element, using an enhanced Wi-Fi triangulation system with an integrated altimeter to zero in on the exact floor and unit where the signal had originated.

A brief interview with the building superintendent had enlightened them as to how the address had not been connected to Howell in any database. Meanwhile, Flint had contacted the same magistrate by video, and he agreed to send an addendum extending the previous warrant to include a secondary residence. Assuming this must have been his base of operations for years, they were eager not only to arrest Howell, but to find still more evidence of his crimes.

Flint's police radio squawked. "Subject not at target location," the ESU team leader said. "No devices found."

"Let's go," Flint said, jogging into the building.

Dani and Wu followed him inside, quickly making their way to the unit, where black-clad tactical personnel held the door open for them. The laptop that had led them here was sitting out in the open on a scarred wooden kitchen table beside Howell's cell phone.

"Why didn't he take the computer with him?" Flint muttered as if thinking out loud. "Or hide it like the computer in his condo?"

Dani connected the dots. "Because he knew we were tracking him and wanted us to come here."

"He left us a trail of breadcrumbs to follow, and we went for it." Flint dragged a hand through his hair. "He could be anywhere by now, and we've got nothing to ping anymore."

"Maybe there's a clue here somewhere," Wu said. "Something that can give us a new place to start looking."

Dani glanced around. The furniture was minimal. It was clear he didn't spend much time here. She walked to the bedroom, which contained only a mattress on the floor and a folding chair. Howell hadn't wasted money on furnishings.

"Get a load of this," she called out after opening the closet door. "I'll bet when we finish going through all his videos, we'll find every one of these disguises."

With dozens of hours of footage to go through, the team had not wasted time screening them all. As soon as they'd identified Howell in the first one, they stopped watching to focus on the hunt to find him.

While Patel used GPS to zero in on the signal, Flint had obtained an arrest warrant charging Howell with murdering Luna Delgado ten years earlier. It would be enough to hold him while they gathered what they needed to place additional charges. A suspect actively fleeing with a warrant on file for homicide provided many more options to law enforcement.

While the NYPD had gathered an ESU team for the takedown, Wu had worked through channels to track Howell's financial transactions, communications, and travel. His name and face were disseminated far and wide, severely hampering his movements.

"These are the moving company overalls he wore in the Delgado case," Flint said, pulling on a pair of latex gloves. "Looks like there was a different company name on the front covered by a Los Brokis logo. And I'll bet his DNA is all over the material."

"For once, he won't be able to mess with the lab results either," Dani added, eyeing the outfits as Flint slid each hanger to the side to reveal the next. "It's amazing how many ways he's found to trick his way into his victims' homes."

"I'll bet he also used these disguises to plant the cameras," Flint said.

"He's a true confidence man," Wu said. "He gains their trust and then takes advantage of them. Only instead of fleecing them for money, he kills them."

She reflected on the discussion, trying to fit the pieces together. "Howell learned the name of her moving company somehow and used that information to fool her into letting him inside." And then recognition dawned, bringing another previously unconnected fact into alignment. "He cons people." She looked at Flint, then Wu. "He's a conner."

"That's why he used that name," Wu said. "And why he spelled it that way. It's not an alias, it's how he sees himself."

"He was taunting us," Flint said. "Like during the interview when he told us the killer would have the video files uploaded to the cloud. He wants us to know how clever he is without coming out and making a confession."

Lost in thought, Dani continued as if he hadn't spoken. "Ever since I realized Howell killed my father, I've been trying to understand what happened. No one connected his murder with Luna Delgado's because they seemed to have nothing in common. But they must have."

"Proximity in time and place," Wu said. "Same building, one day apart."

Dani came to a sudden halt. "Same building," she repeated, then smacked her forehead with the palm of her hand. "Why didn't I see it before?"

Brows raised in question, Wu and Flint waited for an explanation.

"Luna Delgado lived in apartment 5C," she said. "We lived in 4C. Exactly one floor down."

"You think Howell broke into the wrong apartment?" Wu said. "But he stalks his victims in advance. He wouldn't make a mistake like that."

"It was his first time," Dani said. "What if that mistake was the reason he started stalking his victims ahead of time in the future?"

"But he put a pinhole camera in your family's apartment," Flint said. "He'd have to know it didn't belong to Luna."

"Would he?" she said. "What if he saw Luna in the building and thought she went to the fourth floor instead of the fifth? He hasn't developed the stalking part of his MO yet, but he's already a voyeur. He waits until she's at work and picks the lock to what he believes is her apartment. He sneaks straight into the bedroom and starts to install the cameras, but he's interrupted by my father, who was on the sofa sleeping off one of his migraines."

Flint seemed to catch her enthusiasm. "He thought he was in an empty apartment and realizes there's a threat. He heads out of the bedroom, grabs a knife from the block on the kitchen counter, and attacks your father."

"His necklace falls off in the struggle," Wu said, joining the conjecture. "But he either doesn't realize it's gone or can't find it. He takes only enough time to conceal any evidence of his presence, figuring if the crime scene detectives find anything he missed, he'll get rid of it in the lab."

"That's the only way all the seemingly odd facts fit together," Dani said. "We may never be able to prove it in court, but that's how it went down." She resumed her pacing. "Howell took a risk coming to the same location the very next day to kill Luna. He felt confident the cases wouldn't be linked, but it was still a gamble because everyone would be on alert."

"Not after your mother was arrested," Flint said. "People in the building would think it was domestic violence, like we did."

"And Luna Delgado was moving out the next morning," Wu added. "We know he was aware of that fact because he showed up in coveralls with the Los Brokis logo."

"He should have let her go and chosen a backup target," Flint said.

"What if he didn't have anyone else lined up?" Dani started to pace, the rhythmic movement helping her think. "As far as we know, Luna was his first kill. Something about her triggered him to act on whatever urges he'd been suppressing. She was special. Maybe he thought she'd be the only one. He probably didn't evolve into selecting alternate victims until later."

"When he began to view them as targets and developed a murder schedule?" Wu asked, apparently thinking out loud, because he didn't pause for an answer. "And he stayed on course for ten years . . . until we closed in on him."

Dani came to a stop again, sensing Wu's growing excitement.

"He plans for everything." Wu motioned all around them. "This apartment. The way he timed the kills. Collecting evidence to frame someone else. He developed all these strategies over a period of years. Nothing was left to chance."

"Dr. Cattrall figured he was obsessive-compulsive," Flint said. "And she was right."

"He obsesses over the women he targets," Dani said. "And he's compulsive about his timetable to a degree no one had ever seen before. What can we do with that?"

"Do what you do best," Wu said to her. "Filter out the noise and find the pattern."

She considered what they had learned, going from the knowns to work toward the unknowns. "He didn't maintain a perfect schedule. The last one in the proper sequence was Angela Dominguez. Wilfredo Ochoa's murder was a total departure for him in the timeline and in his victimology."

"Because we forced his hand," Flint said. "He gave us a scapegoat when we started closing in. That proves he's a preferential killer but will act out by necessity as well."

"What about Gloria Gomez?" Dani asked. "Howell gave us the Julian date for her murder in the clue at Washington Square Park. That was another deviation, and it came before he killed Ochoa."

They were all silent for a long moment, each struggling to find a pattern that would take them in the right direction.

Wu grew very still. "What was the next Julian date on his agenda after Angela Dominguez?"

Dani had no trouble remembering. "Angela's date was 232. The next one in the sequence he uses is 333."

Flint was already looking it up on his cell phone. "This is a leap year, so that's November 28."

"That would have made the third and final murder this year," Wu said. "And the first two were in Manhattan, which means that's where the one planned for November would occur."

She suddenly understood where he was going. "He always plans ahead, picking out his targets in advance and following them to learn their habits before he plants pinhole cameras in their apartments."

Flint looked from her to Wu and back again. "You two care to take me along on this ride?"

Wu turned to him. "Gloria Gomez lives in Hell's Kitchen, which is in Manhattan."

He didn't need to elaborate. Flint caught on immediately. "Even though we caught the other guy, Howell was stalking Glo too."

"And he already installed the cameras," Dani added.

"Shit," Flint said. "Glo was supposed to die this November, but he moved up her date." He frowned. "Why would he do that?"

"Remember that he sent us the note before he framed Ochoa," Wu said. "My guess is he intended to keep us busy with that investigation while he killed Ms. Gomez. Based on what he did with Ochoa, he'd stage the scene to frame someone else or make it look like a suicide."

Flint looked skeptical. "But he knew we'd be looking for murders on that day."

Dani agreed with Wu's assessment. "Would we?" she said. "Howell was thinking our case would be closed and we'd be deep into the after-action reports and a psychological analysis of Ochoa. If the new murder was different enough, why would it even come to our attention?"

Flint closed his eyes and pinched the bridge of his nose. "If there was no obvious connection and the serial killer case was already closed, they'd work Glo's murder out of the Manhattan Homicide Squad, not the task force."

Wu caught Dani's eye. "He's already locked on to a target. Remember Luna Delgado? His compulsion drives him to take huge risks to fulfill his needs."

And then it clicked. "Glo is the only remaining target."

Wu nodded. "And he's not waiting for November."

CHAPTER 59

Dani watched her boss swing into action.

"I need a team at Ms. Gomez's apartment ASAP," Wu said into his phone. "Detective Flint is on the phone with her now. We're instructing her to lock all the doors and windows and to not answer the door until he tells her to. As soon as you arrive, get her to a safe house."

"That's right, Glo," Flint was saying into his cell. "I'll stay on the line with you until they arrive. In the meantime, pack a few things you'll need in a small bag. We can get anything else later." He listened. "I don't know how long." He listened again. "Until we have him in custody."

Beckoning Dani to follow him, Wu walked out of the bedroom and into the kitchen, ensuring Glo couldn't overhear their conversation through Flint's phone.

"Howell may not go after her right away like he did with Luna Delgado," Wu said. "This time we're onto him and he knows it." Apparently anticipating her objection, he added, "But I agree we should take every precaution."

"What's this about Luna Delgado?" Patel asked.

He had come with them as they zeroed in on the GPS signal, prepared to help with any electronic devices they found in the apartment. Now he sat at the kitchen table with Howell's secondary laptop open to the desktop screen.

Dani explained their reasoning, and Patel readily agreed. "Howell takes his compulsions to a level I've never seen before." He angled the screen to face her. "Now that we have five seconds to breathe, I was reviewing the other files." He gave his head a disgusted shake. "He recorded video of the victims in their apartments, going about their business, for days or weeks before he killed them."

Dani swallowed the bile that had climbed to the back of her throat. "Is each murder recorded?"

Patel nodded. "Of the ones I've watched so far, it's always at the end of each video file. Just like we thought, he records himself killing his victim. Then he uninstalls the pinhole cameras and leaves."

"Is his face visible in any of them?" Wu asked.

"Oh yeah, a jury will be able to tell it's him," Patel said.

"There are three videos that are set apart from the rest," Dani said, indicating files labeled X100, X220, and X333. "The file names start with an X, so they appear at the bottom of the list."

"He clearly did that on purpose to separate them," Patel said. "I haven't gotten to them yet."

"Open X100," Dani said, stomach roiling with a mix of anticipation and dread.

"Don't open that file," Wu said, stepping toward Patel. He turned to Dani. "You're not fooling me." He gentled his tone. "I know what you're thinking, and I don't want you watching your father's murder."

"He's right," Patel said quietly. "The day your father died was the one hundredth day of that year."

"I wonder if that triggered him," Wu said. "We'll see if he talks about it during the post-arrest interview."

"Not if Cassie Flock has anything to say about it," Dani said. "She'll muzzle him before we finish reading him his rights."

"I don't understand why Howell would have video of what happened with your father," Patel said to Dani. "Assuming the pinhole cameras were on during all or part of the attack, why would he keep the evidence of his crime when there's nothing he would enjoy watching."

Dani had a guess. "Training," she said simply. "When we went out on missions, we'd review body cam footage during the after-action debriefing to learn from our mistakes and reinforce our successes. He might have done the same."

"I still don't want you to watch it," Wu said in sympathetic tones. "You'll probably see it during the trial, but not now. Not when I need your head in the game."

She started to say witnessing whatever was in the file would have no effect on her, then shut her mouth to prevent herself from lying to her boss.

Instead, she directed a question to Patel to change the subject. "Let's have a look at X333. If I've got this right, it should be stalking footage of Glo."

"Let's see." Patel clicked on the file.

Streamed footage of Glo in her apartment began to play. They watched as she entered her unit holding a canister of pepper spray. The video cut to follow her to the bathroom, then into the bedroom, where she opened her dresser drawer and froze for an instant before hurrying toward the kitchen. The feed ended when she left the unit.

"Just got off the phone with Glo," Flint said, coming into the room. "Also spoke to the two uniforms who just picked her up in a sector car. They're taking her to a safe house."

Despite her relief that Glo was safe for the moment, Dani didn't feel the dancer would truly be out of danger until Howell was behind bars. With his history of avoiding capture, they'd have to up their game considerably to make that happen.

"We've deployed every available plainclothes police and undercover agent in the area," Wu said. "If Howell gets within a five-block radius of her apartment, he's going down."

"That's not enough," Dani said. "This asshole always finds a way through our net. This time we need to anticipate his next move and intercept him."

Her comment was met with murmured agreement from the others.

"Then we'd better get back to the business of analyzing the suspect's past behavior," Wu said after a long pause. "Insight into how he thinks will help predict his future actions, especially under stress, like he is now."

Patel, ever the computer specialist, looked to the screen for answers. "So did he label Glo's file with an X because he hasn't killed her yet, or because she's off his normal schedule?"

"There's one good way to tell," Dani said. "Let's have a look at X220."

Patel moved his mouse and clicked on the file icon. When it opened, Dani made out a woman's form in semidarkness. Taken from the living room of what appeared to be a nice apartment, the video brightened when the woman turned on the lights.

"What the hell?" Flint said.

Dani was equally stunned to see Howell's attorney, acclaimed defense counsel Cassie Flock, step out of her signature high-heeled pumps with a relieved groan and stride toward the bedroom.

"This makes no sense," Wu said. "She's nothing like any of his other victims. Plus, she's his lawyer. Why would he be spying on her?"

"This recording was made six months ago," Patel said, noting the time and date stamp in the corner. "And the size of this file is huge—much bigger than the others. The most recent footage appears first, but it probably goes back years."

"He's never watched his victims for more than a few weeks before he murders them." Dani glanced at the others. "This is a total deviation from his pattern."

The film cut to Cassie walking through the main bedroom to the en suite bathroom. She stood before the mirror, pulled a comb out of her hair, and shook her long tresses loose to tumble down over her shoulders.

"She's beautiful," Dani offered. "Maybe he chose her because he was attracted to her."

Cassie unzipped her pencil skirt and stepped out of it, then began to unbutton her blouse. This time, Patel didn't wait for the order from Wu to exit the screen.

"I bet she'll have a different take on trying to get her poor innocent client out of the hands of the jackbooted police after she sees this," Flint said. "Maybe she'll stop defending perverts and killers."

"He won't be her client anymore," Wu said. "She can't represent him if she's a victim. We'll subpoena her to testify that this was recorded without her knowledge or consent. She'll have to recuse herself now that she's got a starring role in his videos."

Dani pictured Howell watching Cassie Flock. A nagging sensation filtered in through her subconscious. She'd felt it before while trying to break a code. Something was incomplete. Out of order. Disrupted.

And then she realized what it was.

"We talked about Howell changing his murder schedule when he killed Ochoa and went after Glo," she said. "But he deviated from the sequence of Julian dates one other time." She looked at Flint. "Remember all the lingerie we found in Ochoa's apartment?"

"Everything was in clear plastic tubs," he said. "What's that got to do with—"

"Remember there were only thirty-one containers?"

"The missing case," Flint said with a groan. "We were wondering whether he'd decided to skip that date in the rotation, or if there was something about that particular target that made him . . ." He trailed off, and their eyes met in shared comprehension.

She turned to Patel. "The Julian date for the missing case was 220, right?"

He slid out his laptop and tapped the screen to wake it up. After a quick scan, he touched an icon, opening the spreadsheet. "Yep. That was August 7 in 2020."

"He didn't just want to watch Cassie," Dani said. "She was supposed to be victim twenty, but she was useful to him, so he held off. That's when he gave her the X in the file name. He would take her out of order."

"You're saying he gave her a stay of execution?" Flint asked.

"That's one way to put it," she said. "He didn't kill anyone else for that slot, which means it's still on his agenda. And now he knows we have the video, so she can't represent him. She's no longer of any value to him, except—"

"To take her place on his timetable," Wu said. "He'd feel compelled to fill the only gap."

"And we've denied him access to Glo," Flint said. "He'd have to go after someone else."

"Glo isn't his target," Dani said. "At least not tonight. If I'm right, he'll try to set things right in the order they should be, and Cassie has been on borrowed time since 2020. I think he'll deal with her first and circle back around to Glo next."

Wu cursed. "I sent all our resources to the wrong place." He looked at Patel. "Get me a cell number and a home address for Cassie Flock."

Watching Patel's fingers flash over the keyboard gave Dani an idea. "Howell's surveillance equipment is probably still in her apartment. He only uninstalls it after a kill."

Wu moved to stand beside Patel. "Can you connect to a live feed with his laptop?"

Patel let out a frustrated huff. "What do you want me to do first?"

"Get the phone number," Dani and Wu said in unison. Then Wu went through a brief triage. "First, we warn her. Second, we get boots on the ground at her location to protect her. Third, we look to see if he's already inside her apartment, which we can do after help is on the way."

She agreed. There was no sense in remotely watching Howell strangle Cassie if they had no idea where it was happening and no one was on the way to stop it.

Moments later, Patel called out her cell number to Flint, who tapped in the digits on his phone.

"It's going straight to voice mail," Flint said. "I'll leave a message and keep trying."

When Patel gave them a Carnegie Hill address, Wu exchanged a knowing glance with Dani before he connected the last dot. "Where were the other two murders for 2020 committed?"

Patel tapped in another command. "Manhattan." He looked up, eyes wide. "And Carnegie Hill is in Manhattan."

It had taken Howell four years to rotate back to the same borough, making them believe Glo was the target. But he was operating in Manhattan back in 2020 as well.

Wu was immediately on his phone, redirecting the surveillance units and support personnel.

"I know that building," Dani said, starting for the door.

Wu took the phone from his ear. "Where are you going, Vega?"

"That's only a few blocks from here," she said over her shoulder. "The undercover surveillance team is in Hell's Kitchen. We've wasted valuable time setting up in the wrong place. He's probably already at Cassie's apartment."

"I'll contact the tactical team," Wu said. "They only cleared here twenty minutes ago."

"That means they're twenty minutes out," Dani said, crossing the room. "They might not get there in time."

"I'll get dispatch to send some uniforms over there," Flint said. "They work the beat. They'll be at her place in five."

"I can run there faster than you can explain the situation to the dispatcher, who'll ask you a hundred questions before relaying all the info to the beat cops in the area."

She opened the door, nearly making it out before Wu's stern command brought her up short.

"Stand down, Vega." He joined her on the threshold. "You've got no backup—or, hell, even a plan. You can't underestimate Howell. He's shown us time and again that he's dangerous, smart, and tough."

She faced her boss. "With all due respect, sir, so am I."

Their gazes locked. They both knew what she was capable of. Despite the number of people Howell had murdered, her body count was higher. And her kills had been armed and trained enemy combatants, not defenseless young women alone in their apartments.

"I'll go with her," Flint said. "We'll have each other's backs." He moved to stand beside her. "Besides, this is still an NYPD case. Makes sense for someone with a shield to be there."

Surprised by the offer, she decided to take assistance from wherever it came. "I'm right about the response time from patrol," she said to Wu. "You can make the call to dispatch while we head over to Cassie Flock's building together."

"And if you get there first?" Wu asked.

"We listen at the door. If everything's quiet, we knock and see if she's home." She gestured toward Patel, whose eyes were on his screen. "We might have access to a live feed inside the apartment by then."

"Going as fast as I can," Patel said. "Looks like the live feed is behind a different firewall. I don't want to risk another countdown clock, so I'm being careful."

Wu dragged a hand through his thick, dark hair and turned back to Dani and Flint. "Go," he told them. "Before I change my mind."

CHAPTER 60

Park Avenue
Carnegie Hill, Manhattan

Ten minutes later, Dani pounded to a stop at the front entrance of Cassie's building half a minute ahead of Flint. Barely winded from her sprint, she waved at the doorman, who rushed out from behind his desk when she raised her credentials.

By the time he buzzed her in, Flint had joined her, holding up his gold shield while he caught his breath.

"FBI and NYPD," she said to the doorman. "We need to access Cassandra Flock's unit."

"Police, yes," he said in a thick eastern European accent. "Upstairs." He pointed upward. He hurried to his desk and returned with an electronic passkey.

Taking the proffered card from his outstretched hand, Dani glanced at Flint and saw her own confusion mirrored in his rugged features. "Do you mean the police are already here?" she asked the doorman.

He nodded vigorously. "I give key card."

"Sounds like they made it here ahead of us," Flint said. "But I don't have a patrol radio to find out where they're staging or anything."

She'd been on enough scenes with the police to know they'd likely set up a base of operations to coordinate their response in a situation that involved the potential arrest of a serial killer who might have a hostage. Especially if the special agent in charge from the FBI had called in the request.

Constant media coverage since the news conference had kept the entire city, including its police force, on high alert. They would take no chances while bringing in the suspect, making it likely they might wait for one of the rapid-response tactical units to arrive before attempting contact with Cassie.

"Can you call dispatch to confirm?" she asked Flint, then turned back to the doorman. "What's the unit number?"

Even if patrol officers had already responded, she wanted to talk to Cassie personally.

"Floor is 14," the doorman said, indicating the elevator on the opposite side of the spacious entry area. "Top floor. Only four penthouse suites up there."

"Which one's hers?"

"Unit is 14A. Right side."

"Patrol supervisor requested a rapid deployment ESU," Flint said after disconnecting. "They're staging around the corner to stay out of view until everyone gets there." He gave her a meaningful look. "He wasn't aware of any patrol officers inside the building."

She didn't like where that comment took her but didn't want to alarm the doorman. "Did the police go up in the elevator?" she asked him.

Another nod. "Yes."

Forcing back the wave of dread surging through her, she posed the most important question. "How many police came?"

An index finger went up. "One police."

She pulled out her cell phone, tapped the screen, and turned the device toward the doorman. "This man?"

He squinted, then beamed at her. "Yes."

She grabbed Flint's arm, pulling him away. "Howell's up there," she whispered. "We have to assume he used the key card and got into her apartment."

Flint already had his cell out. "I'll request a patch-through from dispatch to the incident commander." He put the phone to his ear. "This just officially became a clusterfuck."

She grew increasingly frustrated as Flint navigated the NYPD's communication system. While the detective followed proper procedure, Cassie Flock was fourteen stories above them, trapped with a serial killer. Flint's conversation receded into the background as various scenes played out in her mind. Every scenario ended with Cassie dead.

"Let's go," she said to Flint, who had finally connected with a patrol sergeant.

"Hold on, Sarge." Flint glanced up at her. "Where the hell are you going, Vega?"

She let her actions speak for her, pushing the elevator button.

"Oh no," Flint said. "We're not doing that. Patrol is handling this. A captain just arrived to take charge of the situation."

The elevator doors opened, and Dani stepped inside. "You coming?"

After muttering a few obscenities, Flint joined her. "Agent Vega and I are headed up to the vic's unit," he said into the phone. "I know." Pause. "We won't."

Dani mashed the button labeled 14, pressing it until the doors slid shut. "Put your phone on speaker so I can talk to him." As soon as Flint announced her, the sergeant wasted no time making his stance clear.

"Agent Vega, the NYPD is in charge of this operation. I'm with Captain Ahmad. He's now the incident commander, and we're treating this as a hostage-barricade at this point. Crisis negotiators will be here within minutes, and we're coordinating a tactical response."

She appealed to his training. "Would real-time intel about what's going on inside the apartment be of use to you?"

"Of course, but—"

"We won't make entry," she cut in. "We'll listen near the door and advise." Aware communication was critical during an operation, she explained the rest of her strategy. "Detective Flint will leave his phone on speaker. You'll hear everything in real time." The rest probably went without saying, but she spelled it out anyway. "Mute your end so we don't give up our position." She barely stopped herself before adding, "To the enemy."

She had switched to Ranger mode.

"Roger that." The police sergeant's two-word response told her he shared a military past.

The elevator slowed, and Dani slid her Glock from its holster.

Flint followed suit, drawing his Sig Sauer.

The elevator shuddered to a stop, and Dani raised her hand to give the signal for a perimeter check. Flint gave her a curt nod of understanding. When the doors hissed open, they each peeked out to scan the hallway in opposite directions.

All quiet.

Seeing no one, she angled her muzzle down in low-ready position and buttonholed out of the elevator with Flint directly behind her. She bent her knees and took point, crouching to use her body as a shield, protecting Flint, who moved in lockstep, training his weapon above her head.

They advanced, keeping close to the wall, heading to the right as the doorman had instructed. Before coming into view of the apartment door's fish-eye lens, Dani raised her left hand, fist closed, and stopped. Taking the silent cue, Flint came to a halt behind her.

They waited a full minute before Flint bent down, his lips nearly touching her ear. "There's nothing going on in there. Do you think he's already—"

A muffled scream from inside the apartment cut off his words.

There was no mistaking the sound, which was distinctly feminine, and filled with terror.

Dani raised her non—weapon hand again, this time holding up three fingers. She lowered one. Flint was still close enough behind her for Dani to hear his breath quicken. Good. He clearly understood her intentions. She motioned for him to move into position beside her.

When he did, she met his gaze and lowered another finger.

There was no chance to explain her plan to the police staging around the block. The sergeant had hopefully heard the scream. If not, he would certainly hear what was about to happen next.

Law enforcement used two methods to breach a stronghold. The stealth option involved sneaking inside to effect an arrest or luring the suspect out for capture. The alternative was called dynamic entry, in which police crashed inside all at once, often using flash-bang grenades and shouted commands to overwhelm and disorient suspects, lessening the threat to all involved.

She backed up and planted her right foot slightly behind her, preparing to use her powerful hip and thigh muscles to deliver maximum force when she kicked the door. Experience had taught her to heel-strike near the side of the knob, where the lock was mounted, which was always the weakest spot. If Flint followed her lead and timed it right, they could break the door open on the first attempt.

She lowered her third finger.

The force of their simultaneous kicks sent the door flying inward to crash against the interior wall. This was the no-tech equivalent of a flash-bang grenade used by tactical teams to stun and disorient potential attackers prior to making entry. Any hesitation would sacrifice the element of surprise, their most effective weapon.

Assuming he would follow her lead as he had before, she sank back into a crouch and took point, rushing inside ahead of Flint.

CHAPTER 61

Wu crowded in close to Patel, desperate to see the laptop's small screen. He'd been on the phone with the NYPD captain in charge, relaying info from the pinhole camera Howell had planted in the bedroom, when a loud crash sounded in the background.

"Did you hear that?" he asked Captain Ahmad.

Ahmad didn't respond right away, and Wu made out several voices, all apparently speaking to him at once.

"My sergeant tells me it sounds like Flint and Vega broke down the door. Can you get a visual?"

They had been monitoring Cassie, who was bound and gagged on the bed, making sure the captain knew she was still alive while they planned a rescue operation.

"I'm switching to the living room cam," Patel said. "I'll try to split the screen so we can see both feeds at the same time."

A few seconds later, Wu found himself watching Vega dart inside the apartment with Flint directly behind her.

"My agent and your detective just made entry," Wu told the captain.

"They were supposed to maintain their positions," Ahmad said. "Listen and report only."

Wu bit back a curse. "They must've heard Ms. Flock scream through the gag when Howell hit her and figured he was killing her."

Putting himself in Vega's place, that's what he would assume. They didn't have the benefit of the live-streamed video, so they couldn't know Howell was just getting started. In fact, he hadn't even gotten undressed.

At first Wu was shocked to see the police uniform, but, on reflection, it made perfect sense. Over his years of employment with the police department's crime lab, Howell had managed to collect the components of a patrol officer's blues, including a duty weapon. He had used the disguise to con his way past the doorman and into Cassie's apartment.

"What's going on in there?" Ahmad asked. "I've got an entry team ready. I was waiting for negotiators, but it looks like they won't get here in time."

Wu felt like a play-by-play commentator at a ball game. "They're clearing the apartment. Vega's on point. I can see her hand signals. She's telling Flint to stay behind her while they open the hall closet door."

He gritted his teeth. What Vega didn't know was that the only threat was the bedroom, where Howell had positioned himself to shoot the first person who came through the doorway.

Daniela Vega. His agent. His responsibility. He was watching her move toward certain death, and there wasn't a damned thing he could do about it.

Unless . . .

He reached out to Patel. "Give me your cell phone."

Patel's eyes never left the screen as his hand groped for the phone on the table beside him. Locating the device by feel, he pressed his index finger on the screen to unlock it before slapping it onto Wu's outstretched palm.

Wu stared at the contact list and saw Vega's name. Flint's phone was being used as an open mic for the PD to listen in, but not Vega's. She always kept her device stashed in her pocket. If he called, would the sound of an incoming call give away their exact position? If it happened to be on vibrate, would the sudden buzzing against her body distract her at the wrong moment? If she'd taken the precaution of muting the phone before going in, she wouldn't even get the call.

He ran through the options again. A call might save her, get her killed, or go unanswered. The decision was his, and his alone.

"I've split the screen," Patel announced. "We can see the bedroom and the living room in real time now."

"I'm sending an ESU team from the command post now," Ahmad said. "They'll be in the lobby in less than two minutes, but it'll take time for them to ride the elevators up, secure the hallway, and get into position. We can't risk other tenants walking into a crossfire. I need constant status updates on everyone inside the unit until they're all fully deployed."

Wu glanced at the phone in his free hand. "I can call Agent Vega's cell, but I don't think—"

"That could cause tactical problems." Ahmad apparently shared the same concerns. "We'll coordinate in advance if we need you to set off her phone."

Interesting choice of words. Was the captain thinking of the cell phone as a distraction for Vega, or for Howell?

"Howell's on the move." Patel was pointing at the side of the screen, which showed the bedroom.

"Talk to me," Ahmad said. "ESU is in the lobby now."

"Howell left his position by the bedroom door, he walked to the bed." Wu kept up a steady narration for the captain's benefit. "He's still covering the door with his weapon, but he's doing something with his free hand." He leaned in close, then froze at the movement, which was accompanied by a loud smack transmitting through the microphone hidden in the wall. "He just slapped Cassie hard across the face."

"What the fuck?" Patel said over the sound of Cassie's muffled shriek. "He's running back to where he was hiding before."

Vega and Flint stopped their methodical search, heads turning toward the bedroom.

Wu knew exactly what was going on, and so did Ahmad. "He's drawing Flint and Vega to the bedroom," the captain said over the phone. "It's a trap."

Frustration and powerlessness threatened to overwhelm him as he watched Flint dart around Vega, heading toward the source of the noise. Meanwhile, Howell was in a shooting stance with his sights trained on the open bedroom door.

"Flint's going in," Wu told Ahmad. "Vega's trying to stop him, but I don't think she'll get to—"

The sound of gunfire cut off his words. He looked on helplessly as Detective Flint crumpled to the floor.

CHAPTER 62

Dani watched Flint fall in what seemed like slow motion. She was familiar with the standard issue Speer Gold Dot +P 124-grain hollow point NYPD police round, which would have been traveling at over 1,250 feet per second when it slammed into his outer right thigh. As her partner tumbled to the plush carpet, words from the Ranger Creed flooded her thoughts. *"I will never leave a fallen comrade to fall into the hands of the enemy."*

Her first priority was to get Flint out of the kill zone. She couldn't see Howell, but the trajectory of the round told her he was hiding inside the bedroom to the right of the door. She could make out the corner of the king-size bed where Cassie lay spread eagle with one limb tied to each bedpost. Flint was on the floor inside the room, writhing and unable to walk or crawl, so she would have to drag him to safety.

She recognized the tactic. Assuming Flint wore a Kevlar vest, Howell could have taken a headshot. Instead, he'd deliberately chosen a grievous wound that would not only incapacitate the detective but would also prove fatal without first aid.

In battle, enemy forces often took nonlethal shots or planted IEDs designed to maim rather than kill. The idea being that a wounded soldier not only was out of the fight but required two other soldiers for evacuation from the field, sidelining three for the price of one.

Effective, efficient, and ruthless.

Howell had correctly assumed an injured partner would hinder her far more than a dead one, and had acted accordingly. He may have studied tactics, but she doubted Howell had as much real-life urban warfare experience as she did.

She raised her weapon and aimed at the wall to the right of the bedroom door, away from the bed. She gave no warning and offered no chance for surrender before she opened fire.

Bam! Bam! Bam! Bam!

With deadly precision, her rounds perforated the wall with a row of neat circular holes at waist level. When trapped in a live-fire scenario with no means of escape, the options were either cover or concealment. Effective cover offered protection from incoming rounds, but concealment only hid your location.

Howell had been forced to choose the lesser option to ambush Flint, and drywall was no protection at all from the Hornady +P Luger 135-grain Critical Duty ammo in her Glock.

Deafening blasts from her weapon prevented her from hearing if Howell screamed or his body thudded to the floor, so she kept firing until the holes had traversed the length of the wall. She stopped when there were four rounds left and focused on Flint, who had stopped moving.

If Howell had hit Flint's femoral artery, the detective might already be dead. If not, his only hope for survival would be a field dressing until medical help arrived. The thought brought her up short. Where the hell were Flint's fellow officers?

Taking a breath to center herself brought clarity. She was familiar with the way time seemed to expand and contract in combat situations. It felt like an hour but had likely been a little over a minute since Flint had been shot. Assuming his cell phone was still on, everyone knew the situation and backup would be here soon. In the meantime, Flint was her responsibility.

"Never shall I fail my comrades."

Every instinct she possessed demanded that she chase Howell, but she would not sacrifice Flint to make an arrest. She sank to the floor, belly-crawling toward Flint. Reaching forward with her gun hand, she fired to the right of the doorway, using suppressive fire while she peeked her head through the opening.

No sign of Howell. And no telltale bloodstains on the carpet indicating he'd been hit by one of her shots through the drywall.

He was still in the room but could be hiding under the bed, in the bathroom, or in the closet, waiting to cap her when she was distracted by Flint's extraction. She glanced at the bed. Cassie was still bound and gagged, but maybe she could tip her head or cut her eyes toward her captor's hiding place.

But Cassie's eyes were half-closed, and her head lolled to one side. Her bare chest rose and fell, so she wasn't dead, but not fully conscious.

Conflicting duties warred within her. She had no doubt police were rushing to help, but they might end up in a standoff if Howell had extra ammo. She'd learned not to underestimate his cunning or his advance planning. If the situation became protracted, her next actions would decide who lived and who died. She found herself conducting the tactical version of triage. Every choice had a serious downside.

Cassie was an innocent civilian who had taken no oath to serve and protect. Naked and tied to the bed, she was completely unable to defend herself if Howell chose to shoot her from wherever he'd hidden.

Flint was unconscious, and also vulnerable to attack. To make matters worse, he would die without prompt intervention on her part.

Last, she thought of herself, not out of selfishness, but because if Howell eliminated her, he could then kill the other two easily. She was the last line of defense for both of them.

If she took the time for a methodical search of the room, she could neutralize Howell when she found him, preventing him from harming anyone else.

What to do first?

She flung her body forward, exposing herself to fire as she grasped Flint's ankle. Clutching her pistol in her right hand, she had to use her left to haul his inert form out of the bedroom. She'd carried her fellow soldiers before during training and in combat situations, but it was never easy to maneuver someone who was both large and unconscious. She pushed the phrase "dead weight" out of her mind and kept dragging until he was completely out of the room.

A quick check of his vitals revealed a pulse and respiration, but the swath of blood smeared across the carpet and the fresh blood oozing from his thigh alarmed her.

She divided her attention, continuously scanning for Howell as she loosened Flint's tie and slid it from around his neck. She lifted his leg enough to feed the tie underneath, then pulled both ends up, crossing them over each other and pulling them tight to form a knot.

If Howell wanted to kill her, this was his best chance. She'd laid the gun close by, but a makeshift tourniquet required both hands or it would never be secure enough to stop the blood flow. Regardless, she'd made her choice, and would live—or die—with the consequences.

Seconds later, the sound of booted feet thundered around her, accompanied by shouted commands from several voices behind her.

"Hands where I can see them."

"I see a gun!"

"I said hands up, now."

The tactical team would have been told a detective had been shot. They had rushed in to find a woman dressed in street clothes in a position that probably looked like she was pinning Flint down. With her back to them, they couldn't see the credentials around her neck.

"I'm Special Agent Dani Vega," she said. "FBI."

"I don't give a fuck if you're the Queen of England. Get your hands up."

Reluctantly, she released her grip on the tie and raised two bloody hands high above her. "Detective Flint's been shot in the leg. He'll bleed out unless he gets medical attention." She paused. "And the shooter is in the bedroom along with the victim."

The team surged around her, fanning out to search the space. When someone jostled her, she turned to see one of the team members kneeling beside her.

"I've got EMT training," he said, glancing at her creds. "I'll take care of him." He used his comm system to call for an ambulance as he began working on Flint.

"I tried to stop him." She felt compelled to plead her case to his fellow officers. "He blew right past me when he heard the scream." She tipped her head toward the bedroom. "Is she okay?"

"We've got this," he said, not unkindly. "The vic in there is out of it, but I haven't heard anyone saying it's critical." He flicked a glance at Flint. "The round missed his artery. The necktie you cinched around his leg probably saved him."

Four paramedics arrived, flanked by tactical personnel. One pair kneeled beside Flint, while the other two continued into the bedroom.

After a sharp look from one of the EMTs, she moved out of the way. She'd barely gotten to her feet when the team leader came out of the bedroom.

"Perp's gone," he said flatly.

"That's not possible." She walked past him into the bedroom. "I was blocking the doorway. He would have had to literally step over me to get out." She pointed at Flint and the medical team. "That's where I was the whole time."

The team leader swept a hand out to encompass the entire apartment. "Well, I don't see him anywhere." He raised a brow. "You think he's got an invisibility cloak?"

CHAPTER 63

Dani strode past the ESU team leader to check out the bedroom for herself.

"I guess FBI agents have extra-special vision," he said to her. "Maybe you can see things I can't. Then again, maybe not."

The comment deserved no response, so she offered none. Her gaze fell on Cassie, who had been covered by a sheet while a female EMT cut her loose from the bedposts. Dani was pleased to see a woman treating her and imagined Cassie felt the same way.

Dani approached them and spoke in gentle tones. "Can I ask you something, Ms. Flock?"

Cassie still looked groggy. Humiliated, degraded, and brutalized, she was likely still in shock from her brush with death. A forensic psychologist or victim-assistance specialist would eventually interview her prior to Howell's case going to trial, but Dani needed answers now.

Cassie turned in her direction, blinking in apparent confusion.

This part of Dani's job—there was no other way to put it—totally sucked. She tried again. "Ms. Flock, I need to know where Brad Howell went. Did you see him leave?"

Cassie leaned forward and clutched the paramedic who had become her rescuer.

The woman put a comforting arm around Cassie. "I don't think she can answer you," she said to Dani. "She hasn't sustained obvious physical injury, but we'll treat her for shock and run a tox screen. Then we'll keep her overnight for observation."

Dani was debating whether to try another approach when her phone buzzed. Seeing Wu's name, she crossed the room for privacy before answering.

Wu got straight to the point. "How's Flint?"

"I'm told he'll be okay, sir."

"Ms. Flock?"

"Ditto."

"You?"

She summed up her feelings in four words. "My partner got shot."

She was pleased that Wu didn't mention that they worked for different agencies and, therefore, Flint wasn't technically her partner. Details didn't matter. Flint was a fellow law enforcement officer, a comrade in arms.

"We've been monitoring the camera feeds Howell set up in the condo," Wu said. "There's nothing you could have done to—"

"Wait . . . you were watching the whole time?"

"Yes, and we saw you try to—"

"Where the hell did Howell go?"

A long pause. "We don't know."

She recalled watching the video of Cassie Flock getting undressed. "But one of the pinhole cameras covered the bedroom, right?"

"Not the whole room," Wu said. "Just the part with the bed."

Phone still pressed to her ear, Dani walked over to the dresser. She bent down, squinting to see the minute hole in the drywall beside the mirror. The hole for the microphone was concealed behind the mirror.

"We see you looking into the lens right now. Can you see how the edge of the mirror blocks part of the room?"

Howell had wanted to hide the holes as much as possible. There was no need to have the mic hole in view, so that went behind the mirror. To avoid Cassie noticing the other hole, he'd put it as close to the edge of the mirror as possible. For his purposes, all he really needed to see clearly was the bed.

She strode across the room. "Can you see me now?"

"All except your right shoulder."

She moved to her right. "How about now?"

"You're totally blocked," Wu said. "And that's the last place we saw Howell."

She turned around. "There's a balcony."

The ESU team leader had apparently been listening to her half of the conversation. "Already checked it out," he said, loud enough to be heard through the phone. He must have guessed she was on the phone to FBI colleagues and wanted to be sure they didn't think the PD was incompetent or stupid.

He jerked a thumb over his shoulder at the sliding glass door. "There's no way down from there that doesn't end with a loud splat." He paused. "We looked. The perp's not pancaked on the sidewalk." Another pause. "And before you ask, we checked for any signs of a rope, a hook, or a ladder. He didn't climb or rappel down either."

Cassie Flock's penthouse suite was on the fourteenth floor. Unlike Dani's childhood apartment in the Bronx, this elegant, renovated luxury building did not have an unsightly metal fire escape attached to the exterior.

"We can't see the balcony at all," Wu said into her ear.

Dani walked past the team leader and tugged the glass door's handle. "Was this unlocked when you checked it?" she asked over her shoulder when the door slid open easily.

"It was closed," he said. "But the vic probably forgot to lock it. This is the top floor, after all, and there's no access to the balcony except from the bedroom."

She turned to face him. "You're a large, powerfully built man. You've had advanced tactical training. You're well armed."

"Your point?"

"You have no idea what it's like to be petite, untrained, and unarmed." She glanced at Cassie, who was still in no shape to answer questions. "I'd be surprised if she weighs more than a hundred and ten pounds. She's single. Most attorneys put in long hours, so she doesn't have time for a dog. In other words, she's here all alone."

She let the information sink in before driving her main idea home. "Cassie Flock is known for defending the worst of the worst. Murderers, rapists, arsonists, you name it. She studies police reports and interviews her clients about their crimes. No one who spends that much time thinking about crime would ever leave their balcony door unlocked. I don't care if she lives at the top of the Empire State Building, she'd make damn sure her place was secured at all times."

"I agree with you," Wu said over the phone. "But we've isolated a clear picture of Howell. That police uniform he had on was too snug to conceal any climbing equipment, and I don't see how he could've gotten down without even a basic rope."

She walked out onto the balcony to check it out for herself. Maybe Howell had free-climbed his way out or, resourceful as he was, perhaps he'd planned ahead, hiding some climbing gear in case he got cornered in the bedroom.

She'd done plenty of vertical building assaults and knew what to look for. She tilted her head back to see if Howell could have gone up to the roof. At first she thought she was looking at an oversize gutter, then realized what it was.

"The roof's been climb-proofed," she said so both Wu and the team leader could hear. "The management installed one of those smooth bullnose barriers around the perimeter of the roof to prevent anyone from getting up there except through the stair access."

To prevent liability from people getting to the top of buildings and jumping, throwing things, setting up urban campsites, or causing other problems, some city buildings now sported anti-climbing devices.

"She's right," the team leader said, joining her on the balcony. "He for sure didn't go up, and there's no balcony directly below this one, so he couldn't have dropped down to it."

Still not satisfied, she inspected the spindles on the metal railing, which was the only object strong enough to hold Howell's weight. She found no telltale marks left by any kind of climbing gear. Besides, if Howell had rappelled down, he'd have no way to untie the rope and take it with him after reaching a lower balcony or the ground. The same was true of a grappling hook or a portable ladder.

"See what I mean?" the team leader said. "Unless this guy's got Acme rocket shoes like Wile E. Coyote, he had no way off this balcony."

"What about the next unit over?" Wu asked Dani. "Does it have a balcony?"

She looked along the side of the building. "It's about thirty feet away. These penthouse suites are huge."

"Even if he got there somehow, the balcony door would be locked," the team leader said. "I've made entry through patios, and the doors don't shatter like in the movies. The glass is heavy-duty, double paned, and tempered according to code. If he somehow managed to break in, we'd hear him, and so would the people who lived there." He squinted at the other balcony. "And I don't see any broken glass."

She put herself in Howell's shoes. The police had him pinned down, with only one point of egress. Whether he had planned an alternate escape or not, he would retreat to the balcony out of necessity. She was certain he'd stood exactly where she was.

A mewling sound distracted her, and she quickly located the source. A sleek calico cat sat on the railing of a balcony one floor down and to the right.

Could it be?

"I know what you're thinking," the team leader said, following her gaze. "He'd have to go down at an angle to make it. Risky jump."

The cat licked its paw.

"And there's no broken glass there either," he added.

The cat leaped down from its perch . . . and disappeared inside the unit.

Dani exchanged a stunned glance with the team leader. "That's it," she said. "That's how he did it."

"What's going on?" Wu's voice was sharp. "What did you see?"

"The units below the top floor aren't suites. They're closer together, so the balconies aren't directly below the penthouse ones. Howell would have to jump down one level and about ten feet to the right, but it's doable."

"And how would he get inside?" Wu asked. "The sliding glass door leading into the unit—"

"Is open," Dani finished. "The people who live there left their door open a few inches for their cat."

The team leader gave her a knowing look. "Guess they're not petite women who live alone."

She refused to apologize for her earlier statement. "I'm sure they're not."

"Can we get a team down there?" Wu cut in. "Now."

"On it." The team leader tapped the transmitter on his comm system and directed his ESU personnel to meet in the living room of Cassie's suite.

She watched him leave, remaining behind on the balcony. "Howell's long gone, sir. He won't be hanging around in that apartment. He slipped in, made sure the sliding glass door was in the same position as when he found it, and slipped out the front door."

Wu's frustration carried through the phone's speaker. "He was one floor down from all the action. He could easily take the elevator or the stairs down to the lobby and walk right out the main entrance. He'd blend in with the rest of the uniforms. Cops were pouring in from all over the place after the 10-13 went out."

Much as she hated to admit it, Dani had to admire Howell's strategy. He knew once shots were heard in the apartment the dispatcher would broadcast a 10-13 Assist Police Officer call. Cops from everywhere in the vicinity would converge on the building, and Howell could easily get lost in the sea of blue uniforms rushing in every direction until he made it out to the street. In the world's largest police department, strange faces were to be expected, especially when they were coming from various precincts.

"Howell's inside knowledge of the NYPD is a nightmare for us," she said. "He's always one step ahead."

"Then use your inside knowledge against him," Wu said. "Anticipate his next move. Then intercept him before he gets there."

Her boss was right. She'd been playing catch-up the entire time, and it had landed them here. Time to turn the tables.

"I'll call you when I have something."

She disconnected. Looking out at the city from the high balcony, she freed her mind to explore all possibilities. This kind of thinking required a combination of expanded awareness and focused attention. She sank deeper into Howell's mind. Treat him like a puzzle. What were his patterns? What did he do in the past? What were the compulsions that drove him? When he was under extreme pressure, where would he go?

She froze. Her meandering thoughts crystallized into sharp focus. She knew where Howell was headed.

CHAPTER 64

Dani tapped the speed dial number to reconnect with Wu. "How long has it been since you last saw Howell on the live feed?"

"Putting you on speaker," Wu said. "Patel will check the time stamp while you tell me what you've come up with."

"It's only a guess, sir."

"I'd take one of your guesses over an analysis from our profilers."

This was the highest vote of confidence her boss could give. He was counting on her natural abilities and prior training. Codebreaking was all about deductive reasoning and forward progression. You had to start with the constants and extrapolate to find the most likely variables, which was what she'd just done.

Wu was one of the smartest people she knew. If he drew the same conclusion she had, odds were better that she was on the right course.

"Fact-check me," she said. "What did Howell do after he was released pending trial?"

"Headed for his apartment to destroy the evidence."

"And when that didn't work, did he flee the city?"

"No. He went after Cassie Flock."

"We didn't know about the police uniform," she said. "He stood a decent chance of getting away, but he risked going to jail because he decided it was more important to—"

"Keep his schedule," Wu finished for her. "Or at least go back and fill in the blank space."

"Think of it as closing the loop," she said. "The only reason he'd been able to tolerate Cassie being alive this long is because he knew he'd tidy up that loose end later."

"And later is now, because he's a fugitive and his options are limited."

Dani walked back into Cassie's bedroom while she waited for Wu to process the information. "There's only one more loop to close."

After a long moment, Wu uttered a single word. "Shit."

"My thoughts exactly." She kept going past the bed where paramedics were still tending to Cassie, intent on her new mission.

"He thinks we'd never expect him to go back there," Wu said. "After all, it's where you locked him up."

She framed her next question carefully, without any judgment. "You redirected all our resources here, didn't you?"

When Wu spoke, his voice sounded like he was walking away from the phone he'd put on speaker moments earlier. "Call Gloria Gomez," he said to someone in the room with him. "Tell her Howell might be headed to her apartment. See if she can stay in a neighbor's unit until we get there." He paused a beat before the next set of instructions. "Then get Captain Ahmad on the phone again. Brief him and tell him I'm sending my agents back to Ms. Gomez's apartment, but patrol officers already working in that area would get there a hell of a lot faster."

Wu had no authority to order personnel from another agency to respond. He was directing someone to call the PD incident commander and make a request. Dani was confident uniforms would be there "forthwith," in police lingo, but their visible presence might scare Howell off before he could be arrested.

She paused at the place where Flint's blood had begun to coagulate on the carpet. The EMTs had wasted no time getting him to the hospital. She'd done what she could, and now the only thing that remained was to hunt down the man who had shot him.

"Make sure they know Howell's wearing police blues," Wu continued speaking in the background. "And send them a photo of him too."

Patel was obviously still beside the phone when he answered her earlier question. "It's been fifteen minutes since Howell was last on camera at your location," he said to Dani.

She considered his objective and weighed his options as she crossed the living room and exited Cassie's unit. "He has to get from the Upper East Side to Glo's place in Hell's Kitchen," she said. "He doesn't own a vehicle, and he wouldn't steal a sector car or hail a cab."

Howell would know that police cars were equipped with GPS tracking devices that would provide real-time information of his whereabouts to dispatch. Flagging down a taxi in full uniform would cause far too much suspicion.

Apparently still listening to Patel and Dani while he gave orders to someone else, Wu came back to the phone to join the discussion. "He'll have to take public transportation. Not a bad choice, because most people probably can't tell the difference between MTA and NYPD officers. As long as he doesn't run across a crime in progress, he'd make pretty good time on the subway."

"I'm headed in that direction." Dani was walking down the hallway. "I might lose you on the elevator."

"And how are you planning to get there?" Wu asked. "You've got the same problem."

She and Flint had arrived here on foot, but that wouldn't stop her—or slow her down. "I'll ask a cop for a ride. When I explain that I'm after the guy who shot one of their own, there won't be any problem."

"I pulled up a transit map," Patel said, keys tapping in the background. "If Howell ran to the subway at 86th, he could take the 6 to 51st Street and transfer to the E train that takes him right to Hell's Kitchen."

"That'd take about half an hour," Wu said. "There's still time to intercept him."

"He'd get out at 50th Street and walk the rest of the way to Glo's place," Dani said, pleased she hadn't lost the signal in the elevator. "But he might take another route."

She heard Wu in the background again, asking for police to keep an eye out for Howell at all surrounding subway stations, while she left the elevator and wove her way through a mass of blue uniforms crowding the lobby.

"I'll work with the police," Patel said. "We should be able to pick him up on video."

The NYPD's Domain Awareness System combined their own closed-circuit network with private security cameras spread throughout the city. The Metro Transit Authority also monitored passengers using live feeds.

"He'll know about that." She pushed through the front doors and stepped out onto the sidewalk. "I wonder what his escape plan is after he's done with Glo."

"He may not have one," Wu said quietly. "I think it's the endgame for him."

She considered the possibility. "You're saying Howell is willing to go to jail?"

"No, Agent Vega. I'm saying Howell is willing to die."

CHAPTER 65

Seventh Avenue
Hell's Kitchen, Manhattan

Dani pointed to the curb. "Let me out right here."

After disconnecting with Wu back at Cassie's building, she'd located the PD command post and found Captain Ahmad. A brief call from Wu had convinced Ahmad to detail a sector car from the Upper East Side to take her to Glo's building in Hell's Kitchen. No one had any illusion that she'd get there sooner than patrol officers from the 10th and Midtown North Precincts already in the vicinity, but she intended to be the first federal agent on the scene in the event of an arrest.

Boyle, the burly Irish cop behind the wheel, tapped the brakes and maneuvered the marked sector car into the right lane. "We're only on Seventh," he told her. "If he took the E, he'd get off at the next stop on 50th."

She didn't have time to explain. "I've got an idea. Humor me." Glo had already been moved to a safe location, so apprehension was now her prime objective. Accomplishing that mission with someone like Howell demanded creative thinking.

Boyle eased to a stop. "Okay, but I got orders to take you to the target's residence, and that's where I'm headed."

Fine with her. "Go on without me," she said, opening the door. "I'll do the last few blocks on foot."

He shrugged. "Suit yourself."

She got out, walked to the corner, and headed west on 53rd, deliberately taking a parallel street to her destination so Howell wouldn't see her.

She hadn't told the patrol officer she was using pattern recognition to anticipate Howell's next move. He wouldn't make a beeline for Glo's building. He was someone who watched and strategized. If he suspected they were onto him, he'd avoid the nearest subway stop. Instead, he'd surface where they weren't expecting him and start walking. Getting the lay of the land. Keeping an eye out for uniform patrol or plainclothes surveillance teams.

She glanced around, taking in all the places Howell might wait and watch. Was he still wearing the police uniform? Had he worn another outfit underneath so he could shed his disguise like a snake sheds its skin?

Less than ten minutes later, she sensed someone watching her. She was familiar with the phenomenon, known as gaze detection. Scientific studies confirmed that almost all humans could sense when someone was looking at them, even if that person was not in their field of vision. A capacity passed down from our ancestors that had helped them survive.

She had enough personal experience with the phenomenon to take it seriously. She wrapped her hand around her Glock's grip and thumbed open the leather guard that held her service weapon secured in its slender holster and eased it partially out.

She would have "cleared leather," cop-speak for drawing your duty weapon, but no target had yet presented itself. In a crowded urban environment, the risk of collateral damage in a gunfight was a real and tragic possibility.

She had put hundreds of thousands of rounds through various weapons during her military and FBI training. She was fast and deadly accurate, but that would do her no good if Howell sniped at her from behind cover.

When the prickling sensation grew stronger, she raced to the side of the nearest building and put her back to its brick facade, cutting her vulnerability in half. Now she had to watch only 180 degrees around her position.

She caught movement out of the corner of her eye and snapped her head around to focus on a figure partially hidden behind the trunk of one of the trees lining the street.

It was Brad Howell, still wearing the stolen NYPD uniform, aiming his gun directly at her.

Years of training had created muscle memory, enabling her to react reflexively. She dropped to the ground to make herself a smaller target an instant before the distinctive pop of gunfire sounded. A pebble of brickwork tumbled down from a newly formed crater in the wall behind the spot where she'd just been standing. Howell must have spent some time at the range.

Already on her belly, she extended both arms with her elbows resting on the ground. The Glock was in her right hand with her left hand supporting the grip. At the same time, she bent her left knee, pulling it forward slightly to stabilize herself. In less than one second and without conscious thought, she had assumed the pistol prone shooting position used by special forces.

She trained her sights on the wide tree trunk where Howell was hiding and waited for a clear shot. From this position, she could park a round in the center of his forehead if he so much as peeked his head out to take another shot at her.

A woman's shriek, accompanied by a cacophony of shouts, filled the air around them. The single gunshot had drawn attention.

Dani had to keep her eyes locked on target. She may get only one opening and couldn't risk looking around. She had been trained, however, to process information through her peripheral vision, and she caught movement as people began running in all directions, apparently unable to tell where the shot had come from.

"Active shooter!" Howell yelled from behind the tree. "She's got a gun."

Howell was hidden from her vantage point, but he was completely visible to onlookers from various places on either side of the street. Dani had to appreciate the genius of his plan.

People would see a police officer in a standoff with a woman dressed in street clothes. An obviously deranged woman who was aiming a gun at him.

Police in the area would be here in less than two minutes. She could hold her position until then, and they would sort it out. They had been alerted that an impostor was nearby and had been provided a photo of Howell, but this scenario would be called in by passersby who would tell the dispatcher about a female active shooter trying to kill a cop on 53rd Street.

Would the officers rushing to the scene connect the two cases? Would they see her aiming a gun and immediately open fire?

No matter how much she shouted that she was FBI, they would order her to drop her weapon, cuff her, and verify her story before taking any other action. Even if she somehow didn't get shot, Howell could slip away while everyone's attention was directed at her.

If she laid down her weapon now to avoid the confrontation, Howell would have the option of running away or shooting her before backup arrived. There was no time for her to call Wu and have him relay a message to all the king's horses and all the king's men who were doubtlessly converging on her location at this very moment. Howell had reversed a situation in which he was about to be captured or killed, turning his predicament on her.

Brilliant. Efficient. Ruthless.

A skittering piece of gravel close by was all the warning she had. Someone was sneaking along the side of the building, advancing on her from behind. The wail of approaching sirens prevented her from hearing more.

Eyes still on the tree across the street, she called out to whoever was headed toward her. "I'm Special Agent Daniela Vega with the FBI. The man across the street is not a police officer, he's—"

Two large male bodies thudded down on top of her before she could finish.

Howell hadn't needed to wait for the confusion of sector cars screeching to a stop with police jumping out, guns drawn, shouting commands at everyone.

All it took for him to escape was a pair of Good Samaritans.

CHAPTER 66

Dani figured the first man who had landed on her back had the proportions of a defensive lineman—or perhaps a rhinoceros. At least that's how her lungs felt when the impact forced the air out of them.

"Hold her down." The second man who had piled on appeared to be calling the plays. Going with her football analogy, he'd be the quarterback.

She couldn't breathe, much less identify herself and show them her credentials. When the quarterback started grasping for her Glock, Dani realized she had an entirely new threat to deal with. If he wrestled it from her hand, he might use it on her.

She immediately reverted to her weapon-retention training, trying to pull the Glock under her body.

The lineman's job was apparently to immobilize her while the quarterback tried to disarm her. "Give up the fucking gun, bitch."

Flattened as she was, it was impossible to tuck her arms under her body. Rough hands yanked the pistol from her slackening hand. The lack of oxygen was taking a toll, and her vision blurred. She had only a few seconds of consciousness remaining and could only hope the sirens meant the police had arrived in time to save her from asphyxiation.

As the world faded to gray, she managed to make out Howell's back as he raced to the end of the block and turned right, heading north on 10th Avenue.

"You can get off her now," another voice said seconds before darkness overtook her. "We'll take over."

Dani was familiar with the expression about the weight of the world being lifted but had never experienced the sensation in literal terms until the moment the lineman rolled away from her.

She barely had time to suck in two gulps of much-needed air before her hands were jerked behind her back. Steel bracelets were slapped around her wrists and cranked down hard.

Ah, yes. The police were here. She opened her mouth to speak, but managed only a series of coughs as what felt like deflated lungs expanded.

"F . . . ," she finally wheezed, unable to get the other two initials out.

"Yo, what are you doing?" another voice called out from a short distance away. "She's an FBI agent. Let her go."

Still face down on the ground, Dani craned her neck upward to see Officer Boyle, the cop who had dropped her off earlier.

The officer who had handcuffed Dani narrowed his eyes at the newcomer's collar brass. "You're from the 19th Precinct. What the hell are you doing here?"

The police had been alerted that an impostor was in their midst. Anyone they didn't recognize, especially someone coming from another part of the borough, would be suspect.

"Captain Ahmad detailed me to take her to 52nd and 10th," Boyle said. "But she got out early, so I went on ahead."

Mention of the captain had the desired effect. Dani's wrists were freed, and Boyle stepped forward to help her to her feet. After inspecting her creds, one of the Midtown North Precinct cops wordlessly handed back her Glock.

A quick weapon check satisfied her that it was in working order. "Howell's on foot. I saw him turn at the end of the block and run north on 10th."

"Is he still in uniform?" Boyle asked, grabbing the mic attached to his shirt. When she nodded, he keyed it and broadcast a lookout.

The others raced to the corner, turning north on 10th, but Dani took off in the opposite direction, heading south. Picking up speed, she pretended not to hear Boyle calling out to her from behind. She regularly ran five-minute miles and doubted the burly cop could keep up.

Sensing Howell would shift his strategy again, she was playing another hunch. Considering his past behavior, she concluded he would change his appearance. If he didn't have another disguise underneath, ditching the uniform shirt would make a difference. A plain undershirt with blue work pants and boots would help him blend in with the public now that the cop outfit had become a liability.

Nothing in Howell's past pattern and practice indicated he would simply give up and move on. To the contrary, he'd been compelled to close any open loops. Having been denied his two remaining targets, Cassie Flock and Glo Gomez, Howell would have no choice but to shift his focus to a proxy.

Howell was not a random killer. Every murder he'd committed had a singular purpose and had been planned out well in advance.

Every murder but one.

He had intended to begin with Luna Delgado but had mistakenly entered the wrong apartment, where he was confronted by Sergio Vega. He'd made a critical mistake during that unplanned murder, leaving evidence behind that would eventually expose him.

Panicked though he must have been about the missing chain, he still went back the following day to "correct" his mistake. That level of compulsion could not be overcome by logic.

Which was what Dani was counting on as she turned right and crossed onto 52nd Street. Glo had been whisked away to safety, and Howell was spotted in the vicinity. No one would expect him to be at her building, so every cop in the area had fanned out to lock down Hell's Kitchen and start a grid search for the suspect.

Dani pulled out her cell phone and tapped the speed dial.

"SAC Wu."

"I'm at Gloria Gomez's building," she whispered. "I have reason to believe Howell is nearby."

"What?" Wu seemed to be trying to process the new information that must have contradicted everything he'd been told over the past several minutes. "I'll let Captain Ahmad know that you're—"

"No." The word came out sharper than she'd intended, but she had no time for lengthy explanations. "PD is securing the perimeter to make sure Howell doesn't escape. I'm freelancing here." When Wu started to interrupt, she spoke over his objections, getting directly to the reason she'd called. "I'm leaving my cell phone on so you can monitor the situation and keep everyone apprised, but I can't talk anymore."

Flint's phone had provided usable intel during their recon at Cassie's apartment, and she wanted to do the same now, however things turned out.

Her calculations might be completely wrong, which would be good for her, but bad for any future targets Howell might latch on to . . . or they might be right, which would likely result in Howell's arrest, but could be fatal for her.

To lessen that chance, Dani needed to operate without distraction. She slid her phone, still on, back into her pocket and kept scanning the area. Howell was not only a strategist, but a voyeur, as Dr. Cattrall had told them. Voyeurs got their kicks by watching people without being seen.

Howell would find a position where he could see her without her knowledge. Her experience with urban warfare came back to her, including missions where the enemy hunkered down between buildings or on rooftops, waiting until unsuspecting reconnaissance personnel walked into their crosshairs.

Which was precisely why Dani refused to explain her plan to draw Howell out by making a target of herself. A quote from General George

S. Patton came to her. *"A good plan violently executed now is better than a perfect plan executed next week."*

She'd been on similar ops before and knew that no matter how skilled the soldier, sometimes the first sign of an ambush came in the form of a bullet.

CHAPTER 67

West 52nd Street
Hell's Kitchen, Manhattan

Howell picked her out immediately. The sidewalk wasn't crowded, but even if it were, he would have noticed Special Agent Daniela Vega. Her stride was confident, but not arrogant. Purposeful, but not heedless. Wary, but not fearful. Another fifteen steps would put her in the perfect position. With an adversary like her, he would get only one chance, and it had to be a headshot in case she was wearing body armor.

Unlike with Detective Flint, this time he'd shoot to kill.

The planter bordering the patio in front of the building offered the perfect cover. Made of poured cement, the three-foot-tall structure contained a row of privacy hedges that screened him from view. Even if she managed to return fire, her Glock's rounds couldn't penetrate the barrier. The foliage, on the other hand, concealed his movements as he poked his pistol between the leaves. When she was in position, no one would see him pull the trigger.

The blast would draw attention but would also cause panic, a tool he'd learned to use well. People were essentially afraid. With the rare exception of individuals like those two buffoons who had tackled Vega earlier, most folks scattered and ran for cover at the sound of gunfire. All of which served his purpose.

And now he was free to settle a long-overdue debt. A debt he hadn't been aware of until recently. In the span of several heartbeats, he considered the day his fate had become inextricably intertwined with Vega's.

He'd gone to the wrong floor of Luna Delgado's building. He'd broken into the unit located one floor below Luna's and had nearly paid for his mistake with his life. When he read Sergio Vega's obit a few days later, he'd nearly shit himself. The man was a decorated combat veteran and a badass special forces soldier. If Vega hadn't been so severely injured by an IED, Howell was honest enough to admit that he couldn't have taken him out.

And now Vega's daughter had followed in his footsteps in more ways than one. Despite Howell's training and fitness regimen, she'd beaten him in a fair fight. He'd never known a woman like her. Under different circumstances, with the luxury of time, he might have studied her. Watched her. Added a video of her to his collection. He would have spent hours alone with her, recording her slow but inevitable surrender—first to him, and then to death.

But right now his only objective was to kill her as quickly and efficiently as possible. She was nearly in position. Only a few more steps. He moved the gun's muzzle a fraction so the lush greenery wasn't in the way.

And then it happened.

As he started to pull the trigger, Vega dropped down. Instinctively, he rose from his knees to get a bead on her, but she'd scrambled below the level of the planters, and he couldn't tell where she was.

When she popped up into a crouch an instant later, he found himself looking directly into the barrel of her gun. Panic threw his pounding heart into overdrive. Even as he adjusted his aim, he knew it was futile. He'd thought of everything. Planned for everything. But he hadn't planned for her.

Dani. Fucking. Vega.

His chest exploded when her bullet found its mark. Crushing pain consumed him. He knew the devastation from a hollow point round tumbling around inside his upper torso was not survivable.

Even so, he was determined to leave this life on his terms. Which meant taking Vega with him. He started to squeeze the trigger again, but before the impulse could cross the synaptic gap in his brain to deliver the command to his finger, something slammed into his forehead. As his legs gave out from under him, his final thought was of the chain of events that had brought him to this moment.

A silver chain whose links had connected the past to the present. Perhaps this had all been inevitable.

CHAPTER 68

West 52nd Street
Hell's Kitchen, Manhattan

Dani rose to her feet, keeping her weapon trained on Howell through the thin wisp of smoke curling up from the muzzle as he crumpled to the ground. Still in combat mode, she assessed the enemy to be sure he no longer posed a threat.

She'd planned to draw him out to force his surrender, but Howell had sealed his fate when he set up an ambush. Frequently assigned to reconnaissance, Army Rangers received advanced training in detecting and defeating these traps.

Which was how she had seen Howell.

Taking care to maintain a steady pace, Dani had been careful to show no overt reaction when she glimpsed his reflection in the massive windows spanning the lobby of Glo's building. She could see only his back, and he was crouched behind a row of cement planters surrounding a small courtyard near the entrance. A row of lush green plants sprouted up from the planters, providing the perfect screen to conceal him from the street.

But not his reflection.

Howell was a clever strategist, but he had never been at the tip of the spear in hostile territory. He had never secured a space where well-armed enemies plotted traps. In short, he had never been a Ranger.

But she had.

Before her arrival, she'd assumed Howell would be lying in wait because he'd seen her anticipate his movements three times. First, at Glo's apartment when she arrested him. Second, at Cassie's place. And third, on 53rd Street less than twenty minutes earlier.

They had figured each other out, and neither of them could walk away.

Howell was an obsessed killer. He would continue to take lives if he escaped. According to her personal code of honor, if she had the ability to stop him, then it fell to her to do so, regardless of personal risk. Warriors brought the battle to the enemy to keep others safe, and she was a warrior.

If that involved sacrificing herself, so be it.

Once she'd made up her mind, switching into tactical mode had been a simple matter of observation and planning. She'd kept up a covert observation of the tall windows and soon spotted Howell's back reflected in the glass-fronted building behind him. She'd watched him dart through an opening in the low wall of cement planters and squat down, no longer visible from the sidewalk or the street, but very apparent to her.

Judging by his position, Howell had taken up a shooting stance. If she'd turned to run, he might have fired potshots at her, hitting innocent bystanders. Her only play was the element of surprise, often the best tactic.

No one with combat experience would have made the grave tactical error of hiding near a reflective surface. Howell hadn't seen her tracking his movements and was no doubt surprised when she dropped to her belly an instant before he shot her. She'd low-crawled forward, then popped up to a kneeling shooter position as she lifted her Glock out and up. Howell had reacted an instant later, surging to his feet and taking aim.

Dani and Howell had ended up face-to-face, their weapons pointed at each other. According to FBI protocol, she should have announced herself and offered him one last chance to give up.

But Howell had given up that opportunity when he'd aimed a gun at her. She had less than a second to make a decision others would spend months evaluating from the comfort of their padded swivel chairs.

She had fired twice in rapid succession, the first round hitting Howell center mass and the second piercing the middle of his forehead. The lethal chest and headshot combo was referred to as a double tap.

She had taken no pleasure in what she did, only in the knowledge that she had stopped a deadly predator. She'd known she would answer for her actions and would accept whatever came. Regardless of her fate, the man who had destroyed so many lives would never hurt anyone else.

CHAPTER 69

August 23, 2024
FBI New York Field Office
26 Federal Plaza
Lower Manhattan

The following morning Wu sat at a mahogany table in Assistant Director Hargrave's private conference room. Dr. Cattrall occupied the chair to his right, while Ruben Silver, associate counsel for the Office of Professional Responsibility, was to his left.

Hargrave, directly across from him, had wasted no time distancing himself from Wu's decision-making during the previous day's events as they reviewed footage from the hidden cameras inside Cassie Flock's penthouse apartment.

"I have the police commissioner calling to ask why one of his best detectives got shot while accompanying your agent on a takedown that should have involved a SWAT team," Hargrave said.

Wu noticed his boss had referred to Vega as *his* agent, meaning he was responsible for her actions. What Hargrave didn't know was that he was fine with that. He would take one Dani Vega over ten other field agents and consider himself lucky.

He'd been worried about Flint, however, and had used his considerable influence to check on him last night. "Detective Flint is out of surgery and has an excellent prognosis," he said. "According to the surgeon, the round missed his femoral artery and didn't cause nerve damage. He should have a full recovery after physical therapy."

Associate Counsel Silver had apparently also been keeping tabs on the situation. "Chief Ivan Dobransky is at the hospital keeping the commissioner up to date."

Wu remembered the three-star chief of detectives who had given the press conference in front of One Police Plaza days ago. As head of the Detective Bureau, Flint fell under his command. Clearly the NYPD was taking care of their own. A lesson in leadership.

"It looks like Detective Flint will recover," Hargrave said, confirming Wu's information. "But I'm also fielding calls from the media about Cassie Flock."

This was news to him. "I understood her injuries were only minor. Physically, at least. Did something change?"

"She put out a statement as soon as she left the hospital. Said she made a deal with God that if she got out of this alive, she'd leave her law practice to set up a nonprofit legal firm representing victims of abuse and violence free of charge."

He marveled at the unexpected change in one of the fiercest criminal defense attorneys in the wake of Howell's attack. How many lives could she change for the better by putting her considerable talent to use for victims?

"Right now I'm interested in Agent Vega's use of force," Silver said, redirecting the discussion. "I've seen the video and heard the audio, and she never identified herself as a federal agent or offered Mr. Howell a chance to surrender. Is that true?"

Patel had synced the recording captured from her phone call to him with video from area security cams. She had shot and killed someone, and her actions would be reviewed by everyone from forensic techs specializing in ballistics to prosecutors at the US Attorney's Office. If things went badly, she would find herself at the Southern District Courthouse, awaiting arraignment.

Wu couldn't tell if Silver was trying to nail Vega or catch him lying to defend her. He would certainly defend her, but he wouldn't lie to do it. He kept his tone matter of fact as he responded.

"Howell knew precisely who Agent Vega was. He'd already shot at her a few minutes earlier down the street and, as you saw in the video, his weapon was aimed directly at her, and he was about to pull the trigger—at point-blank range." He paused for emphasis. "Are we going to hold her in violation because she was simply quicker on the draw?"

Silver opened his mouth to respond, but Dr. Cattrall preempted him. "If I may, sir?" When he nodded, she offered her opinion. "Howell could've gotten away, but he sacrificed his chance at escape to lie in wait for Vega. I believe he couldn't fulfill his needs with the targets he'd planned, so he used her as a substitute." She glanced at Wu. "I also agree that Howell had concluded he might not survive and was okay with that outcome. I wouldn't describe him as suicidal—he wanted to get away—but only after completing his ritual. To put it plainly, he would have kept on killing if she hadn't stopped him."

Silver regarded them a long moment before responding. "I served twenty years in the Army Reserve before retiring as a colonel. My time in the military included eighteen months of active duty deployed overseas." His gaze met Wu's. "We had rules of engagement, but there were times when following strict protocol would have gotten us all killed." He looked around at the others. "I can accept that Agent Vega had no opportunity to announce herself."

"That may work on an internal memo," Hargrave cut in. "But I'm supposed to call Director Franklin with an update so he can make a statement to the media. I don't know what the hell I'm supposed to say."

"How about telling the director we put a stop to a serial killer responsible for the deaths of thirty-three people?" Wu included Sergio Vega and Wilfredo Ochoa in the count, though they were separate from the series. "Or maybe explain that Vega and Flint saved the women who would have been his thirty-fourth and thirty-fifth victims?"

He bit his tongue before mentioning that Hargrave should stand up for his personnel when they had done the right thing, regardless of the impact it might have on his career.

Hargrave rounded on him. "None of this would've happened if Agent Vega hadn't been there." His face grew ruddy with irritation. "What part of 'keep Vega at arm's length from the investigation' did you not understand?"

Hargrave had told Wu to distance Vega from the investigation of her father's murder, but the case had turned out to be inextricably involved with the serial murders. Now that OPR didn't intend to go after Vega, they might be looking for a different scapegoat, and the assistant director was offering up his second-in-command.

Wu had been raised to be respectful of his elders and those in authority, but he refused to be cowed by his boss. "The situation developed rapidly. There was no time to find another agent and, frankly, no one else could have read his patterns and found him the way she did."

Hargrave's eyes narrowed. "You've lost your objectivity when it comes to Agent Vega. Perhaps you need a transfer?"

Stunned into silence, Wu had no response. Hargrave hadn't dared to make a direct accusation, but he'd implied Wu had feelings for Vega. She was several ranks beneath him, but her position fell within his chain of command. If they were to have a relationship, one of them would have to leave the JTTF.

Denying any romantic interest in Vega would give Hargrave the opportunity to pretend Wu had misunderstood him, making Wu come off as guilty and defensive. If they all thought he was hiding something, he'd have to submit his request for reassignment immediately. Hargrave had skillfully maneuvered him into a corner.

He longed to wipe the smug expression off the man's face, but that would only give his assertion more credibility. Aware both Dr. Cattrall and Silver were watching him, he schooled his features and forced calm into his voice when he spoke.

"The only thing between Agent Vega and myself is mutual respect," he said quietly. "The kind a true leader has for those he supervises. The kind that is rewarded with loyalty because his subordinates know he'll watch their back instead of sticking a knife into it."

Wu knew he'd pay for the retort, but Silver's almost imperceptible nod of appreciation meant his message had been received.

CHAPTER 70

FBI Joint Operations Center
Lower Manhattan

Dani sat with the group in the Joint Operations Center conference room. After the debriefing, they would stand down the JOC and disband the task force. There was still plenty of follow-up work to be done, but it no longer required an all-hands-on-deck deployment of resources.

Patel had started the meeting an hour earlier, explaining that Wu was in a meeting with Assistant Director Hargrave, Dr. Cattrall, and someone from the Office of Professional Responsibility. When Wu finally walked in, she noticed the tension tightening his features and assumed things hadn't gone well in the corner office.

She'd caught him looking her way but couldn't read his expression. Was he waiting until the debriefing ended to tell her she was facing disciplinary action or, worse, criminal charges? Whatever happened, she trusted him to look out for her, but knew she had colored outside the lines a few times. She was prepared to accept whatever discipline he gave her but hoped it didn't involve a transfer.

While Wu took a seat, Patel advised him they'd already reviewed a compilation of videos from various patrol officers' body-worn cameras. The police had provided more than a dozen digital video files showing Dani's temporary handcuffing on 53rd Street.

"I thought those two monsters would crush me to death," Dani said, recalling the men who could have passed for NFL starters rolling off her back before one of New York's finest slapped a pair of cuffs on her wrists.

"You could see an indentation in the shape of your body where they smushed you into the ground," Chapman said.

A chuckle went around the room. It was an exaggeration, but not by much, judging from her aching rib cage.

"I edited footage from all the cams together in the proper sequence of events," Patel said. "Had to get a clear picture of Vega's badassery in action."

Embarrassed, Dani was grateful for her tan skin that concealed what surely would have been a vivid blush on someone paler. "I did what I had to do according to my training."

Wu raised a brow. "Best not to ask whether it was law enforcement or military training." Apparently sensing they were getting into territory that should be reserved for internal review, he changed the subject. "Did we ever figure out exactly how he framed Ochoa?"

"Going through the rest of Howell's computer files answered a lot of questions," Patel said, splitting the screen and opening documents. "He gathered material to set up three potential candidates. Makes sense in case one of them unexpectedly died or moved out of the country or something. He selected men who had been charged with any combination of stalking, assault, peeping, burglary, or sex-related crimes."

"He's heard enough behavioral profiling to know that we would look for someone with those things in their background to escalate to rape and murder," Dr. Cattrall said. "And he could look it up if he didn't. He had access to police databases and criminal arrest information. It wouldn't be hard to locate the perfect candidate."

"He saved samples of their DNA from when they were arrested," Flint added. "Crime Scene detectives went through his apartment and found two labeled containers with carefully preserved forensic material.

He knew what he was doing. The perishable stuff was in the fridge and the rest was in evidence bags in a climate-controlled cabinet. The names on the labels matched the other two men Patel found in his computer files. When he was ready to frame someone, he had everything he needed to plant the evidence. Unfortunately for Ochoa, he was first up at bat."

"His only mistake was Ochoa's trip to Florida," Chapman said. "If not for that one minor slipup, Gloria Gomez might be dead right now."

"I don't know," Dani said. "Glo is a survivor."

"We recovered a burner phone from Howell's body," Wu said. "One of the numbers comes back to Donovan Dewitt. According to NYPD, he's a small-time wannabe crime boss who specializes in collections and enforcement. We're guessing you can pick out the three hoods who tried to rob you from his associates." He air-quoted the last word.

"So we were right about that?" Dani said. "Howell's not in the underworld. How did he recruit them then?"

"They're part of a crew," Flint said. "The head guy, Donovan, got on the wrong side of a drug beef. Howell reached out to him. He arranged for the forensic evidence tying Donovan to a fentanyl-distribution operation to be lost. Saved him a long stretch in prison."

"Donovan owed him," Dani said. "And he called in the favor."

"We also found a lot of research about cryptanalysis on his computer," Patel said. "Looks like it wasn't his hobby, but he pulled a code together to suck you in."

"And it worked," Dani said. "It took me a long time to connect him to the case he didn't want me looking into."

"Your father's murder," Chapman said quietly. "Howell had managed to scrub himself from every crime scene except his first. And you were running around with the one piece of evidence he couldn't get his hands on."

"I'm guessing he was buying time by keeping you busy until he could get that necklace," Flint said. "In the end, he would have killed you for it."

Dani's hand drifted to her bare throat. "Did the Quantico lab extract Howell's DNA from the chain?"

Wu nodded. "Even after ten years, there was enough material to get a solid match." He hesitated. "We reviewed video file X100," he said. "You were right. Part of your father's murder was captured by the surveillance equipment he had planned to install. The camera had dropped on the floor, but you can see most of what happened."

"I want to see it," Dani said.

"There won't be a trial," Wu said. "So it's not going to be shown in court. There's no reason for you to put yourself through—"

"He's my father," Dani persisted. "I owe it to him to bear witness to his final moments."

The video had played out nearly exactly as they had thought it would. Howell's reflection had been captured in the full-length mirror across from the dresser as he put the video equipment on the bed and began poking a small hole in the wall in the main bedroom.

He hadn't activated the microphone yet, so the scene played out like a silent movie.

Howell suddenly straightened, his head snapping around. He must have made enough noise to awaken her father, and heard him call out, perhaps wondering if her mother had returned from her weekly trip to the laundromat.

Howell snatched up the camera, darted into the closet, and closed the door. Several minutes later, he emerged from the closet and went into the kitchen. He must have realized that her father was between him and the front door and grabbed a knife from the butcher block.

Creeping forward, he jumped when her father sat up from where he had been lying on the couch. Her father's eyes narrowed, and he appeared to shout something at the intruder. Then he clutched his head and staggered, clearly suffering from the vertigo that plagued him.

Howell's arm came into view, his left hand holding the knife. He rushed forward and plunged the blade into her father's chest.

Dani felt the steely blade pierce her heart as she watched, her hand reflexively covering her mouth to stifle a howl of rage. Rage at the man who had viciously taken the life of someone so noble. Rage at the bomb that had rendered her father nearly defenseless.

Howell yanked the knife out and thrust it into her father's body again. She had witnessed the bloody aftermath of Howell's attack, a sight that had broken her mother, and believed nothing could be worse.

But she'd been wrong.

Blood poured from her father's wounds, soaking his shirt. Mortally wounded, he still found the strength to reach under the sofa cushion and pull out the baseball bat he kept there for self-defense. He and her mother kept his military weapons in a lockbox safe from the children, and Sergio wanted something close at hand in an emergency.

He swung the bat, clearly making contact and causing Howell to drop the camera on the floor. The rest of the video was from an obstructed angle, but Dani could tell her father had put up a valiant fight despite being hampered by his war injuries and blood loss from the knife attack. According to the autopsy report, he had been stabbed four times. Three were fatal blows, but he swung the bat again and again before he went down.

"He used a bat to defend himself." Chapman's voice was thick with emotion. "I thought there were no bruises or scrapes on his knuckles because he wouldn't hit your mother, but I was wrong. So wrong."

"Your father was a brave man," Wu said after the screen went dark. "I can see why you admired him so much. He tried to protect his family with his last breath."

Violence wasn't new to her, but this was something altogether different.

She did not trust herself to speak.

Her father had a favorite line from the Ranger Creed. *"Surrender is not a Ranger word."* He'd seen enough combat to know he was mortally wounded, yet he pushed himself to endure what must have been agonizing pain to stay in the fight well past what should have been possible. In fact, his valiant struggle had eventually led to justice.

But it had taken far too long.

As had happened many times over the years, she sensed his spirit beside her, urging her on. She had set the whole sequence of events in motion, and he would not rest in peace until she made things right.

"I have to see my family." She heard the rasp in her own voice as she spoke.

Wu's gaze was uncharacteristically intense. "Can I drive you?"

For a moment his eyes seemed to glimmer with emotion, but she decided it had been a trick of the light and turned to leave.

"This is something I have to do alone."

CHAPTER 71

Benedict Avenue
Castle Hill, Bronx

Dani had driven straight from the JOC to the Bronx, her vision occasionally blurring with unshed tears. Not one to show her feelings, she hadn't cried since her father's funeral, but witnessing his death had brought the long-buried grief back to the surface.

Standing outside her aunt Manuela's apartment, she tried, and failed yet again, to come up with a gentle way to explain everything she had learned. She'd had no contact with her family since rushing out the door after confronting her aunt about the necklace. They would certainly suspect her questions had something to do with their father's death, but they wouldn't have any answers.

Her sister, Erica, opened the door at Dani's knock.

"We were all wondering when you would show up again," Erica said without any censure in her voice. "We're all in the living room, watching the news."

By "all" Dani assumed Erica meant she was with Axel and their aunt, and she was correct. She was also right about the scowl with which Manuela greeted her.

". . . expect the live news conference to begin at any minute," a reporter standing in front of police headquarters was saying into the camera. "The police commissioner will be joined by the assistant director in charge of the FBI's New York field office to provide further information about yesterday's shooting of a suspected serial killer by a federal agent."

Her brother motioned toward the screen. "Weren't you helping with that investigation?" His eyes narrowed on her. "The agent involved in the shooting. That was you, wasn't it?"

She had a lot to share. And none of it was good. "That case is part of the reason I'm here." Sidestepping the question, she took a seat in the wingback across from the sofa. "We all need to talk."

Axel remoted off the television and turned to her. "What's up?"

Manuela got to her feet. "I've got things to do."

"I'd like you to stay," Dani said. "You should hear this too."

Manuela sat back down and turned suspicious eyes on Dani. Erica and Axel exchanged puzzled glances before leaning forward in their seats, clearly anxious to hear what news had caused this unprecedented outreach from their big sister.

Dani spent the next hour taking them through the investigation into the murders Howell had committed—beginning with their former neighbor, Luna Delgado. As her boss had indicated, there would be no prosecution and no trial, so there was no need to hold back.

She waited until the end to explain how the silver necklace that had been hidden inside the family Bible ultimately tied Howell to their father's murder.

They stared at her in stunned silence for a full minute. Seeing their anguish, Dani spared them the details surrounding their father's death but made sure they understood how heroically he had fought.

At the mention of her brother's bravery, tears flowed down Manuela's cheeks. She accepted a tissue from Erica and dabbed at her face. "I never knew," she choked out. "I always thought . . ."

The dam Manuela had built around her heart seemed to burst. Her whole body shook with sobs until Erica put a comforting arm around her.

Finally, Manuela lifted her head to meet Dani's gaze. "I was wrong," she said, her voice thick with emotion. "About you. About your mother. About everything."

Her aunt had stewed in a soup of toxic grief for so long that she might never fully recover from the darkness it had imprinted on her soul. For this, Dani could feel sorry for her.

"Speaking of Mom," Axel said quietly. "What's going to happen to her now?"

Axel's pleading expression as he looked at her with total trust nearly broke her. He had no way of knowing how much pain his question had caused. How much she wished she could go back to the one day that had changed all their lives and do things differently.

She could indulge in self-recrimination later. Right now her family was looking to her for answers. She had discussed her mother's situation with Flint and Chapman before the debriefing had started. Wu had offered to help in any way he could, but the crime, the charges, and the sentencing had all been in the city's jurisdiction.

"I have friends at the NYPD who are working on it," she said. "The police will have to reopen the case based on new evidence and conduct the investigation all over again. When they're finished, they'll take the information to the District Attorney's Office. That's who will decide what to do about Mom."

"They'll all have to admit they were wrong," Axel said. "And that an innocent person has been locked up for the past ten years. That's not going to go over well."

"I'll make damn sure they do it," Dani said. "But it will take time."

Erica frowned. "But she has to stay in there while we wait?"

Dani would gladly take her mother's place if she could, but Camila needed constant care. Of course, if she were home in a familiar environment, maybe she'd make faster progress.

"They treat her well." Dani tried to put a good face on the situation. "She only has a few lucid moments now and then. She's not ready to live a normal life yet."

"But she wouldn't have to be in the locked ward," Axel persisted. "And we could take her out on visits and trips."

"As soon as her status changes, we'll do that." Another thought occurred to her. "You know, all this happened because of our mother. When I went to see her, she was clear for a minute and told me she didn't kill Dad. If it hadn't been for her, I wouldn't have started investigating." She didn't add that a killer would have continued to make the city his hunting ground.

"And your investigation took you to Detective Chapman," Axel said, seeming to read her mind, as he often did. "And that led you to discover the serial murders."

"You're right," Manuela spoke again, catching them all off guard. "Your mother had to fight through all her confusion to get a message to you." She turned to Dani and, for the first time, smiled at her with genuine warmth. "Because she knew you would never stop until you found the truth."

"Maybe we can have some closure now," Erica said, her voice hopeful, then studied Dani. "Something else is bothering you."

Dani was wondering how long it would take her brother and sister to realize the full extent of the damage her statement to Detective Chapman had done to the family. She had borne the brunt of her aunt's anger for something she *didn't* do, and now braced herself for the justified anger of her siblings for something she *did* do.

"I told the police what happened," Dani began. "That is to say, what I thought happened. But I was wrong. So very wrong." She looked from her sister to her brother. "I'm sorry. That sounds pretty weak after all this time, but—"

Two bodies pressed against her, the pressure from their hugs cutting off her words.

"Is that what this is about?" Axel shook his head. "You think we blame you for telling the truth?"

"Then why does it feel like I betrayed her?"

Erica squeezed her harder. "Because you love her."

"Just like your father did," Manuela added from across the room. "I never understood it before, but I do now."

Deep inside, Dani had harbored a secret fear that her father was deeply disappointed in her. On the day her mother had needed her most, Dani had failed her.

Failed to love her enough to see the truth.

Failed to take care of her as he had always done.

Erica reached out to touch Dani's cheek. "Parents aren't supposed to have favorites, but you were Dad's." Her expression showed no resentment. "You begged him to take you camping, teach you soldier drills, and let you polish his boots." She glanced at Axel. "We weren't into that stuff, but you were like his shadow whenever he was home from his deployments."

"And you were there for the bad times too," Axel added quietly. "When he left the Army and came home injured, you were the one who took care of him. We were too young and Mom just . . . couldn't."

She remembered organizing her father's many pills, rushing to his side when he woke up screaming at night, and holding a bucket while he vomited, nauseated from vertigo and migraines. Those had indeed been difficult times, but she would give anything to have them back, just to be near him again.

Manuela sniffled and drew closer. "You're a lot like him."

Her aunt could offer no higher praise.

"He would have understood what happened with Mom," Axel said. "And thanks to you, she'll come home when she's ready. All those people who gossiped about our family, well, you've shut them up. And you'll never admit it, but I'm guessing you risked your life to set things right."

"Dad was always proud of you, Dani," Erica said. "He's still proud of you now. Don't ever doubt that."

In that moment, a weight lifted from her. Those she held dearest, those who had the most reason to judge and despise her, had forgiven her instead. Perhaps now she could forgive herself and become worthy of her father's legacy.

Her mind went back to the video of their father's final moments. As Wu said, he had protected his family with his last breath. Now that job fell to her. She glanced upward and made a silent vow she hoped would finally bring him peace. A sacred vow from one warrior to another.

Rest easy, soldier. Your mission is completed. I'll take it from here.

ACKNOWLEDGMENTS

My husband, Mike, has been incredibly supportive through all my endeavors. The best partner and friend anyone could want, he is my rock.

My son, Max, brings me joy every day. How blessed I am to play a part in his journey.

So much more than an agent, Liza Fleissig shares my vision and makes miracles happen. Her advice, support, and outstanding professionalism have been life changing for me and many others.

My other agent, Ginger Harris-Dontzin, spent countless hours reviewing the manuscript to make sure the New York City facts and locations rang true, bringing the venue to life. When writing about such an iconic place, there's no substitute for the authenticity that can come only from a native.

Several scenes in this story take place at the United States Courthouse at 500 Pearl Street in Manhattan. I am extremely grateful to the Honorable Jill Konviser for her generosity in providing details about the venue and legal proceedings from a judge's perspective. Any liberties taken in service of the plot or mistakes made are my own.

A special thanks to retired NYPD detective turned author Vic Ferrari, who gave me a true insider's (often hilarious) insight into how investigations are handled in the Big Apple. Any liberties taken in service of the plot or mistakes made are my own.

Retired NYPD detective turned author Marco Conelli helped ensure locations and police procedures were accurate. Any liberties taken in service of the plot or mistakes made are my own.

The men and women of the FBI work without expectation of fame or fortune. They dedicate themselves to upholding their motto, "Fidelity, Bravery, Integrity." A special thanks goes out to Ret. Special Agent Jerri Williams, who shares their stories in her award-winning *FBI Retired Case File Review* podcast.

To create a fictional story with an authentic feel, it's imperative to speak to those who were there. Former FBI executive Lauren C. Anderson, who served in New York City, was generous with her time and considerable expertise. Any liberties taken in service of the plot or mistakes made are my own.

Creating codes, riddles, and clues for this story was both challenging and fun. When one of the clues involved a complex polynomial equation with trigonometry, I needed an expert to check the answer. Jagger Fleissig used his mad math skills, performing the calculation in his head in about thirty seconds (because he's brilliant) to solve for X.

Senior Editor Megha Parekh, my acquiring editor, has been with me throughout my journey with Thomas & Mercer. Her strong advocacy, continued support, and keen instinct for story have made all the difference. Always ready to discuss new ideas, her creative collaboration has been invaluable.

My developmental editor, Charlotte Herscher, put her impressive talent toward making this story better. Her incisive observations, well-thought-out critiques, and sharp eye for detail kept me on track through many iterations of the manuscript.

The amazing team of marketing, editing, and artwork professionals at Thomas & Mercer is second to none. This story is particularly complex, and they worked with me tirelessly to double-check each component of the unfolding mystery. I am incredibly blessed to have such talented professionals by my side.

ABOUT THE AUTHOR

Wall Street Journal bestselling and award-winning author Isabella Maldonado wore a gun and badge in real life before turning to crime writing. A graduate of the FBI National Academy in Quantico and the first Latina to attain the rank of captain in her police department, she retired as the Commander of Special Investigations and Forensics. During more than two decades on the force, her assignments included hostage negotiator, department spokesperson, and precinct commander. She uses her law enforcement background to bring a realistic edge to her writing, which includes the bestselling Nina Guerrera series (optioned by Netflix for a feature film starring Jennifer Lopez), the Daniela Vega series, the Veranda Cruz series, and the Sanchez and Heron series, coauthored with #1 *New York Times* bestselling author Jeffery Deaver. Her books are published in twenty-four languages. For more information, visit www.isabellamaldonado.com.